About the Author

GUY BOLTON is a screenwriter and author who has worked in publishing, film and television. *The Pictures* is his first novel, and he lives in London.

Praise for *The Pictures*

Shortlisted for the John Creasey (New Blood) Dagger Award 2017

'Craine is not the usual maverick cop and his ambiguous nature makes this novel tick…Place and period are lovingly described.'

Spectator

'It's one of those books which you pick up idly – and don't put down. I read it in a couple of days and I'm still thinking about a couple of the characters. Definitely recommended…. There's a real pace to the story and an effortless evocation of the Hollywood of the nineteen thirties…It's his first novel and is particularly assured for a debut.'

The Bookbag

'A skilfully written, atmospheric tale.' *Literary Review*

'*The Pictures* is well-constructed adventure and detection in a manner reminiscent of the Hardboiled detective novels of the period…Mystery fans and fans of old-time Hollywood are likely to enjoy Bolton's novel.'

Pop Culture Association/American Culture Association

'Bolton has clearly done his homework on pre-WWII Hollywood… Bolton has imagination to spare.' *Publishers Weekly*

THE PICTURES

Guy Bolton

A Point Blank Book

First published in North America, Great Britain and Australia by
Point Blank, an imprint of Oneworld Publications, 2017
This paperback edition published 2017
Reprinted, 2017

ISBN 978-1-78607-245-0
ISBN 978-1-78607-040-1 (eBook)

Typeset by Hewer Text UK Ltd, Edinburgh
Printed and bound in Great Britain by Clays Ltd, St Ives plc

This book is a work of fiction. Names, characters, businesses,
organisations, places and events are either the product of the author's
imagination or are used fictitiously. Any resemblance to actual
persons, living or dead, events or locales is entirely coincidental.

Oneworld Publications
10 Bloomsbury Street
London WC1B 3SR
England

For my mother

PROLOGUE

West Hollywood, Los Angeles
May 10th, 1939

The roads were busy for a Wednesday night. The evening sky was drawn and overcast and most Angelenos were heading home before the rain came. In a radio car smelling of cheap coffee and paper-bag dinners, Officers Becker and Cassidy took a disturbance call from Dispatch, a last pickup twenty minutes before the midnight changeover.

They were both local product, rare in the department, with over thirty years of service between them and a working partnership for almost half that. A disturbance report meant very little but the address was a tony neighborhood three miles west of Hollywood and Becker suspected nothing more than a domestic dispute, maybe assault and battery if they were unlucky. He slouched in the passenger seat, his partner steering slowly and carefully down a row of detached houses surrounded by neatly sheared hedgerows and freshly trimmed lawns.

"You got the house number?"

"One-ten. Looks like the third on the right."

Becker peered through the windshield. A porch light revealed a woman sitting hunched on the steps leading up to the front door.

They parked in the shadow of a coral tree, Becker pulling out his notebook before they'd even killed the engine. They could wrap this up in fifteen minutes easy, type it up in the morning.

They stepped out onto the asphalt, glancing sideways at the adjacent houses, noticing the curtains twitch and a second later the lights go out. This was a quiet neighborhood and people weren't used to police cars pulling into driveways this late at night.

"You Mrs. Greer?" Cassidy asked the woman. She looked to be seventy or so, with thin, almost wispy hair and sharp elbows hiding beneath a woolen housecoat. When they stepped closer they could see her face was twisted in fright.

"Excuse me?" Cassidy repeated. "Are you Dolores Greer? You called the police a few minutes ago?"

The woman looked at each of them in turn without recognition or surprise. She blinked several times but said nothing.

Becker looked at Cassidy then back again. He had to hide the irritation in his voice. "Ma'am, are you Dolores Greer? Did you call the police department about a disturbance at one-ten Longbrook?"

"I called," she said at last. "Something terrible has happened." There was a shrill ring of fear in her voice.

"You live here? This your place?"

A shake, and then a nod. "This is my house. I own it."

"Can you tell us what happened? You reported a disturbance."

She looked back at the door and flinched, nervous by proximity.

Exasperated, Cassidy lit a cigarette. "Everything alright? You had an argument with your husband?"

"It's awful." Her voice sounded like a child's whisper. "Look at what they did. Dead. And for what?"

Becker's eyebrows arched. He wasn't sure he heard her correctly. He pointed his notepad at the doorway. "Someone's died in the house? There's a body inside?"

"Yes," she said. "Inside."

Becker pondered the possibility of murder. No—unlikely in these parts. He envisioned instead some old-timer rigored in his armchair. Mr. Greer, probably eighty years old, resting peacefully in a puddle of his own piss and shit.

He turned to his partner. "You want to stay with her?"

He went up without waiting for a response, stepping around the old lady as he made his way up to the front door.

The screen door was wide open, the front door unlocked. Inside, the house was dark, with only a dull tungsten glow coming in from the front windows facing the street. He reached for the light switch and the hallway lit up.

Becker left the front door ajar and moved through the house. The corridor was empty but picture frames had been pulled off the walls, glass and wood laying across soiled footprints on the floorboards. There was a soft hissing sound like running water but it didn't look like anyone was inside.

Becker put his hand on his pistol and tilted his head back toward the front door. "Looks like we got a robbery."

The first room he entered was the living room. The room had been turned over, that much was clear. The couch was cut open, more pictures broken from their frames. The floor was covered in shattered glass and one or two of the floorboards had been jimmied up.

He scanned the room but there was no dead body. The kitchen was the same, drawers and cupboards torn open but no corpse and no sign of blood. There was a bathroom at the end of the hall, some jewelry visible on a side cabinet, which seemed strange for a robbery.

He found the source of the noise at the end of the hallway, outside what must be the bedroom. On a dresser was a phonograph, the needle prodding aimlessly at the end of the record. He left it there and approached the bedroom door, taking out a handkerchief to turn the knob.

When the door opened his stomach concaved. His heart rose in his chest and he felt his pulse throbbing in his ears. For a long minute he saw red spots and dark concentric circles. Dizzy, he steadied himself on the doorway.

Officer Eric Becker had thought he was hardened to death. He had lost two fellow officers in his tenure and believed he'd seen enough dead hoods and dope peddlers to keep his head at the sight of blood. He was wrong.

The butchered remains of a pale, lithe body lay on a double bed in the middle of the room. A woman, if not a girl, was sprawled on her back, surrounded by a pool of coagulating blood. She was naked but for the tattered remains of a once-white nightgown clinging to her midriff. Both arms and legs were extended into a spread-eagle, her ankles and wrists trussed tightly against each of the four bedposts. Her pale limbs and torso were swollen and bruised, her neck criss-crossed from a ligature. But where the body's head should be sat only a loose jaw with a small ovate hole in it. The body had no eyes, no nose, no face: the remains of her skull littered the pillow like bloody eggshells. Whoever she was and whatever she'd done to deserve such an end, the victim had been cuffed, beaten, strangled, and then finally killed.

After the shock receded, Becker looked back through the door at the needle dancing on the phonograph. They must have played the music to drown out the screams.

CHAPTER I

Fred Astaire was performing at the Lilac Club.

A black tie supper club on the eastern end of Sunset Boulevard, the Lilac Club was a venue synonymous with stars and stardom. It was owned by William Wilson, the wealthy publisher of *The Hollywood Enquirer*. Not content with running Hollywood's most popular trade newspaper, Wilson had bought seven highly profitable clubs on the Sunset Strip, catering specifically to the Hollywood rich and famous. The Lilac Club was the largest and grandest of them all.

Jonathan Craine was sitting at a table not far from the bar. Resisting the recent trend for white jackets, he wore a plain black New York drape suit with the legs tapered at the ankle. To look at, he was at once both appealing and unremarkable. Standing a little under six feet, Craine was fairly tall and reasonably broad but not quite either. He remained to most people who met him quiet, measured and reserved, a harmless nobody.

The evening was in full swing, the room alive with chatter and laughter, but Craine sat alone. He bowed his head as a few familiar faces passed by, anxious to avoid their awkward nods and smiles. He tried to ignore the hushed whispers of strangers who knew him only by reputation, the hairs standing tall on the back of his neck as he imagined how they gossiped about the widower of the late actress Celia Raymond.

"Detective Craine?"

Craine looked up to see a waiter he recognized. Being referred to by his profession always put him on edge when he was off-duty.

"Hullo."

"Good to see you again. Have you been away?"

"I was in New York."

The waiter lowered his voice. "Are you back working the studios?"

Craine was a little taken aback by the directness of the question but he recovered his composure. "No," he answered truthfully. "I don't do that anymore."

"Well, it's nice to have you back, sir. And I wanted to say—" the waiter paused, trying to find the right words. "I wanted to say I was very sorry about your wife. She was a lovely lady."

Craine tilted his head to acknowledge what he'd said then replied simply, "I'll have a French 75 whenever you're ready."

The waiter stiffened. They returned to their roles as server and guest. "Oh, yessir, right away."

On stage "Cheek to Cheek" was brought to an end and the club audience broke into applause. A tall, olive-skinned man came on stage to shake Astaire's hand: the club manager, Benjamin Carell. They hadn't met before but Craine knew he was a Chicago-bred Italian with criminal ties. He wondered why William Wilson had ever hired him.

"Jonathan Craine? *Detective* Jonathan Craine?"

He was expecting his cocktail but when Craine turned around the concierge was standing over him. "Yes," he said.

"There's a call for you, sir."

Craine sighed. He knew exactly who it would be.

"Thank you, I'll be right over. Cancel my drinks order."

"Yes, sir, right away."

Craine took the call at the front desk. Two studio executives were moving through the foyer and Craine caught them staring at him. He heard his name mentioned and one of them laughed. His ears burned and Craine contemplated why, after almost five months away, he'd decided to come back from New York to a place that left him feeling injured and empty.

"This is Craine," he said after they'd gone.

"Good evening, Detective," said a young man's voice. As expected: it was Dispatch. "I apologize for calling you. Your secretary said you might be at the Lilac Club."

"Yes," added Craine impatiently.

"We have a report of a robbery-homicide in West Hollywood."

"Who's on duty? I'm not due in until nine."

"I'm afraid all our night officers are out on calls."

Craine sighed quietly. The homicide unit was understaffed and overstretched. It was little surprise Captain Simms had been so keen to have him back.

"Do you know the name of the first officer?"

"I'm sorry?"

"The first uniform officer on the scene."

"One second, please." The line went quiet and Craine heard a ruffle of papers. Outside, four security guards pushed back a rank of photographers gathering beside the double glass doors. Craine followed their gaze. A woman entered the foyer and walked briskly toward the main hall. He recognized her as the actress Gale Goodwin. Her latest picture, *The Tainted Feather*, had topped the box office— she must be celebrating.

The dispatcher came back on the line. "I'm sorry, I don't have that information, sir."

Craine rolled his eyes. "Do you have the address?"

"Yes, Detective, the address is—"

"Hold on one second." He cradled the receiver between cheek and neck and stretched across the desk for a pen and pad. "Go on."

"Address is one-ten Longbrook Avenue."

Craine scrawled it down then checked his watch. Just after midnight. He let out a long sigh. "Tell the first officer I'll be there in twenty minutes." He put the phone down, rubbed his eyes and asked the concierge to retrieve his coat and hat.

*   *   *

A gray and dusty Los Angeles reeled through the windows like a broken strip of celluloid. Although the motion picture industry had helped prop up Los Angeles in the lean years since the Wall Street Crash, visible shocks of depression were not in short supply. Craine wound up the window as he drove past a slum of tarpaper shacks and a group of homeless men fretting over a garbage fire. He passed vacant lots and filling stations, mile after mile of billboards selling God, bank loans and beauty creams.

He accelerated west down Sunset before turning south toward Hollywood, the neon nightlife receding in his rearview mirror. He was driving the V-16 Cadillac Fleetwood that Celia had bought him for their ten-year anniversary. The car radio was playing an Ella Fitzgerald record and he turned it up so loud that thoughts of Celia were buried in the song.

The slum receded, quickly forgotten to palm trees, flowering plants and the stucco-walled homes of the Hollywood middle class. This is a city of contradictions, Craine thought, a metropolis where sepia and Technicolor play side by side.

He turned into Longbrook where the roads were quiet now, almost empty, with barely a Buick or Packard in sight. Craine looked at the address Dispatch had given him, counting the house numbers on his right. He spotted a squad car parked outside a single-story and pulled up behind it in the driveway.

The porch light flicked on and the front door opened. A squat uniform officer with a thick mustache and a flashlight cradled under one arm stepped outside.

"Evening, Detective," he said as Craine got out of his car. His eyes widened when he caught a glimpse of the Fleetwood but he kept his thoughts to himself. He probably thought all detectives drove two-thousand-dollar Cadillacs.

"You the first officer?"

"Yes, sir. Becker. Arrived about an hour ago. My partner, Cassidy, went to take a statement from the neighbor. She called it in."

Craine took a pencil and notepad from his jacket pocket. "Did you touch the body, move it at all?"

"Didn't get further than her doorway."

"A woman?"

"Yessir. Shot dead."

He sighed inwardly. A dead girl meant unwanted media interest.

Craine paused to examine the door and windows on the front of the house. All intact, no signs of forced entry.

"Door was unlocked when I got here," said the uniform, taking off his hat to wipe his brow. "I went all around with the flashlight but there's no windows broken either."

"Make sure that's in your report."

Craine noticed Becker was staring at him. "Have we met before?" Becker asked. "Yeah, we have. That assault charge on that actor. They called you—"

"I remember."

"He beat her up real bad. Broke her nose, stitches across her cheek where he'd split it right open. What was she, sixteen? I'm surprised the charges didn't stick."

They didn't stick because the actor in question was two days away from shooting a million-dollar motion picture and City Hall had asked Craine to have the charges dropped.

"Why don't we concentrate on the task ahead, Officer Becker?" said Craine sharply. "Let's head inside."

Bare ceiling bulbs lit a wide hallway leading onto a checkered kitchen floor to their left and what must be the living room to their right. Craine could see the bathroom further down the corridor, opposite a white door. The house was spacious and well decorated inside but the kitchen and hallway had been ransacked.

The officer pushed open the living-room door. There were no lights on but the mess was evident in the half-light. Framed pictures had been pulled off the walls and the couches had been cut open. Even a wall clock lay on the floor in pieces. "All the rooms are the same."

"Looks like a botched robbery. Where is she?"

"Bedroom. Down the end there."

"You got her name?"

Becker pushed a cigarette between his teeth and lit it while talking: "Florence Lloyd. White female. Thirty years old."

Craine wrote down F/W/30 on a new page in his notepad.

"Did she live here alone?"

"Far as we know. Rents it from her neighbor, a Dolores Greer. Says she noticed the door open and went inside."

"What time?"

"A little after eleven."

"Did she hear the shot?"

"No, she didn't."

"Canvass the other houses here, see if anyone else saw anything or heard the shooting. Anyone else here yet?"

"Techs are on their way." Becker checked his watch. "Medical examiner should be here any minute."

Craine noted the kitchen in disarray: the pantry shelves swept clear, the canned food tossed on the kitchen floor. Broken dishes and pans were scattered across the sideboard and the refrigerator had been pulled away from the wall.

He didn't go into the bathroom but he could see the medicine cabinet had been pulled open. A bottle of pills was scattered across the floor. Sleeping pills. Must have been hundreds of them.

"Lot of pills she's got."

"Nothing unusual," Craine said. At times it felt like the whole town was existing in a narcotic delirium.

"There's a gold watch on the side of the sink there. Seems funny the intruder would leave it."

Craine wasn't listening. He flanked into the corridor. "Let's see it then."

Becker followed close behind, lighting a second cigarette from the first as they reached the bedroom door. "It's pretty messy. Not much left of her, that's for damn sure."

The door was ajar; Craine pushed the door back and surveyed the bedroom.

Florence Lloyd's remains were enough to make him gag. He suddenly felt hot, a bracing sweat forming on his forehead. He wiped his brow with his handkerchief and used it to protect his nose from the stench of fresh meat. Murder scenes never became easier, no matter what people said.

Becker was still loitering in the doorway. "Can I get you anything? Think there's some coffee back there on the kitchen floor. I can put a pot on?"

"That won't be necessary."

"I'll leave you to it, then." Becker didn't want to see the body. He left him alone in the bedroom.

Craine started working the crime scene from the periphery, walking around the perimeter of the bedroom and making notes. All her clothes had been pulled out of the drawers and lay scattered around the base of the bed. The burglar looking for a safe or money box, he reasoned.

There was a photo framed on the sideboard. Same fair hair, same skin tone. Must be the victim. She was attractive, stunning even. It was a professional photograph, a three-quarter shot of Florence Lloyd in a décolleté cocktail dress. White pearls hung low around her neckline. He imagined the budget lines: "BLOND BEAUTY BUTCHERED IN HOLLYWOOD." More fuel for the tabloids.

He looked for other signs of disturbance, anything that didn't fit in with the surroundings, before taking a long look at the body. The bleeding was still pronounced and the sheets were glistening crimson. Copper wire was wrapped tight around her wrists and feet, a ring shank nail pinning her palms against the bedposts. Bruising round her collarbone suggested her throat had been constricted and there were bloody ligature marks ribboned around her neck. The M.E. would determine if she was raped but there was no doubt she had been beaten and tortured—for what means he couldn't be sure. The papers would have a field day.

Shards of skull and brain matter framed a bullet hole in the head-board. Craine held his handkerchief to his face and breathed through his mouth. *God, this was awful.* He'd have the lab techs remove the bullet and run some ballistic tests. The damage done to the head indicated a large-caliber weapon and he wondered how the neighbors had failed to hear the gunfire.

Craine quickly sketched the position of the corpse in the room and the angle of fire before touching the back of the dead girl's arm. Cool. He looked at her hands. The fingers were rigid but the body had yet to fully enter rigor mortis. She had died less than two hours ago.

Leaning back against the wall, Craine went through the attack in his head. Robbery turned foul. The intruder, if indeed there was only one, had entered the bedroom when Florence Lloyd was asleep. He had tied her ankles and wrists to the bedposts, beaten her to a pulp then shot her dead. He must have ransacked the house for most of an hour, probably left not long before the uniforms arrived.

Craine flipped his notepad shut and breathed a sigh of relief.

He found Becker in the kitchen sipping coffee and writing up his case notes.

"All done, Detective?"

"Robbery-homicide. As expected."

"You don't think it was planned out? Maybe someone came here to kill her, I mean."

Craine tensed. He detested speculation, particularly from the lower ranks. Abstract theories and conjectures served no one. Most murder convictions were of young black men local to the area; consequently, it was logical to assume that this murder was committed by a young black male.

"No," he said. "The intruder saw Lloyd in bed, had his fun then shot her dead. He'll be a Negro male, twenties or early thirties. I'll ask Dispatch to put a call out for young Negroes known to the area."

"How can you be sure?"

Craine struggled to remain calm. "Because that's the typical profile," he said, his eyes drilling into him.

"What about the wire? The nails in her wrists? She was beaten half to death, raped probably—"

"Don't include it in your report."

Becker frowned. "Why wouldn't I—"

"It only complicates matters. She was shot in her bed, her house robbed. That's all you need to include."

Craine deposited the notepad in his outside jacket pocket and walked back into the hallway toward the front door. He was glad to get out of the house.

"Detective?"

Craine turned at the door. Becker stood in the hallway.

"I was thinking that it seems so odd the robber would leave that watch in the bathroom but go through the whole house like this. I also found a bit of cash in the freezer. Why would he take the time to turn over every room but not take all the money? And why torture the girl? I mean, Jesus, the things he did to her. Doesn't seem to fit to a botched robbery—"

"It fits perfectly," said Craine with finality. "Good night, Officer."

Craine walked out into the night and crossed the driveway toward his Fleetwood. He could be home in less than thirty minutes.

Pulling out of the driveway, he saw Becker staring at him from the front door, shaking his head. Years ago, when I was new to the Bureau, I used to be like that, thought Craine. I wanted every stone turned over, every fact and theory examined.

That time has long since passed.

CHAPTER 2

May 11th

Louis B. Mayer sat in the back seat of his Lincoln, drew a deep breath and squeezed his eyes shut. He had a headache.

He took a small bottle of aspirin from his jacket pocket and swallowed two pills dry. Christ, his head hurt. Too many Dubonnets last night. He didn't normally drink more than the occasional aperitif but Gable kept ordering round after round, and he hadn't the heart to turn them away. Still, Gable had a good night and that's all that mattered. Clark Gable and his new wife Carole Lombard were trying for a baby and Mayer was delighted—that kind of press did wonders for a man's image.

"Are you excited about your party, Mr. Mayer?" his driver asked through the divide.

"Absolutely. It's going to be terrific. We even have the Dandridge Sisters playing."

"Oh, my wife loves them," his driver said, particularly chatty this morning. "What M.G.M. has done for all of us, it means a lot."

"Well that's kind of you to say, Artie. Very kind indeed."

This weekend was M.G.M.'s fifteenth anniversary. Fifteen years since Louis Mayer had first walked onto the lot as head of the newly formed M.G.M. He'd started with six hundred employees, a few dozen actors and a handful of stars. Now he had six thousand employees and over one hundred contract players on his books, a third of whom he categorized as "stars." M.G.M. had come out of the recession as the only studio to make profits year on year and the anniversary was a great excuse to celebrate.

Mayer started to relax when they approached Culver City and saw the M.G.M. lot looming ahead. "You know," he said, feeling unusually generous, "why don't you and your wife come join us at Loew House for a glass of champagne? You can pick her up after you've dropped us off."

Mayer saw a wide smile through the rearview mirror. "Oh, that's so generous, sir. We'd be absolutely delighted. My wife, she'll be over the moon."

The car passed through the M.G.M. gate between two large Corinthian columns and pulled up outside the Thalberg Building, the home for all senior M.G.M. executives.

Ida, his executive secretary, met him from the elevator on the third floor. She looked pale and her mascara was running. She'd been crying.

"Morning, Ida. You look sick. Are you ill? Do you need to go home? Dr. Hendricks is downstairs."

Ida held back tears. "No, Mr. Mayer. It's—"

"It's what?"

They'd reached the walnut doors of Mayer's office. Ida reached for the doorknob and composed herself.

"I'm fine. Russell Peterson is inside waiting for you."

Good, thought Mayer. Peterson could set up a press release about Gable and Lombard trying for a baby.

Mayer's office was newly decorated in the Art Moderne style: the walls were white leather, a white floor carpet had only recently been laid and all the furniture was painted magnolia. The national flag and an atlas globe were almost the only items of color. Standing beside Mayer's white kidney-shaped desk was Russell Peterson, M.G.M.'s Publicity Chief and one of Mayer's closest confidants. He was tall but slight, with a thick pencil mustache that resembled Errol Flynn's.

Ida closed the door behind them. Peterson looked unusually anxious.

"How are you this morning, Mr. Mayer?"

"Peterson, why are you in my office?" Mayer barked, striding around his desk toward his chair.

Peterson didn't reply. He waited for Mayer to take a seat but Mayer stayed standing. Despite never reaching a height above five foot seven, he still hated the feeling of being smaller than someone else, especially in his own office.

"Well?" said Mayer, scanning the morning mail. "Come on, out with it, Peterson. I have a meeting with LeRoy in a quarter-hour."

Peterson spoke slowly, his voice low and even. "Ida had a phone call ten minutes ago from the maid at Herbert Stanley's home."

Mayer felt the blood drain from his face. He already knew what Peterson would say next.

"Sir, she found him ... she found his body earlier this morning hanging from the ceiling fan. He's dead, Mr. Mayer."

Mayer steadied himself on his chair then sat down. Herbert Stanley was among Mayer's most talented producers. He was also married to Gale Goodwin, one of M.G.M.'s most valued movie stars.

"Has anyone been told?"

"Ida rang me as soon as she found out. She'd tried phoning you at home but you'd already left."

"What about anyone else?"

"Only Gale. She wasn't there."

"Jesus. She was with us at the Lilac Club. Where did she stay last night?"

"She's been staying at Joan Crawford's."

"She there now?"

"To my knowledge."

"I'll go over there this afternoon." Mayer ran through his options. *The Tainted Feather* was top of the box office this week but was a costly production that might struggle to recoup its costs if Gale got caught up in a scandal.

Peterson coughed. "Shall we call the police?"

"Not yet. Get Whitey Hendry and organize a car. We'll call the police after. Ask for Craine."

"He's back?"

"Margaret saw him at the Lilac Club last night. See if he's back at the Bureau."

Peterson seemed hesitant. "Are you sure you want Craine?" He shifted his weight between his feet. "After what happened ... with Celia Raymond, I mean."

Mayer had always thought Jonathan Craine something of a fool but he'd consistently proven a loyal and invaluable supporter of the M.G.M. cause. For longer than he could remember, Craine had been tasked by City Hall to clear all indictments against studio employees by any means possible. He was, in essence, the studio "fixer," the man who made criminal charges disappear.

Then, five months ago, Celia Raymond had died at their home from a drugs overdose and Craine's swift departure after his wife's funeral had left everyone unsure of where his allegiances lay. Did he know that Mayer had ended Celia's contract with M.G.M. only a few days prior to her death?

"Ask for Craine—"

"Sir, is that wise?"

"Don't argue with me, Peterson, it doesn't suit you. Ask for Craine but make sure he stays out of the public eye. And I don't want any mention of Celia Raymond. We have enough on our plate with Stanley."

Peterson looked wounded. "Anything else?"

"Prep a statement."

"Same approach as Paul Bern? Homosexual. Depressed. Suicidal tendencies."

"Agreed," Mayer confirmed. "Something along those lines."

"Thank you, sir. I'll call Captain Simms immediately and have Craine assigned." Russell Peterson nodded and left the room.

Mayer twisted around in his seat until he faced the window. His headache was gone. Through the glass he could see a line of cars pulling into the parking lot below. The working day was about to begin. He spotted Judy Garland's limousine approach the gates. He'd completely forgotten—they were doing reshoots on *The Wizard of Oz* today. Herbert had been one of the producers.

CHAPTER 3

When the telephone rang at eight in the morning, Craine was still awake. He hadn't slept properly in months. Although the house had six bedrooms, he'd spent most nights since his return from New York in the drawing room, lying on a velvet divan by the fireplace and staring down the long corridor that led to Celia's bedroom. Their bedroom once, but now forever known as hers. He hadn't been inside yet, hadn't dared.

Craine reached over for the rotary phone and lifted up the receiver. "Hello—" He cleared his throat. "Hello."

The operator: "Mr. Craine?"

"Yes."

"One moment, please." Craine rubbed his eyes and turned toward the double French doors as he waited for the line to connect. The lawn outside was long and unkempt, the surface of the pool covered in white pear blossom. The gardener, like the house staff, had been given indefinite paid leave the morning of Celia's funeral. If he was being sensible he'd put the house on the market, but even though he was behind on their mortgage payments, he knew he could never bring himself to go through with a sale. This was all he had left of her.

"Detective Craine." It was his secretary, Elaine. "I thought you might like to know, patrol picked up a Negro youth, Leonard Stone, asleep in his car on Highland in a Model B Ford. They found what looks like stolen goods in his trunk."

"Any priors?"

"One conviction for theft in June last year."

"Good. Is he at the precinct?"

"Yes, Detective, he's in the holding cell."

"Thank you, Elaine. Move him into the interview room. I'll be in shortly."

Craine put the phone down and sat back on the divan. The room was a mess. Dust sheets lay over the furniture like shawls covering a massacre; rows of skeletal lilies stood limp in glass vases and an empty bookshelf was pushed against the far wall, flanked by two cardboard boxes filled with paperbacks and movie scripts. He noticed a picture hanging unevenly on the wall above the fireplace. It was a picture of a small boy sitting cross-legged underneath a Christmas tree. It was a picture of his son.

Sunset Boulevard was quiet for a Thursday morning. The crisp May air whipped through the open windows but did nothing to ease his anxiety. The picture of Michael at Christmas was still firm in his mind and the guilt over how he had treated him since Celia's death sat deep in his chest. The last time he'd seen his son was when he left him at boarding school the day of Celia's funeral, Michael standing at the school gates, watching his father drive away. He hadn't cried. He hadn't even said a word. Craine had never told him where he was going or when he'd be coming back.

It was Michael who found Celia, face up in her nightgown beneath the surface of the bathwater. It was Michael who tried to save her, his little hands tearing at her wrists, desperate to pull her out. And it was Michael who called the police, crying down the phone, begging for help because his mother wouldn't wake up.

As Craine navigated toward City Hall, another memory flickered in his mind, clinging on too long for him to ignore. He remembered the police officer who had first arrived at the scene later telling him that he'd had to break through the back door to get inside the house. He'd followed the sound of a scream through the empty corridors until he'd got to their bedroom door. He found Michael sitting on the bathroom tiles, soaked through, his knees pulled up to his chest and his hands held tight over his ears as if he was trying to protect himself from the noise. But it was Michael who was screaming.

The homicide unit, the L.A.P.D. section responsible for the investigation of all unexplained deaths within the City of Los Angeles, was situated on the fifth floor of the Central Headquarters building opposite downtown's Civic Center.

Entering the Detective Bureau, Craine walked along the waxed linoleum corridor that led past the briefing hall and the holding cells and into the homicide unit.

The squad room was a half-lit office bullpen crowded with empty desks and deserted workstations. As Craine entered, he noticed a handful of unfamiliar faces sat slumped in chairs, fingering at typewriters. New recruits, Craine thought. He saw a row of eyes look up from their desks, watching him sidelong as he passed. He recognized two detectives, Henson and Kingsley, laughing and joking by the coffee pot. They fell silent when they saw him. Other investigators resented Craine's role in the department. Working studio cases seemed an easy assignment, with generous rewards that came from grateful studio heads.

Henson tilted his chin, said "Detective." Craine gave them a polite nod. Keep walking, he told himself, don't think about it. He felt their critical eyes following him as he crossed toward the interview rooms. He hated how they made him feel. Like he was different, worse somehow. An outsider in his own office.

When he'd turned the corner, he heard Henson say, "Who knows why he's back? Some investigator. Surprised they don't put his office in M.G.M."

Interview Room C was a small square cell with bare concrete walls and no windows. The door was plate steel and bolt-locked from the outside. A uniform guard stood by the door at all times.

Leonard Stone was seated on one side of a wooden table, his hands manacled and chained to the chair between his legs. Sinewy arms shivered as Craine entered and took a seat opposite.

Craine placed two thin folders on the table beside a pen and shorthand pad. In one was Leonard Stone's record of arrests and prosecutions, his known employment history and the first officer's report outlining how Stone was found. It had a red band across it and a legend on one side that read STONE, LEONARD. In the other file was a pre-typed statement of confession, a formal declaration of guilt that needed to be signed by the suspect to guarantee a court conviction. Craine didn't need to open it to know what it said; it was a template he knew well: "Between 9 P.M. and 11 P.M. of Wednesday May 10th, 1939, I, LEONARD STONE, entered the property of FLORENCE ELIZABETH LLOYD with ambitions to rob said property to the value of less than one hundred dollars. During this episode, I encountered Miss Lloyd in her bedroom. A fracas ensued and I shot Lloyd with a .38-caliber weapon . . ."

Craine stared across the table at Stone's boyish black face. He was young, maybe early twenties, perhaps even younger. His wiry hair was greasy and coiled, matting into a dirty Polish plait. He was thin, gaunt even, but he had marred, knotted forearms and bulbous shoulders, probably from years of manual labor.

"Am I right in thinking you're from Oklahoma originally, Mr. Stone?" Craine asked politely, opening proceedings. He picked up Stone's police file and scanned his employment records. Stone's life story was short and familiar. He could have been any other of the thousands of itinerant Negroes driven West after years of drought and dust storms turned prairie lands into a desert. "Okies" was what most Angelenos called them.

Craine sat back and tapped his pen against the table. "Mr. Stone? I said are you from Oklahoma?"

"Yes-suh," Stone mumbled. His voice was deep but soft. Two bloodshot eyes rolled from side to side, roaming aimlessly around the room. Craine could smell old alcohol on his breath.

"I see here you moved West eighteen months ago. I assume you were part of the F.S.A.'s rural rehabilitation program," he suggested, the model of dispassion.

Stone shrugged.

Craine thumbed through the file and removed Stone's criminal record. "And you stole from a foreman, on June 17th last year," he said plainly. "You stole a bag of oranges from his cellar and you were sentenced to three months' labor at Kent Penitentiary."

There was a silence, during which Craine leaned forward in his chair and turned the R.A.P. sheet around so Stone could see the printed conviction typed across his criminal record. Stone chewed the side of his mouth. His eyes started to water. He tried to wipe them with his hands but the chains wouldn't stretch. He turned away as Craine continued to read from the file.

"Mr. Officer-suh, can I please have something to eat," he whimpered, "I'm so hungry."

"In a minute. We're not done yet. I'm curious as to where you have been living since your release."

No reply.

"Mr. Stone, it's not a difficult question. Where have you been staying? Mr. Stone!" Craine was shouting now.

"Here and there, suh." Stone's voice was high and stretched. He cleared his throat and tried to compose himself. "I been with friends, mostly. In my car sometimes."

"That would be the 1932 Model B Ford that you were found in?"

Stone squeezed his eyes shut. His face grimaced and his body trembled. He took quick, shallow breaths and tried his best not to cry. There was no hope now. He began to see how this would end.

"Yes," he said.

"And can you tell me what was in the trunk of your car? Would you like me to remind you? The officers at the scene found two rolls of dollar bills, a bag of silverware and various items of jewelry. Can you tell me who those goods belonged to?"

"I'm hungry, I'm so hungry."

"Leonard. Let's start with the basics and then I'll get somebody to bring you a hot plate. The items in your car: where did you get them from?"

Leonard tilted his head back and studied the ceiling. When he lowered his gaze Craine could see tears crawling down his cheeks.

"I took them."

"You stole them? From the house on Longbrook."

"Maybe, I don't remember."

"The house on Longbrook, Leonard."

"I'm not sure. Yes, maybe. I didn't know the name of the street."

"And you shot Florence Lloyd? You were in her house, she saw you and you shot her in her bed, is that right?"

"No."

"Yes, you did, Leonard," Craine persisted. "You shot her in her bed. You said it yourself, you robbed Miss Lloyd's house." He'd reached the concluding verse of his well-practiced routine. He took a breath for the finale: "Come on, Leonard, either you went in there and shot Florence Lloyd in malice before robbing her entire household or you shot her in self-defense. Which is it?"

Craine opened the second folder and laid out the confession form. His voice was softer now: "Look, it says it right here, 'self-defense'— we know you didn't mean to do it, Leonard. We know it was a mistake. No one will be angry with you. You shot her by accident, didn't you Leonard?"

"No—"

"Leonard."

"I didn't shoot her. I didn't shoot nobody. I'm hungry. I'm so hungry. Please, suh—"

"I'm trying to be transparent with you here, Leonard," Craine interrupted, growing impatient. "I'm trying to be honest and I'm trying to be fair. If you sign this form now, I can ask for a reduced sentence. No death penalty. It was an accident; she tried to shoot you, you acted in self-defense. The jury will take pity on you, it wasn't your fault—they'll know that. You'll do a stint back East, go to work on some road. You've done it before; it's easier the second time around."

Leonard Stone was crying freely now and Craine gave him a moment. Stone looked distraught, broken even, and Craine felt a twinge of sympathy. He wanted his confession but he didn't want to destroy the boy. Maybe I'm getting soft in my old age, he thought.

Craine spoke gently, trying to reassure him.

"You won't have any trouble, Leonard, I know it. How old are you now? Leonard, stop crying. How old are you now?"

"Twenty-one."

"Twenty-one," he repeated. "I remember being twenty-one. It's young. And you know what, Leonard, you'll come out and you'll still be young. You might not even be middle-aged. That's still plenty of time to get married, start a family. Is that what you want, Leonard, to start a family? Everyone wants to start a family. You want a wife? You want children?"

"Yes."

"Well then, that is what you'll do. I'm sure of it. Come on then, let's get this signed and we can find you some breakfast."

Stone sank in his chair, defeated. Craine nodded to the guard to unlock the cuffs.

"Sign this, Leonard." He pushed the form in front of him and placed the pen on the other side of the table.

Leonard lifted his large, blistered hands onto the table and rubbed his swollen wrists.

"Go on, don't be afraid, Leonard."

Leonard slowly wrapped his fist around the pen and looked across for approval.

"Well done, Leonard. Well done," Craine repeated graciously. "You did good. Can you spell your name? You want me to help you? Here, I'll print it, you just do a little cross right above it. Right there. That's it. Congratulations, Leonard, you did the right thing.

Everything is going to work out fine for you, I promise, everything will be fine. Now, let's get you something to eat."

As Craine stood up, the door opened and a clerk appeared in the doorway.

"Detective Craine. When you're finished Captain Simms would like to see you in his office."

There was no one in Simms' outer office, so Craine checked himself briefly in the reflection of the glass doors. He looked tired, dark circles forming around his eyes. He pushed his hair back and straightened his jacket before heading inside.

He found Simms sitting alone in his corner office, talking quietly into a phone resting on his lap. Behind him morning rain was slashing against two broad windows that overlooked the City Hall tower.

Simms looked up, motioning with his hand that he should come in and take a seat in the chair opposite. Craine shut the door behind him and sat down, taking the opportunity to glance at his watch. It was almost twelve o'clock.

Simms ended his conversation then placed the phone back on his desk. Without saying hello, he took a cigarette from a pack in his jacket pocket and lit one, drawing in a long satisfying breath. He was smoking Chesterfields. Craine knew this because Celia had smoked Chesterfields and because every breath Simms exhaled reminded him of her.

Roger Simms was a quiet and considered leader for a paramilitary organization and with his thick-rimmed bifocals looked more like a bookish schoolteacher than a police captain.

"How are you settling back in?" Simms said eventually, sitting up in his chair and pushing his glasses up his nose.

Craine shrugged. "I'm pleased to be back."

"Good. And your interview this morning?" he asked with some apprehension. As head of the Hollywood division, Captain Simms was in place to ensure that criminal activity in his district conformed to predetermined levels set by senior personnel. Police work was no longer about protecting county citizens. It was about maintaining trends, reducing crime levels, increasing conviction rates. The bureaucrats had seen to it that crime was not merely recorded, it was budgeted. Failure to convict a suspect would not be tolerated. These were the rules. If you didn't comply, you were simply transferred to another unit.

Craine handed Simms the signed confession. "He expressed remorse for what he had done and signed it willingly."

"Already?" Simms looked relieved but not surprised. Craine succeeded where other detectives failed because he was a yes-man, well-practiced at maneuvering the political structure of the division. "As always, your efficiency is very impressive, Craine. Who was the victim?"

"A nobody. Florence Lloyd. Employment unknown."

"A woman? Such a tragedy." Simms sighed. "Dead men are so much easier to deal with. Have the Attorney's Office set a court date for this Leonard Stone. He may even hang before the next quarter."

Craine shifted in his seat. This wasn't what he'd expected. "I offered him concessions," Craine said. "Manslaughter doesn't carry the death penalty. I told him he wouldn't be executed."

"You shouldn't have. New guidelines are no plea without a lawyer present. From now on, a confession guarantees a conviction, not a reduced sentence. The Chief is demanding murderers be made examples of. Apparently City Hall don't want to seem soft on crime." Simms rolled his eyes. "But I wouldn't worry about it. He may get lucky. What matters is that he's a suitable conviction."

Simms tapped a thin manila file on the center of his desk to signal the end of the matter.

"My apologies for dragging you in here, Craine. I wanted to talk to you before the press got hold of it. I had a call from M.G.M. about an hour ago." Craine stiffened. He felt an apprehensive drumming in his chest. He'd asked not to be involved with any more studio crimes, so why was he here?

"Herbert Stanley's body was found at ten o'clock this morning. He hanged himself late last night."

A ruminative silence filled the room. Craine knew who Stanley was. He knew he worked for M.G.M. and he was starting to understand why Simms had brought him in.

"Did you know him?"

"We'd met a few times. Briefly. His wife is—"

"The actress, Gale Goodwin. Yes, M.G.M. made her importance very clear."

Craine became conscious of Simms' probing stare. "Were there any suspicious circumstances?" he said eventually.

"I'm not familiar with the details of the crime scene, but none that I'm aware of."

"Who found him?"

"His maid. He hanged himself from a ceiling fan in his study. We'll have a formal statement from her shortly."

"And Stanley's wife?"

"She wasn't there."

"I saw her at the Lilac Club."

"That matches Louis Mayer's report. We haven't had a full statement from her yet but as far as we know she was staying with a friend of hers, Joan Crawford."

Craine nodded. "Thank you for letting me know." His posture didn't alter by a fraction. "Is there anything else?"

Simms frowned. "You don't look surprised?"

He didn't reply.

"Would you say he had suicidal tendencies?"

"I didn't know him particularly well."

"Then what do you know about Herbert Stanley?" Emphasis on the "do." He was peering down at him through bifocals.

"He was a producer, must have worked for M.G.M. for most of the past twelve years. One of Louis Mayer's top men; supposedly had a real talent for story." He paused but Simms waited for him to continue. "I know he started off as a writer, then started producing musicals.

Last I heard, he was shortlisted to head his own production unit but he had an argument with Peterson over marketing."

"Russell Peterson from Publicity?"

"Mayer's right-hand man," Craine replied with another nod.

"When was all this?"

"Past year or so."

Simms took this all in. "I spoke with Peterson a few minutes ago," he said, leaning forward in his chair. "He told me Stanley was a depressive homosexual who'd tried to kill himself several times before. That's their line exactly, and we're going to read about it in the papers tomorrow. Is it true?"

"I wouldn't know." He raised his voice. He had to calm himself. He softened, continued: "I heard he had issues in his personal life, I know that much but I wasn't aware of any previous suicide attempts."

"Do you know if either of them had affairs?"

"I don't."

"Well, was he a queer, like they say?"

"There were rumors. No substantial evidence."

"But you think he was?"

"As I said, I didn't know him well."

"Do you know his wife?"

"We've met before. A long time ago. Rarely since. Look, where are you going with this? If he hanged himself, this isn't a murder so why is this even being discussed like one?"

The room fell silent except for the rain beating against the windows. Simms stubbed out his cigarette then looked at Craine steadily. "There was no note."

There it was. The sole reason for this conversation. Not curiosity but necessity. In Craine, Simms had always found a loyal disciple, an investigator who followed his very own maxim that it was more important that a case be closed than solved. Now he wanted Craine's help to ensure Stanley's suicide remained that way.

"The papers will jump all over it," Simms continued. "Yellow press will probably start shouting from the rooftops that he was murdered, that it's a cover-up and the L.A.P.D. are blind to it or in on it. Either way we're culpable. I've been asked to use someone who can take control of this situation. Someone with the necessary contacts, someone capable of exercising discretion."

"By who?"

"Message from higher tiers suggests this is important. Chief Davidson wants to make a good impression with the new administration. We've been instructed to keep this a filed case, nothing cold, nothing open. Straight-up suicide, which is exactly what this is and you know it."

"You need a fixer."

Simms shook his head. "I need someone who can operate alongside both the studio heads and the press—it's not the same. City Hall doesn't want any tantrums, absolutely no press hysteria."

"You know my return to the department was contingent on me being assigned regular cases. I asked not to be involved with the studios."

"It is; it will be," said Simms, mustering his persuasive talents. "I need this one last favor. Use your better judgment to smooth things over with the press. A simple explanation of fact is all I ask."

"Is no one else available? Who's the primary?"

"Patrick O'Neill. He arrived a few weeks before you left. He's a good investigator, nine homicides since he arrived, all in the black but he doesn't know the industry like you do. You're part of it."

"Not anymore."

"Craine, your presence in this investigation would be invaluable. Look, I'm not oblivious to the fact that your own personal history with M.G.M. is somewhat tied. I appreciate that there are elements of this case you may find difficult . . . with Celia, I mean. But there's no reason for you to become emotionally involved. All I'm asking you to do is take some statements, supervise the press releases, monitor the newspapers and liaise with the necessaries over the coming week. Your role is merely to oversee the case and hold the M.G.M.

line—that's not much of a request. There's also the matter of remuneration." Simms slid across a small piece of paper. Several inked zeros lay exposed on the page. It was enough money to keep the bank at bay. "Two thousand now, another two if they're satisfied with your work. And you know they always are."

Craine stared at him for a long moment before reaching across the desk and picking up the file.

"Detective," said Simms, "I don't need to tell you how important it is that Stanley's death pass untroubled. This has been expressed clearly through chain of command. Do you understand what I'm asking of you?"

Craine understood. In the unending battle to avoid scandal, he was the crucial pawn.

"Yes, Captain," he said as he stood up and straightened his jacket. "I understand perfectly."

CHAPTER 4

Any type of crime scene involving a celebrity is almost immediately a public stage. The stakes are higher, the exposure greater, the scrutiny all the more intense. Everyone involved in this little play was putting their reputation on the line. Craine had promised himself he'd no longer work studio cases and it didn't matter what Simms said about staying in the background. By being there at all Craine was putting his name into the hat. I want no part of this, he told himself. This has to be the last time.

The road swept around the green foothills of Herbert Stanley's hillside estate on Easton Drive. It was still raining, and Craine tried to focus on holding his car in the center of the road. He stifled a yawn. He found himself following the rhythm of the rain drumming on the roof of the car and his mind began to wander. He'd found himself dreaming increasingly during the day, struggling to concentrate on simple tasks yet still unable to sleep at night. The white nights kept the nightmares out, though, something could be said for that. Daydreams, his imagination, memories: these could be controlled. But nightmares? There was no telling what the Sandman offered if you let him in.

A mob of photographers was gathered outside Stanley's gates, flashbulbs popping beneath black umbrellas. Craine sank in his seat and tipped his hat low. He was spotted by Whitey Hendry, head of M.G.M.'s private police force, who quickly ordered the cameramen away from the gates.

"Out of the way! Get them gates open. L.A.P.D. is here. Get them gates open!"

Hendry was a bulldog of a man with a fierce allegiance to M.G.M. He was there at every M.G.M. crime scene, barking orders and beating photographers who dared to expose the scandal on celluloid.

"Oh, come on! Jesus!" one cameraman protested as he was pushed to the floor. He stood up and picked up his umbrella, frowning when he saw Craine through the driver's window.

"Hey, that's Celia Raymond's husband," he said, darting in front of the car. He lifted up his camera. "Hey you—Detective!"

Craine quickly accelerated through the open gates before he could push his camera against the glass.

Stanley's driveway curled round a circular lawn. The house was dull white, with a red tile roof and a wrought iron finish in the Californian style. Craine parked outside the garages and stepped out into the rain. He narrowed his eyes against the drizzle and put on his hat.

"How are you, Craine?"

He turned to see Russell Peterson standing on the stone steps leading up to the front door, an umbrella held firmly above his head.

Craine studied his ever-ready smile and wondered what he wanted. He had never had much time for Peterson, M.G.M.'s Head of Publicity. It was always Peterson who was there waiting at the scene of the crime, ready to launch himself at Craine with a list of demands. Maybe it was his canine obedience to Louis Mayer that bothered him. Or maybe it was because he was a shameless manipulator with a superficial charm. But then again, maybe it was their similarities that troubled Craine the most. With his well-coiffed hair and rigid grace, Peterson was the shinier side of the same coin.

"I'm fine, Mr. Peterson."

Peterson strode over to the car and covered them both with his umbrella. They walked slowly to the front door. "I hope you weren't held up at the gate."

"I wasn't expecting so many photographers here."

"The story was leaked," he said quickly. "It doesn't bother us, we're well prepared."

"Do you need me to bring more uniforms?"

"We've got plenty of studio police here. We'd like to keep this an internal affair as much as possible." Craine noticed he'd lost his usual sangfroid. There was an anxiety in Peterson that he hadn't seen before. His forehead was wet. It could be rainwater. "And what about the L.A.P.D.? Will you be holding a news conference anytime soon?"

"Later today."

"What time?"

"Six."

"And I trust Miss Goodwin's police statement will be adequate?"

"It will be."

Peterson leaned in closer. "East Coast publications will have their own perspective on events, they always do, but that isn't of real concern. We're not anticipating much trouble with the press." That didn't surprise Craine. Most print articles were provided to newspapers by outside sources. With a publicity department of over one hundred staff, Peterson had more than enough resources to control the flow of information to the general public.

Peterson smiled. He had large white teeth. "We are, however, uncertain as to what angle *The Hollywood Enquirer* will take. Our relationship with the paper is a little strained at the moment. We're renegotiating the terms of our advertising costs. There's a chance they may use this opportunity to embarrass us."

"I'll wait until tomorrow. If the headlines aren't favorable, I'll go speak to them personally."

"Much obliged, Detective Craine. We'll be using all our own resources to make this situation easier. I've already made calls to City Hall. The District Attorney is fully aware of the situation. You're not working alone on this."

No, Craine thought, I could never claim to work alone. I'm merely one of hundreds of people positioned to maintain harmony in the motion picture industry. The newspapers, the City Mayor, the Chief of Police—all of them recognize that the seed that grew this prosperous town has to be protected at all costs. Without the motion picture industry, there would be no Los Angeles.

"I'll keep you informed," Craine said. "If this is a suicide as you say, the D.A. shouldn't need any further involvement."

"Good," Peterson looked visibly relieved. "I should mention that Louis Mayer would like to offer his appreciation for your contribution to the case. M.G.M.'s fifteen-year anniversary is a few days away. There's a celebratory evening planned at Loew House. He'd be very grateful if you'd accept his invitation. It's the least we can do."

"The invitation isn't necessary," Craine replied. "Where is Stanley's body?"

"The study is at the end of the corridor to your left. You'll see the double doors."

"Thank you," he said, reaching for the front door.

"One last thing." Peterson held his arm across the doorjamb. "That young detective, O'Neill. Can we rely on him as we can rely on you?"

Craine the reliable. The mention of the word threw him back five months to when he'd stood with Peterson outside the doors to the L.A.P.D. press briefing room. "No one needs to know," Peterson had said. "They'll think it's an accident. Forget about the pills. She took one or two too many, she fell asleep and she drowned. Why make a storm in a teacup? Let the whole thing blow over. It'll be better for you and better for us. Let her memory be of pictures and awards. Don't let her be remembered for a weak moment of hysteria."

Yes, Craine was reliable; reliable to the end. Relied upon to cover up his own wife's suicide.

He pushed Peterson's arm away and stepped inside. "I'll make sure of it."

Herbert Stanley's lifeless body hung rigid from the ceiling fan of his study. He was in the early stages of rigor mortis, his arms stiff by his sides and his socked feet pointing toward the floor below him. A leather belt was wrapped tight around his neck, angling his head to one side. His face was swollen and cyanotic through lack of oxygen, and although his eyes were closed, his mouth was wide open, twisted into an awkward grin with his gray tongue protruding from between his teeth.

Detective Patrick O'Neill stood in the shadow of the dead man, making notes on a small pad. He circled around the body, careful to avoid stepping on a pair of Stanley's slippers and a wooden desk chair lying on its side as he tried to log every detail of the crime scene. He'd lost track of how long he had been here. Maybe two hours, maybe longer.

"Watch your eyes, Detective," said Crickley, the ruddy-faced crime tech photographing the scene. Closed French shutters covered both of the study's windows so the tech was using flashbulbs to get the right exposure. O'Neill was tempted to open the shutters to light up the room but he didn't want to disturb the crime scene any more than he had to. Experience had taught him that you only ever get one chance at a crime scene and it deteriorated very quickly. The body would remain there untouched until the morgue wagon took it away, but the crime scene itself was vulnerable as soon as the first person entered the room.

"Shall I get one with the slippers, Detective?"

"I'm sorry? Oh, um, yes, yeah—if you can."

Crickley steadied his camera. "Patrick O'Neill. Any relation to Quinlan?"

O'Neill covered his eyes as another flashbulb popped. "He's my father. *Was* my father. He passed on about a year ago."

"I'm sorry to hear that, kid. I worked with him a while back in San Francisco." Crickley looked at him and frowned. "Can't say I can see the family resemblance."

"Yes, thank you," O'Neill said, not wanting to dwell on it. Patrick had both his father's eye for detail and his detective's intuition. He had not, however, inherited his father's impressive physical stature; he was short and stringy, with his mother's round, cherub-like face and an astigmatism that forced him to wear thick, horn-rimmed glasses at all times. "Do you mind getting ... can you get another snap of the slippers with the chair ... with the chair in there?" He was tripping over his words so he cleared his throat. "I mean, if that's not too much trouble. Thank you. But please—I mean, please be careful. Don't touch anything."

"Are you okay, Detective? You seem a little jittery."

"Yes, I'm fine. I'm swell, thank you." O'Neill shifted on his feet. He was sweating. Maybe he was overdressed again. In defiance of the warm Los Angeles climate, O'Neill tended to dress in thick Donegal tweed suits with woolen waistcoats. Today's humidity only made it worse.

"You seem a little puzzled. Like you're confused." Crickley was at his side now, sizing up the crime scene as he unscrewed a flashbulb and placed it in his pocket.

"Sorry," O'Neill said, unsmiling, "I'm only ... I'm trying to figure out what happened here."

"You kidding?" Crickley pointed a sideward thumb at the deceased. "You don't think this is straight-up suicide?"

"I'm not sure. Looks like it but it's too early to be certain."

"I know," said Crickley, jumping on an idea. "It's 'cause of those slippers." Crickley pointed his boot toward Stanley's slippers. "They're the wrong way round. He's got the right one below his left foot, the left one under his right. You're thinking someone put them there, make it look like he'd done it to himself."

O'Neill had already considered this. "No. If you didn't have laces, or if you were wearing slippers, you'd use your feet to slip off your shoes. One heel on the back of the other. Like this. That'd leave your shoes the wrong way round."

Crickley pondered that, running his tongue around the inside of his cheek. "Yeah, I guess that makes sense. So what's the problem?"

O'Neill put his pad in his pocket and folded his arms. Something about this crime scene had irked him from the outset. One small detail that didn't sit right with him: "There's no note."

O'Neill had been working in homicide for just a year and a half and had admittedly only ever seen two other suicides, but in both cases the victims had left a note: one was a drunken apology, and the other was a desperate goodbye, but they were indicators of willing departure nonetheless.

"Huh." Crickley had stopped taking pictures now. He looked around and pursed his lips in agreement. "I guess you're right. So you think someone did this to him? Strung him up like that?"

"Forcing a man to—um—*hang* himself is harder than it sounds. Even if they'd put a bag over his head, he'd have lashed out. They'd have had to restrain him. We'll get a full autopsy tomorrow but I don't see any bruises on his face or hands, no marks on his wrist either. Think about it: if you were really going to hang someone, you'd never get them to climb onto a chair or a ladder, not unless he was . . ."

Crickley picked up on O'Neill's line of thought. "Unless he was drugged?"

O'Neill nodded his head. That was exactly what he was thinking. "Unless he was drugged."

Crickley packed up his equipment. "I only take the pictures. But you ask me, it's pretty hard to figure it's anything but suicide. You always been so suspicious, Detective?"

"Always," replied O'Neill without smiling. He knew that Crickley was poking fun at him but if anything he took it as a compliment. Maybe being suspicious made him question everything, but being suspicious also made him good at his job.

O'Neill noticed Crickley's eyes flick toward the door. His face paled.

"Detective O'Neill?"

At the sound of his name, O'Neill turned to see a man in a long coat and hat standing in the doorway. He recognized him as a detective from the Bureau. They hadn't met yet. Craine, he thought his name was. He was the man whose wife died a few months ago. He was the man they said used to be assigned to studio cases. O'Neill wondered how long he'd been standing there watching them.

Craine addressed Crickley: "Would you give us a minute?"

"No problem, Detective."

Craine waited for Crickley to leave the room before he approached. He looked up at Stanley's corpse and waited silently for a moment. O'Neill thought he heard him sigh under his breath.

"You know who I am?" he said, his voice slow and clear. "You know why I'm here?"

"You're Jonathan Craine. Did Simms send you? I'm the primary detective—"

"Are you all done here?" Craine interrupted. "It looks to me like you're all done here."

"Yes, almost. But I haven't found a note yet. I should really check the house, in case. Seems odd to me he wouldn't leave a suicide note."

Craine ran the thick of his palm along his jaw. "Mr. Peterson and his security team have checked the entire house and no one found a note. If they do, you'll be the first to know, I promise you. I suggest you finish up."

"I was hoping to talk to the maid at the precinct. I'd like to give her a formal interview."

"Why?"

"She said she found Stanley's body a few hours ago. I mean, she didn't speak English that well but she said she found the body at ten o'clock. Stanley died sometime during the night so I can't understand why was he found so late in the morning. He had three house staff who live on site—"

"It's a large house. There are a dozen rooms on the first floor alone."

"But the double doors to the study were wide open. Anyone could see his body from the foyer or the living room."

"Does it look like suicide?"

"Well, at first, maybe—"

"Then why are you questioning it?"

The room fell silent. Patrick O'Neill was a good police investigator but had always struggled to assert himself in the presence of others. Although he was twenty-nine years old, thirty this coming

September, he had the fresh-faced polish and nervous gait of a much younger man and was rarely taken seriously among other adults.

Craine continued: "If you undermine my efforts to ensure this case passes smoothly I'll have you removed from the Bureau. You'll be working auto theft for the remainder of your career. Is that clear?"

O'Neill nodded. Any further investigation into Herbert Stanley's death was prohibited. There were larger forces at work here.

"This crime scene is closed. Type up your report, put it on my desk. I'll prepare you a statement to be released to the press this afternoon."

"But I still have to interview some people."

"I'll take care of it."

"What about his wife, Gale Goodwin?" O'Neill was skittish now, the octaves of his own voice unpredictable.

"I'll take a statement from her myself."

"But Craine—"

"Finish up here. This crime scene is closed."

CHAPTER 5

At thirty-three, Gale Goodwin was increasingly aware that her time as an actress was running short. She stared at herself in the gilt-framed mirror in Joan Crawford's spare bedroom and wiped her eyes with a handkerchief. She'd been crying. Her nose was raw, her eyelids bloated and there were firm prints of crow's feet in the corners of her eyes. She wondered why anyone had ever found her attractive; why the papers had ever thought of her as a poster girl.

Her thoughts turned to Herbert. She pictured his slack body hanging from his study. She hadn't seen him, couldn't bring herself to go to the house or even to the mortuary. She knew she'd have to go and identify the body—his corpse. The chill realization that he was gone made her miss him. She stopped hating him, pitied him, wanted him to be there with her.

Gale heard a man's voice from downstairs and knew immediately who it was even before the maid came upstairs to find her. She'd thought that another detective had already been assigned but Joan had warned her that they'd send Craine. They'd met briefly a number of years ago at a private screening at Loew House for one of M.G.M.'s first "talkies," his wife Celia Raymond in her first and only starring role. They'd seen each other in passing since but never shared more than a few polite words. She knew him mainly by reputation, as the inside man at the L.A.P.D., the man mostly seen having a quiet word in the corner. She wondered now whether Craine had had any part in Celia's death, whether he was involved in some form of cover-up. She'd heard the stories.

Gale stepped out of the bedroom. She took a long, deep breath and composed herself before starting down the stairs, holding the banister lightly with one hand. Above her head a cut-glass chandelier lit the checkered hallway floor. She became aware of another figure in the room and when she turned she saw Craine's silhouette in the doorway of the living room.

She stopped three steps from the bottom. He turned and she saw his face. There he was, Jonathan Craine. Jonathan the widower, Jonathan the investigator, Jonathan the keeper of secrets. He had changed since she'd last seen him; his face had grayed and there was a hardness in his eyes, a wounded gaze that made her feel unnerved. His very presence shook her.

"Hello, Miss Goodwin, I'm here to talk to you about your husband," he said. His low voice slid down her spine, clinging onto every nerve. She couldn't speak, her throat was squeezed closed.

"I didn't know you were coming," was all she could manage. Good, her voice was steady and controlled. She tried to keep it that way. "I hope I haven't kept you waiting. I wasn't expecting to see anyone until tomorrow."

"There's another detective investigating. I've been asked to oversee the file. Has Peterson spoken to you yet?"

"He said someone from the police would be coming. He didn't say any more than that."

"I'm afraid I need to take a statement."

"Right now?"

He nodded. "The quicker we do this, the best chance we have of quelling any rumors about your husband's death. It will also help us to avoid a deposition if for any reason this goes to court."

"Deposition?"

"Further questioning. A court reporter would be present. We want to avoid that if we can."

"Should I call my lawyer?"

"Consider me your lawyer in this situation, Miss Goodwin. This isn't an interrogation. I just want to take a witness testimony."

"Do I have to go to the precinct?"

"No, I can take a statement here."

"Then I suppose we should get on with it. Joan will be back shortly," Gale said, turning her back to him as she crossed the hallway toward a dark-stained door in the far corner.

The drawing room was dark, lit only by a single green desk lamp on a bureau against the wall. Queen Anne chairs and a Davenport sofa formed a half-circle around a broad fireplace but Gale didn't take a seat. She made her way across the room toward a small circular side table holding a whiskey decanter and three lowballs. She pulled out the stopper and poured herself a glass.

"When was the last time you saw your husband?" he asked with a formality that she hoped would make the questions that followed easier. She could act the part, pretend this was simply a scene in a picture.

"Last night. We had an argument, no reason to deny it I suppose." She avoided eye contact but her hand was shaking so she left the lowball on the table. She noticed a cigarette box on the piano.

"Can you describe the confrontation?"

"It was bitter. We'd been arguing a lot recently."

"What about?"

"His mood swings were becoming unbearable. He was drinking too much. I told him I wanted a divorce."

"What did he say?"

"He said no. He wouldn't grant me one." She lit a cigarette and leaned against the wall.

"Did he become violent?"

"He never touched me. Never had."

"Did he threaten you?"

"In a way. He said that if I tried to divorce him he'd make sure my contract wasn't renewed and that I'd get nothing."

"What happened after?"

"After what?"

"After the argument."

43

"I left the house. He must have gone into the study. I saw him at the window when I got in the car. We were supposed to go out for dinner so I was all dressed up. I went to the Lilac Club." She smiled faintly, as best she could, as if the idea itself was ridiculous. She was dancing at the Lilac Club when her husband was taking his own life.

Craine checked his pad for what looked like nothing in particular. "Around what time did you leave?"

"I'm not sure. Ten. No, later—eleven maybe."

"Who drove you?"

"I don't usually drive but I drove myself."

"Why?"

"Herbert had sent everyone home, told them to come back in the morning." She saw Craine frown then write on his pad.

"There was no one else in the house. The dailies may pick up on that. They'll try to weave it into their headlines. When was this last night? At what point did he send them home?"

"When we were arguing. Ask the maid if you don't believe me. He said for once I wouldn't get my audience."

"But at what time was this?"

"That must have been a little after nine."

"So you argued for almost two hours before you left the house?"

"Yes. He was drunk and there was no point talking to him; nothing was getting through so I left."

"Your husband left no note before he died. Certain areas of the press may try to use this to suggest foul play. As a countermeasure, the studio will release their own statement today saying that Herbert was a depressive homosexual with suicidal tendencies," Craine said in a matter-of-fact tone. "Would you say that was accurate?"

A long pause. She could feel the blood drain from her face. How could they turn their back on her husband so easily? She remained composed. She found a voice. "I suppose he was depressed," she said at last.

"Did you think he would hang himself?"

She shook her head. "No."

"But you weren't surprised?"

She shook her head. "Herbert had threatened to before." She turned away from him now, hands shaking as she tried to lift her drink to her mouth.

"I would regard that as suicidal tendencies. Had he tried to kill himself before?"

"No, not that I'm aware of."

"And was he a homosexual?"

"I don't know," she whispered. In truth, she'd always been suspicious but never been sure. Herbert had never looked at her as a sexual being. Their relationship had always been more concerned with business than love. But despite this, idle gossip on the studio lot angered her. How dare they presume to know about Herbert? And so what if he was a homosexual—was it really so foul to have feelings for the same sex?

Craine persisted. "Miss Goodwin, the studio will use your husband's sexuality to limit the damage to your reputation. You're more likely to be viewed sympathetically by the public."

"I told you I don't know. Maybe. I'd heard rumors but nothing I genuinely believed to be true."

Craine stood still for a long moment then put his pad in his jacket pocket. "We'll be releasing your statement at a news conference later on today. Expect to see your name in the newspapers tomorrow."

She tried to stop herself from clenching her fists and balled her feet instead. "I was hoping that it might not make the news—"

She searched Craine's face but there was no sympathy there. Only emptiness. "Miss Goodwin, you're in the public eye. I can assure you it will make the morning print. That can't be helped. It's better to get your side of the story across first, that way we have more control over the press."

"So everything I tell you now will be splashed across the headlines?"

"No, only what we see fit to print."

"You'll censor me."

"Something to that effect."

Gale looked at Craine for a long moment. She could read nothing in his face. How could he be so cold? She needed kindness, not cruelty. Why couldn't they find fellow-feeling in the face of shared difficulties, two people whose husband and wife had lost their lives? "Did you know I was friendly with your wife?" she said. "We knew each other."

A moment of paralysis as Craine didn't reply. Then: "I didn't see you at the funeral."

Gale hadn't anticipated such a sharp reply. She turned so that he faced her back. "Is there anything else, Detective Craine? I'm not sure I'm ready for any more of your questions."

"There's nothing else."

"Then please, would you mind leaving?"

Craine stalled. For the first time he spoke to her as a human being. "You must understand my job is to protect you. Everything I say or do is directed with that in mind."

"I don't need your help. Now get out, please."

"I'll have someone collect you tomorrow and bring you to the Bureau. I'll need you to identify your husband's body."

"Fine."

Craine nodded, and turned on his heels. At the doorway he said quietly, "I've been where you're standing. It gets better. You think it never will but it does. Slowly, day by day, it gets better." He left the room without saying another word. Gale heard him stride out of the room and across the hallway.

She waited for the front door to close before bursting into tears.

CHAPTER 6

"You finished?" asked Craine, making a show of checking his watch. "We don't have a lot of time."

O'Neill wriggled in his suit—a tweed suit. It was like he was dressed for a cold snap. "I'm sorry. I'll just be a second. Do you mind if we run through it one more time? I mean, in case there are a few things that we haven't covered yet."

Craine had provided a typed transcript of his conversation with Gale, edited as he had seen necessary. Together they were finalizing a statement to be read out to the press. O'Neill was making hard work of it, fingering at his typewriter with those chubby hands of his and questioning Craine's notes line by line.

He found O'Neill a strange boy. He looked about twelve but dressed like a sixty-year-old man. They'd never worked together but Craine vaguely remembered him from when he started. People said he used to have a big-shot father in San Francisco.

Craine leaned over the typewriter and pointed at two lines above the ribbon. "Cut the part about Gale's whereabouts," he said. "It'll only draw attention to her. If they want to know, they'll ask. Add a sentence stating that there were no suspicious circumstances."

When O'Neill looked at him, clutching at words, Craine said, "What is it?"

O'Neill took off his glasses and wiped them with the end of his necktie. "It's just . . . all of this feels like . . ."

"Like what?"

"All I'm saying is . . . It doesn't feel very objective. Gale Goodwin's statement, for example."

"What about it?"

O'Neill looked nervous under Craine's stare. "I wondered whether we might consider writing out what she said . . . in its complete form."

"I took a statement myself."

"But Craine, with all due respect, this is not a transcript."

"It's an edited account of our conversation. She's going to sign it."

O'Neill shrank lower in his chair. He looked at his hands when he spoke. "In San Francisco, any statement we give to the press sticks strictly to the known facts. We don't make conjecture."

"This isn't San Francisco," Craine snapped. "And we're under a lot of pressure here to see this is done right."

O'Neill didn't say anything but Craine could tell this was bothering him. He looked at the young detective with his palms held open. "O'Neill, what is it about this scenario makes you question that this isn't suicide?"

O'Neill swallowed. "I'll admit it looked like a suicide. At first, anyway. But then I got to thinking. We don't know that for sure. Have you thought maybe we could look at other options?"

"Such as?"

O'Neill took a deep breath. "What if he'd been drugged?"

Craine closed his eyes. Patrick O'Neill's endless questions were exhausting. "I don't want that mentioned in the statement. We can wait for an autopsy."

O'Neill nodded slowly.

"Anything else?"

"There's one last thing," O'Neill said delicately. "I think the press will ask about the note. Who doesn't leave a note?"

Craine could feel his temper rise then fall again. He thought carefully about how he was going to respond before asking coolly, "Have you seen cases like this where there hasn't been a note?"

O'Neill was resolute. "No. Never."

"And how many have suicides have you seen?"

O'Neill scratched a beard he didn't have. "Two."

It was the answer Craine was hoping for. "Only two? Are you trying to tell me that two suicides are enough to predict a definite trend? That all suicides must write their family a self-satisfied goodbye?"

"No, but—"

"But nothing. Haven't you ever heard of Occam's Razor? Sometimes the simplest explanation is the right one. It looked like suicide because it *was* suicide."

O'Neill didn't reply, and Craine could see that he was faltering. Craine was persuasive like that. Manipulative, even. Could make you change your mind about pretty much anything. He knew people sometimes found him intimidating. And he knew too he frequently took advantage of that fact.

Craine pulled the statement from the platen as if to draw the matter to a close. "We have twenty minutes before we brief the press. Give a copy to my secretary and I'll see you downstairs."

"Wait—who's reading this?"

"You are."

O'Neill blanched. "You mean, outside? I'm going to stand there and read all this to the press?"

"That's right."

"I'm not . . . I'm not a big fan of public speaking."

"Nothing to worry about. Just read the statement."

Craine reached for his coat and hat. He was already half-way out the door when O'Neill said: "And what if they don't believe it?"

Craine didn't turn back. "That's my problem," he said.

The Los Angeles Police Department news conference was held on the steps outside Central Headquarters, opposite City Hall.

Detective Patrick O'Neill addressed a noisy and restless press corps shortly after 6 P.M., Craine's secretary holding an umbrella high above his head to protect his typed statement from the rain. He shivered but despite the cold he could feel sweat on his forehead. Standing directly behind him were Captain Simms and, a little further behind him, Russell Peterson, the Publicity Chief at M.G.M. that he'd met briefly at Stanley's house.

O'Neill noticed Jonathan Craine standing discreetly at the back of the crowd but tried his best to avoid his gaze.

"Good afternoon, good evening," O'Neill began, leaning over the plinth. "My name is Detective Patrick O'Neill. As many of you—" He paused when he saw his hands start to tremble. He gripped the paper firmly between his fingers. "As many of you are now aware, this morning, at approximately ten o'clock, the body of M.G.M. producer Herbert Stanley was discovered by his maid at his home on Easton Drive. His death was promptly reported to the police by Russell Peterson, Head of Publicity at Metro-Goldwyn-Mayer, and uniform officers and a paramedic team arrived on the scene shortly after 10:30 A.M. Mr. Stanley was pronounced dead at 10:40 A.M. The crime scene has now been examined by county police and I can confirm that Herbert Stanley hanged himself from a leather waist-belt tied to the ceiling fan in his study. Estimated time of death is between midnight and 2 A.M. At present there are no . . ." O'Neill took a deep breath. *Was he really going to say it?* He caught Craine staring at him. He didn't have a choice. "At present," he said again, "there are no suspicious circumstances surrounding Mr. Stanley's death."

There was a furor of desperate pleas and waving hands as reporters shouted out their questions. O'Neill continued talking over the noise and the crowd fell silent, their pencils scratching furiously at their pads.

"This is a very tragic case. Herbert Stanley, fifty-two years old, was a motion picture producer at M.G.M. studios, well liked and respected by his peers. He is survived by his wife, the actress Gale Goodwin, who has asked that the media respect her privacy during this difficult time. She will not be making a public statement to the press in the near future.

"I can confirm that—" O'Neill paused. His notes seemed strangely blurry and unclear. He blinked to correct his vision but instead all he saw were the faces of the men in the crowd staring at him.

He swallowed drily and tried to continue: "I can confirm, however, that Miss Goodwin was interviewed this afternoon and that we do have a police statement that will be provided to the press. She indicated that her husband had been suffering from depression for some time and had made previous attempts on his own life. His suicide was not unexpected."

"Detective! Detective, over here!"

Flashbulbs popped. O'Neill flinched as magnesium flash powder flared near his face. He coughed, the plumes of white smoke burning at his throat. He tried to distinguish the questions fired at him by reporters. A small man darted forward and took a picture. His face bobbed up from behind his camera.

"Detective O'Neill," he said, before others could jump in. "Are you certain it was Stanley's body?"

"There seems to be no doubt that the body was that of Herbert Stanley, but he will be formally identified by his wife tomorrow."

". . . Was there a suicide note found at his house?"

". . . Do the L.A.P.D. believe there was a cover-up?"

". . . What about M.G.M.'s role in his death?"

Another flashbulb popped. O'Neill couldn't see. He squeezed his eyelids together. "There was no suicide note but there was no sign of foul play."

". . . Did his wife say what made him kill himself?"

". . . Where was Gale Goodwin at the time?"

"Miss Goodwin wasn't present at their house on Easton Drive last night. She stated that she believed her husband's death was the culmination of months of deep depression. We will be providing you with her full statement shortly."

". . . Will you be conducting a full autopsy?"

The reporters were pushing closer. O'Neill felt jostled by the encroaching crowd. His legs began to shudder with nerves.

"The body . . . Stanley . . . Mr. Stanley's body has been removed from his house by representatives of the medical examiner's office. A pathologist will be completing a full autopsy in the coming days."

". . . Do we know if he was on any prescription medication?"

"That, I am unaware of."

". . . What about rumors of Stanley's sexuality?"

"Miss Goodwin did not deny the rumors."

". . . Was she planning on divorcing her husband? Was that why he killed himself?"

Simms stepped forward and pulled O'Neill away. "Gentlemen, no more questions. Thank you, we're out of time. No more questions, please."

Jonathan Craine watched as the herd of umbrellas dispersed and the shaken figure of O'Neill was ushered into the safety of the police department. He had reason to be pleased. The fruits of his labor had paid off. Still, he wasn't sure if he trusted O'Neill. He was always two steps ahead, always questioning the facts. What was he angling for? Did he want a promotion? Money? The Detective Bureau wasn't known for its ethical idealism.

Craine's Fleetwood was parked in the road. When he reached his driver's door, a hand leaned out and opened it for him.

"Allow me," said Russell Peterson, standing a little too closely by Craine's side with his umbrella held over both of them. There was rain on his stubble like dew on freshly cut grass and Craine thought it odd he hadn't shaved that morning.

"Satisfied, Mr. Peterson?"

Peterson smiled in slow motion. "Aren't we always, Detective Craine? Your efforts to make good on our arrangement are appreciated."

Craine took the door from his hand. "I'll contact you tomorrow then."

"Will you be speaking to Wilson?"

He was referring to Billy Wilson, owner of *The Hollywood Enquirer*. They shared a long history, and the thought of seeing Wilson filled Craine with unease. "Tomorrow morning," he said, "pending the outcome of today's press release."

"We're expecting negative press. Insider talk on *The Enquirer's* budget lines has been nothing but scathing and Mr. Mayer is anxious."

"Do you have something to offer Wilson in return?"

Peterson inclined his head. "We'll review our position over advertising costs. A favorable deal if Wilson amends his stance."

"I'll pass on the message."

A nod signaled the end of their conversation and Craine slid into the driver's seat. As Peterson walked back toward his waiting car, Craine's eye was caught by a man wearing a long beige coat over a dark, chalk-striped suit. He was standing near the top of the steps and remained so as the press broke away, staring at him with a look delivering recognition yet completely devoid of expression. Did he know him? Beneath a petrol-blue hat, Craine saw russet-brown hair, almost red. An unfashionably trim ginger beard halted at the jawline where a long scar ran up to his temple.

There was a tap on the window to his left. "Detective Craine?"

Craine's secretary, Elaine, stood on the sidewalk, wrapped tight in a clutch coat with her hands tucked under her armpits. She didn't have an umbrella, and a scarf around her head did little to protect her hair from the rain.

"Don't you have an umbrella?" he said, winding down the window.

"I left it with Detective O'Neill. There was a call for you from your son's school. Father Calloway."

"Is something wrong? Has something happened to Michael?"

Elaine turned against the wind as rain buffeted her face. "He didn't mention anything. He asked if you could visit. He's been calling here—"

"Fine, if he calls again you can tell him I'm on my way. Get inside or you'll catch a cold."

"Good night, Detective Craine."

As he turned the ignition, Craine looked back again at the steps but the man with the red hair had disappeared.

CHAPTER 7

"I'm not worried about his studies," said Father Calloway, pushing a prayer book to one side so he could rest his elbows on the desk. "Michael is by far the brightest pupil in his class." Calloway's face was wide and round, framed by a thick beard and wispy gray hair that had begun its slow retreat up his forehead. His office was in an old bell tower that overlooked the school courtyard. The room was small and dark, with wood-paneled walls and a low ceiling. It reminded Craine of a confession booth.

Craine was quiet for a moment, head bowed, staring at the knuckles on his right hand. He knew Calloway was studying his face.

"Then what is the problem, Father?"

"We're worried about his social development. He remains reclusive, his behavior troubles his teachers. I've left messages at your work."

"I've been away."

"I wrote to you in New York."

"I received your letters." The letters explained that Michael was having trouble adapting to the death of his mother. They suggested that it wasn't good for Michael to be without a parental figure. The inference was clear: Craine had abandoned his son.

"Then you know he won't talk to anyone. He still hasn't."

"He's quiet, that's all. I was a quiet child."

"He's not quiet, he's mute, Mr. Craine. He hasn't said a word since the accident. Not to his peers, not to anyone. I've seen him mumble his prayers to himself, but that's about all. Mostly he rereads the same chapters in the Old Testament or plays marbles with the other boys, but he'll never talk to them. He plays completely silently, one hand always clinging onto his bag of marbles. You know the one I mean?"

"I know it." It was a gift from Celia, given to Michael at Christmas a few days before she died.

"One of our boys took a marble off him this morning. Wouldn't give it back, so Michael clean broke his nose. Boy's parents are in an uproar, came in here demanding Michael be expelled." Tired of sitting, he pushed himself off his chair and swung himself toward the window. "I said that wasn't possible, that I couldn't do anything of the sort without talking to his father first. But I've had no word from you, Mr. Craine. I didn't even know you were back from New York."

Craine had been in denial about his responsibilities, he knew that. But he wanted to get his life in order first. Celia had been such a good mother and he would be so weak in comparison. Better to have no father than a bad one, surely? "I was planning on coming to see you," he tried to explain. "I apologize if I've been difficult to get hold of. I wasn't aware of the urgency of the situation."

"Look, I have no intention of expelling Michael," said Calloway. "He belongs here, and if you don't mind me saying, that other idiot had it coming to him. But in all seriousness, Michael needs help. I'm not in a position to—"

"He found his mother," said Craine, interrupting. "Did you know that? He found her dead. You can understand he'd be upset. They were very close."

Calloway ran a finger between his neck and clerical collar. He looked hot, uncomfortable. "We know," he said, "but there are things he needs that we can't help him with. What I mean is there are things we can't offer him."

"If he needs extra help, if he needs to see a doctor, I'll pay for it. I'll donate to the archdiocese if necessary. Money isn't an issue."

Calloway shook his head. "That's not what I meant."

"Then what do you mean? Look, I'll speak to this other boy's parents. What's his name? What's their address?"

"He needs his father, Mr. Craine. What Michael needs is you."

Craine sat upright, straightening himself. "I'm here, aren't I? I'm here to spend time with him. He's why I came back."

"Then do you think he should return to his family home? The summer break is fast approaching."

Craine flustered. Michael couldn't stay with him. He wasn't ready. And even if he brought the maid or the nanny back he wasn't sure it would be good for Michael. Good for either of them, in fact.

He glanced toward the door to make sure it was still shut. Michael was sitting on a bench outside. He lowered his voice: "I'm busy with work. Things are a little difficult for me right now. I want to take him out. Tonight. We'll go to the pictures."

"I think he would really benefit from spending some time with you, Mr. Craine—more than the occasional evening visit and the odd excursion."

Craine's nostrils flared, blood coming to his face. "I think I know what's best for him; I am after all his father. This is a boarding school, isn't it? Or was I misinformed?"

Calloway nodded. "This is a boarding school."

"Then I assume Michael is one of many boarders of his age."

"He's not alone, no." Calloway stepped back to his chair and took a seat.

"And you say he's not expelled."

"I won't be taking the matter any further."

"Then I see no reason why he shouldn't continue as he is."

Father Calloway sat back, defeated. For a long moment he said nothing. "Yes, Mr. Craine," he said, picking up the prayer book on his desk and placing it in his lap, "Michael is more than welcome to stay."

Craine drove them to a picture house on Broadway and asked for two tickets to whatever was showing. When he collected his tickets he spotted Michael facing across the street, staring at a breadline trailing two blocks south. The Depression was most visible here downtown, where panhandlers and indigent transients sold oranges and pencils to make enough money for a decent meal and maybe a bottle of something.

Craine tapped his shoulder. "Come on, Michael, let's go inside."

Craine followed the blue neon strips to their seats. The vendor had told him *The Tainted Feather* was ten minutes in but the name of the picture didn't resonate until he saw Gale Goodwin's face projected in close-up onto a thirty-foot square. He considered leaving but it was late now and he was tired. Even though he doubted he'd sleep tonight, he had no intention of staying out any longer than necessary and he chose two seats near the back of the screening room so they could make a timely exit when the curtains closed.

When they were seated, Craine leaned down, whispering, "Are you alright? Do you want anything to eat? Popcorn? Peanuts?"

Michael shook his head, eyes staring intently at the screen.

"You know, Father Calloway said you were fighting. You shouldn't hit people, you know that. But if you're standing up for what you believe in then that's different. That's important."

Again, Michael didn't reply and Craine realized that what Calloway had told him was true: Michael was mute. He wondered how long he would stay that way and whether he should take him to a doctor. But doctors in L.A. would likely put him on medication and that wasn't what Craine wanted. Michael wasn't mentally ill. He didn't need his brain fixing. He was sad.

It was a good picture, one that Celia would have liked. She was one of the few actors he knew who genuinely enjoyed going to the movie theater. She loved pictures, would go twice a week if she could. Craine was apathetic, as he was increasingly to most things in life. Michael sat quietly throughout the whole movie. Like his mother, he loved every second, would ask to go every night when he was younger. Craine scanned Michael's face quickly, noticing a light on behind those narrow eyes, his pupils glowing brightly at the movement on the screen.

When the picture ended they drove for forty minutes without saying a word. The rain had stopped and Broadway was buzzing with nightlife. They passed drunk college boys staggering out of bars; a barker was yelling about a midnight showing of some B-picture; a little further down the street a gang of Mexicans were fighting outside a drugstore. You didn't see many Latinos in this part of Hollywood. Most Mexicans lived in the flats or toward Happy Valley, relegated to a new social substructure beneath the white working classes.

On the quiet road that twisted toward Michael's school, Craine said, "When I left, I know I didn't really tell you when I was coming back. I should have told you how long I was going away for. I realize that. But I'm back now. I have my job back."

He was making excuses. He was always making excuses without ever really apologizing. He shot Michael a side glance but he was staring at the footwell. "I would have come to see you sooner but I've been busy," he went on. "There's something I've been meaning to talk to you about. I thought about writing but in the end I figured it would be easier if we talked about it. I've been thinking about selling the house."

This seemed to get Michael's attention. He looked at him. A blank expression but a look nonetheless.

Encouraged, Craine continued: "You remember before Christmas your mother mentioned about moving East? Do you remember that? We discussed it a few times."

Discussed was the polite term. They'd fought about it for weeks. He tried to recall the argument they'd had that final night. He could remember Celia's incessant pleas that they leave California and move to New York, but his memory was blurred and unclear and he couldn't quite envisage the scene or remember the words.

"I've been talking with real estate agents about putting the house on the market. Just to see what happens. It could free up some money. And it's a big place, too big for the two of us. Besides, I thought a change of scene would do us good. Maybe move out of the city. Maybe move East like your mother wanted." In truth, he had no idea. He only knew he didn't want the life he had anymore. "I was brought up in New York. Did you know that?"

Michael stared at him. A long pause, then finally a tilt of the head. So slight Craine wasn't sure if it was a nod or not.

Craine broached the next part carefully. "You could come with me, but I was wondering whether you wanted to stay here." He couldn't picture their life together, is what he meant. There was too much that hadn't been said and being with Michael just reminded him of everything he'd lost. Both of them were still coming to terms with what happened that night. But rather than bring them closer together, Celia's death had somehow created a greater rift between them. And now, whenever he looked at Michael, he saw Celia's eyes looking back at him. Judging him. So it became easier, perhaps even for both of them, if they spent time apart. Craine would allow Michael to process the loss of his mother as he himself dealt with the passing of his wife. There didn't need to be any crossover. "You have your school here," he explained, "and your friends. I don't want this to disrupt your education unnecessarily. But you could come visit . . ."

Whatever expression was on Michael's face changed into something darker.

"Think about it. We don't have to decide now."

It was a lot for Michael to take on board, he knew that. And he was ignoring the bigger issue, the elephant in the room. The boy had found his mother dead and they needed to talk about it. But for someone so skilled in the art of interviews and interrogation, Craine found it remarkably hard to talk to his son on an emotional level. He knew that he loved Michael, knew that he cared for his well-being, but he worried so much about his abilities as a father that he couldn't communicate that love in any way. He didn't hug him and couldn't speak to him earnestly without both of them feeling uncomfortable; at times it seemed to him that he was merely Michael's parent by proxy, little more than a legal guardian.

They reached Michael's school and Craine pulled up outside the main gates and sat behind the wheel with the engine running.

There were many things he wanted to tell his son, but in that moment the words failed him. "When your mother . . ." he began before he changed his mind. He couldn't talk about what had happened. He wasn't ready. For what felt like a long time it was silent in the car except for the sound of the engine humming. "Father Calloway says you're doing well at school," he said eventually. "That's good. Your mother would be pleased."

Michael didn't look at him. He fingered the inside passenger handle and opened the door, using his arms to push himself out. He shut the door behind him then walked through the school gates toward the double doors of his dormitory.

"I'm sorry you found your mother," he wanted to say. "I'm sorry that you blame yourself for my failings as a husband. It's not your fault she died. It's mine."

But Craine didn't say anything. He put the car in gear and drove away. He didn't even say goodbye.

Seven miles away, the tall, lean figure of Paul Kamona walked through the foyer of the Morden Hotel carrying a small leather brief-case. He wore a large felt fedora and a single-breasted gray suit with a plain white shirt. Perhaps his face was paler than most, his hair cropped unfashionably short at the temples but, that aside, he looked like any one of the many traveling salesmen who stayed at the Morden. He nodded to the young night clerk sitting at reception then took the cage elevator up to his room on the first floor.

The room was spacious but spartan. Kamona put the briefcase on the floor near where his other luggage stood, took off his jacket and checked his pocket watch. A little after midnight. He had ten hours to wait for his phone call. He went over to the window and looked out at the rear parking lot. Good: his rented Ford was parked directly below, a few feet from the fire exit door.

Kamona was always very particular about where he stayed when he was working. Like most of the hotels he stayed at, the Morden was mid-price, busy enough that he didn't stand out, quiet enough that he was left alone. Most importantly, however, the Morden had more than one entrance and exit. Kamona had been absolutely insistent that he had a room on the first floor that was as near to the emergency stairway as possible.

He pulled the curtains closed, fastened the chain on the door and placed the briefcase on the bed. He undid the brass latches, lifted the lid and pulled out a long-barreled Mauser pistol fitted with a steel Maxim suppressor. Then, with the same meticulous approach he had with everything in life, Paul Kamona set about cleaning his favorite weapon.

CHAPTER 8

May 12th

At a glance, press coverage of Stanley's death was better than expected. Although his suicide was front-page news in all the major West Coast dailies, most editorials avoided any unnecessary mudslinging and in Mayer-aligned papers, the headlines tended to follow the M.G.M. line. William Hearst's the *Los Angeles Examiner* ran the headline "GALE GOODWIN'S HUSBAND FOUND DEAD," with a subheading that read "Depressive Homosexual Herbert Stanley Takes His Own Life At Easton Drive Mansion."

Early that morning, Craine scanned the lead paragraphs.

Hollywood, Cal. May 12—Herbert Stanley, motion picture executive at M.G.M., ended his life in the $60,000 home in Easton Drive he shared with his actress wife, Gale Goodwin. Mr. Stanley, who was 52 years old, hanged himself in his study and left no note. The police reported that Stanley's maid found the body and called M.G.M. The suicide was reported to the police by Russell Peterson, Publicity Chief at Metro-Goldwyn-Mayer Film Corporation. "Stanley was alone in their home on the picturesque Benedict canyon estate," Peterson stated.

Miss Goodwin, staying at the home of friend and fellow M.G.M. actress Joan Crawford, was said to have been devastated by the news. Although she has yet to release a formal statement to the press, in a police interview Goodwin denied there had been any quarrels between herself and Stanley, stating: "My husband has suffered from severe depression for some time."

Police are not treating the case as suspicious.

The rest of the article continued on page eight. It outlined both Stanley's and Goodwin's careers at M.G.M., and there was a full paragraph on Gale Goodwin's most recent film *The Tainted Feather.* Interesting, thought Craine, considering Stanley had nothing to do with the picture. Beside the article were photographs of Herbert with Gale and photos of them separately. One picture saw Herbert looking particularly solemn and gray in his office, another saw him frowning at a party at the Lilac Club. That was contrasted with several photographs of Gale looking radiant on a film set. The subheading read: "Widowed, Award-winning Actress Gale Goodwin On The Set Of *The Tainted Feather.*" Peterson had always been very shrewd with the photographs he provided to the press. He knew that many Americans struggled to read and would flick through newspapers to the pictures.

Other, less M.G.M.-friendly papers were reluctant to follow the trend. *The Hollywood Enquirer* ran with "WILL HUSBAND'S SUICIDE END GALE GOODWIN'S FILM CAREER?" Subheadings included "Goodwin's Affairs Drove Husband To Suicide" and "Stanley Betrayed By Movie Star Wife." In his *Tradeviews* column, Billy Wilson had even written that Gale was a poisoned chalice who had driven her husband to an untimely death.

Published six days a week, *The Hollywood Enquirer* was the first—and most popular—daily trade newspaper dedicated to Hollywood's motion picture industry. Written almost entirely by Wilson himself, the paper reported on studio news and town gossip, not only covering the minutiae of show business but writing scandalous exposés of the illicit activities of Hollywood's movie stars. Wilson was a constant irritation to studio publicity departments.

Craine sat in the reception area of *The Hollywood Enquirer*'s offices on Sunset Boulevard, a stone's throw from Billy Wilson's many nightclubs and restaurants. He was here to meet Wilson to try to come to some kind of agreement over *The Enquirer*'s coverage of Stanley's death. Wilson's relationship with Louis Mayer had always been a little tumultuous, but the two men had recently fallen foul of each other when Wilson doubled his fee for an annual advertising account with *The Enquirer* and M.G.M. had refused to extend their contract.

Craine stifled a yawn and glanced at the wall clock to his left. A little after nine. He was exhausted. He still found sleep elusive and had considered taking the morning off to rest but he knew he had to see Wilson this morning before they ran their budget lines for tomorrow's print and besides, Gale Goodwin was due at the precinct at noon to formally identify her husband's body.

"Detective Craine?" It was Wilson's secretary, a slight redhead, holding a tray of Coca-Cola bottles. Wilson was known to drink fifteen to twenty a day.

"Good morning."

"Apologies for keeping you waiting. Mr. Wilson will see you now."

Billy Wilson was sitting behind a wide mahogany desk with a telephone receiver in one hand and a bottle of cola in the other. There were two chairs opposite him. Craine sat in one of them.

"Well I won almost fifty grand on the horses last week, Reuben, so capital shouldn't be a problem," he said unnecessarily loudly into the receiver. He rolled his eyes toward Craine and mouthed "sorry," but Craine knew he enjoyed having him wait. "Well, I can't deny I like a flutter from time to time myself, but the way I see it, the only way to beat the house is to own it!" Wilson laughed, snorting briefly before catching himself. Craine had already heard that Wilson was planning to sell off his club and restaurant assets and build hotels in Nevada. More than that, he also knew that he was talking to Chicago mafia rings about sharing the costs. He was hoping the latter information might give him some leverage in negotiation.

Wilson placed the receiver back on the cradle. He spoke quickly, punctuating rapid sentences with small sips from the soda bottle. "My apologies, important call from my accountant. How are you anyway, Craine? It's been a while, hasn't it? Six months, if not more. Simms taken you off the studio roll?"

Wilson was baiting him but Craine wasn't going to rise to it. They'd known each other for years, had gone through this charade countless times. "I've been on leave," Craine replied.

A lowering of the tone. "Your wife, yes of course. My condolences. I always liked her."

Craine balled his fists. The day after she died, Wilson printed an article stating that Celia was a drug addict. He then published an exposé of studio practices that encouraged actors and actresses to use psychostimulants such as methamphetamines to enhance performance and control weight gain. It also said that most contracted talent then relied on sedatives to get to sleep at night. It wasn't the article itself that bothered Craine—the accusations were mostly true. But Wilson also had a photographer break into his house and take pictures of Celia's empty bath. This, and another picture of his wife's body being loaded into a morgue truck, accompanied the text under the subheading "Celia Raymond: Victim Of Her Addictions."

"Anyway, are you still a regular at the Lilac Club?" Wilson went on, switching effortlessly into cheerier gears. "I'm surprised we haven't bumped into each other recently."

If he'd have seen Wilson at all Craine might have throttled him at his table. "Mr. Wilson, I was hoping to talk to you about your latest issue."

"Of course," said Wilson, still smiling inanely, "I digress. Did you enjoy it?"

"There were aspects of it I thought we could discuss."

Wilson let out an exaggerated sigh. "You mean you were hoping to persuade me to change my stance on Stanley's death? Well you won't. Mayer thinks he can run Los Angeles with an iron fist but you won't get me pandering to his demands. Do you know what tomorrow's headlines will be? I worked on them all night. Let me read you the proofs."

"That won't be necessary. I appreciate your personal position on M.G.M. All I'm asking is that you protect yourself from libel."

"Libel? Is that what you think it was? Nothing defamatory about it.

And why is it that you deem it necessary to come into my office and threaten me with libel, Detective?"

"It's not a threat."

"Then you're simply here to forewarn me. How kind," he said drily. "I didn't know the L.A.P.D. were so thoughtful." Wilson loved to rile people. Craine knew having him groveling in his office would be something of a minor triumph. "Mayer's been involved in cover-ups for years, Craine. You think I didn't know that Gable's got illegitimates scattered across America and that Spencer Tracy wakes himself up in the morning with a quart of bourbon. I know everything. And you? Don't think I don't know about your involvement, coming in here every few months begging favors like some kind of L.A.P.D. poodle."

Wilson leaned forward across his desk, speaking softly as he baited Craine for a reaction. "Smoothing out those little criminal crinkles, isn't that what they have you do? Magician, that's what they call you, isn't it? Make all those little convictions disappear. That rape case eighteen months ago with the girl at that M.G.M. party—after you replaced the lead detective, all the key evidence for the prosecution went missing. How exactly did you manage that? Louis Mayer must have been delighted to settle out of court."

Wilson leaned back, content with his little speech, but he could read nothing in Craine's face. He wouldn't give him the satisfaction.

"Mr. Wilson, I'm sure you're busy and I don't want to waste your time. In your column you suggested that Stanley was driven to suicide by his wife. What evidence do you have to support such a claim?"

"I have my sources."

"Well, who are they?"

"They're viable. And anonymous. As all of yours seem to be. What did Hearst's paper say? Quoting from unnamed sources, as always: 'Witnesses close to the victim say he was a closet homosexual who suffered from depression.' Delightful."

"There's no sign of foul play here, Billy."

"There was no note, Craine," Wilson went on, speaking quickly: "What about that little piece of information all the other papers have skirted over so neatly? Who doesn't leave a note before they kill themselves?"

"You're fabricating conspiracies out of nothing," Craine replied just as quickly, grateful O'Neill wasn't here. "There was no sign of a struggle, no evidence that he was murdered. And absolutely nothing to suggest that Gale Goodwin had any involvement."

"You're coming in here, telling me it's scurrilous to write that Gale Goodwin drove her husband to suicide when you don't even know the real reason he killed himself. Depressed? Queer? That's all hearsay. Goodwin must have been involved."

"You don't need to write that in your papers."

"Why? Because City Hall needs M.G.M.'s help in the polls and no one wants to upset Mayer?"

Craine ignored this. Both of them knew it was true. "I'm asking for your help."

"You're asking a favor from me but you have nothing to offer in return. Why would I support a studio that has gone out of its way to drive me out of business? M.G.M. used to burn my newspapers at the studio gates. Why should I help them? Why should I help you?"

Craine had anticipated this remark. He knew that promises of advertising revenue alone weren't going to change Wilson's mind. No, he had only one crucial bargaining tool. Please let it work. "In return for your compliance," he said, "I will have the police department turn a blind eye to your hotel ventures in Las Vegas."

"Blind eye?" Wilson laughed. "What makes you think I have anything to hide? So what if I'm expanding operations out there? The business plan is entirely legal. Ingeniously, the State of Nevada does not prohibit gambling or the sale of liquor. It's going to be my mecca for the free spirits of America. Christ, even prostitution is legal. Tell me, Detective, in America's last free state, what illegal activity could I possibly be involved in?"

"I could ask Frank Nitti."

Wilson's grin dropped away like a picture falling off a wall. He put his hands in his lap and slid back in his chair.

"Nitti?" he said finally, "I don't even know who you're talking about." He took a deep breath and tried to sit up straight.

Frank Nitti had become head of the Chicago syndicate when Al Capone was put in prison for tax evasion. He controlled narcotic and gambling rackets but had supposedly been trying to branch out into California. There was barely a person in America who hadn't at least seen his name in the tabloids.

"Do you think the L.A.P.D. isn't aware of your ties with the Chicago syndicates? I hear you've been having conversations with Frank Nitti about expanding operations out there. You'll never get the money together alone, will you? You need help, I can understand that. But Nitti's sitting on a pretty high branch in the mafia, Billy. Hoover's got the F.B.I. running a war on crime all over America. Do you really want Hoover knocking on your door? Do you think Nitti would like that?"

Wilson's long fingers pulled at his shirt collar. "Is this a threat? Is this blackmail?"

"This is a conversation. You could consider it an offer."

"What do you want?"

"You know exactly what I want."

Wilson sat back in his chair. Craine had to wait a full minute before he said, "When a member of the Hollywood family dies, Detective Craine, it affects all of us." He nodded his head and assumed a judicious frown. "Stanley's death is a tragedy and deserves a full tribute. I think tomorrow we'll even dedicate a few pages to his poor widow. How about that?"

"That sounds suitable."

"She has a picture out at the moment, doesn't she? Maybe we could write a few paragraphs on it."

"I think that would be decent of you."

Wilson's cheeks twitched momentarily before he resumed a coat-hanger grin. He rose from his desk and looked at his watch. "I'd love to offer you more of my time, Craine, but I'm afraid I have some very important meetings to attend to."

"Thank you. Expect a call from Russell Peterson in the coming days. I understand M.G.M. are looking for some advertising space. If the price is right."

Craine stood up, satisfied, and walked to the door. Simms would be pleased. He imagined Peterson would send over a case of champagne, as he so often did. Craine left the room before Wilson could offer his hand. If only they'd found Wilson's body hanging from his ceiling fan, he thought. Now that would be worth reading about in the papers.

CHAPTER 9

Kamona woke at nine. He washed his hands, showered and dressed then sat on the edge of the bed, waiting for the phone to ring. He always had an arrangement with the client whereby they would call him two times daily at prearranged times: usually ten in the morning, and ten at night. He would try to answer the phone on both occasions but might miss a call if he was preoccupied with work. He never took the client's number or met them face to face. Anonymity was a vital part of the process. If it was truly necessary, the client could call outside of the scheduled times but Kamona preferred to stick to the set routine. He lived by routine.

The telephone rang at ten.

"Kamona?" The client's accent was hard to place. Usually they were Italian-American but this time Kamona couldn't be sure and to be honest, he didn't care.

"Yes."

"I called you last night. And the night before."

"I was occupied."

"Did you get the pictures?"

"They weren't there."

A hint of annoyance. "You're certain?"

"I'm certain."

"What did she tell you?"

"That she didn't have them."

A long silence.

"What about Campbell? Did you find Jimmy Campbell?" As with the client, Kamona knew almost nothing of the target apart from what he looked like and where he lived. His occupation was unknown, his revoked raison d'être completely irrelevant. Most of the time, the targets were low-level mobsters who'd done something to upset one of the six families. More often than not they were informants, police witnesses or turncoats, but what they'd done, why they'd done it and who they'd done it to was never relayed to Kamona by his superiors and he preferred it that way. The rules were put in place for a reason: were he to come in contact with the police, there would be nothing to tie him to the target and vice versa.

"He wasn't at the given address. I waited two days. He never returned."

The client seemed concerned. "I need you to find him. Do you have a day rate?"

"Five hundred."

"I'll double it. Find Campbell. Find the pictures." The line went dead and Kamona put the phone down.

His Mauser was on the nightstand, cocked and loaded. Kamona picked it up and checked that a round was chambered. It was. He wiped the handle down and packed it in its leather briefcase. He'd be sure to need it again today.

Shortly before eleven o'clock, O'Neill parked his Plymouth behind the Los Angeles Theatre, ignoring the street kids who laughed at his rusted hubcaps and broken fender. It was his mother's car—she'd given it to him when he'd moved out of home, claiming she didn't like to drive at her age anyway. "Save your money and try and buy a house," she'd said to him, and a few months ago he'd done exactly that, combining his own savings with his father's inheritance to put a deposit down on a one-story on the southern fringes of Cypress Park.

It was earlier that morning when he was making breakfast at home that O'Neill had started to think more about what his father would have said about the Herbert Stanley case. He would never have disobeyed chain of command. And yet, he would probably have argued that it was worth presenting his findings again at a later date, pursuing independent investigation before providing his superiors with more information on which to base a conclusion.

The decision made, O'Neill had a uniform car pick up Herbert Stanley's housemaid, Rosa Martinez, for questioning at Central Headquarters, and took her up to the interview room himself, taking the service elevator in case Simms or Craine were around.

Mrs. Martinez wouldn't speak English when he tried to talk to her, so O'Neill brought in one of the secretaries from the pool and had her translate. She spoke tenderly of her employer and three times kissed the silver cross hanging around her neck, repeating again and again that he was a good man; he deserved to go to heaven. But Stanley's passage through purgatory was of no interest to O'Neill. What mattered was building up enough evidence to warrant a formal inquest into Stanley's death.

It took some persuasion and threats of deportation, but eventually she confided that Herbert Stanley received a package on the morning of his death and not long after, an anonymous phone call. She stated on record that the package, a sealed five-by-seven envelope, was delivered by a black sedan but couldn't give any indication of the age, model or license plate of the car. The phone call came thirty minutes after, when a male voice who wouldn't give his name asked to speak to her employer. Mr. Stanley, who was working from home, took the call in his study but she had no knowledge of what was said or how long the conversation lasted.

When asked about his reaction to the call, Martinez stated simply that Stanley remained in his study all day and that she hadn't heard from him again until Gale Goodwin arrived that evening, at which point he instructed her to go home. She admitted that she could smell alcohol on his breath and also that this wasn't unusual—her employer often seemed drunk during the day. But she also told O'Neill that Stanley had been in good spirits of late and had made weekend plans at the racetrack. Crucially, there had been no indication in the days preceding his death that he was depressed or suicidal. So either something had happened to make him change his mind, or something else happened that night. O'Neill was convinced that only the caller would know.

At ten, he'd driven to the Pacific Bell Telephone Company on Grand Avenue and after much persuasion, a supervisor in the billing department took him down to the archives to retrieve the telephone records for Herbert Stanley's house on Easton Drive. He received only one phone call the day of his death, an incoming call at eleven thirty in the morning. The supervisor had a nine-digit code, which after some searching was found to correspond to an address off West 7th Street.

Standing beside his Plymouth, O'Neill looked at the painted sign hanging in an alleyway not far from the corner of 7th and Hill Street, then glanced down at the billing sheet from the telephone company. "The Shamrock Pub and Grub," both said.

The door was shut, so O'Neill knocked softly then took a step back.

There was vomit beside the gutter and the smell of something awful coming from three garbage sacks by the door. Half-way down the alley, another fifteen yards from the street, three homeless men sat watching him from beneath a shelter constructed of corrugated iron and trash cans. One of them said something and another one laughed, wheezing loudly then spitting dark phlegm into his lap.

After a minute O'Neill knocked again, louder this time, and then a third time a minute later. Eventually he heard a faint scraping sound and the door opened an inch. Two eyes and a cigarette cherry peered at him from the darkness.

"Hello? Hi, my name is—"

"We're closed," said a voice in an Irish brogue. "Read the sign."

The door closed as quickly as it had opened. O'Neill glanced around. There was no sign.

He knocked again, talking loudly at the door.

"Sir, my name is Detective O'Neill. I'm with the Los Angeles Police Department. Sir—"

He heard a bolt slide, the door opening just enough for smoke to come out.

"What is it? Can't you read the sign? We're closed." His accent was first generation Irish-American, like his father's, only darker.

"There is no sign! Sir, my name is Detective O'Neill—"

"So?"

"May I come in?"

"No, we're closed. Come back later."

"I was hoping to speak to you."

"We're closed."

"I'm a police officer."

"Then why are you coming to a bar? It's eleven o'clock. Don't cops have scruples?"

"I'm not here to drink."

"Then why *are* you here?"

"Police business. I have a few questions that relate to a murder investigation."

The door opened so quickly it almost knocked O'Neill off his feet. A heavyset man in his forties or fifties stood in the doorway with a long-handled club held down by one leg. He had lumpy shoulders and a hunchback that looked as if it had been earned rather than inherited, a consequence of a life of hard graft.

"Murder?"

The man measured him with curious eyes weighed down with liquor. It took him less than a second to assess O'Neill. Half his weight, four or five inches shorter. Skinny arms with no punch behind them. He knew he wasn't a threat. "What did you say your name was again?"

"O'Neill. Detective O'Neill."

"You Irish?" His breath smelt like his tongue was rotting.

"Yeah."

The man grinned and held the door open. "Well, why didn't you say so? Come on in. I'm Sean McGinn, the owner."

O'Neill tentatively stepped through the door.

"I thought you were closed."

"We were, we just opened."

The Shamrock was long and narrow, a wooden bar traveling the length of the room and only enough tables to seat two dozen or so privileged customers. It was dark inside, but two faint orange bulbs hanging from the ceiling guided him toward a barstool. There were empty glasses and peanut shells along the bar top, a jar of boiled eggs and another of pickles stood in front of him. From behind the bar, McGinn drew himself a pint of dark ale. In his mouth was a half-smoked cigarette that he didn't take out when he spoke.

"Drink?"

O'Neill tried to avoid his eyes in case he could see how apprehensive he was. It always happened when he was talking to strangers, as if he was waiting for them to ask how old he was or wonder out loud if he was too young to be a police officer. "Not right now," he said, staring at his shoes. "No, thank you."

"What do you want, then? Hasn't been no trouble here. No killings, not since I opened and that's been twelve years."

"I'm not accusing you of anything."

"What then?"

"Do you have a phone here?"

McGinn stared at him with disdain. "You blind?" he said, waving a tattooed arm to one side. "We got two of them."

O'Neill's eyes adjusted to the light. At the back of the room was a wooden phone cubicle crafted out of a confession booth.

"People use them a lot?"

"What's a lot?"

"Well, do the same people come by to use the phone, or is it different people?"

"Depends. We got regulars. People in this neighborhood, most of 'em don't have phones."

"So they use yours?"

"Some of them."

"Any of these people you know?"

He shrugged. "The regulars. Why?"

"I'm interested in a phone call that was made from here at eleven thirty on Wednesday."

"We don't open before noon," he said in a flat voice. "There couldn't have been any phone calls."

"You see this? This is from the Pacific Bell Telephone Company. Says a call was made from here eleven thirty Wednesday."

"We were closed at eleven thirty."

O'Neill was finding this incredibly frustrating. They were getting nowhere. "Which means," he said as firmly as he could, "that it was either you or a member of your staff using the phone, am I right?"

"I don't have any staff."

"That leaves you, then."

McGinn stiffened visibly and shook his head. He took another swig of beer and wiped his face with the back of his arm. "There's a guy who comes in here most weeks," he said, the cigarette jiggling between his lips. "The other day, he came knocking on my door asking to use the phone."

"You let him in?"

"Slipped me a dollar if I left him to it. Said it was important."

"You know his name?"

"Yeah, I know his name. And for five bucks, I'll even tell you where he lives."

CHAPTER 10

"Is this your husband, Miss Goodwin?"

Gale Goodwin stood over the body of her deceased husband, her eyes wide and unblinking. She was in the police department's pathologists' examination room, a small, confined chamber with green tile walls and polished linoleum flooring. Standing the other side of the table was Dr. Richard Collins, Los Angeles' chief medical examiner. Craine stood against the wall beside the door, turning his hat in his hands.

She had arrived at the precinct not long after Craine had returned from *The Hollywood Enquirer*. He'd offered her a cup of coffee but when Gale declined he led her toward the elevator. They'd sunk down six floors to the basement pathology department in silence and when the thought crossed his mind to ask her how she was feeling or how her morning had been, it dawned on him that he hadn't properly spoken with anyone in months. He was incapable of polite conversation.

"Is this your husband?" Collins repeated more delicately when Gale hadn't replied.

Craine kept his eyes on Gale before glimpsing the body on the table. Stanley lay on his back, wrapped in a white sheet from the shoulders down. He remained fully clothed but the belt had been removed from his neck and his tongue had been pushed back into his mouth. Purple bruising hung around his neckline but his skin was that pale yellow unique to the dead, sallow with a hint of gray. The image came to him of Celia lying on the very same table, her skin

77

blanched white and crisscrossed with blue veins. He remembered that her blond hair had seemed so thin, so colorless. There were scratches on her arms where Michael had tried to pull her out of the water.

"Yes, yes that's him." Gale said eventually. "That's Herbert."

People reacted differently in the identification chamber. Some people liked to touch the body, to explore what they once knew and see how it had changed. Others obsessed over the narrative details, wanting to reconstruct the events leading up to someone's death. It wasn't so much about completing the biography of a loved one as much as it was their wanting to know exactly where they were and what they were doing themselves when that other person died.

Collins pulled the sheet back over Stanley's face before taking Craine to one side. Gale stood staring at the sheeted figure, arms tensed in front of her, one hand clutching the other.

"That Irish detective—" Collins whispered.

"You mean O'Neill?"

"He's been asking about doing an autopsy."

"I know. Is it strictly necessary? Legally, that is?"

"It's advised in these circumstances."

"What circumstances?"

"Where cause of death isn't clear."

"It is clear—he hanged himself."

"I can stall him, but in cases of suicide it's the normal protocol."

"Fine. I want to know what the outcome is before anyone else hears about it."

Collins nodded. "One last thing, Detective. That G.S.W. cadaver you brought in. The girl—Florence Lloyd. You want to be present for the autopsy?"

"No, just file the report with R. and I. It's closed."

"No one's come to claim the body."

Strange, Craine thought. *How could a girl that looked like her go completely unclaimed?*

"I'll have my secretary track down her next of kin."

When Craine turned back to the table Gale was crying. She rested her hand on Stanley's chest for a second then stepped back. He could see that she was hurting. It was something most people never have to go through and he shared that pain with her. Seeing Celia was one of the worst experiences of his life. It didn't matter how much you argued, how much your relationship was strained, how bitter things got between you; when you see someone you love lying dead in front of you it makes everything else irrelevant. It was something he wouldn't wish on anyone.

"Is there anything else? Can I go, please?"

She should have had a friend with her today. This wasn't something you should go through alone. "Would you like a ride home, Miss Goodwin?"

"Please," she said through tears, "take him away. I don't want to be here anymore."

"We're done, Miss Goodwin," said Collins. "My deepest condolences to you and your family. When you come to make funeral arrangements, you can tell the parlor they can collect your husband from here. Please don't hesitate to contact me if you have any questions."

Craine opened the door. "Miss Goodwin, I'll drive you home."

Gale nodded then looked away. She seemed smaller than she did yesterday and more delicate and fragile than the self-possessed movie star he'd seen on the screen only last night. There was a sorrowful, almost pathetic look in her face that he recognized in himself.

It was a five-minute walk through the lower corridors to the parking lot and they shared it in silence. When they reached his car, Craine held the door open and helped her inside. He shut it softly behind her and walked round to the driver's seat.

"Craine?"

It was dark in the basement parking lot, but he recognized O'Neill instantly in his three-piece suit and thick-rimmed spectacles.

"What is it, O'Neill?"

O'Neill glanced toward the car and spoke quietly. "I wanted to tell you that I spoke to Stanley's maid."

"And?"

"She told me Stanley had seemed normal this week. He didn't seem suicidal."

"Depressives often don't." Craine waved the matter aside, his tone telling O'Neill that this wasn't the time.

"Wait, there's more. The morning he died he received an unsigned package. Then a phone call. She said it really spooked him. He locked himself in his study for the rest of the day."

Craine ushered O'Neill to one side to be certain they were out of earshot. "Who from?"

"She couldn't say. But I traced the call to a bar the other side of town." O'Neill handed him a folded piece of paper. "The caller's name is at the top."

Craine took it reluctantly. He looked back at the car. Gale was looking at them. He couldn't leave her waiting.

"Have you told Simms?"

"Not yet."

"Then leave it with me. It's probably nothing."

"Wait, I'll come with you. I thought we could go together."

Craine held up a hand. "Go to the autopsy, O'Neill," he whispered so Gale couldn't hear. "It'll put your mind at rest. But I don't want you running around Los Angeles asking any more questions about Stanley. I mean that. I'll handle this myself."

He unfolded the paper and glanced at it as he reached the driver's door. It was a telephone bill with an address off Main Street penciled in the margin. The listed tenant was scrawled in capitals. His name was James Campbell.

Craine's Fleetwood drove up 2nd Street before turning onto Grand Avenue, with its long blocks of retail buildings, apartments, and commercial offices. It was dry outside; the roads were washed clean by the rain but there was a pressure in the air and he knew it would rain again soon.

Gale sat quietly in the passenger seat, staring at the comings and goings of the curbside and Craine remained content to drive in silence. The Fleetwood inched through the northern edges of downtown, passing food lines, restless teenagers playing dice on street corners and old men stretched across liquor store doorways. Craine saw a line of newspaper vendors on the giant square paving slabs beyond the curb. He noticed Gale turn her head to read the headlines inked out on a sandwich board: "GALE GOODWIN'S HUSBAND COMMITS SUICIDE."

She sank low in her seat, and there was a slight tremor in her hands as she pulled a pack of cigarettes from her purse.

"Do you mind if I smoke?" she said at last.

"Please, go ahead," he said, although he regretted it as soon as he realized that she was smoking Chesterfields.

Craine kept his eyes on the road ahead. Out of the corner of his eye, he noticed Gale's slender fingers fumbling over a lighter. She lit the cigarette and wound down the window, balancing her wrist on the doorframe. She was trembling.

"Are you alright, Miss Goodwin?"

"It's Gale, but yes, thank you."

Twenty minutes passed in silence. They began crawling up the winding roads into Brentwood. Joan Crawford's house was only a few miles away. Finally Gale said: "I'm sorry, I didn't mean to be short before. I didn't mean to make a scene like that."

"You don't need to apologize. I know it can be difficult."

"No. No, it was completely uncalled for." She drew on a fresh cigarette and sighed. "It was just . . . being in that room, I guess. I haven't really thought about where he was. I'd assumed I'd never see him again. Then seeing him lying there, on that table . . . I'm so embarrassed, I'm sorry."

"Don't be. I understand."

"You must have done that so many times."

Craine nodded.

"I suppose you get used to it."

"I can appreciate—I've been in your position. I know how difficult it is."

"Of course—Celia. I wasn't thinking. When she died, you went down there? You went down to see her?"

"Yes, yes I did."

"And was it easier, knowing what to expect?"

"No," he replied, "it wasn't easier." Worse, in a way; he didn't tell her. The anticipation of seeing Celia's body was almost unbearable because he already knew what she'd look like dead. He almost didn't go in there.

"I didn't want to go there today, not alone. I've been dreading it really, but there was no one else."

"Herbert doesn't have any family?"

"No. No one. He was an only child. His parents died before I met him. And he never wanted children. Do you have any children? I'm sorry, that's none of my business. What I was going to say was that I'm glad you were there. Joan drove me down but she had to be on set today so she couldn't stay. And Russell— Peterson—promised he would come with me but I called his office this morning and they said he wasn't available. His secretary said he'd be in meetings all day. I left a message but he never called. I guess he was too busy."

"He's a busy man," Craine said, although really there was no excuse. Peterson only did what was good for him and M.G.M. He couldn't care less about how Gale actually felt.

"Do you know him?"

"Not well. We're acquainted. Through work matters."

"Do you like him?"

"He's very good at what he does." I despise him, he could have said.

"How very fair of you, Detective," Gale said, smiling. "For more time than I can remember, Russell Peterson has been telling me what to say, what to eat, what to wear, where to be seen. For my last picture he even gave me my own dietician and a dressmaker. Then he hired this girl to sign my photos for fan magazines, can you believe that?"

"Celia had the same, once."

"It's ridiculous, really; no one needs so much, not with so many people in need." She spoke quickly, with an earnest intensity he found unexpected. "And he may call me three times a day about this and that but when it comes to actually being there when you want him to? No, he'll tell you exactly what you want to hear but he's never actually there when you need him most. And he's such a creep around L.B. I mean really, the endless flattery. Herbert used to say, 'Louis Mayer doesn't use toilet paper, he just rings for Peterson.'"

They both laughed and Craine had to catch himself.

"I'm sorry, I'm being vile, aren't I? But it's nice to see you smile. It suits you."

Craine suddenly felt self-conscious. He couldn't remember the last time he'd smiled.

Relieved that the mood had lifted, Gale said, "Herbert was so funny, he was always making me laugh. Most of the jokes in those early Busby Berkeley musicals were his, did you know that? He had a wicked sense of humor. Well, he used to. He lost it somewhere along the way."

Neither of them spoke for some time. Gale turned and stared at him, taking a moment to work up the courage before asking, "What was she like—Celia, I mean? If you don't mind me asking. I only met her a few times."

Taken aback by her directness, Craine hesitated. He let the question linger before saying, "She was very kind. Most people know she was an actress, few people know anything else about her. But she was incredibly selfless; she always wanted to help people."

"I remember going to a charity gala she hosted. For the homeless."

"At St. Vibiana's. Celia was a big part of the church."

It was a long time since Craine had discussed Celia with anyone.

As the investigator, he rarely felt the spotlight. Gale must have sensed his unease and didn't probe him any further.

They slowed as the car approached the main gates to Crawford's estate on Bristol Avenue. Craine steered into the driveway, moving between a tended row of cypress trees toward the front door of the Georgian-styled residence.

"Detective Craine, you've been very kind. You didn't have to drive me home."

"I felt obliged."

"You shouldn't have. But thank you. For your concern, I mean."

He slowed to a stop beneath the pepper tree beside the front door. He left the engine running and stared at the backs of his hands. For a reason he couldn't put his finger on, he wanted to share something with her.

"A son."

"I'm sorry?"

"You asked me if I have any children," he said, looking at her. "I have a son."

"Yes, I think I knew that. Does he live with you?"

"He stays at his school. A boarding school."

"I always wanted children. Herbert had no interest. I don't suppose I ever will now, but who knows, maybe it wasn't meant to be. I expect Celia was a wonderful mother."

"She was, yes."

"Do you mind talking about her?"

"I haven't spoken about her in quite a while."

"Your little boy must miss her immensely."

"He does."

"And how about you? Do you miss your wife? Do you think about her often?"

"All the time," he muttered.

"I miss Herbert. I don't know why but I do. I miss the old Herbert. Is it difficult, being alone? Being lonely?"

"Being alone and being lonely aren't the same thing."

Craine found himself blushing slightly and closed up. Why was he sharing such personal thoughts with a stranger? His eyes darted away and he found himself staring toward the front door.

"I trust someone is here to let you in," he said a little too coldly.

"Yes," Gale said, gathering herself. "Clara, the housekeeper, is here. I'm almost certain of it. Well, goodbye, Detective Craine." She opened the car door but before she could step out Craine put a hand on her arm and turned toward her so that they were face to face.

"It's Jonathan," he said with a sense of propriety that almost seemed absurd. "You can call me Jonathan."

"Goodbye, Jonathan."

Gale Goodwin walked briskly to the front door. Craine put the car in gear and steered toward the gates.

As he met the crest of the hill he looked soberly down toward the urban sprawl that made up the ever-growing city basin. It was starting to rain again.

CHAPTER 11

"O'Neill. Is that an Irish name?" asked Dr. Collins, rolling on a pair of black rubber gloves.

"My parents are Irish. Were. They became American citizens."

They were standing in the mortuary, or the examination office, as the pathologists preferred to call it. Herbert Stanley's body was on a metal gurney between them.

"Why are there so many Irish in the department?"

"I'm not sure."

"Every day another fresh-faced Paddy comes down to see me, throwing his little Irish guts up all over my shiny linoleum floor. *Every day*, always Irish. They put you on the same boat?"

"No. I mean, I hadn't noticed."

O'Neill hadn't been with the homicide department long enough to develop a close working relationship with any of the pathologists, but he found Collins particularly intimidating. He was a large, imposing figure with hard features and close-cropped blond hair balding at the crown. Like most moneyed East Coast Anglo-Saxons he encountered, Collins had a deep, serious voice with a clearly defined, cutglass accent that made O'Neill feel like a sham American.

"I must say," said Collins, "I'm not quite sure why this is so urgent. Did the family request it?"

"No, I did. I wanted to be sure."

"You have doubts?"

"Stanley didn't leave a suicide note," he answered. He wasn't going to mention the phone call or the package. "It didn't feel right."

"It didn't *feel* right? You had a *feeling*. I see." Collins pulled over the dissection table and instrument tray. O'Neill caught a glimpse of the bone saw and chest shears used to remove the breastplate. He started to sweat. "Let's get started. There's a clipboard on the side there. Spell the big words as best you can."

O'Neill took a clipboard and pencil hanging from a wall peg. From the corner of his eye he saw Collins pull back the sheet covering the body. He took long, deep breaths and tried to prepare himself for what he was about to see. His first few autopsies had ended in quick exits to the lavatory down the corridor and only over time had the process become familiar. O'Neill had to tell himself that it was a cadaver lying on a table, not a body, not a someone.

"Detective?"

"Sorry—yes, I'm ready, Dr. Collins." After a few seconds he turned and looked at the naked body on the table. He felt relieved: Stanley's corpse wasn't difficult to look at. He had always found it easier to see men on the table. Women and children were the worst.

"White male, 164 pounds, seventy-three inches in length by my tape. Where was he found?"

"In his study, hanging from a ceiling fan."

Collins moved slowly around the corpse, occasionally probing the body with a gloved hand. He spoke in the dull, monotonous voice of a man who has spent the best part of his life describing the deceased. "Hair color is brown, short, graying. Victim has small birthmark on right upper forearm, two moles on lower abdominal, no other distinguishing features. No signs of bruising on face, limbs or torso, no other contortions or visible signs of trauma other than his neck." Collins waited for O'Neill to finish writing. He smiled weakly, adding, "He wasn't shot or stabbed, but I suppose you knew that."

Collins continued with his view and grant, using a finger to raise each eyelid in turn. Stanley's pupils were fixed and dilated. They betrayed nothing. "Green eyes. Note also both sclerae look hyperemic. You see the burst capillaries on his face and in the whites of his eyes? It indicates cause of death: *cerebral ischemia*, the blood flow was cut to his brain and he had a stroke. It wouldn't be agonizing but it certainly wasn't instant either. Does that satisfy your investigation? What homicide scenarios had you considered, Detective?"

"Either that he was forced to hang himself or that he was choked to death first and strung up afterward to make it look like suicide."

"I don't know if I've seen any examples of someone being forced to hang themselves. At least none that I'm aware of."

"It's difficult to make someone take their own life, not without a struggle. I didn't notice any evidence of an attack at his home. Nothing on the body to show he was assaulted either."

Collins used a pair of wide forceps to lift Stanley's hands by the wrist. O'Neill bent down for a better look.

"Correct. No physical alterations on his hands. Fingernails undamaged, no bruising on either set of knuckles."

"His palms?"

"No fingernail markings on his palms."

"No signs of stress, you mean?"

"Exactly." If Collins was impressed, he didn't show it. "So you think he was choked?"

"I think it's possible. Or that he was drugged."

"Not a scenario I've seen before."

"But it could explain why there's no sign of struggle."

Collins breathed deeply and leaned in closer to the victim's neck. "Severe bruising and abrasive ligature marks circling the neckline. The abrasions on the side here match a belt strap. You can see where the buckle has cut into his skin."

"Is there any indication that he could have been strangled by someone else? Is there any way you can tell?"

"We'll need to take a closer look. Help me move him onto the slab, would you? There are some gloves by the sink."

The wall nearest the door was lined with sinks and stainless steel benches used for dissecting organs. The smell of ammonium disinfectant was overwhelming. O'Neill gloved up and they lifted Stanley onto an autopsy table, O'Neill carrying Stanley by the shoulders. His skin was softer than he'd expected. He'd never actually touched a dead body himself before. O'Neill kept hold of Stanley as Collins slid the body block, a large rubber brick, under the center of Stanley's back. His body arched, Stanley's chest was pushed toward the ceiling and his long neck was stretched out for maximum exposure. Collins pulled a tray of surgical tools toward him. O'Neil started to feel light-headed. He loosened his collar.

"Something wrong, Detective? Would you like a chair, a stool perhaps?"

"No. No, I'm okay."

Collins picked out a scalpel and cut a deep incision across the top of Stanley's neck, right above the Adam's apple. Without the heart pumping, bleeding was minimal—small trickles ran down either side of Stanley's neck and formed in shallow pools. O'Neill took a small step back. He couldn't breathe.

"The way to tell if someone has been hanged or strangled is by looking at the hyoid bone." Collins was leaning over the body and using his forceps to open the incision for examination. He was slow and precise, careful not to open the wound any more than necessary. "It's a small horseshoe-shaped bone that isn't connected to any other bones in the body. It's right above the larynx here. In cases of strangulation, direct pressure from someone's hands or from a belt or noose normally snaps it on either side. I've never seen it broken from a short suspension drop before."

O'Neill caught sight of Collins cutting away the sinew around the small bone and looked away. He waited for the sound of the scalpel to stop before clearing his throat. "Does it look damaged, Doctor?"

"No, it's not broken," said Collins with finality, straightening his back and wiping his brow with the back of his arm. "It looks absolutely fine. As far as I can tell, the victim's cause of death was hanging by a short drop from a belt ligature. He wasn't choked or strangled. As for whether he was drugged first, only blood tests and the internal exam will tell."

O'Neill felt somewhat defeated, wondering whether he'd truly let his imagination get the better of him. Worse, he was beginning to feel nauseous. He stepped away from the table but had to steady himself with his hands. His legs felt heavy. Beads of sweat ran down his back. He could feel himself buckling at the knee.

"Is everything alright, Detective?"

"Yes, absolutely. Everything's fine." O'Neill held his breath, a knot forming in his stomach.

"I'll need to complete a full internal autopsy. Let's examine his organs, shall we?"

"Yes, go ahead." The room was starting to look fuzzy. He could hear a high-pitched humming in his ears. He took two long, deep breaths and tried to concentrate on the procedure. He watched Collins pick out another scalpel and make a deep Y-shaped incision from the top of each shoulder, down across the chest, meeting at the lower sternum and continuing to the navel. He felt the vomit rise in his throat, held it there as Collins picked up a pair of steel shears and prepared to cut open Stanley's chest cavity. In a moment he would remove Stanley's entire breastplate and take out his organs one by one.

He felt his chest swell. He could taste the gastric acid filling his mouth. He couldn't stop it.

Patrick O'Neill made it half-way to the sinks before he heaved the contents of his little Irish guts all over Dr. Collins' shiny linoleum floor.

Although he'd lived in New York for most of his life, Kamona was born in rural Ontario and still held his Canadian passport. So when the Great War broke out in Europe in 1914, Kamona took a train to Toronto, lied about his age and volunteered himself for military service.

Kamona was one of the few soldiers he knew who actually enjoyed the war. He relished the opportunity to fire his rifle; he loved tossing grenades and fixing bayonets. He was living out his childhood fantasies, where killing was not only encouraged, it was actively rewarded. Kamona flourished. Over the course of the war, he became the most decorated soldier in his unit and was given consecutive battlefield promotions until he reached the appointment of Sergeant Major, the highest rank available to a non-commissioned officer.

Sitting in downtown traffic not far from James Campbell's apartment building, Kamona wondered what was different about what he did then to what he did now. All that had changed was that he worked privately rather than for the government; he was a self-employed contract worker, a mercenary, rather than an enlisted soldier. His approach to killing remained the same and he never felt guilty when the job was done. Once, a few years ago, the target had been a woman who reminded him of his mother. He'd hesitated briefly but still had no moral qualms about finishing the task at hand. She, like all the others, was solely a victim of circumstance. He was only a messenger. If it wasn't him, it would have been someone else.

Kamona drove up Broadway and headed north toward the jewelry district on 6th Street. It was raining again and the wind was growing stronger. Campbell's apartment building was opposite the Los Angeles Theatre but he'd park a few blocks away, as he always did, in case there were witnesses. He was driving a rental car but the plates could be traced and he rarely took unnecessary risks.

He wound down the window and let the air cool his brow. If he was efficient, he could make the evening train back to New York. He rippled his fingers on the steering wheel and let out a long sigh. Not much longer now. In twenty minutes he'd be in the apartment building. In less than an hour, Campbell would be telling him everything he needed and begging to die. In two hours, Kamona would oblige him.

He wished he'd packed more clean shirts.

CHAPTER I2

Craine had lunch at the Ambassador Hotel's Cocoanut Grove, ordering a salmon loaf with a potato salad followed by French peach pie and several cups of coffee. With the studio money coming in, he could afford to treat himself.

"Good to have you back, Detective Craine," the waiter said as he left. Everyone knows me, Craine thought. And for all the wrong reasons.

Sitting across the room were the actors Clark Gable and Humphrey Bogart. He thought of the time he'd helped Gable avoid scrutiny from the press when he'd crashed his car leaving Joan Crawford's house during one of their late-night flings; the time a year ago when he'd pacified Bogart's drunk wife after she'd tried to stab her husband with a kitchen knife and burn their house down with a can of gasoline. I've spent too much of my life playing moral gatekeeper to the stars, he said to himself. All of it so I can eat in fancy restaurants and go to exclusive clubs.

Craine asked to use the telephone and a waiter brought him over to a private booth. He dialed his own office and had Elaine patch him down to Dr. Collins' office.

"Pathology," a man's voice said woodenly.

"Collins?"

"Yes."

"It's Craine. Have you completed an autopsy on Stanley?"

"Finished a few minutes ago. As expected, cause of death was hanging from a belt ligature."

"And O'Neill?"

"Was there with me until he passed out. Vomit everywhere. Whole place stinks to high heaven and this is coming from a man who's spent the past twenty years opening up the dead."

"Thank you. I appreciate it."

"There's something you should know," Collins said, his voice lowering. "While it looked like suicide, I noticed some powdery residue in Stanley's stomach lining. Could be Demerol, but from the residue in his liver and throat looks to be more likely oxycodone."

"Sedatives?"

"Strong sedatives."

Craine felt his insides sink. This wasn't what he needed to hear. "You saying he was drugged?"

"I'm saying there were drugs in his system. It's not my place to say how or why. It's perfectly plausible that it was for personal consumption."

"I understand. Does O'Neill know?"

"Couldn't lie to him. Seemed to get over his nausea pretty quick once I told him."

Not good news, Craine thought. It would hardly abate O'Neill's doubts about the case. "Can you omit it from the report?"

Collins spoke quietly. "If you deem it necessary."

"Thank you. I'll let Russell Peterson know that you've been very efficient. I hope that in the past he's shown his appreciation for the work that you do."

"Sometimes I think he needs reminding," Collins muttered before ringing off.

When the waiter brought him the check, his mind returned to the day ahead. An autopsy confirming suicide should bring an end to the press speculation over Stanley's death but the sedatives were a concern, especially if O'Neill knew. The last thing he needed was that Irish upstart undermining his efforts to have the whole thing blow over by talking to the press about drugs, mysterious packages and unexplained phone calls. He took a deep breath, knowing he would have to go and talk to Campbell. Whoever he was—a friend, acquaintance or work associate—he needed to confirm his irrelevance to this case once and for all. After that, maybe he could persuade O'Neill to forget about the whole thing.

Craine checked the address O'Neill had given him. He was on the fourth floor of a six-story apartment building off Main Street. He'd lived in a similar block when he'd first moved to L.A. himself. Fifty apartments filled with out-of-work writers and actors, each of them clinging onto the hope that their break was next.

Campbell lived in apartment 409. The corridor was empty; no cracks of light coming from under the doorways he passed. It was quiet, almost silent but for the rattle of the Red Cars on the street below.

Craine found the apartment at the end of the corridor and knocked at the door. There was no response, and he began brooding instead over his conversation with Gale Goodwin. Asked about Celia, he'd bared his most private thoughts to a woman he barely knew before panicking, suddenly overcome with an instinctive need to protect himself from all forms of intimacy.

Craine knocked again but there was still no answer. He couldn't break down the door without a warrant. That could take days. He turned to go downstairs to find the building manager, then hesitated. He might as well try the door in case it wasn't locked. He turned the handle and the door opened.

Inside a man in a long gray coat and shiny black shoes stood by a telephone. He was tall and thin. Short hair, no particular age. Forty maybe. Nothing about him was particularly remarkable.

"Mr. Campbell?"

A pause then: "Yes."

"I'm sorry, I tried knocking."

"I was in the bedroom. Can I help you?"

"My name is Detective Craine." He showed Campbell his identification.

"Yes?"

"You're a friend of Herbert Stanley?"

A long pause, then, "Yes, we knew each other."

"You may have heard. It's in the papers." He always talked in elliptical sentences in these scenarios, told people only enough that they understood. Talking too much only made them more anxious. "I hate to be the one to tell you. Herbert Stanley was found dead yesterday morning. He hanged himself in his home."

Another long silence. Campbell's face betrayed no emotion. Shock, perhaps. People take bad news differently. Craine had to do this a lot over the years. It became easier over time to tell people but it never got easier watching their reactions. He wondered how Simms had felt when he'd told him about Celia.

"Yes, I was aware, thank you for coming by to tell me," he said, a little too casually. "It really wasn't necessary."

"We're treating it as a suicide. There was nothing suspicious about his death that we're aware of."

"Is there anything I can do to help?"

"Yes, I was hoping you might be able to tell me the nature of your phone call with Stanley the morning of his death."

"My phone call?"

"I have a record from the telephone company. You called Stanley's home at approximately eleven thirty Wednesday morning."

"Wednesday?" he said tentatively, as if he was half asleep.

"Yes."

"Oh yeah, I remember now. Yes, it wasn't important. A quick call. He's an old acquaintance."

Campbell's behavior was odd. Craine wasn't a fool—he was clearly hiding something. He probed further. "Can you tell me what you spoke about?"

"Oh, you know. Not much. Nothing in particular. I can't really remember."

"Perhaps it would be easier if you came down to the precinct. We could take a formal statement."

Campbell took a moment to answer: "Is that necessary?"

"I think in this case it would be for the best. It's important we clear these things up. Stanley was a public figure, as is his wife. Questions will be asked at a later date if we don't get all the details down on paper now."

"Right now?"

"If possible."

"Not a problem," Campbell said, smiling broadly. "Would you give me a minute? I need to go to the bathroom first."

Craine waited by the front door and surveyed the apartment. One bedroom, a dimly lit, open-planned living area with a small kitchenette in the corner. The apartment was small but well furnished: new furniture, European throw-rugs covering polished wood floors. Odd pieces of camera equipment were dotted around the room: lenses, tripods, flashbulbs—no cameras, though. There were books on the shelves alongside one wall and framed photographs on a rolltop bureau in the corner. More photos hung on the wall beside the bathroom door.

He called out: "Would you mind if I made a quick phone call?"

No reply.

Craine crossed over to the bureau. There were two photographs standing in frames beside a candlestick telephone, a blotter and a notepad. One of the pictures was a sepia-toned albumen print of a middle-aged woman outside a farmhouse. His mother, he presumed. The other was a large monochrome black-and-white photograph of a young man in a suit sitting at a table in a restaurant. The man was tall and angular. Campbell, Craine thought. He looked closer. No, this wasn't the same man as the one in the bathroom. His nose was wider, ears far bigger. Who was he? A friend, a brother? A lover, perhaps? That certainly wasn't out of the question.

He lifted up the phone receiver and asked the operator for the publicity department at M.G.M. There was a brief silence. He could hear trucks grumbling and Red Car bells jangling outside.

"Publicity," a girl's voice said.

"Hello, Russell Peterson, please."

"May I ask who is calling?"

"Detective Craine."

"One moment."

A long pause before the line crackled.

"Craine, how are you?" Peterson's unctuous voice was unmistakable.

"I wanted to let you know you won't be having any more problems with *The Hollywood Enquirer*. You should also find Wilson more amenable to your advertising expenses."

"Well, that's good to hear indeed. Very impressive."

"And Gale Goodwin positively identified the body this morning."

"Ah, yes—of course. And the autopsy?"

"Confirmed suicide." He didn't mention the drugs. There was no need to worry Peterson unnecessarily.

"Splendid." He sounded relieved.

"I trust that Collins' assistance in this matter will be rewarded."

"You don't even have to ask. How about O'Neill?"

"I'm not sure that would interest him. O'Neill is less keen than we are to see this closed."

"Strange one, that boy. Well, perhaps he'll be appeased by an invitation to M.G.M.'s party tomorrow evening. I hope we can expect to see you there?"

"Goodbye, Mr. Peterson."

Craine put the receiver down. As he did so, he noticed a larger photograph on the wall beside the window. It was a picture of a woman in a black décolleté dress. She had her hands posed under her chin, a chain of pearls around her neck. It was the exact same picture he'd seen only two days before.

It was a photograph of Florence Lloyd.

Kamona stood in Campbell's bathroom with his foot pressed against the bottom of the door. The deadlock was broken and there was no key in the keyhole. He stood at the door listening, the Mauser clenched in one hand. He could hear the detective moving around the living room. He felt foolish for leaving the Mauser in the bath-room as he searched the apartment, but at least being found unarmed confused the detective. For now, at least.

Kamona had arrived at the apartment building an hour earlier. He'd picked the front door as he had the previous night and entered without alerting the neighbors. He searched the bedroom first, but there were no clothes on the hangers and nothing but a stolen hotel Bible in the bedside cabinet. He'd pulled up the flounced cover and looked under the bed but there was nothing there. From the chest of drawers he took out a deck of cards and a cardboard box but the box was empty except for a few loose coins.

He'd gone through the bathroom next, leaving the Mauser in the sink so he could reach under the bath. Nothing there.

The living room was exactly the same.

After going through all the drawers and cupboards in the small kitchenette, he'd picked up the phone in the living room and asked the operator to connect him to the last call made.

"I'll have to put you through to the San Bernardino switchboard."

"Thank you," he said. There was a brief pause before a male voice answered.

"St. Louis Hotel, can I help you?"

"Hello. My name is James Campbell. I'm calling to check my reservation."

"Campbell? That's right, we have your reservation. In fact, we're expecting you shortly."

Kamona rang off. That was all he needed to know. That was when he heard two firm knocks at the door.

Kamona still had his ear to the bathroom door. The detective had stopped moving. He pushed himself away from the doorjamb and pulled back the hammer on the Mauser. He checked the suppressor was screwed on tight and flicked the safety off with his thumb. He had to get out.

*   *   *

Craine crossed the living room and tapped on the bathroom door.

"Mr. Campbell? Mr. Campbell? Hello? Are you in there?"

There no was reply.

"Mr. Campbell? Mr. Campbell?" There was no sound from inside. Why would Campbell have photographs of Florence Lloyd? There had to be a logical explanation. They were friends, relatives perhaps. Campbell would provide a perfectly good reason, he was sure of it. But something half-buried in his mind told Craine he was lying to himself.

He drew his service pistol, a Browning nine-millimeter unused since the day he bought it. *Did it even work?* He was nervous. He steadied his hands, racked back the top-slide to chamber a round and kicked open the bathroom door.

The room was empty. The man was gone. Cool air blew through an open sash window. Craine stepped inside, his clammy hands gripping the Browning firm. The window led out onto a fire escape, a set of steel platforms and ladders mounted to the building's exterior wall that led down to the ground four stories below. Innocent people don't run, he thought. He pulled back the hammer on his pistol, leaned forward and peered down the fire ladder. Nothing. He leaned out further for a clearer line of sight. The fire escape below ended two flights down, over thirty feet from the street. Scrappers must have stolen it to sell. Had Campbell jumped?

Craine felt the metal platform vibrate, heard movement from above. He looked up in time to see the gray figure twenty feet above him, hanging from a rung with one hand and leveling a long-barreled pistol down toward him with the other.

Craine's knees flinched; he dropped away from the window just as six muffled shots rained down on the window ledge, ricocheting off the platform and shattering the window glass. *Jesus Christ.* Craine fell to the floor, protecting his head with his arms until the firing stopped. He was covered in broken glass. His hands shaking, he aimed his pistol back at the window. He was lucky to be alive—he should have known Campbell would head to the floors above. It was a miracle he hadn't been hit.

Craine got to his feet. He struggled to keep hold of the Browning in his hand as he stepped toward the window. He hesitated. If he followed Campbell he'd be shot at. He'd been more than willing to fire on a police officer; he wouldn't have any hesitation in killing him cold if he got the chance. Doubt seeded in his mind and rooted firm. No, he should stay put, call for police backup and wait until more officers arrived on the scene. That would be the safest option. People would understand. This didn't make him a coward.

With his gun trained on the window, he slowly backed into the living room. He left the bathroom door open and crossed over to the phone. *Was he doing the right thing?* As he picked up the receiver, he felt a late surge of adrenaline pump through his veins. He could feel the blood rushing back into his limbs. His legs steadied, biceps tightened. He felt more alert. Confidence replaced anxiety, reason replaced fear. He knew what he had to do. He couldn't let him get away.

A female switchboard operator held the line. "Operator. How may I connect your call. Hello? Hello?"

But Craine was already out the door and sprinting for the stairs.

Craine's heart jolted when he reached the stairwell at the end of the hallway; he could feel his pulse twitching in his neck. He stopped to the right of the door and stood pressed against the wall, listening for movement on the stairs. Hearing distant footsteps echo through the stairwell, he inched the door open with his free hand until he could see the way ahead was clear.

The stairwell was dark. A single bulb hung over the stairway on a seven-foot wire and the windows at each floor were boarded up. There were rapid footsteps coming from below—Campbell was already making his way down to street level. Craine leaned over the banister and trained his gun on the moving shadows.

His arm was trembling. With little conviction, he called, "Don't go any further. I'm armed—"

Muzzle flash and suppressed gunfire snapped a reply. Craine dropped flat against the stairs as bullets ricocheted off the handrail and clanged overhead. His ribs cracked on the risers. *Sweet Jesus*, he thought. What am I doing? You're not dying on these stairs—get up. He rolled onto his side and pointed his pistol down through the balusters. Gripping the butt tight, he thumbed back the hammer and squeezed off two rounds. The bullets rattled off the railings below. He fired again, straightening to his knees. His gun was loud, aggressive. It had been so long since he'd fired his pistol he'd forgotten that the trigger was stiff, a resistance you had to push past. He fired again and the stairwell lit up with fleeting muzzle flash. In the strobe light, he could see the gunman reloading, backing into a corridor doorway on the second floor before firing back. Craine dropped low as bullets whistled overhead and embedded themselves into the wall just above him.

He waited for quiet then listened out for signs of movement: the door banged open two floors below. He heard screams from the lower corridors. Doors opened and slammed as anxious mothers pulled their children from the hallways and locked themselves in their apartments. He must be heading for another stairway down to the front entrance. If he managed to reach Main Street Craine would never find him—he'd be lost in the melee of afternoon traffic.

Against all inclinations to stay put, Craine pushed off the steps and ran down after him.

When he reached the second floor he stood with his back to the wall, the open door to his right. He closed his eyes for a second, swallowed thick phlegm and let the adrenaline wash through his blood. His heart was pounding. He took a long, deep breath then pivoted into the corridor.

The gunman was running straight down, toward a window at the other end of the hallway. There were no other stairs. The corridor was a dead end.

Craine shouted: "There's no way down!"

The man stopped running, turned and looked at him. He knew he was caught.

Craine stared at him, his pistol outstreched.

"Put the gun on the floor."

The man lowered his gun. His shoulders sank, defeated. Both he and Craine stood still for a long moment, their chests rising and falling as they gathered breath. Neither man moved an inch, neither man said a word.

After almost a minute had passed in silence, Craine took a step forward, keeping his arm raised at the shoulder. He could still feel the vibrations in his arm from firing his pistol and struggled to keep it held out in front of him. Or was it the nerves?

There were barely thirty feet between them. The man looked over his shoulder toward the window at the end of the corridor and then turned back. Craine spoke calmly through deep breaths:

"Come on. Put the gun on the floor and raise your hands. Please. Don't make me shoot you."

The man slowly raised his arms but the pistol was still held in his right hand. Craine took another step forward, lowered his Browning for a brief second as he reached for his handcuffs.

His throat was so constricted he had to swallow twice to speak. "If you don't drop the gun—"

But before he could say anything more an apartment door in the space between them opened.

Craine stammered, "Whoever you are, stay inside," but the six-year-old who stepped out either didn't hear or didn't understand him.

Both men looked at each other and then at the boy in turn. Craine realized with a rush of horror what was going to happen next. There was a moment where he should have pulled the trigger, but he couldn't do it. Something—*fear*—held him back. His muscles locked and he watched impotently as the gunman lunged forward in a single darting movement and grabbed the boy by the waist before Craine could stop him.

"He's just a kid," Craine said uselessly, his pulse beating so wildly in his ears he couldn't even hear himself speak. "You don't have to do this."

The man in the coat didn't say a word, even when the boy started crying. He pulled the child toward him and began to back away, glancing from Craine to the boy, brow knotted, his pistol arm now squarely aimed at Craine's chest. Craine couldn't understand why he was sidling backward until he looked past him and registered the windowpane.

Craine took a step forward, aiming down his pistol, trying to find a clear shot. As if in response, the boy began squirming, unaware of the complexity of the situation. If he closed one eye down the muzzle, Craine could see the man's head in his sights but his hand was shaking. If he squeezed the trigger he might kill the boy.

Like the twisting climax of a play, a woman stepped out into the hallway from the same door, confused but not alarmed by the shouting. Blankly she looked around. It wasn't until she realized her son was being held at gunpoint that she began screaming.

The shooter seemed as startled as Craine was and the two of them shared an exchange of looks that might in another situation have produced laughter. There was a disbelieving pause before he put his pistol to the child's temple—a boy even younger than Michael was—and continued moving backward.

The situation now apparent, the woman focused her shouting at the gunman, spitting words at him in some Eastern European tongue that did nothing to ease the situation. Every time she took a step toward the gunman he pointed his long-barreled pistol in her direction, provoking what looked like an electric shock as she shuddered on the spot with her hands held outward, yelling obscenities they didn't understand. What language was she speaking? Polish? Russian? The words were wild and unformed, evidence she was struggling to put into sentences what she was feeling right now.

Neither Craine nor the gunman said anything back. At this point, words only seemed like a distraction. Although his eyes darted from the woman to Craine, the man's attention was now focused solely on Craine's pistol. He pulled the boy tighter into his shoulder and threw Craine an unmistakable look that warned him as well as words would have done that if he stepped any closer he was going to end all of their lives, starting with the boy's.

Craine stopped moving and lowered his pistol just enough that he wasn't escalating things any further. All of it—the screaming, the crying, his ringing ears—was somehow bouncing off the walls, the room seeming to swell then shrink like a Surrealistic nightmare. Everything that was happening felt like it was in slow motion, his mind alert, his muscles taught, the adrenaline so rich in his veins he felt almost drunk with it. He couldn't see any way out of this situation, and part of him was relieved that the shooter had found an exit because otherwise there was no way for this scene to play out peacefully.

By now the boy's mother was chalk white, her guttural shouting had segued into a steady sob, and her frightened eyes began to sweep across the hallway as if one of the other doors might hold her salvation. Her eyes snared Craine's and in a half-moment, when Craine's attention was diverted, the gunman dropped the boy with open arms and fired wildly down the corridor, splintering the doorframe a few inches above Craine's head.

The report was so loud that Craine sank to the floor with a violent shudder, almost dropping his pistol entirely. Ignoring him, the gunman spun full circle, sprinting straight toward the window at the end of the corridor.

The woman, jolted into life, threw herself onto her son and pushed him hard against the wall. Craine had a free shot.

Lying prone, he fired back, grazing the man's thigh and taking the glass out of the window before his clip emptied. Still winded, breathing hard, he dropped the magazine out of the butt and grabbed for a fresh one. The man didn't stop. He limped on, wrapping his arms around his head and throwing himself at the broken window, his body punching through the remains of the glass and dropping out of sight onto the street below.

Craine got up and ran to the end of the corridor. They were still two stories up; the fall would have broken both his legs or knocked him out cold.

He got to the window. There was a truck parked below, a blood-stained dent in its roof. He spotted a jagged pool of blood trailing across the sidewalk but it was quickly lost in the thick crowd of hats and umbrellas. It was raining hard now; the road was busy and the sidewalks were starting to fill with commuters anxious to get home. A half-mile up the street, an electric trolley was pulling out of the Red Car shed and there were traffic queues in both directions. Craine looked up and down the street but there was no sign of the man in the long gray coat anywhere.

Kamona managed to get through the hotel lobby without dripping any blood on the floorboards. He walked quickly past reception so no one could see the bloodstains covering his pants leg but the clerk never even took his eyes off his newspaper. Kamona took the cage elevator up to his floor and limped to his room.

Once inside, Kamona set the Mauser on the bed and took a bottle of whiskey and his army medical kit out of his suitcase. Slowly, he unwrapped the strips of shirtsleeve that he had tied around his thigh. Blood started to run down his calves and form a pool by his feet. He quickly washed his hands then inspected his leg: a surface wound. The bullet hadn't penetrated deep into his thigh, only torn through the skin layers and grazed his outer quadriceps muscle, a finger-width canyon trailing across the outside of his leg.

Kamona cleaned the wound with warm water and sulfa powder but there were still small pieces of cloth stuck to the flesh so he propped his leg up on the bath and used the tip of his razor blade to remove the fibers. The pain was sharp and he felt nauseous. He sat on the floor with his back against the bath and waited for the pain to ease, taking slow, deep breaths and swigging from the whiskey bottle.

He thought of the detective at the apartment. By now he would have returned to his precinct and instructed search teams to go out and canvass hotels in the area or set up watches at the bus and rail stations. He wasn't particularly worried that the police would be looking for him: it would take hours to draw up a profile picture, and there were over a hundred hotels in Los Angeles to choose from. Door-to-doors could take days. No doubt the client would be concerned but these events were inevitable—you couldn't kill people without the police becoming involved, not anymore anyway. If they had really thought it an issue they would have had him dump Lloyd's body somewhere in the first place. His rates were worth the trouble.

But anyway, if they were still looking for a James Campbell, and to be honest they probably would be, they'd likely have already figured he was headed for San Bernardino and try to take him at the motel. He'd have to make sure he found Campbell before they did.

After a few minutes he pulled himself up and prepared himself for the next step. He'd stopped the bleeding, cleaned the wound and protected himself against infection. Now he had to stitch the wound shut.

CHAPTER 13

"So I already put an A.P.B. out for known felons in the area. Nine names came up. But it'll take me half the week to grind one of them down to sign a confession."

Detective Henson was pacing back and forth in front of O'Neill's desk, smoking furiously. Henson was older than O'Neill by ten years. He was friendly and approachable but a little brash too. That seemed to be the most common trait of detectives in the Bureau.

"That may not be necessary," O'Neill said.

"You found something?"

O'Neill was helping Henson on a homicide case. An accountant from the Hollywood Hills had come home from a golf weekend to find his house broken into and his wife stabbed to death. Henson was trawling through known burglars in the area. O'Neill wasn't convinced that was necessary.

"You said her husband found her dead around midnight?"

"That's what he said. Seemed pretty cut up about it. Autopsy put T.O.D. around eleven."

"And he'd been away?"

"Went away the whole weekend. Witnesses corroborated it. Came home and found her butchered like that. Uniforms got there maybe one in the morning, I got there an hour later."

O'Neill shook his head and held up the case notes for Henson to see. "In the evidence slip it says he had a bottle of bourbon in a brown bag."

"I saw it when I got there. Said he got a bottle of something nice from the liquor store near his house."

"Liquor stores close at eleven. So either he spent an awful long time driving around or he was home earlier than he told you." As Henson mulled this over, O'Neill added: "One last thing—your autopsy report indicates she had intercourse a few hours previous."

"Really?"

"I think maybe your husband knew that."

Henson nodded, suddenly understanding. "So she's banging some guy all weekend, husband comes home, they argue, he stabs her then frames it to look like a break-in."

"Exactly."

Henson smiled, impressed. "I've been working this case over two days. You got all of that from scanning the reports for ten minutes?"

O'Neill shrugged. Some people didn't pay attention; too busy trying to get things done quickly than get things done right. "Easy to miss, I guess."

Henson seemed genuinely pleased, not in the slightest bit embarrassed. "Hell, saves me pounding some poor wetback for two days."

"Glad to be of help." O'Neill gathered the photographs together and put them back in their file. "Might want to bring the husband in before he consolidates his statement, gets his alibi straight."

Henson laughed. "You're too smart for your own good, O'Neill. You'll be running this place one day."

Another detective wandered over with his coat under one arm. He lifted his chin to Henson. "Drink?"

"Absolutely." Henson stood up and grabbed his jacket off the back of his chair. O'Neill heard him whisper, "Shall I invite him?" The other detective glanced at O'Neill. A side shake of the head—no, Patrick O'Neill wasn't going to join them for a drink.

Henson turned to O'Neill and smiled apologetically. "Thanks for your help, kid, have a good night. I'll be sure to mention it to the Captain."

The other detective made to leave then said to Henson, "Hey, you hear about Craine? Got himself in a shoot-out in some apartment building off Main Street."

Henson guffawed. "*Craven* Craine? Didn't even know they let him have a service pistol."

O'Neill's ears pricked. "What was that?"

They didn't hear him so he called after them. "What was that you said about a shoot-out?"

This time both detectives turned round. "Jonathan Craine. Been in a shoot-out."

"Where?" O'Neill asked, frantically checking his desk for the keys to his Plymouth. "What happened?"

"Who knows?" the detective said. "All I heard is he got shot at by some perp downtown."

The two deaths were unrelated: Lloyd's murder, Stanley's suicide. The two of them had no connection, no obvious association. Surely it was simply a coincidence that Campbell was acquainted with both of them?

"We'll get him, don't you worry," Simms reassured him. "I won't have hard-working police getting shot at. Not in my district."

Craine was walking through the corridors of the apartment building, Simms keeping step. Inebriated with lassitude, Craine didn't reply. Around them were uniforms and ballistics, a few lab techs taking prints, all wondering what had happened here. He was surprised Simms had come at all. You didn't see brass show up at crime scenes unless they had to.

Craine yawned, feeling the ache of insomnia in his chest. Or was it something else? Something that felt a lot like guilt. He had sentenced a man to death for Lloyd's murder and convinced the general public that Stanley's death was a willing suicide. Now he couldn't rid himself of the feeling that maybe it was James Campbell who had killed Lloyd, that Campbell might also have had something to do with Stanley's death. Was O'Neill right to be suspicious? Had Stanley been murdered?

"So . . ." Simms went on, taking a deep breath. "We've put out calls to all hotels and local hospitals for the name Campbell. Nothing has turned up yet but we'll keep you in the loop."

Craine nodded. The shooter would need immediate medical attention, that was almost certain. But something about him had been so desperate to avoid being caught—would he risk going to a hospital knowing that Craine would try and track him down?

"He was injured. He took a round to his leg."

"It's on the bulletin. But you should include that in your report."

The two of them continued down the corridor, passing uniformed officers ushering people back into their apartments. "Stay inside please, ma'am," he heard one of them say. "This whole area is a crime scene."

Craine looked up and down the corridor. "There was a woman and a young boy here—"

"Uniforms downstairs said they interviewed them. Couldn't give a positive I.D. Different floor."

"Were they okay?" His own hesitation had almost got that boy killed. He'd been afraid to pull the trigger when he had the chance. A braver man would have taken that shot.

Simms shrugged. "They didn't ask to go to hospital. We had a Polish uniform take a statement. Were you hurt?"

"No, nothing but a few bruises."

Simms lifted up police rope and moved toward the stairwell door at the end of the corridor. "Do you want me to call anyone for you? Michael's school, perhaps?"

"No, that's not necessary."

"Then I think there's nothing else we can do today. I suggest you go home and get some rest, try and put this behind you. Although I have to say I'm still a little confused as to what you were doing here in the first place."

"Patrick O'Neill came to me earlier with this address." Craine spoke carefully, unsure of how Simms would react. "It seems James Campbell called Herbert Stanley the morning he died. I was looking into it."

Simms blinked twice. "Huh. I see. A horrible coincidence."

Craine was unconvinced. He wanted to agree with Simms, but a part of him couldn't dismiss what had happened so easily. "Do you think there's something more to this?"

Simms visibly tensed. "In what way?"

"Maybe something relating to Stanley's death."

"Because of the phone call?"

"I can't help but think ... Why would Campbell call Herbert Stanley? How did they know each other? If there's a simple reason, then I can't think of it. And if it weren't important, why would he fire at me? He panicked and ran when I asked him about Stanley. Doesn't that imply ... guilt?"

"Guilt for what? Look, Craine," Simms said, almost bemused by the whole thing, "who knows why he shot at you? There could be a hundred reasons. He might be some crook got annoyed you were knocking on his door."

"What about the phone call?"

"Maybe he was some jilted writer desperate to get his script made, determined he was sitting on the story of the year. Or some actor convinced he's the next Spencer Tracy. Throw a ball out the window and you'll hit someone desperate to make it in the movies. That doesn't make them all murderers. Are you going to drag up everyone Stanley's ever spoken to? Every studio worker? Every dreamer in town?"

"There's something else you should know about Campbell. I found a picture of Florence Lloyd in his apartment. She was the girl killed two nights ago. He had a photograph of her."

Simms looked at Craine like he was cracked. "And?"

Craine continued tentatively. "I'm starting to think that maybe ... Well, what if Campbell also killed Florence Lloyd, and that somehow they're both connected to Herbert Stanley's death?"

"This is ludicrous," Simms broke in. "You don't have a shred of evidence, no proof whatsoever for any of this."

A short silence passed and Simms' voice softened. "In every case there are a few loose ends, Craine. You yourself closed both investigations. Why would you want them reopened?"

Craine thought for a long time about that. Simms was right. It was out of character for him to question a closed case. He wasn't thinking straight. "I'm sorry," he said. "I forgot myself."

Simms slowed and put his hand on Craine's shoulder. "I've put you under a lot of pressure. Maybe it was too early to bring you back."

"I can handle this, Captain," Craine said protectively.

"You're sure?"

"Really, I'm fine. I wanted to make sure that we weren't missing anything that might be problematic later, that's all." He felt angry with himself for losing focus on what was important and for speaking so freely in front of Simms. It was O'Neill's fault. He'd made him second-guess his instincts.

Simms smiled graciously. "You're a good detective, Craine. I know you were looking out for our best interests. But don't let O'Neill's paranoia play into the hands of the press. He's been sniffing around for trouble ever since he got here and I won't have it."

"Yes, sir. I'll keep him in check. Thank you again for coming down. I'm sorry if I've wasted your time."

"Not at all, Detective. Not at all."

They stopped at the stairwell and Simms checked his watch. "I have to get back to the office. Senior command panicking about the next quarter. Budget cuts inevitable, targets most definitely raised. Do more with less seems to be the call. You happy to wrap this up?"

"Yes, Captain. Not a problem."

As Simms began climbing down the stairs, Craine remembered something. It had been sitting in the back of his mind ever since he was last in Simms' office. "Captain, what about Leonard Stone? If Florence Lloyd did know Campbell, is it worth us questioning him again? To establish whether he knew Campbell at all or where he might be?"

"I wouldn't worry yourself." There was a brief pause as Simms took off his glasses and sighed. "Leonard Stone cut his wrists with a piece of broken glass. They found him dead in his cell this morning."

*　　*　　*

Craine closed the crime scene and left the apartment building not long after the last of the uniformed officers. His mind was weighed down by what Simms had told him. *Leonard Stone.* He couldn't believe it.

Outside, the first thing he noticed was that the streets were unusually quiet. There was no sound of sirens, no crowds gathered. Even the homeless had cleared the streets. It was as if the entire neighborhood had heard about the shooting and wanted nothing to do with it.

The second thing he noticed was O'Neill standing by the curb. He was waiting for him with two paper cups of coffee in his hands.

O'Neill stepped forward. "Craine. You want a coffee?"

"No thanks. Surprised to see you here, O'Neill. I understand you've been a little ... unwell."

Craine started walking toward where his car was parked. He was in no mood for conversation, least of all with O'Neill, but the young detective was determined. He kept step, sipping at both coffees so they wouldn't spill.

"Did Dr. Collins tell you that?" O'Neill said, clearly embarrassed. "It was a passing stomach bug, maybe something I ate, that's all. Anyway, I was wondering ..." he formed his words carefully like he was treading on eggshells.

"What is it you want, O'Neill?"

"I heard about the shooting."

"It was nothing. A minor incident."

But it wasn't nothing. Underneath he knew it wasn't and O'Neill was no fool either.

"It was Campbell, wasn't it? The man who called Stanley shot at you." There was a steel in O'Neill's voice but it lacked conviction.

"It's possible it was a misunderstanding," Craine replied, trying his best to sound calm, with nothing to hide. "Probably a carjacker or pickpocket worried he was going to get pulled in." Craine was sounding more and more like Simms and he didn't like it.

"I'm sorry. I don't want to bother you about it. I only ... I only wanted to know if you'd asked him anything about the phone call. About Stanley."

Craine slowed but didn't stop walking. "He escaped before I could bring him in for questioning. Honestly, I barely mentioned Stanley. I'm not even sure he knew who he was." Craine was tempted to expand on what had happened and Campbell's connection to Florence Lloyd but he knew no good would come of it. He'd already said too much so he clamped his mouth shut.

"Don't you think we should maybe ... try and find him? You should—I mean—have you put a search order out?"

They'd reached his car. Craine fished in his pocket for his keys. "Everything that needs to be done is being done already."

The young detective was red from effort. "I'm concerned we're not doing enough. Did Collins tell you that Stanley had drugs in his system? Why not pursue this Campbell character? We could do a background check, see where it leads. Or we could talk to the studio."

"You stay away from M.G.M."

"What is it with you and the studio? I know your wife worked for them but—"

Craine twisted around and jabbed a finger in O'Neill's face. He was uncommonly angry. "Don't ever mention her again, do you understand?"

Detective O'Neill was almost quaking. He dropped one of his coffees and stepped back. "Craine, I'm sorry—"

"Do you understand?"

"Yes, I'm sorry. I didn't mean to—"

But Craine had no interest in O'Neill's apology, the words plowing past him as he pulled open his car door and slammed it shut again. A few seconds later and he was gone, his Fleetwood fast accelerating north toward Beverly Hills.

One hundred and fifteen miles east of Los Angeles, Jimmy Campbell lay on his hotel bed in Barstow, contemplating his future. He was booked under his own name in room 24 of the St. Louis Motel. "Louis" pronounced "Lewis," the manager kept telling him when he said it wrong. His room was a cubic cell on the first floor, with three windows facing the parking lot and a glimpse of the San Bernardino mountain range if you pulled the drapes all the way back. A moth-eaten chenille bedspread lay loosely over a single mattress and the bathroom faucet leaked cold water, deep brown puddles already spreading across the tile and making their way into the bedroom.

He tensed when he heard a car pull off the gravel track and onto the forecourt. The room lit up momentarily as the headlights flickered against the net curtains. He heard the engine cut and then the sound of a car door opening. Calm yourself, Jimmy, it's the third car in the last thirty minutes. The manager said people turned up at all hours.

Campbell slid further down the bed and tried to relax. The bedside clock said it was two in the morning and the night manager had promised he'd call by to fix the leak in the bathroom hours ago. Where was he?

He took out a cigarette and lit it, hoping the smoke would put off the flies. He wished he could afford to stay somewhere better but things hadn't panned out and he needed to save his money where he could. He calculated he had about a hundred dollars in his case, at least a hundred more stored in a security box at the Pacific National Bank in Chicago. Over two hundred dollars in total. The sum of his entire life's earnings. It didn't matter; he wouldn't let it get to him.

He looked at the suitcase sitting next to him and took out a set of pictures. He looked at them intently, one after another, grainy flesh-on-flesh photographs that had brought him nothing but a lifetime alone. He drew hard on the cigarette. Christ, what had they been thinking? How could Florence have died for a set of lousy photographs?

He knew that keeping the pictures was a risk. He should burn them, destroy the photographs completely. He should have done this weeks ago.

Campbell took out his lighter and ran his thumb against the flint. A flame sparked then died. He shook it and tried again but it wouldn't light. It was out of fuel.

Before he could search through his pockets for matches there came a soft double knock at the door.

Campbell slid off the bed and leaned his head toward the window. There were no lights on outside but he could see someone standing by the door.

"Who is it?"

"Management."

A small sigh of relief. "One second."

Back toward the bed, he slipped the photos in the case with his camera and latched it shut. He'd squared a chair under the doorknob and pulled it away now before twisting the knob and opening the door.

"Thanks for coming. I was worried the whole place would flood—"

Campbell stopped still. The roof of his mouth went suddenly dry and he felt his cheeks start to burn. Barely three feet away, the tall silhouette of a man in a long gray coat stared at him through the darkness.

It wasn't the manager.

CHAPTER 14

May 13th

Returning to Beverly Hills feeling dejected, Craine pushed his anxieties about the case aside and ate a light meal with a bottle of claret.

As the evening endured, however, the doubt seeded. He drank another bottle of wine but there was no ridding himself of the feeling that something about these two cases wasn't right.

When daylight gave way to darkness, he took his place on the living-room divan and drifted toward half-sleep, waking at hour-long intervals without ever knowing if his eyes had even been shut. Images flitted across his eyes. Celia. Michael. Then Leonard Stone. Thoughts of what had happened to that boy had been silently nagging him all night. Leonard Stone was dead, and it was his fault. He tried not to think about Stone dead in his cell but it was easier to think of Leonard than it was of Celia. She would have hated him for what had happened, he knew that much. The man she fell in love with used to really believe in the merits of police work. Or at least he pretended to. Craine wondered at what point he'd stopped caring about his job. Or if he ever truly had. Because no detective with any self-worth would ever agree to cover up his own wife's suicide simply to satisfy the needs of a motion picture studio.

To clear his mind of self-loathing, Craine began to concentrate instead on the investigation. At some unknown hour of the night he came to the conclusion that he would never satisfy his conscience if he didn't delve into the two cases further. Not just find a story to fit the theory but piece together what really happened the night Stanley and Lloyd died.

It was clear now that he would have to start from the very beginning. For the first time he could remember, Jonathan Craine was approaching a case with no preconceived agenda, no certainty of outcome.

Knowing that he would need to talk to Gale Goodwin, Craine thought back on the conversation they'd had yesterday in his car. He felt strangely excited at the prospect of seeing her again and lidded his eyes to evoke an image of her face. When he opened them again it was light outside.

At five, Craine drove back to the Bureau. At six he was in his office, calling down to the Records and Identification Division and asking the female admin clerk to track down R.A.P. sheets on James Campbell and Florence Lloyd. An arrest and prosecution record might provide a photograph or an address. It might even give some clue as to what Campbell was looking for at Lloyd's house. Or not—it could also lead to nothing.

After retrieving Florence Lloyd's homicide file, Craine went into his office and locked the door. The Bureau worked on rotating shifts and although four detectives were always on duty between midnight and 8 A.M., the steno pool only worked a regular day and without their fevered chatter the office floor felt unusually quiet.

Within the pages of the red binder, a one-page missive written by himself only two days ago highlighted the key elements of the case. ROBBERY-HOMICIDE it said in bold letters at the top. Turning to Lloyd's autopsy report, he considered instead what he now believed to be the essential facts: cause of death was gunshot wound to the head—precisely as predicted. The medical examiner had determined that Lloyd was not sexually assaulted but the report stated that there were signs of physical abuse. Torture, it meant. Florence Lloyd was tied up and beaten then finally shot dead. There was no casing found on the scene but the slug had been pulled out of the wall and sent off for examination. Was there any way to compare it to yesterday's shooting?

Shortly after 8 A.M., Craine picked up the phone and asked to be connected to the ballistics unit on the second floor. The ballistics team was barely six years old, a team of three responsible for logging and analyzing weapons, cartridge cases and projectiles recovered at crime scenes.

"Ballistics," said a gravelly voice at the other end of the line. "This is Noakes."

"Noakes, Craine. Have you made any headway on those casings I asked to be sent in?"

"From the Main Street apartment block?"

"That's the one."

"Yeah, came in last night. Some firefight I hear. You alright?"

"I'm fine. We have a positive I.D. but he hasn't turned up. I was hoping you could match the projectiles."

"Well, we made some comparisons with the ammunition located in the stairwell. I assume you were firing a Browning P-35 with nine-millimeter rounds?"

"I was. I don't know how many."

"Doesn't matter. The other casings belong to a nine-by-nineteen Parabellum round. Likely a German manufacturer, D.W.M., probably from a Luger semi-automatic or perhaps a Mauser."

"Are they common?"

"Not really, not in California State. But I saw some the other day. Which was it—?"

Craine let out a breath slowly. "Was it the Lloyd file?" he asked tentatively. "From the house on Longbrook Avenue?"

"Yeah, that's the one. Same ammunition used in that robbery-homicide. Except there was no casing. Slug went straight through the headboard and into the wall. It was all in one piece, if I remember."

"You're certain? I need to know there's absolutely no doubt."

"I'd have to run some more tests on the projectiles to make sure there's an exact match, but yes, I'm almost definite."

"Thank you, Noakes."

Craine put the receiver on the hook and tapped his foot against the floor. His theory was gaining credibility. He contended that Campbell had entered Lloyd's house somewhere around 10 P.M. There was a struggle and Lloyd was trussed to the bed and shot dead. Campbell then went through the house and robbed her.

Probing through the first officer's report, Craine remembered what Officer Becker had said about the watch in the bathroom and the forgotten money in the kitchen. Even at the time he knew it was strange but he'd chosen to dismiss it. He seized on a new theory now. Florence Lloyd's murder was planned, premeditated. She was tortured, killed and her house searched. But why? And for what?

His secretary Elaine was outside his office, nibbling at a muffin. She wiped her mouth and sat up straight when she saw him. He hated how he had that effect on people.

"I'm sorry, I was just eating. How are you feeling today?"

Craine ignored the question. "Has Detective O'Neill come in this morning?"

"He's not due in until noon. Do you want me to call him?"

"No, it's fine. Hold my calls. I'll be out for the rest of the day."

"If the Captain asks for you?"

"Tell him I've gone home."

Craine took the elevator down to R. & I.—the Records and Identification Division—a network of rooms filled with shelves and file cabinets that took up most of the second floor.

When he entered, a neatly turned-out girl at reception looked up and smiled a little desperately. She was sat at a wide desk beneath a row of bare, hanging bulbs. There was no one else in the room.

"I'm Detective Craine."

"Oh, hi, hello—we spoke earlier, didn't we?" she said, with the flustered desperation of a girl who'd never imagined spending her better years sitting locked up alone. She looked to be early twenties, with mousy brown hair and a broad, toothy smile.

"So did you find the R.A.P. sheets for Florence Lloyd and James Campbell?"

She stared at him for a second, her mouth a little open. "Oh, yes. I mean, I couldn't find anything on Lloyd—"

"Nothing?"

"Well, nothing in California State," she said, handing him the file.

"And Campbell?"

"I'm sorry, I haven't had a chance to—"

"Then let's find it together."

He followed her into the archive hall, a low-ceilinged room filled with long rows of metal shelves stacked with manila files. The room smelt of paper, the thin dust clinging to his throat.

"Gets awful stuffy in here. And dark," the girl said sadly as they moved down a line of shelves. Craine looked around. There were no windows.

The files on the shelves were ordered alphabetically. Each letter spanned between ten and fifteen shelves, with each shelf containing an average of eighty or ninety folders, each marked with a name.

They reached "C," eleven shelves and a thousand files of liars, thieves and murderers. The girl consulted her notepad and stopped. Craine waited as she ran her fingers across the spines, first the top shelf and then the second before selecting a thin manila file and sliding it out. She held it under the light: CAMPBELL, J. L. was carbon-printed across a small white label on the front. "Here we are—that's Campbell."

Craine took it from her and removed the paper from the file. A summary report stated that James Campbell was born in Chicago in March 1903 and on a charge sheet for a recent drunk-driving misdemeanor he'd stated his profession as photographer. His description was listed as white male, thirty-six. He was five-ten, brown and green but there were no photographs clipped to the file.

"What about prints and mug shots?"

"We only store those if the subject has a state conviction. If there are no yellow pages then he doesn't have any. We'd have to track them down from other counties."

Craine was already turning pages. "There aren't any. What about out-of-state convictions?"

"They're at the back there. I'm Maggie, by the way," the girl added when Craine didn't say anything for a few minutes. "You look tired. Would you like some coffee?"

"No. No, thank you," he said, turning one final page before he found the R.A.P. sheet.

James Campbell had a conviction dating back to '31, a two-year sentence at the Joliet Correctional Center in Illinois for distributing illegal narcotics, detailed as two ounces of street-produced diamorphine powder. He was convicted alongside another man, Jackson T. Rochelle.

Rochelle. A figure from Craine's past now creeping into his present. Jack Rochelle was a bootlegger who'd run speakeasies in Boston during Prohibition then moved over to California seven years ago, running rum from Mexico into Los Angeles before M.G.M. hired him to manage their barbershop, a front for illegal activity. Craine considered the relevance of this new piece of information. Campbell knew Jack Rochelle, who in turn knew almost everyone on the M.G.M. studio lot, including Stanley. So what was their connection? Drugs?

"Could you call Chicago, get me what they have on either Campbell or Lloyd? And try and get a mug shot of Campbell. We'll need it to track him down."

"Yes, Detective," she said, looking at him with something that looked like despair. "But it might take a week or so."

"Does Campbell have a separate employment record?"

"Should be something on the second or third page in . . ."

Craine flicked backward, thumbing through closely typed sheets of court reports until he found what he was looking for.

Two pages after the appendix, an employment notation listed his name, temporary address and date of birth. A single line stated that he was employed as a nightclub photographer between May and November of last year. It was a club Craine knew only too well.

CHAPTER 15

Craine was met by the Lilac Club's head of security outside the main entrance doors. Vincent Kinney, as he introduced himself, was about Craine's height but with broader shoulders and a deep barrel chest that filled every inch of his double-breasted suit. His face was large, his features slack and his voice, when he did speak, was low and feral, the accent of a man brought up in untamed neighborhoods.

"You should call two hours ahead in future, Mr. Craine. The manager is a very busy man."

Craine handed Kinney his police identification. "It's Detective Craine, and I won't take up much of his time."

Two thick, knotted arms held the badge out for inspection before handing it back. "Are you carrying a weapon? We don't allow fire-arms inside the building."

"I'm a law officer. I'm required to carry one at all times." Not strictly true, and rarely taken as gospel. Craine had to remind himself most days to take it out from under his driver's seat.

Kinney grunted and for a moment it looked like he wanted to spit. He swallowed heavily instead and walked briskly through reception. "Come with me," he said without turning back.

Craine followed Kinney through the club restaurant, past empty tables and stacked chairs as they walked toward the rear of the building. They continued on through a door to the left of the stage, leading into a long corridor with glass-fronted offices to either side. Despite coming to the club almost weekly for the past few years, Craine had never met the manager, Benjamin Carell. It seemed strange, considering that Craine was acquainted with almost every person of note in this city, that their paths had never crossed. More than that, he could find no records of arrests or prosecutions on Carell. He'd heard the rumors of Carell's history in Chicago, whisperings of friendships with Al Capone and his successor, Frank Nitti, and yet what people said had never seemed to amount to anything more than hearsay. In a town where everybody knew everybody, Benjamin Carell should be congratulated on keeping his personal history locked up behind closed doors.

Carell had an attractive office with wood-paneled walls and mullioned windows through which you could see the Hollywood Hills.

"Jonathan Craine, it's a pleasure to finally meet you," said Carell in a warm, if slightly controlled voice.

Craine shook him by the hand. Carell's palm was damp and spongy and he noticed a row of gold rings rippling over his knuckles that betrayed a meager upbringing. His father told him once, "A gentleman never wears jewelry."

"Please come in. Thank you, Vincent. You can leave Detective Craine in my hands."

Kinney grunted again and left them alone. When the door closed behind them, Carell took his place behind his desk and offered his guest one of the two leather-backed chairs opposite, which Craine noticed were slightly lower and smaller than Carell's.

"Apologies for my head of security. 'Taciturn' is a polite way to describe him. Hot, isn't it? All this rain seems to make it worse. Can I offer you anything?" he asked hospitably. "Iced tea? Coffee? Something stronger?" Two of the rings clicked against each other as a long arm swept toward a hidden corner where a bow-fronted sideboard held bottles of liquor, crystal glasses and a silver ice bucket. Craine examined Carell as his gaze turned away, contemplating his easy confidence and cared-for features. His olive skin betrayed Italian heritage and he reasoned that Carell was an anglicized version of Carelli or Carello. Craine had assumed at first that he was in his early forties but he had the childish eyes and incipient stubble of a much younger man. He couldn't have been much older than thirty-four or thirty-five.

"I'm fine, thank you," Craine replied eventually, taking a notepad and pen from his pocket.

"I've heard so much about you. I understand you're one of our regulars." The accent was hard to place. If he was born in Chicago then he'd tried hard to lose his northern city vowel shift. "You were married to Celia Raymond, isn't that right? My deepest condolences. A wonderful actress. A genuine loss."

"You knew my wife personally?"

Carell lit a cigarette. "I'm afraid I never met her myself. But I've seen a lot of her pictures. I was so sorry to hear about her accident."

That final word tripped off Carell's tongue like foreign vocabulary. Craine wasn't sure if it was intentional or not. "Thank you," he said anyway. "It's not necessary. Mr. Carell, I appreciate you seeing me at such short notice."

"Not a problem. I assume this isn't a social visit?"

"I'm afraid not. I was hoping to talk to you about an employee of yours, a Mr. James Campbell."

"Campbell?" he said, visibly discomfited but feigning otherwise. "Are you sure?"

"Campbell's employment records state he worked here as a photographer."

"The name rings a bell. I could have my secretary find out for you." He pressed a button on the underside of his desk and leaned sideways into a hidden microphone. "Emily?"

"Yes, Mr. Carell," a young voice said.

"Would you be so kind as to look through our personnel files to see if we employ someone called Campbell, John Campbell?"

"James Campbell," Craine quickly corrected.

"Sorry, James Campbell."

"I can tell you right away that we did, Mr. Carell, but his contract ended some time ago. He was the young gentleman who—"

Carell cut her off before she could finish. "Well there you have it; it appears we did. Wait a minute, yes, Campbell—I know him. He worked here, of course he did. We have a number of photographers, you see, and I'm not necessarily the best person to ask about our staff rota."

"How many photographers do you have?"

"A different number at different times. Four, maybe."

"Can you explain exactly what a club photographer does here at the Lilac Club?"

Carell's mouth pursed. "The photographers? Well, they take pictures of guests at tables," he explained airily.

Craine wanted to believe him but he was too well versed in lies not to recognize one said to his face. "What for?" he asked.

"What for?" Carell took his time to answer. Time to remember? Or time to imagine? "For framed photographs in the reception hall." Carell blew his smoke out sideways. "That kind of thing."

"I didn't see any photographs in the hall."

A second or two of hesitation, then: "Well, I will admit the photos are sometimes used for other means."

"Could you be more specific?"

Carell smiled thinly. "Motion picture studios procure them from our club and provide the pictures to newspapers. We take a small commission, of course. They're mainly for publicity purposes." He waved his hand in the air. "Gary Cooper out with his wife the night before his picture is to be released, that type of thing."

"You do that for all the studios?"

"In this town, different hands feed different mouths. We all help each other to get by. Isn't that true, Detective?"

Craine didn't answer him. "Campbell's employment record says he was working here until November. Can you expand on why he left?"

"I'm afraid I don't recall. We have over a hundred staff," Carell offered by way of explanation. "Some people stay months, others weeks. Contracts are often fixed-term or they leave on their own accord. These things happen. I'm sorry I can't be more helpful. You must understand I'm a very busy man."

"So your head of security told me."

"Is this Campbell someone you're looking for?"

Craine nodded: "There was an incident." He paused, uncertain as to how much he should give away. He decided to tell Carell about Florence Lloyd, without mentioning the connection to Herbert Stanley. "A young woman was found shot dead in her home a few days ago," he went on, candidly. "You could say that Campbell is considered a suspect."

"That's awful. Who was she?"

"Florence Lloyd. Does her name sound familiar?"

The club manager shook his head. "No. Not at all."

"You're sure? She's never worked here?"

"Never."

"You don't want to check with your secretary?"

"This time I'm certain. But do you know why Campbell would do that? Murder her, I mean."

Craine didn't answer straight away. "I'm not sure yet," he admitted quietly.

Carell seemed pleased by this fact and didn't bother to hide it. "My, my, you do have a lot of strings to tie. I don't envy you, Detective Craine."

The phone rang and Carell answered it at once.

"Yes?"

A pause as he listened. "Then try and book him for the week after. We'll be amenable," he said before ringing off.

"Apologies."

The phone rang again. This time Carell listened intently when he answered. It was evidently important. His face strained and twisted.

"Detective Craine, I have to take this. I'm afraid our conversation will have to continue another time."

Craine managed a smile to meet Carell's. "I understand," he said, standing. "Thank you for meeting with me at such short notice."

"Absolutely. Anything you need, please don't hesitate to call."

I've learned nothing, Craine reflected as he made his back way through the corridors, that gorilla Kinney inches from his side. He knew he could have demanded more time but had decided not to. He had nothing left to ask. Some questions are traps, he thought, and some are merely enquiries. Today I have nothing but the latter. Besides, it's too premature to offer an interrogation. Why act like the hangman when you're not even sure who the right man is for the gallows?

CHAPTER 16

Louis Mayer was standing on the yellow brick road in Munchkinland, shifting uncomfortably from foot to foot in a stiff navy blazer and cream flannel slacks. It was hot under the arc lights on Sound Stage Eleven, and only the blossoming sweat patches under his arms kept him from taking off his jacket.

Mervyn LeRoy, the picture's primary producer, came and stood officiously at his side. He was a genius, that boy, as smart and creative as any he'd ever met. But Jesus Christ if a monkey wasn't more business-minded. If only Herbert were here. He was always good at keeping the accounts in order.

"They're almost ready for another take, sir."

Mayer squinted as an arc light turned his way. "What is it, take twelve?"

LeRoy cleared his throat. "The Technicolor cameras are proving more complex than we expected."

"Mervyn, the budget for the reshoots is almost as high as our original shooting budget."

"Yes, I know our ledger is a little heavy. Unforeseen circumstances."

"Thank God we don't have to worry about the unions. But I don't want the press to find out about this. This will not be a box-office flop before it's even out."

"We're working closely with Peterson. The publicity campaign is well underway."

"Good," said Mayer, making his way toward the exit before he had reason to throttle his producer. "And don't ever ask me to come down to the studio lot again. It's giving me a headache just standing here."

Outside, the sun was high in the sky and the heat was unbearable. Mayer took out his handkerchief and wiped his face and neck. He could smell the hot, wet concrete so distinct to Los Angeles. At least that clammy rain had stopped.

Russell Peterson was standing beside the rear passenger door of Mayer's limousine, looking even more flustered and tense than he normally did.

"Sir?"

"What is it now, Peterson?"

"I've made a discretionary donation to the D.A.'s re-election campaign. He also has a niece who wants to be an actress. I'm going over to speak to him shortly."

"Give her a basic three-month contract. B-pictures only. And invite both him and the Chief of Police to Loew House. Make sure they have a good time."

Peterson looked around. "There's something else."

"Can it wait? I'm due to meet Margaret for lunch in ten minutes."

"I want to talk about Jonathan Craine."

Mayer leaned inside the door and said to his driver, "One second, Artie," before shutting the door behind him and taking a few paces back away from the car. "What about him?" he said quietly, beckoning Peterson toward him with a small, cupped hand. "He's done his job; I don't know what's left to talk about."

"I'm talking about Craine asking questions he doesn't need to ask. I'm talking about Craine meeting Gale Goodwin at the Brown Derby."

"When?"

"Right now. He called her at Joan Crawford's house an hour ago."

"Well, let's not get dramatic. What's the problem?"

"We don't want any unnecessary complications."

Mayer squeezed his hands into fists and stood in thought. It was crucial to keep up appearances of success and happiness at all times because more than anything, Mayer understood that audiences came to see his stars. And the only way M.G.M. could rise above its peers would be to make sure it filled its wholesome pictures with wholesome people.

"Craine's onside, he's one of us," he said eventually to Peterson. "But keep an eye on him. I don't want the press to find out Gale Goodwin is still speaking to the police department. It'll send out the wrong impression. Make some calls, find out what Craine's up to. But whatever happens, for God's sake make sure City Hall has our back."

Craine sipped a coffee in one of a long line of curved leather dining booths. He was tired. He was always tired. He could no longer bear to yawn, and when the urge came he held his jaw shut and breathed heavily through his nose.

He was sitting in the Hollywood Brown Derby on Vine Street. Craine had chosen the Derby because it was quieter and less formal than the Trocadero or Cocoanut Grove but he was starting to wish he'd booked somewhere even less conspicuous. The restaurant was busier than he remembered, packed with publicity-hungry socialites and debutantes keen to catch the eye of press hounds and movie producers. I should have gone to the house, he thought. I should never have asked her to come somewhere so public.

A few minutes after two, Gale came into the restaurant. Her hair was waved smoothly and underneath a long black coat she was wearing a dark gray gabardine dress with matching gloves. She looked gaunt, but not as solemn as he might have thought. He saw the maître d' point her toward his table and felt his stomach knot. He was uneasy about talking to Gale. Interviewing Carell was one thing, but putting probing questions to one of M.G.M.'s biggest stars was an entirely different matter. But there was something else too. Just Gale being here made him a nervous. A little on edge. He wasn't sure why.

Gale took a seat nearest the entrance doors, folding herself behind the table. She removed her coat and gloves then laid her hands on the tabletop. An actor's gesture: I have nothing to hide, it said.

"Hello, Jonathan," she said breezily, "you're looking very tired. Are you sleeping?" Turning the attention away from herself, opening the conversation with a question. He'd seen actors do this a hundred times.

An Italian waiter appeared pushing a tea wagon before he could muster an answer. "Can I get you a drink?"

"Pall Mall, please. Are you having anything?"

"Another coffee, please."

Gale seemed to have prepared herself. Her confidence took him by surprise. "How's your son? Did you see him last night?" she said when the waiter had gone.

Most people he knew liked nothing more than an opportunity to talk about their children. For Craine it served only to remind him that he was a terrible parent. "Michael's doing well. He's enjoying school."

"Michael. What a lovely name. What school does he attend?"

"St. Thomas's."

"I'm pleased he's enjoying it. It's very well regarded among people I know." She smiled, changing the subject. "Actually, I've been meaning to ask you. Are you going to Loew House?"

"Loew House?"

"Yes, for the party—M.G.M.'s anniversary. Louis said he's asked you."

"I haven't decided," he answered truthfully.

"Nor me. It feels very premature, but I know Louis and Peterson would prefer it if I did. I'll see how I feel." Gale opened her purse and searched for something. She brought out a palm-sized metal case and a thin lighter.

"You don't smoke, do you?" she said, taking out a Chesterfield and lighting it.

Craine shook his head. "Thank you for coming. I'm sorry if this is a little public."

"I wasn't bothered. Louis must have put the press on a leash. Besides, it's good to get out."

"I know it's very soon. You must be busy making arrangements."

Gale looked down at the table, as if talking to herself. "Yes, it's been complete chaos but we've finally picked a date. The funeral is Thursday. You're very welcome. I haven't sent out invitations as yet. Do you call them invitations? I suppose I've always associated the word with birthdays and celebrations. It seems so inappropriate. Anyway," she said, puffing at her cigarette, "I'm blabbering again. I'm sure that's of little interest. I never asked you; did you read the papers? Of course you have, what am I saying? Are you pleased? Is Louis satisfied?"

Gale was fidgeting, her hands moving from lap to table and back again. I shouldn't have chosen somewhere so public, Craine thought. This is making her anxious.

"Yes," he said, trying to reassure her, "M.G.M. are happy. Although you'll feature more heavily in the coming week. I don't know if you'll be reading the papers yourself."

"I'll ask Joan to tell me. I won't read them myself, I rarely do. You never really get used to what people write about you."

Just as he thought they were incapable of skirting around inanities any longer the waiter arrived with their drinks. They smiled their thank yous but neither looked up. When the two of them were alone again, he cleared his throat, pulled his cup toward him.

"I wanted to ask you a few more questions," he began cautiously. "About Herbert."

Gale ground out her cigarette in the ashtray then lit another. He noticed the fixed smile disappear and her eyes narrow ever so slightly.

"I thought you'd taken your statement? Is that not enough for the press agents?"

"This is something . . . separate. Another matter. Your maid spoke with Detective O'Neill. She mentioned that your husband had received a package the morning he died. And a while later he had a telephone call from an unnamed caller."

"I wasn't aware of either."

"He didn't mention them? When you argued?"

"No, why would he? It was probably work-related. We often had scripts sent to us. And when Herbert worked from home the phone rang all day."

Craine trod carefully, conscious that she was becoming defensive. "I'm merely looking into it. But I wanted to know if Herbert . . ." He paused, then decided on a more direct approach. "Gale, have you ever heard of someone called James Campbell?"

The question surprised her. "I've never heard of him. Should I?"

She smiled briefly but she wasn't looking at him anymore.

"I think Herbert knew him. Or at least, he knew Herbert. What about Lloyd? Florence Lloyd?"

"I'm sorry. There are many people he knew that I'm not familiar with. Who is she?"

"She's a girl who was murdered few days ago. James Campbell is a suspect. Or at least a person of interest."

Gale stopped smiling and frowned. "That's horrible. How could this Campbell possibly know Herbert?"

"I'm not sure. He called your husband the day he died. I'm trying to work out why."

"Are you saying Herbert was involved in a murder?"

Craine was anxious not to scare Gale. "No. Not necessarily. I'm just establishing a line of enquiry. Thank you for clearing that up."

"Should I be worried?"

"No, not at all. As you say, the call was probably work-related. It's likely a coincidence." Gale seemed nervy and he tried to move the conversation on quickly. "I'm sorry if I've asked you this before, but you previously mentioned Herbert had been depressed. You said that he drank, that he was drinking a lot."

Gale held her lower lip between her teeth and nodded. His questions were making her uncomfortable.

"Was Herbert taking anything for his depression? Was he on sedatives or other forms of medication?"

Her eyes flicked down then quickly up again. "What makes you think he took sedatives?"

Craine had been reluctant to mention the internal autopsy but now saw no way of avoiding it.

"There was a medical examination. An autopsy, Gale."

"Oh," she whispered. "Is that normal? To do . . . that?"

"It's an option open to us. In circumstances such as these."

She shifted in her seat and puffed harder on her cigarette. He saw now that her air of calm was a facade. She was delicate, splintered, so close to breaking.

"Sometimes he had trouble sleeping. And he got these terrible migraines. Dreadful, they were. It got so bad sometimes that he couldn't even leave the house. He took some medication. For the pain, you see."

So she'd known about the drugs. Why hadn't she told him? He wondered whether that ruled out O'Neill's theory that Stanley had been drugged. It looked like Collins was right—they were for personal consumption.

"When did he start taking them, that you're aware of?"

"A few years ago when Mayer made him a producer." There was a tremor in her hands. She slipped them off the table and laid them in her lap. The cigarette sat uselessly in the ashtray; the smoke trailed across the table and scratched at his throat. "The pressure was overwhelming; it was for all of us. It still is. Everyone has seen what's happened to Columbia, to United Artists, to R.K.O. The studios that we all thought were invincible suddenly started going into receivership. It's frightening. Mayer wants us to raise our standards, work harder, perform better, whatever that means. We have to make the best pictures—there's no room for failure, especially if you're a producer. Herbert was working for weeks on end without a break and if he wasn't at the studio he'd be at home rewriting scripts. He couldn't sleep. He would lie awake worrying until it was light outside."

Now it was Craine's turn to twist in his seat. He and Stanley shared a habit. Maybe in a few years' time he'd get to the same point of desperation, decide the best way to get some rest would be to tie himself to the ceiling fan.

"After a few months I told him to see somebody," she continued, picking up the cigarette and pressing it between her lips. "He didn't want to see the studio doctor because he didn't want Mayer to know."

"If it wasn't the studio doctor, then where did he get them from? Were they all prescribed?"

"I expect they weren't. Everyone knows there's a man on the lot who has ways of getting things."

"Rochelle. His name is Jack Rochelle."

"Yes, I think that's him."

Craine regarded her through the smoke. She looked nervous now, her face flushed with panic. "Why didn't you tell me this before?" he said.

"I didn't think it mattered."

"To an investigation into your husband's death? Why would you lie?"

Gale's eyes darkened, her face contracted. "I wasn't lying," she snapped, keeping her voice from rising. "It simply didn't cross my mind to tell you. And you of all people have no right to call me a liar."

Their waiter approached the table with two lunch menus. "Can I get you anything else to drink? Will you be eating with us today?"

"No, I won't be staying, thank you," said Gale. The waiter nodded and moved on to the next table.

"What is it you want from me, Jonathan?" she asked resentfully. "What is it you're insinuating?"

"I'm not insinuating anything."

"Then why did you drag me here? Why are you asking me all these ridiculous questions? First it's a murder. Then it's drugs. My husband killed himself—why does any of this matter?"

"I'm only interested in the truth, Gale."

"Truth?" she hissed, slamming her glass down so hard people on the adjacent table started to stare. "You don't even know the meaning of the word. You've spent most of your life feeding Mayer's little stories to the press. Don't even deny it. So why are you trying to spin something out of nothing?" She was shouting now, anger clinging to her throat. People on other tables stopped eating, their eyes wandering toward their table. They whispered Gale's name.

"I told you I don't know those people," she went on, "I told you I don't know what Herbert was taking but you're looking at me like I'm a liar. Like I'm covering something up. How dare you? How *dare* you?"

At last he spoke, slowly but sharply. "Stop it, Gale. Please, stop it."

Somewhere in the restaurant a woman shrieked with delight. A table of guests applauded. Two waiters brought out a birthday cake on a silver trolley. The table started singing "Happy Birthday." Other tables joined in. Another theatric had pushed the spotlight away from them.

Craine and Gale sat in silence.

"I should go," she said quietly.

"Gale—"

"I have to go. Please, I'm sorry." She stood up and swathed herself in her coat.

"Gale, don't go—"

Craine watched Gale stride toward the exit doors. He called out her name again but the sound was drowned beneath the cheers of "happy birthday" and for a second he wasn't even sure if he'd said anything at all.

CHAPTER 17

O'Neill had thought long and hard about the repercussions of going behind Craine's back but he knew that something wasn't right about Stanley's connection to James Campbell. Maybe it was the stress of losing his wife or something else entirely, but Craine wasn't adequately performing his duty as an investigator. Captain Simms could make things right, overrule Craine and open an inquest. O'Neill was counting on his support.

"So what is it I can do for you?" Simms asked when O'Neill had finally managed to find five minutes in his schedule. He'd been waiting for almost an hour outside Simms' office before his secretary told him to go in.

O'Neill twisted in the small chair in front of Simms' desk. Talking to senior officers tended to make his anxiety flare up and he was worried he'd stutter and slip over his words. To calm his nerves, he'd rehearsed what he was going to say several times last night.

"Well, Captain," he began slowly, "while the pathology report concluded that Stanley's death was probably suicide, it failed to mention that the internal examination revealed Stanley had a high dose of sedatives in his stomach. As you may also know, no suicide note was found at Stanley's address after he died."

O'Neill handed over a green folder and Simms' stiff white eyebrows creased together. "Explain to me why you think this is important?"

"Well, you'll see in there—that is, on the second page—a transcript from my interview ... my interview with Stanley's housemaid."

Simms opened the folder and scanned through the report. "Go on."

"Page three, half-way down—yes, yes, right there—she said Stanley received a package the morning of his death. And shortly after the package was delivered he got an anonymous phone call."

Simms squinted his eyes. "What was her name?"

"The maid? Ana Mercado, I think. Yes, definitely. Ana Mercado."

"Mexican?" The corners of his mouth turned down disapprovingly. "That doesn't sound like a reliable witness."

"She's reliable. She worked for Stanley."

Simms shrugged without stirring. "Either way, Craine has already highlighted this to me. I'm sure Stanley received dozens of letters and phone calls every day."

"Let me go through this from the beginning," O'Neill said, trying to engage Simms' interest. "It starts with the phone call and the package—it's all in the maid's interview. A package was delivered and less than an hour later a phone call received. Twelve hours later, Herbert Stanley is dead. The key question is: what was it that was said in the call? And where is the package that Stanley received? It's not listed in the evidence submissions slip."

Simms gave the document a cursory glance and raised a quizzical eyebrow. When he spoke his voice remained impassive. "Craine spoke with the caller. The matter is dealt with."

"There was a shooting—"

"Unrelated."

"I think—I mean, aren't there areas of gray surrounding Stanley's death that need to be investigated? Suspicious circumstances?"

Simms picked up a pair of half-moon spectacles. "Nothing you've said convinces me an inquest is necessary."

O'Neill swallowed hard. His ears were burning. "Well, surely it's my job—*our* job—to look into these matters."

Simms drummed his fingers against the desk. "Detective, outline your reasons why I should be spending resources we don't have looking into a confirmed suicide and upsetting M.G.M. and half the town at the same time."

O'Neill was losing his bearing. "Captain, I—I mean, the note . . ."

"Go on. I'm giving you the opportunity to make your case. Outline your reasons."

But in that moment, Patrick O'Neill knew what he wanted to say but somehow couldn't say it. Under the glare of Captain Simms he became increasingly self-conscious, his confidence disappearing as quickly as it had arrived. It was as if he'd walked out on stage and forgotten what play he was in.

"Sir, I apologize, I . . . I—"

"Speak up, Detective."

"There's the phone call . . ." he began reeling off words at random, ". . . the package . . . and the drugs . . . the shooting at the apartment . . ."

"None of which implies anything of significance. The package could have been anything. The phone call could have been business-related. The drugs might have been his own. Either way, Stanley's death was a suicide; nothing here tells us otherwise."

"But Captain—"

"But nothing." Simms stood, transcript in hand. "O'Neill, you're new here and I had a lot of respect for your father so I'm not going to caution you. But don't expect special treatment because of your police pedigree. This is my department and I won't have you getting ahead of yourself."

O'Neill hadn't moved. He felt like he was drowning. "Yes, Captain."

"Now is there anything else I can help you with, Detective?"

"No, no thank you."

Simms was already holding the door open. There was nothing more to say. There would be no inquest—this investigation was over.

When O'Neill pushed himself out of his seat, Simms said, "Detective Henson is primary investigator on a gangland shooting in Echo Park. Chief Davidson and I believe a second detective may help close the case."

"You're taking me off the studio?"

"Stanley's case is closed. I suggest you report to Henson immediately."

Craine parked on M.G.M. Studio Lot 1, the square mile along Washington Boulevard that housed the executive offices, sound stages and dressing rooms. He was annoyed with himself for upsetting Gale, but too many questions remained unanswered for him to stop now. He was here to see Jack Rochelle, studio barber and designated bootlegger on the M.G.M. lot. If Stanley had known Campbell, then Rochelle was more than likely the man who introduced them.

Most of the buildings on the lot were long, two-story huts that looked like military barracks and the barbershop was no different except for the helix pole in the window and the small sandwich board beside the doorway that read "HAIRCUT 10¢, SHAVE 5¢".

Craine stepped inside and let the door close softly behind him. Jack Rochelle was stood in the corner of the room, wet-shaving a man propped back in a lever chair.

"Come on in, sir," Rochelle said, without glancing back, when the entrance bell rang. "Take a seat over by the corner. Won't be a minute." Rochelle was heavyset and chubby-faced, his forehead etched with lines and his jowls red with broken capillaries.

Craine took off his hat but remained standing. The small barbershop smelt of wax and wet hair. At the back there was a cash register and a door in the center of the wall half-covered by a curtain. A white-shirted man holding a broom in one hand stood in front of it. He smiled awkwardly then looked away. He was tall and rangy with slicked blond hair and a pale, vacant face. He looked like Laurel to Rochelle's Hardy.

"How's that for you, Eddie?" said Rochelle, levering the barber's chair forward so that the customer could inspect himself in the mirror.

"That's a job well done."

"You working today?"

"*Wizard of Oz*. Still doing pickups."

Craine watched as the customer paid Denny at the cash register. Rochelle threw the shaving towel in a tin wash basket and picked up a broom. Finally, he turned to the door. "Sorry about the wait. Would you like a shave or a—" He froze mid-sentence when he saw who he was talking to.

"Hello, Rochelle," said Craine once the customer had left.

Rochelle's ruddy face hardened, his wide shoulders sagged. He had a right to feel nervous. There was a time after Celia died that Craine could have killed Rochelle. He'd thought about it plenty of times over the last few months.

"Denny," Rochelle said, his voice low and burry, "why don't you pop out and get us some of that chicken soup Mrs. Edwards makes at the commissary?"

"I had lunch already," the skinny man said, his voice high and frog-like.

"Go and get the soup, Denny," he said, gripping his broom with his stout, fleshy arms. "Go get the soup."

Rochelle stood there with his eyes locked on Craine until Denny had left the shop. When the front door closed, he put the broom to one side and ran the back of his palm over his forehead. He coughed, unclogged the phlegm from his mouth then swallowed. "What do you want?" he said eventually.

"I'm looking for a photographer called James Campbell. Have you seen him recently?"

"I haven't seen him in years," Rochelle answered immediately.

"But you knew each other, didn't you?"

He shrugged. "A long time back."

"You sold dope, didn't you? Did time in Illinois."

"Different chapter of my life."

"What about his girlfriend? What about Florence Lloyd?"

"Never heard of her."

"She was murdered two nights ago in her house. Campbell knew her."

"*I* didn't. And if you think he killed her that's nothing to do with me." Rochelle took several deep breaths. "Now if you'll excuse me, I've got a business to run."

Craine wasn't finished. "How well did you know Herbert Stanley?"

The question caught him off guard. "You asking about Stanley now?"

"This is important. I'm not accusing you of anything but I need to ask a few questions. Now can you help me or not?"

Rochelle held his gaze long enough to know that he couldn't talk himself free of the situation then shrugged. "The guy killed himself, what could I possibly tell you that you don't already know?"

"I hear Stanley was a good customer. A regular."

"I get a lot of regulars from the lot. My wet-shaves are only five cents."

"But he wasn't that type of customer, was he?"

"I don't know what you're talking about."

"We both know that isn't true. A bottle of pills at my house tells me that isn't true."

Rochelle bristled. "That wasn't my fault. I help people, is all." It was the dismissive way Rochelle said it that got to Craine. Rochelle didn't care what happened to people he sold to. He must have been making a killing. Pills to bring you up. Pills to bring you down. Pills to counteract the pills you just took. On the night of her death, Celia had taken a dozen sleeping pills and a handful of Rochelle's opiates. Dr. Collins had said after the autopsy that even if she hadn't drowned, the cocktail of drugs would still have killed her.

"You feed their addictions, Jack. You give them the tools they need to destroy themselves."

"Don't blame me for what happened! You go see Judy Garland dancing on Stage Four and then come and accuse me of ruining lives," he said thickly, his nostrils flaring. "Mayer needs them up at dawn, on set 'til gone midnight. Six days a week, seven if they fall behind schedule. I keep them awake when they're running on fumes."

"And Stanley? You sold to him?"

Rochelle sighed, a hard crease forming above his nose. He took a seat on one of the lever chairs and patted his pockets, pulling out a half-smoked cigar. He lit it without offering another one. "He bought off me maybe half a dozen times. Never large amounts, small doses here and there. Said he had trouble sleeping."

"What did you sell him?"

He spoke calmly but trembling hands and darting eyes combined to suggest disquiet. "Bluebirds mostly: barbiturates. Sometimes oxycodone. But he stopped coming by here months ago."

"And you haven't seen him since then?"

Rochelle removed the cigar from his mouth and examined its sodden end. "Why would I lie, Craine? Tell me one reason why I would lie to you? Look, Stanley, he was a nutball, he hanged himself because he was a depressive whose wife outgrew him. What else is there to know?"

"Did he know James Campbell?"

Rochelle wasn't expecting that. "How should I know? I told you already," he said slowly, to emphasize the point. "I haven't seen Jimmy in years."

They were interrupted by the bell above the door. Both men turned to see Whitey Hendry, the studio security chief, standing on the small porch step.

"Detective Craine," he said, tapping on the door as an afterthought. "Mr. Mayer would like to see you in his office."

"Thank you, I'll be over in a minute."

"I'll take you over," Hendry said, less an offer than a command. "He said it was important."

Craine's shoulders rolled forward. Mayer wants me out of here immediately, he means. He's heard I've been asking questions about Stanley and now he wants my nose out of the trough. He wants the detective hired to keep the peace to stop what he's doing and remember who he is and who he works for.

"Then let's not keep him waiting."

Outside, Craine saw Denny strolling toward the barber shop with a brown paper bag under one arm.

He smiled when he saw Craine. "I got you a soup," he said.

"Craine, how are you?" bellowed Louis Mayer, pounding down the hallway, arm extended, grin wide-set. "I haven't seen you since—oh, let's not." He clasped Craine's right hand in both of his and dropped his voice. For a moment Craine thought he saw a tear in his eye. "Celia was like a daughter to us. Great actress, real heart. We all have very fond memories. You should read some of the letters we get sent. Honestly, her pictures touched so many. She's a star in heaven, she really is. Margaret sends her love. Did you get our flowers?"

"Yes, thank you Mr. Mayer."

"Come in, come in. Shut the door. Don't want you to catch a cold. Ida's been coughing and spluttering all morning. How about the weather we've been having?"

Mayer's room had been redecorated since Craine had last been here. White walls, ivory drapes, a cream carpet and a curved white desk centered against one wall. It felt sterile, cold and unimaginative.

"You asked to see me?"

"How was New York?" Mayer said, ignoring him. "Completely understood. Would have done the same myself. Don't listen to the naysayers, doesn't make you a coward and definitely not a fool, running away like that. You wouldn't have heard those words in these halls, oh lord, no. Steadfast, there's one. Dignified, there's another." New vocabulary for Mayer. Probably lifted straight from the dictionary on his desk only minutes ago. Celia used to say he tried to use a new word every day, whether he understood its correct meaning or not.

"It's nice to be back."

"Well, bravo on showing a face so soon. You sure you're alright? Looking tired. You sleeping?"

"I'm fine, thank you."

Craine had known Mayer casually for most of ten years. They'd shake hands and mumble pleasantries at parties but Mayer had only ever acknowledged their secret alliance in his own office, away from the glare of others.

"Anyway, you're back in the thick of it, that's the main thing," Mayer said, taking a seat behind his curved desk and motioning for Craine to do the same. "It's good to see you. Did you know we're celebrating our anniversary this weekend at M.G.M.?"

"I'd heard."

"Well, we're having a little soirée up at Loew House this evening. You should come. Wait a second, where are my manners? Would you like a drink? Coffee?"

"No, thank you."

"You're right. Shouldn't touch the stuff, it's dehydrating." He pressed the intercom. "Ida, can I have a coffee please?"

A muffled reply. "Certainly, Mr. Mayer."

"Whitey Hendry said you wanted to see me."

"Yes, of course. About Herbert—I wanted to thank you. Heartbreaking, isn't it?" A tilt of the head, a roll of the shoulders. "I mean, really, as if we haven't suffered enough. Can you believe it? Right in the middle of everything, he signs out. Left with his entire slate: *Gone With the Wind*, the new Andy Hardy picture; *The Wizard of Oz*—"

"What exactly did you want to discuss about Stanley, Mr. Mayer? Whitey Hendry was insistent I come see you."

"Well, Craine," Mayer said, coming to the point with a strained smile, "a little birdy told me you had lunch with Gale Goodwin and I wanted to know what made you think that was necessary?"

"I had a few more questions about Stanley. An autopsy was performed yesterday morning. I wanted to follow up on a few things."

"Oh really? Dotting the i's and crossing the t's, I assume?"

"The results indicate that he had consumed a large quantity of sedatives. O'Neill suggested he might have been drugged. However, I'm now confident that they were for personal use."

"Didn't know anything about drug use," Mayer said dismissively. "Not on my watch. No, classic case of depression with Stanley—he was a sick man who gave it all up. We needed that to translate into print and you performed brilliantly. What more is there to say? And O'Neill—that boy with the baby face? Christ, how old are you recruiting them these days?"

"Stanley's own wife said that he was an addict."

"Why do you insist on dragging her into this?"

"There'll be questions from the press. She knew him more than anyone."

"Stanley didn't use drugs, no one here does. And I don't want anyone saying otherwise. He was a hard-working man who suffered from severe depression. He drank, we can say he drank. And he was a homosexual. I'm not judging but we all had our suspicions. And, let's be honest, something like that, him being that way, it goes to show what Gale Goodwin went through, doesn't it? What girl reading the papers isn't going to feel sorry for—"

"—Mr. Mayer." Craine was more forthright now, holding up a hand to cut Mayer mid-sentence. The head of M.G.M. wasn't used to that. "This isn't just about Gale," Craine said. "There's something else. A woman was killed. Florence Lloyd. She knew another man—James Campbell. It appears they may be connected to this. To Stanley's death."

"Never heard of either of them. How are they possibly related to Herbert?"

"I'm not sure yet," Craine admitted. "But it might be the drugs element. I'd like to look into it further. I'm confident I can make a connection."

"That's not necessary, surely."

Craine wasn't planning on kowtowing to Mayer's bullying tactics. "If there's nothing to hide then there's nothing to worry about."

A silence crept between them, broken only by Mayer tapping a pen against his desk. "If you run with this, with the drugs angle, then people will start to question whether it's a one-off. If Gale herself isn't some kind of addict; if half the studio isn't on drugs; if there isn't some kind of drugs problem on the lot. And to link Stanley's suicide to some murder? It's not only foolish, it's dangerous."

"I'm not asking for permission," Craine said as calmly as he could.

"Well you should, Craine!" Mayer banged a closed fist on the table. "Don't forget where your bread's been buttered for the past ten years. Your job is to make things easier for us. You've always been good with that, Craine, it's why you're here. So why in God's name are you suddenly trying to make it more difficult?"

There was a pause as Craine registered what Mayer was telling him. If he was honest with himself, he had known all along where this conversation was headed. Like the best of his own interrogations, their dialogue had a fixed destination. I'm meddling, he thought, I'm upsetting the balance. This meeting has been about stopping me in my tracks.

Mayer smiled, holding up his hands and leaning forward in a conciliatory gesture. "Who knows what he was taking?" he said softly. "Who knows what was going through his mind at the time? And to be honest, at this point, who cares? What's done is done. Do the details really matter? You come to a point, after all the shit-stirring and the conspiracies, where you simply have to accept the obvious. He took his belt, he wrapped it around his neck and he hanged himself. Let's leave it at that, okay? No unnecessary fuss. And as for those other two names you mentioned—never heard of them. Never heard of them at all."

Craine was considering whether he believed Mayer when there was a tap at the door and a half-second later two men walked in. Craine recognized them both immediately and felt the fulcrum shift. The first was Russell Peterson. The second was the Chief of Police.

Mayer pushed himself away from his desk. "Chief Davidson, so good to see you. Peterson giving you the grand tour?"

The Chief of Police held two hands up and grinned. "Thought I'd stop by to thank you personally for your invitation."

"To Loew House? Think nothing of it. Delighted to have you and—"

"—Betty."

"Delighted to have you both. Come on in. Detective Craine and I were just discussing Herbert Stanley."

Chief Davidson didn't look surprised to see Craine, as if he already knew he was there. It was clear to Craine that the Chief of Police's arrival was no coincidence.

"Oh, I'm sure there's no need for that," Chief Davidson said boldly. "Detective Craine, I think you've taken up enough of Mr. Mayer's time." Davidson's mouth was smiling but his eyes were squeezed into a scowl. "Why don't we leave these gentlemen to run their studio?"

"Sir—"

Chief Davidson's voice was loud. It filled the room. "Craine, Russell Peterson has kindly outlined all the necessary details regarding Herbert Stanley's suicide. I've reviewed the case notes provided by Captain Simms and have concluded that there will be no inquest. As far as I'm concerned, the matter is closed. I suggest we leave it at that."

"Gentlemen, I want to underline how much M.G.M. values the support of the police department. Detective Craine's contribution has been invaluable." This from Peterson, that smile never leaving his face for one second.

Several seconds passed awkwardly in silence before Mayer looked at Craine. "We'll see you tonight for the party, I hope, Detective?"

Craine waited for a long time before leaving silently, ignoring Peterson's outstretched hand as he left the room.

Whitey Hendry walked Craine to the elevators but neither one of them said anything. In the elevator he felt his face begin to burn and his arms start to shake. He noticed the elevator attendant give him a side glance.

"Are you okay, suh?"

No, he was pretty far from okay. "Yes. Yes, I'm fine."

It was rare that Craine lost his cool but the wall he'd come up against in the past few days had stirred something in him. It wasn't merely the trammels of the studio and the police department, it was the knowledge that he was no better than they were. He'd spent years loading the dice, so what justification did he have for his sudden moral resolve?

Driving home, he was angry at first but exhaustion soon drained him of all feeling. Once the adrenaline had left his body, his determination went with it, replaced by a dull resignation that Captain Simms and the Chief of Police would always consider Stanley's death as palindromic: to their eyes, it looked the same whichever way you looked at it. I have reached the end of the road because nothing I could ever say or do would prevent City Hall from protecting their precious studios. Further enquiry would be fruitless. Besides, Louis Mayer was right, of course: the why or the how of Stanley's death didn't matter. I should accept that Stanley's death was suicide, his own personal problems irrelevant. I should accept this because M.G.M. studio is my livelihood.

CHAPTER 18

By the time Craine pulled into his driveway, the evening sun had declined and the air was cool, a light breeze stirring the grass blades on the front lawn. He parked his car in the house's attached garage and placed his pistol under the car seat as he always did.

Inside, the house was dark. A long corridor led from the garage to the lobby and Craine groped his way through the empty house toward the maid's old bathroom. It was a single-storied house but widely set and Craine had to cross through their chandeliered foyer, past the music room, study and the poolroom until he reached the unlit hallway that took him to the maid's quarters.

When Celia was alive, they had guests around for dinner most weeknights and held drinks parties at least twice a month. Before Celia's depression, the house was overrun with screaming children at the weekends, Celia doing her best to make cakes and buns and he doing his best to stay out of everybody's way. But now, after so many months absent, Craine had come back to an empty household. Without Celia, the house felt desolate.

He passed the grandfather clock in the lobby. Almost 7 P.M.— M.G.M.'s party would be starting soon. Craine took a clean towel from a wall cupboard and went into the maid's bathroom. Standing under the hot shower, he pushed his face into the water until it burned. Maybe he wanted to feel something other than self-pity. He'd failed today on all fronts. His attempts to investigate the deaths of Herbert Stanley and Florence Lloyd had done nothing but anger his superiors, frustrate the very studio that supplemented his income and upset the one person he had felt any connection to since Celia died.

When he'd washed, dressed and shaved, he poured himself a drink and moved into the living room. Switching on the lights, he steeled himself against all the things in the room that reminded him of Celia. He drained his glass. Then, without thinking, he picked up a card-board box and started to fill it with the remains of her possessions. The dead flowers went in with the books and scripts. Pictures on the wall, trophies, awards: he didn't want any of it. He ran his arm along the mantelpiece and swept all her useless trinkets into the box. He would burn it all.

Louis Mayer finished buttoning up his shirt and put on his white dinner jacket. At the other end of the long dressing room, Margaret was examining herself in her triple-mirrored dressing table, fussing over her hair. God knows what takes her so long, he said to himself. Looks the same whatever she does to it.

Tonight's dress was black tie, not white tie, but he still wanted to look his best. He stood in front of the long cheval mirror then twisted to see his profile. He was looking a little heavy. He sucked in his stomach then let out a long sigh. Too many prime steaks for supper. His wife was always warning him about his weight. Still, it didn't matter; he'd never been much to look at anyway. It was his personality that was important. One of the few things God had given him was a persuasive charm and tonight he'd need it more than ever. The Loew House party wasn't simply an opportunity to celebrate M.G.M.'s success over the past fifteen years, it was also an important networking event. Some of California's most influential figures were on the guest list and Mayer knew he had to ingratiate himself with Randolph Hearst and the other newspaper owners if he wanted the studio to survive the damage Stanley's suicide had done to their stock value this week. He also had to think long term, and needed the ear of city politicians and policymakers if he wanted a chance at better motion picture tax breaks in the next annual budget. Tonight was the most important event of his social calendar this year.

"What is wrong with this thing?" Mayer's stubby fingers were still struggling with his bow tie. "Margaret, can you help me tie this. It's not even—does this look even to you?"

"Give me five minutes, Louis."

"We don't have five minutes. We should have left ten minutes ago."

"Don't rush me, Louis! I'm rushed as it is. Do you want me to look good tonight?"

"I want to be on time tonight. Christ, how do you tie these things?"

Mayer quickly tied the bow tie then glanced at his watch. *Dammit*, they were definitely going to be late. Where was his speech? He scanned the floor then patted himself down. In his back pocket. He'd go over it in the car. What else did he need for tonight? His notes on *The Wizard of Oz*.

"Margaret, have you seen my briefcase?"

"Which one?"

"My work case. The brown one with *The Wizard of Oz* binder in it."

"By the door, Louis, right where you left it."

"What would I ever do without you?"

Margaret let out a skeptical humming noise, a verbal rolling of the eyes. "You're not working tonight, are you?"

"'Course not, honey." Actually, he needed to have a quick screening of *Oz* with his producers tonight. Ten or fifteen minutes at most. He'd tell Margaret once they arrived and she had a few drinks inside her. She'd understand. Discussions were taking place over whether to cut another musical number in the first reel of the movie, a scene where Garland is singing in a barnyard: "Over the Rainbow," the song was called. Mayer was pushing toward removing it completely but last week the producers kept begging him to keep it in the picture.

*   *   *

Gale was not long out of the bath when the maid came to say that there was a telephone call for her.

She'd been lying in the tub for an hour, sifting through the reasons for and against going to M.G.M.'s party tonight. Mayer and Peterson had given her the choice but implied that, while very soon after Herbert's death, the evening was the perfect opportunity to rebuild her image and publicize *The Tainted Feather*.

Mayer had warned her there would be no mention of Herbert in his speech tonight. Use the occasion to move forward, he'd said. Apparently there was great debate in Peterson's department over the requisite duration of mourning and no doubt more conservative parties would consider it too premature for a public appearance. The message was to forgo a black mourning dress in place of something a little more glamorous but discard her usual jewelry in favor of black jet beads. She should be seen to be solemn but not forlorn, somber but not dramatically so. It was crucial to find that perfect balance between grieving and keening.

Worse than having to perform to the studio's instructions was Gale's uncertainty about her own feelings. Although she was upset, the past few years with Herbert had been so difficult that she couldn't help but feel a little relieved too, even if that in turn made her feel guilty.

Gale had met her future husband at M.G.M.'s Christmas party at the end of '32. At the time she was Gale Gretsberg, a contract actress playing supporting roles in low-budget B-pictures for fifty dollars a week. Herbert Stanley, on the other hand, was a successful screenwriter who had recently been promoted, his "pencil broken" so that he could now produce pictures for one of M.G.M.'s new musical units. Herbert wasn't handsome in a conventional way. He was older, too, almost by twenty years, but Gale found his interest in her charming and his fierce intelligence attractive. She wanted to learn from him and he in turn relished the role of mentor and pedagogue. Herbert helped her to understand the technical aspects of motion pictures, the importance of lighting and framing and how she could best perform for the screen. He used his influence with Mayer to extend her contract with the studio. She signed a four-year deal worth two thousand dollars a week and was given her first leading role. Shortly before she signed, Herbert and Mayer persuaded her to change her name. Gale Gretsberg became Gale Goodwin.

The maid tapped twice on the door and Gale almost forgot where she was. "Miss Goodwin, shall I tell the gentleman to call back?"

"No, I'll be right out," she said, jumping out of the water. "Sorry, I was half asleep. Give me a moment."

Gale told the maid she'd take the call in the bedroom and sat on the edge of her bed in a silk petticoat, her maroon Crêpe de chine evening dress spread out beside her. She suspected it would be Peterson. She hoped it wasn't. "Hello?" she said, lifting up the receiver.

"Hello, this is Jonathan Craine."

When she heard his voice her stomach tingled. "Hello, Jonathan," she replied, shuffling back onto the bed. Gale suddenly felt exposed, as if he was in the room with her, scrutinizing her freckled face and weak, pallid body.

"How was the rest of your afternoon?" was all she could think to say.

"I felt bad about what happened. I wanted to call to apologize."

"You don't need to."

"I do," he said earnestly. "I shouldn't have put you on the spot like that. And not in such a public place. I thought it would be more relaxed. The two of us having coffee. I wasn't only there in an official capacity. I wanted to be there as—"

"—a friend?"

"Yes. Exactly. As someone who knows what you're going through. But you seem like you're dealing with it fine on your own, so I won't bother you any longer."

Although he'd upset her today there was something about Jonathan that intrigued her. And Celia's death . . . it meant he understood what she was going through. There was no one else she knew who could relate.

There was a long pause as neither of them said anything. "Anyway," Jonathan said, "I only called to apologize."

"Are you going to Loew House?" she asked quickly. "I was hoping to but I can't quite decide. There'll be so many people there."

"I'm not sure either. Maybe. There are some friends I'd like to see," he added. "A few people I should catch up with."

"Well, perhaps we'll bump into each other. If we both go."

"Yes, perhaps."

"And thank you for calling."

"Good night, Gale."

Gale put the receiver down and lay back on the bed, her arms spread and her head resting on the pillow. She said his name in her head. *Jonathan.* She repeated it.

Gale rolled over onto her side and tried to understand the anger he had stoked today. Was it the accusing questions that made her angry? Or was it because it was Jonathan who had asked them? He was a strange man. Not as stern as she had first thought. There was a hidden fragility to him she'd sensed when he'd driven her home—he wasn't the intimidating figure she'd always imagined he was. Something about Jonathan intrigued her. She wanted to understand him.

When Kamona arrived back at the hotel, there was a letter waiting for him at reception. Hand-delivered, the clerk said. It was a large rectangular envelope—no stamp, no return address, only his name printed in plain black lettering on the front. He thanked the desk clerk and went up to his room.

Kamona locked and chained the door and sat on the edge of the bed. He squeezed the manila envelope between thumb and forefinger. Nothing but thick paper inside, possibly card. He sniffed the seal. No noticeable scent apart from the sealing gum. He took a stiletto knife from his coat pocket and used it to slice the envelope open. He noticed Campbell's blood was still on the blade.

The envelope contained two photographs, one a standard-issue identification photograph taken from a passport or identity card, the other a monochrome picture of the same man standing among a group of men at what looked like a party. Kamona didn't recognize any of the faces. He turned the pictures over. One of them was blank. On the other, a name and an address were scrawled in pencil.

The telephone rang. He checked his watch. It was eight o'clock, two hours earlier than expected. He'd barely slept in thirty-six hours. He'd spent the day traveling back from San Bernardino. It had taken all morning to dispose of the body. He'd got so much blood in his car that he'd ditched it by the side of the road and taken Campbell's Packard 120 instead. His leg was throbbing again—the wound would need cleaning. His arms ached too from the work he'd done. Campbell had proved very stubborn. He hadn't made things easy.

"Kamona?" said the urgent voice on the other end of the line.

"Yes."

"Did you find Campbell?"

"I found him."

An audible sigh of relief. "And the pictures?"

"He had a case full of film. A few photographs."

"What did you do with them?"

"I burned everything, as you asked."

"You're sure?"

Kamona exhaled. He didn't like being second-guessed.

"I'm sorry. I didn't mean to—I had to be sure. Will I be reading about Campbell in the papers?"

"Not likely."

"Good. I have one more I need. I'm sorry, I didn't know. Did you get the envelope?"

"I have it in my hand."

"His name is on the back."

"And my fee?"

"Are your rates the same?"

"They're the same."

"It'll be transferred to your account tomorrow morning. Plus a bonus. This one has some urgency attached. I can't stress that enough—"

Kamona put the telephone down. He looked at his hands. There was still dried blood under his fingernails. He laid the photos on the bed, went into the bathroom and picked up the soap.

CHAPTER 19

Louis Mayer had every reason to be pleased with himself. All the preparations had paid off: most of the guests had arrived, music was playing, champagne coupes tinkled and everyone looked like they were enjoying themselves.

He was standing in the reception hall of Loew House, a vast studio property in the Hollywood Hills used for hosting corporate parties or for housing the board of directors when they visited from New York. Mayer had ordered two hundred cases of champagne for three hundred guests. White-gloved waiters were on hand with trays of hors d'oeuvres and drinks and there were two dozen kitchen staff preparing an evening buffet.

Mayer started moving around the room, greeting men in black and white tuxedos and women in long gowns that showed off bare backs and naked shoulders. He shook hands, pecked cheeks and made polite chitchat before stopping servers carrying trays to offer around coupes of champagne and lowballs of whiskey.

"Good to see you. How's your mother? Send her my best."

"Great party, L.B."

"Thank you. Here, have some champagne. Scotch for you, Groucho."

Out of the corner of his eye, he spotted Margaret by the long staircase talking to Chief Davidson and the District Attorney. Good, Davidson was laughing. Well done, Margaret. "Apologies, Groucho, I must say hello to our guests. If I don't top up the Chief of Police's glass he'll have me arrested."

Mayer joined Margaret, shaking hands in turn with Chief Davidson and the District Attorney.

"Gentlemen, great to see you here."

"Louis, I was telling them both about your horses."

"Oh, don't get me started. The money it costs me."

"Thank you so much for the invitation," said the D.A. "This is quite some place you have here."

Mayer squeezed his wife's shoulder. "Well, thank Margaret, she organized everything."

Davidson grinned awkwardly at Margaret. "You know what they say. Behind every great man . . ."

The District Attorney raised his glass. "And with the week you've been having."

Before Mayer could answer a waiter without a tray hovered by his shoulder.

"The screening room is all set up for you upstairs, Mr. Mayer."

"I'm sorry? Oh, of course. Is LeRoy up there?"

"Yes, sir, he's waiting for you." The waiter leaned in closer. "One other thing. You asked me to tell you when Gale Goodwin arrived."

"She's here?"

The waiter nodded, the model of discretion.

"Thank you. Tell LeRoy I'll be up in five minutes."

"Oh, Louis," Margaret said with a dramatic roll of her eyes. "Surely you're not working now? I'm coming to keep an eye on you."

"Apologies," Mayer said to his two guests. "No rest for the wicked."

"Please don't apologize. And L.B.—" Davidson winked clumsily. "No need to worry about this Stanley business. We'll make sure of it."

Mayer managed a smile back and took Margaret's hand. "Thank you. Have a great evening, both of you."

As they walked toward the staircase, Mayer spotted Benjamin Carell, the club manager at the Lilac Club. He'd never much liked that man. Didn't trust him either. But some people in this town simply had to be invited.

Craine parked his Fleetwood in the large parking lot outside Loew House. He checked his reflection in the driver's window. He was wearing a single-breasted black dinner jacket with a silk bow tie. He looked smart but his eyes were red and bloodshot and there were still black grains of gunpowder embedded in his chin from the apartment shoot-out. *What was he doing here?*

He stood there dumbly, contemplating the house ahead, with its uplit turrets and stained-glass windows. He strained to listen to the noise coming from the house as if he could distinguish Gale's voice from the distant murmurs inside.

He had spent the hours at home trying not to think about her, convincing himself not to come, but with nothing else to distract him, he had started drinking. The alcohol fueled his curiosity. He knew that he was making a mistake by coming, that nothing good would come from seeing her. The phone call too was unplanned, a spur-of-the-moment decision made after two more glasses of Scotch. He regretted it as soon as the maid answered but it was too late by then. And he couldn't help but feel that he had to see her, that there was something between them. Or if there wasn't, he needed to know.

He stood there, eyes fixed and staring as he wavered between leaving and staying. He breathed deeply and ran a hand through his hair. He was staying.

Craine didn't have a written invitation but the M.G.M. doormen standing under the porte cochère recognized him immediately and let him pass inside.

"Nice to see you again, Detective Craine."

From the entrance lobby, Craine walked down a long corridor toward a huge, sunken reception hall with a white marble staircase curving up to the second floor. A tray of drinks went by and he helped himself to a glass of champagne.

As he entered the reception room the band segued into a rousing Glenn Miller tune. A black bandleader was singing, clutching the microphone with one hand and clicking his fingers with the other. Craine moved through couples on the dance floor and scanned the room: *was Gale here?* It was the usual M.G.M. crowd, a mix of top-tier stars and bottom-rung bit-part players. He knew them all by name, usually introduced at their most vulnerable: drunk at a curbside; weeping in a jail cell; wide-eyed behind the wheel of a crashed car. Most of them turned their gaze as he passed.

Benjamin Carell was there with Kinney, his head of security. As he looked around, Craine recognized some girls from the Lilac Club drinking and dancing but couldn't name the faces. Who were they? Newly contracted ingénues? Part of Carell's entourage?

A bartender in a tuxedo poured coupes of champagne at a bar. Two servers with trays stood to one side on standby. Behind them, twenty-year-old Scotch whiskey bottles were lined up between tall glass vases filled with ice. The waiter answered Craine's brief wave. "French 75," he said.

Craine spotted O'Neill at an adjacent buffet table, tentatively placing two oyster bisques on a plate of Waldorf salad. His boyish face looked as if it had been shaved within the hour and he was wearing a wrinkled dinner jacket one size too big for him.

"Enjoying yourself, O'Neill?"

"Oh, good evening, Craine." O'Neill shrank back, as if Craine might launch at him at any moment.

"Relax, O'Neill. I'm not going to hurt you. I shouldn't have snapped at you yesterday."

"I'm sorry. I only wanted to understand the connection."

"I get it. You're a details guy. Once upon a time I was too." The waiter placed Craine's order on the bar and he quickly knocked half of it back. "But it doesn't matter. I looked into a few leads and got nowhere. I promise you, it's a dead end—a waste of time."

O'Neill put his drink down, his interest piqued. "Really? Because

Simms won't let me anywhere near it. The Chief of Police personally requested I was reassigned—"

"I told you. I came up with nothing. Stanley was an addict, O'Neill. He wasn't drugged."

O'Neill looked disappointed. "You know that for certain? Did you speak to Gale Goodwin?"

Craine turned around. "Why? Is she here? Have you seen her?"

"I don't think so. I mean, I doubt she's here, if I'm honest. But don't you think we should bring her in for questioning? Who else is really going to know what happened to Stanley better than his wife?"

Craine leaned in closer, his speech a little slurred. "Stanley's dead, O'Neill. You were there at the autopsy—he killed himself. When all's said and done, who cares why? Pick the story you like best." As he spoke, he became aware of a familiar figure at the edge of his periphery and turned to see Gale talking on the stairway's mezzanine beneath a heavy crystal chandelier. Her hair was down past her shoulders and she was wearing a maroon evening gown, halter-necked and backless with a bias cut that accentuated her figure. She looked beautiful.

"Look, forget it. I have to go." He took a long pull from his champagne cocktail and walked away.

"Craine. There was a guy looking for you—"

"Enjoy your night, O'Neill," Craine called back, handing his half-empty glass to a passing waiter as he crossed the hall toward the sweeping staircase.

Gale was already walking lightly across the landing, politely declining entreaties from approaching waiters, only pausing when she crossed Katharine Hepburn and Mae West on the stairs. Craine watched as exaggerated, teary-eyed pity ensued, empty words of condolence for a sorrow they didn't really understand. "Our condolences," they'd be saying; "We're all thinking of you," they'd fuss, with a kiss on the cheek and a lingering touch on the shoulder.

Gale was half-way down the stairs when he reached the volute at the bottom step. She stopped when she saw him waiting for her but she didn't seem surprised.

"Hello," she said.

"Good evening."

She put her hand on the banister and carefully stepped down to the floor. Craine had prepared nothing to say. For what seemed like a long time, they stood there without saying a word. The swing tune reached its climax and the room burst into applause. Gale went to step past him before the room fell quiet and the music's tempo changed. The four-piece band started playing a slow waltz and couples across the floor came together. Gale remained standing completely still; Craine said nothing. Then, with his jaw locked firmly shut and his eyes betraying nothing, Craine held out one hand. Gale paused and considered the offer before tentatively stepping forward. In strained silence, the two of them drew together. He placed his right hand in the center of her back; she rested her left firmly on his right shoulder. With two hands lightly clasped together, they slipped into the rhythm of the song and began gliding across the floor, turning slowly in time with other couples around them.

Craine was a good dancer and Gale let him lead. He kept his back straight and held her eyes as they swayed and turned with the music. Their heads remained just a few inches apart but if he wanted to say something, apologize or compliment her, he never once gave it away. Craine remained mute, satisfied in holding her close without discussion or debate.

Gale was the first to break eye contact. She opened her mouth to speak before shaking her head, defeated.

Craine said, "I didn't know whether you'd come here. Tonight, I mean."

"I couldn't be at home alone. Joan offered to have me stay but I needed to get out. I couldn't sit there doing nothing, stewing."

"It's good to keep busy. I found it helps."

Craine waited until the awkwardness had passed then added, "Well, you seem to be very popular here tonight." He had been conscious of the dismayed stares for some time but was too drunk to care.

"The gawping looks, you mean? People are staring, aren't they? They've been doing it all night."

"They're looking out for your interests. It's good to have support."

"I feel like a caged animal out on display for all the prying eyes to see. They want to know that I'm still here in one piece. I bet you they're dying to see me break down in tears. I've spent all evening hearing people say how sorry they are but it's all for show. Why are they sorry? Sorry for what? That he's dead, or I'm alone? Most of them didn't even like Herbert."

"People never know what to say."

"Then why say anything at all? Why not tell me it's good to see me? Why not talk about something else? Don't they think I've thought enough about Herbert?"

"It makes them feel better about themselves. It makes them feel like they've done their duty."

"Then you'd think they'd come across as a little more sincere. I mean, honestly, they're supposed to be actors."

Craine stifled a laugh.

"There's that smile of yours again. What's funny? You think I'm joking."

"I'm agreeing with you."

"Nonsense. You're too polite to tell me I don't appreciate my friends."

Craine changed the subject. "You know, I think this is where we were first introduced."

"Really?"

"Years ago. Only in passing, I think."

"It seems funny that we've never really spoken."

"Funny, how?"

"Just odd. Considering our proximity: your work; Celia."

"I see what you mean."

"And you're different. Than what I thought; than how I expected."

"In what way?"

"I don't know. Just different. You look different now, already, without your coat and your hat, your policeman's glare. Here you are in a dinner suit, and I barely recognize you."

"How am I different to what you expected?"

"I can't explain it. It will sound silly." She laughed then bit her lip. She considered him with steady eyes then stated sincerely, "You're kinder than I thought."

"Kinder?"

"Oh, don't push me into saying something ridiculous." She smiled. "Kindness is very underrated these days. I should know."

"I'm grateful," he said, the corners of his mouth curling slightly.

"You should be. Anyway," she continued, "why did you come tonight? Don't you have work to attend to? Other ... crimes? No; cases. Isn't that what you say?"

"I'm not working tonight," Craine replied. "I was asked to come. I was invited."

"Why did you come tonight, Jonathan?" she asked him again with a sudden seriousness, knowing he was drunk enough to be confessional. There would be no avoiding it now. They could both drop the polite facade. A part of him felt relieved, the tension purged.

"I wanted to talk to you," he conceded. "To apologize for today."

"You apologized already. You called me."

"I wanted to apologize face to face. I wanted to see you."

"You wanted to see me," she repeated. "You know, I should have been the one apologizing. I was rude. You were perfectly cordial—a gentleman." Her throat constricted and she had to pause. "It's difficult, you see." She lowered her eyes again, embarrassed. He was close enough now to see the tears glaze her eyes. When she spoke again she looked around the room. "You were asking me questions and I should have known the answers, but Herbert and I were living separate lives. There was so much we didn't know about each other. Our marriage has been ... had been ... over for years. Neither of us was brave enough to admit it." The curve of her cheek fluttered and her voice became high and strained. "Christ, it's all such a mess," she went on. "It's a mess and I don't know how to cope with it." Her eyes started to well but Craine said nothing. She placed her head on his shoulder and they swayed together until the band brought the song to an end. Couples stepped apart and politely applauded. Gale wiped her eyes, pulled away and silently turned toward the stairs.

"Gale?"

"I have to go."

"Gale, please——" he called out after her but his words were lost to the noise of the hall.

She walked straight into Russell Peterson and Whitey Hendry. Craine watched as Peterson twisted her to one side and whispered urgently into her ear. Hendry stood firm in front of them, a curtain to the scene. Craine saw Peterson hiss at her emphatically. *What was he saying?* Gale nodded acquiescence, all the while shrinking away and wiping her cheeks with the side of her hand. He watched Peterson put an arm around her by way of reconciliation but Gale recoiled, as if afraid that the small gesture of intimacy wouldn't escape attention. She lifted her dress from the knee and escaped up the staircase.

Peterson seethed red but quickly flashed a reassuring smile to enquiring guests. He caught Craine's glare and held it for a fraction of a second before Hendry herded him away.

Craine moved to follow Gale but felt a tug at his arm. It was Jack Rochelle. He looked tense, a bow tie loose around his neck, his eyes dark and wild.

"Craine, I've been looking for you——"

"One minute, Rochelle."

"Craine, I need to talk to you."

"Let's talk later."

"Please. It's important."

"I'll come find you and we'll talk," Craine said, uninterested.

"Please, Craine, come on. I need your help."

"Why, Rochelle?" Craine was drunk and spoke bluntly. "Tell me why I should help you of all people?"

Rochelle implored him. "Please. I wouldn't come to you if it wasn't important."

Craine pulled away. "If it's so important we can talk tomorrow. This isn't the time or the place—"

"It's something you need to know."

Craine looked at Rochelle. Why was there so much desperation in his face? "Okay, fine," he said to placate him, "but give me a few minutes."

"Craine, it's the pictures—"

"I'll be back in two minutes, I promise." He gave Rochelle a conciliatory squeeze on the shoulder and skirted the edges of the dance floor toward the stairs.

He found Gale alone on the rooftop terrace overlooking the rear gardens. She was hunched over the balcony railings, studying the dark shapes of distant trees with a cigarette between her fingers. It was cool outside, and he could see her shivering with the leaves.

"Gale?" he said to her profile as she stared at the night.

She flinched, taken aback. "You startled me."

"Are you okay?"

"Yes, I'm fine, I just needed a little space," she said, looking away. "I couldn't be down there any longer. And all the rooms are taken. There's barely a corner not occupied by someone I know."

"What did Peterson want from you?"

"Nothing, it's not important."

"He upset you."

"I was already upset."

"He told you something. He was angry with you. Why?"

She faced him again. "He has concerns; he wants to protect me. Protect my image. We have a picture to promote and I'm supposed to start rehearsals next week for a new production. I shouldn't be out there dancing with everyone watching. This isn't the time to make a scene."

"You should do whatever you feel like. It's nothing to do with Peterson or Mayer."

"Oh, I don't know," she pressed a balled fist to the corners of her eyes then wrapped her arms around herself. "I'm so tired with the whole thing. I should never have come tonight."

He moved nearer, taking off his jacket and draping it around her shoulders.

"Thank you. I'm sorry. Please understand, it's been a difficult few days. I want to be alone."

"Do you, honestly?"

"I don't know." She let out a long breath and dropped her cigarette to the floor. "No, not really; not from you. But all night people have been coming up to me murmuring condolences when all I really want to do is forget about everything. I think that because I'm an actress people treat me like a character in a tragedy, expecting me to be locked away in mourning but really I think that life moves on. The truth of the matter is I feel like I've been a single woman for years, held back because I never wanted to upset anybody. Now I'm sad and upset but I also feel so guilty because I can't help but feel liberated. Did you feel the same?"

"No, I didn't feel liberated. But I know what it's like to be the outsider. When you feel people staring, hear them whispering." She was trembling. He wanted to hold her in his arms, tell her it would be alright, that she'd get through this and move on, but he couldn't lie to her. He could barely get through the days, let alone the sleepless hours that haunted him each and every night. The truth was that the hurt had never stopped. The guilt seemed endless. "I understand what you're going through."

"You seem to understand more than anyone," she said honestly, before she leaned forward and kissed Craine on the lips. Craine felt strangely warm, caught off guard; instinctively, he pulled her toward him and held her tight. She twisted away, catching herself but left her hand resting on his shirt. He wondered if she could feel his heart thumping in his chest.

When he said nothing, she said, "Something's happened so quickly and it's come at the most inopportune time. I keep telling myself I'm being foolish but I can't help how I feel."

Her eyes started to well again but still Craine said nothing. "I'm being silly," she said, biting her lip. "Herbert's just died and I'm kissing a stranger." She held his stare for a few seconds before saying, "It's getting cold. We should go inside."

"Yes, we should go inside." He breathed in deeply and tried to avoid those dark, contemplative eyes. What were they doing? "It's cold. Too cold for May."

As they reached the door, Craine leaned in toward her and kissed her again. She was reluctant at first, then slowly, her body shaking, Gale's lips opened under his.

CHAPTER 20

Margaret sat next to her husband in the small upstairs screening room. Sitting to their right were the producers Mervyn LeRoy and Arthur Freed, who had threaded the reel himself in the small projection room behind them. When Louis had told her they wanted to have a screening tonight she begged him to let her join them. Although it bothered her how stressful the production was on her husband, Margaret loved the picture and thought "Over the Rainbow" was the best part. Why would anyone want to cut it?

Four minutes in and that sweet girl Judy started singing. Margaret held on tight to Louis' arm and leaned on his shoulder. She whispered the words to herself, wondering how such a young girl could sing lyrics she couldn't yet know the real meaning of. "Somewhere, over the rainbow, skies are blue. And the dreams that you dare to dream really do come true . . ."

Hidden in the dark projectionist's booth behind the screening room, Craine and Gale stood face to face in the flickering light with their bodies pressed against the wall.

There were no bedroom doors they could find open, although neither could admit to really searching. The door to the small projectionist's booth was closest and both had gone inside without either asking the other.

Inside, he drew his face to hers, uncertain whether she might pull away at any moment, and kissed her gently on the lips. She drew back for a second, looked down as if to stop then kissed him again.

Their lips opened and as the tips of their tongues touched she let out a soft sigh before pulling him toward her. He shut his eyes then opened them again. Hers were closed. He wondered what she was thinking.

He put his hands on her shoulders then gently ran his fingers down her back. Her spine arched and she stopped still for a moment before frantically pulling at his shirt and tugging at his cummerbund.

He couldn't really think about what he was doing or why. He hadn't been with anyone else since Celia. Hadn't touched another woman's body in all the time he was married. And now here he was, with a virtual stranger. And all he could think of was how natural it felt. How there was no guilt.

He pushed her hard against the wall and grabbed her around the waist. She bit his ear then gnawed at his neck. He pulled back, clenched her waist tighter and kissed her again. Their heads rolled and turned, she grasping at his hair and he running his fingers up her thigh and pulling up her dress. His hands were shaking now, his palms sweaty with the anticipation of what was about to come.

They locked eyes and she nodded without moving. She wanted the same thing and it was exhilarating to know. I remember this feeling, Craine said to himself. I'd forgotten it existed.

Without speaking, he positioned himself below her. He thought she might hesitate but she remained still, biting his neck with her arms clasped tight behind his head as he slowly loosened her underwear.

Kamona pulled into the driveway of Loew House and parked his car near the exit gates. He turned off the engine and reached over for his case. Checking he wasn't being watched, Kamona took out the Mauser and two fully loaded magazines fitted with large-bore Parabellums. He inserted one of the clips and chambered a round.

He looked again at the pictures of the target the client had given him. Where he'd got them from he'd never know. He memorized the target's key features then ripped up the photos. He tossed the remains in the footwell and stepped out into the darkness.

Treading lightly on his wounded leg, he crossed the parking lot and headed toward the back door to the kitchen at the side of the building.

The kitchen was loud and busy and the line cooks barely noticed as a man in a long gray trench coat came through the back entrance. Kamona moved through untroubled with the Mauser holstered under one arm. The double doors into the main house at the end swung back and forth as servers came in and out carrying trays of hors d'oeuvres and canapés. He checked for security guards then strode through into the reception room.

O'Neill stood at the bar and watched the party unfold. The band was playing swing jazz again and couples everywhere were dancing the Lindy Hop. O'Neill never danced. Maybe he should try. No; he'd need someone to dance with first.

He looked around the room. There were plenty of girls here. Pretty girls too. He'd definitely seen some things tonight, that was for sure. There were men dragging girls into the washrooms, people so drunk they had to be carried out by security. He'd even seen a group of midgets swimming naked in the outside swimming pool. He hadn't expected this level of debauchery. Where was the old-fashioned Hollywood glamour he'd heard so much about? And why had Gale Goodwin been dancing with Craine? It didn't seem appropriate. Did they already know each other? Were they friends?

A blond woman walked over to the bar. As she waited to be served, O'Neill took a moment to look at her. She was younger than him, perhaps no more than nineteen or twenty. She had sharply penciled eyebrows and platinum blond tresses curled tight around her ears. She caught him staring.

"Hey," she said, smiling. Her voice was shrill and buttery.

"Hi. Hullo."

She fanned her face with a paper napkin. "Hot in here, isn't it?" she chirped. "Makes me so thirsty!"

The barman handed O'Neill a whiskey straight then turned to the woman.

"Good evenin', ma'am."

"Can I get a brandy highball, please? Thank you."

As he left, she looked back over at O'Neill. She took a step toward him and held out her hand.

"I'm Delilah, by the way, Delilah Deschamps."

O'Neill took her hand in his palm and shook it clumsily. He felt so suddenly self-conscious he could barely remember his own name.

"O'Neill. Patrick. That is, Patrick O'Neill."

She leaned into him and smiled. "So, what do you do?" she asked. "Are you in the movies?"

O'Neill blushed. "No."

"Oh?" she seemed disappointed. "You're not one of Louis' boys? You're not part of the club?" A moment of silence hung in the air as she waited for an answer.

"Um, no," he stuttered. "I work for the, um . . . for the L.A.P.D. The police. I'm a detective."

She squealed with delight. "A detective! Like those guys in those Hammett books? I love those stories!"

O'Neill smiled politely as the barman passed over her drink. "Something like that."

"Aren't you a little young to be a detective?"

He was still blushing. Christ, it was hot in here. "I'm older than I look," he said, succeeding only in sounding younger.

She took her drink and immediately turned to leave. "Well . . . nice meeting you, Patrick."

O'Neill thought about following her but knew he would never have the nerve to ask her to dance; he watched as she glided over to a scattering of M.G.M. contract players and draped her arm around one of them, whispering in his ear.

He leaned on the bar and nodded his head in time to the music. One last drink for the road and he'd go home. He gulped the Scotch down but the liquor burned his throat. He wasn't used to drinking so much and he began to feel dizzy, unsteady on his feet. He needed the bathroom.

O'Neill pushed away from the bar and waded through the crowd gathering in the reception room toward the washrooms.

Kamona followed the target as he left the reception hall. He watched him out of sight as he pressed through circles of guests into an adjacent corridor beside the kitchen. He saw him squeeze ahead of another man and then tumble through a door at the end of the hall. Kamona looked around for security guards but couldn't see any. He strode down the corridor, stepped into the doorway and closed the door behind him.

A tiled washroom. Two brass sinks to his left, a row of cubicles to his right and a line of urinals fifteen feet straight ahead. The target was standing at the urinal to the far left, facing the wall in front.

Kamona reached under his arm and drew his Mauser. He inhaled deeply, leveled the pistol and aimed at the back of the target's head. He steadied his arm, held his breath and squeezed the trigger. The pistol coughed; the brass casing tinged as it bounced off the marble flooring. He watched as the man's head bounced off the tiled walls in a haze of red mist and his body slumped to the floor. The rich tang of gunpowder hung in the air.

Kamona bent down to pick up the empty casing off the floor. As he went to put it in his pocket he heard movement to his right. A cubicle door was half ajar. He pushed the door open. A small man in glasses was standing over a toilet bowl. His head turned toward him but he didn't say a word, just stared at Kamona's pistol with his mouth agape.

Kamona raised his gun to fire. Before he could pull the trigger he heard the washroom door open behind him. And then almost immediately a woman screamed.

In the projectionist's room, two bodies drew together in the half-light. Gale heard Jonathan's breath in her ear, rhythmic and urgent. Her breathing too was harder now. She bit her lip and held her mouth shut. She was trying not to cry out. His head was buried in her neck and she could feel it as his face flared and burned. Her arms were looped around his neck and she pulled him closer, clinging onto him.

This isn't me, she thought. But she knew why she was doing it. It wasn't only that she found Jonathan attractive in a way that surprised her, although that was true. It was because she wanted to feel something, anything but what she had been feeling for the past two days. Was it too much to ask—an answer to a desperate calling to feel something other than shame?

Judy Garland's song reached its climax, the last few feet of celluloid ran through the sprockets and the projector's douser closed. The room fell silent but for the ruffle of heavy breathing. Then, from downstairs, they could hear the band stop playing and the sound of people running and shouting. Finally they heard the screaming.

A crowd had gathered in the doorway of the washrooms but Craine pushed past. In the corner of the room, a man was slumped against the urinal wall in a spreading pool of blood. He lay there half headless on the washroom floor with his arms outflung. He twitched and lifted one hand up to his throat but the blood pumped steadily through his fingers. Craine stepped nearer, careful not to slip in the pools forming at his feet. He looked closer at the man with half a face: it was Rochelle.

Jack Rochelle had been shot through the back of the head but the round had entered through the base of his skull and exited through his jaw, spreading most of the lower part of his face across the wall tiles behind him. He was bleeding heavily. He tried to speak but the bullet had torn open his windpipe and the air bubbles just gurgled through the hole in his neck.

"Rochelle? Rochelle, can you hear me? Rochelle, look at me."

Rochelle's eyes were open but glazed, the capillaries broken open and his pupils dilated. His body started to shiver and convulse before his hand fell away from his throat and his arm went slack. Within seconds the blood pouring out of his neck slowed to a steady trickle, dribbling down his chest and collecting in his lap. He was dead.

Craine turned to face the growing crowd of onlookers. They looked at him to resolve their situation, like children staring imploringly at an adult. One of them even said, "Aren't you going to do something?"

Craine said, "Did anybody see the shooter?"

No reply. Just a row of glaring faces and opened mouths.

"Nobody at all? Nobody saw what he looked like?"

A woman in her early fifties stepped forward and nodded her head at the open cubicle door beside her.

"Sir, there's a man in here."

Craine rushed over and peered in. Patrick O'Neill sat on the cubicle floor with his head in his hands. His knees were shaking, his shoes dancing on the tiles. A man in spectacles stood over him with a glass of water.

"I'm a doctor. He's okay but he's in shock."

Craine pushed him aside and grabbed O'Neill by the shoulders. "O'Neill? O'Neill, look at me. What did you see?"

"I saw him, I saw him," he said quickly, his eyes wide and red-rimmed.

"Who was he?"

"I'm not sure. He had a gun. I didn't see the shot. I thought he was going to—"

"Where did he go?"

"I don't know—"

The doctor interrupted, "We saw him run out the door, through the kitchen. I think he was headed toward the parking lot."

CHAPTER 21

Craine hurried out of the washroom and went back through the reception hall, pushing his way into the kitchen.

When he reached the outside door he peered around: the main entrance doors were along the wall to his right, the parking lot fifty feet ahead. He looked for signs of movement: nothing. I should never have come, he told himself. I could have been safe and sound at home. Instead I'm going to get myself killed.

Against his better judgment, he stepped out and sprinted toward the line of parked cars, the evening breeze cooling his sweaty temples. He was half-way to his Cadillac Fleetwood when he heard the slam of a door to his left. He turned in time to see a black Packard sedan reverse out of the darkness then screech to a stop, scattering loose pebbles across the parking lot. Before he could make out the driver, there was a faint flicker of muzzle flash from the driver's window, then a muffled pop as three silenced pistol shots whistled by, two pinging off nearby cars and one snapping off the wing mirror of his Cadillac. He dropped down, keeping low as he reached the Fleetwood's driver's door. More shots rattled off the ground by his feet before the Packard was thrust into gear and hared off toward the entrance gates, rubber tires screeching as they dry-skidded against the gravel.

Craine climbed into the Fleetwood, slotting in the key and turning the ignition. The engine coughed and died. He turned the key again—nothing. He pulled out the choke, tried again—*come on*—and the engine finally answered. Putting the car into gear, he pressed down hard on the throttle and accelerated toward the driveway's gates, looking out for the red taillights of the Packard as they sped toward the L.A. basin.

Once on the two-lane road, he went through the gears, pushing the car to sixty then on to seventy. He could make out the Packard sedan ahead, the distant headlights boring through the sky then disappearing as the Packard entered the first curves of Mulholland Highway.

Craine struggled to keep his Fleetwood in the center of the road, his tires alternately grazing the sheer rock walls to his right and the lip of the steep hillside drop to his left. He gripped the wheel and pushed his foot against the accelerator, allowing his adrenaline to wash away the worst effects of the alcohol. He tried to stop his thoughts from wandering toward Gale, sucking in air and concentrating on the car ahead. Now was the time to calm down and think about what was going to happen. If they made it to the busy coastal roads, he'd lose the Packard in traffic. All he could do was to try to gain on him on the first length of straight road, and hope a well-aimed shot might burst a tire or, even better, penetrate the fuel tank and blow the car clean off the road. But who was the driver? Was he James Campbell? It was starting to make sense. Rochelle must have known Florence Lloyd. But how? And what did they do to warrant being killed?

On a short piece of straight, Craine lowered himself and, with his free hand, reached below the seat for the holster he kept in the car. He pulled out his Browning semi-automatic and dropped it into his lap.

Ahead in the Packard, Kamona was driving with a calm urgency. There was no traffic on the road but once the police had been called, they'd start to block all connecting routes to the highway. He might have ten minutes' head start if he was lucky.

His eyes flicked between the road ahead and the glare of his pursuer's headlights in the rearview mirror. He hadn't expected to be followed, and cursed himself for failing to check the bathroom stalls before shooting Rochelle. He should have killed that boy with the glasses but the screaming woman had thrown him and he'd run out. It didn't matter now. All that mattered was getting away.

Craine entered the last camber in a low gear and rammed his foot down to close the gap between the cars. Fifty yards away. Forty, thirty, twenty. Just as he lined his car directly behind the Packard, he saw muzzle flash light up the night. He whipped the steering wheel right to avoid the gunfire but his reactions were too slow and his assailant too accurate; before he could correct the slew of his tail the front windshield was blown inward, two bullets angling past and thudding into the leather passenger seat barely a few inches to his right.

Holding back the urge to vomit, Craine lowered himself behind the steering wheel, pulled back the hammer of the Browning and rapid-fired four shots through the open window. The first two pinged off the car door, the third and fourth cracked the front passenger window. He saw the driver drop his gun and twist in pain. Using his left hand to hold the steering wheel firm, Craine held his breath and raised the pistol to fire again. Only the wail of an approaching juggernaut's horn broke his concentration.

A hundred feet ahead and straddling the crown of the road, a four-ton, six-wheel truck charged toward them like a freight train. The horn blared again, the giant headlamps blinding both drivers. Craine dropped his pistol, hauling himself onto the steering wheel and swerving to his right. The diesel behemoth plowed between both cars, missing Craine's Fleetwood by inches but catching the Packard's rear bumper—the car skidded across the asphalt, the tires sidling out toward the edge of the road.

Craine regained control of his car but his pistol was out of reach. Desperate, his only hope in stopping the shooter now lay in battering the Packard off the highway and down the mountain slope. If he could control the impact, he might keep his car on the road.

It was a decision fueled by alcohol but it was too late now. He aimed his punctured hood toward the Packard's vulnerable passenger door, tensed his forearms against the wheel and braced himself for the collision.

Between the oxbow lanes that curved around the base of the Santa Monica Mountains were quarter-mile expanses of barren hillside, littered only with loose rock and stunted chaparral.

The Fleetwood and the Packard came off the road's escarpment with their front wheels angled downhill and dropped down the steep hillside toward a house at the very bottom of the slope.

Through the darkness, all Craine could see were the tumbling headlights of the Packard below him. His engine stalled, his clutch gave way; Craine could do nothing but cover his face with his arms as loose shards of rubble tore through the remains of his windshield. He watched as, twenty feet downhill, the Packard jackknifed and flipped onto its side. His steering column broken, Craine's Fleetwood careered into it, smashing into the Packard's belly and sending it barreling downward, turning over and over toward the rear walls of the house only yards below.

For a few seconds Kamona's body had refused to acknowledge any pain but it had arrived now in heavy waves, each one strong enough to knock him unconscious. His energy was waning, his life ebbing out of him. The wall of the house below grew larger. He knew then that he was going to die but there was no hair-raising fear, simply acceptance. There was a sound of impact, of bending, breaking, shearing metal and then finally nothing.

Craine's tires were flayed from his wheels, his rims screaming against the rocks and sparks flaring up to either side of him. He saw the Packard pile into the rear wall of the house as his Fleetwood veered to the right and charged onward, hurdling a hedge and, after a brief moment of free flight, landing in the house's courtyard swimming pool.

In a hard second, the Fleetwood's hood hit the base of the pool and the grille and fenders were instantly crushed. Craine's body was flung forward with the momentum of the collision. His head cracked against the steering wheel and everything went black.

CHAPTER 22

Craine opened his eyes. He couldn't see anything. His body was convulsing, his arms lashing out against the darkness. He remembered where he was and tried to push through the water toward the surface. No use; he couldn't move his legs. His lungs were screaming for air, the pain in his chest sharp and raw. Unable to see, he groped blindly at his pants. His legs were trapped, pinned between the dashboard and the driver's seat. His chest started heaving. He could feel himself slipping back into unconsciousness. He had to get to the surface of the pool. He focused, using the last of his strength to reach under his thighs and tug just under the knees. His legs loosened. He pulled again and they came free.

Dizzy now, Craine couldn't hold his breath any longer. He pushed away from the driver's seat, kicked out with his feet and propelled himself through the broken windshield. With his arms and legs flailing against the water, Craine lunged desperately toward the pool's surface.

He choked on the first breath, the clean air too much for his lungs to bear. By the time he pulled himself to the side, he was coughing and retching on each and every breath. Too weak to pull himself out of the pool, he hugged the lip of the concrete edge and let his chest rise and fall with the motions of the water. Only a bright flashlight stopped him from drifting asleep.

"Stay where you are."

Standing at the edge of the pool with a Winchester shotgun was a wispy-haired retiree in a velvet dressing gown. His wrists were shaking, struggling to hold the shotgun butt firm in his shoulder.

"Don't move—I said stay where you are. I've already called the police."

Craine reached for his police identification.

"What are you doing? I said don't move."

"I'm . . . my badge . . ."

"I'll shoot you."

"I'm trying to find my badge."

The tin insignia was still there, held tight in the wet remains of his inside breast pocket. He tossed the badge at the man's feet.

"Los Angeles Police Department."

The man slowly put the shotgun on the ground and helped pull Craine out of the water.

"I'm sorry. The other car—"

"Is the driver still inside?"

"I'm not sure."

Craine patted his pockets. Where was his gun? He stared back at the remains of his car at the bottom of the pool. The Browning was still in the footwell.

"Your shotgun, is it loaded?"

"Yes, sir. Buckshot. Take it."

Craine picked up the Winchester, cocked it and limped around to the back of the house. The building was designed in the international style, a stark cubic form with a set of right-angled facades and windows in long, horizontal rows. He pulled tight against the exterior wall, climbing up the dozen or so steps that angled up and around to the rear of the house.

What remained of the Packard's shattered frame was resting on its side. The radiator was crushed, the paint and nickel dented and grazed. Smoke hissed out of the engine and the cabin was already catching alight. Craine moved closer, the shotgun tight in his shoulder, index finger stroking the trigger. Through the flames, he could make out the driver draped around the steering column. He wasn't moving. Craine shouted out to him but there was no response. Only when he was certain that he was dead did he slowly lower his weapon.

Kamona hadn't survived the impact. He remained trapped behind the wheel, the steering column pushed so far into his chest that his upper vertebrae had split open his back and protruded through his shoulder blades. His face was resting on the dashboard, his eyes open, gray and glazed. One of his arms was half-severed, hanging off at the elbow where Craine's bullet had broken the skin, ripped through the articular cartilage and splintered his humerus bone. The other arm lay rigid by his side, his Mauser still grasped tight in his hand.

In the distance, Craine heard the wail of police sirens as they made their way up the hill. He waited by the car until he saw the headlights pull into the driveway.

The county newspaper reporters arrived shortly after downtown's homicide division had cordoned off the hillside estate. By then the fire department had doused the fire and removed the body in the car. A contingent of uniform police quickly began scouring the hillside, returning with bags of scrap metal and glass recovered from the wreckage. Two yellow press photographers managed to creep under the police rope and take a picture of Craine's Fleetwood being hoisted out of the swimming pool, the hood crumpled, the coachwork in pieces.

Craine sat in the back of an ambulance wrapped in a coarse wool blanket as a doctor examined his injuries. He shuddered when he touched his ribs.

"Sorry—I know it's painful, but would you mind lifting up your arm? Can you clench your fist, please? And open it again. Good. You said you felt a little nauseous. That's normal, it's the adrenaline left in your body. Any headaches? Did you black out since the accident?"

He always had a headache. "No. I'm a little lightheaded, that's all." Craine was admiring the doctor's stethoscope. He pictured himself in a white coat, rushing to the emergency room as an ambulance came in, saving lives, being a hero. He would have made a good doctor.

He watched as the doctor took a brass penlight out of his pocket and trailed it in front of Craine's eyes. "Could you follow my pen please? Okay, thank you, that's great." The light went off, the penlight tucked back inside his pocket. "Well, there's a slight bump on your head and your eyes are a little bloodshot, but you don't seem to have any serious concussion. You may find heavy breathing a little painful for the next week or so. Try to avoid any strenuous physical exercise if you can." The doctor reached inside his jacket pocket for a cigarette tin then placed one between his teeth. "Cigarette?" he said, patting his pants pockets before bringing out a Ronson lighter.

Craine shook his head. "Am I done here?"

"All done. Are you having trouble sleeping, Detective? You look tired."

"I don't sleep much."

"I advise you get some rest in the next few days. Do you the world of good."

When the doctor had left, Craine propped himself up. It hurt to move. In the glass of the windshield he could see his entire reflection. He wasn't wearing his shirt and a ring of purple bruising was visible across his chest. His shoulder was a grayish purple, his lower ribs on his right side swollen and tender to the touch.

Craine shivered against the chill. He was cold, almost numb, and his vulnerable mind began to wander. He looked at his two pale, bruised forearms and thought of Celia's body in the morgue. He washed the thought away with a swig from the bottle of Tennessee the first officer had given him. He was starting to think about Michael when Simms knocked on the open ambulance door and took a seat on the wooden bench opposite. He was dressed in an open shirt collar and thick winter coat.

"Craine, how are you?" he said, with a tenderness that had always seemed lacking.

"I'll be okay."

"Nothing broken?"

He shook his head.

"You should really be checked for hypothermia. We should get you down to the hospital."

Craine attempted to talk coherently: "Doctor said there's nothing wrong with me." He recoiled against a sudden pain in his back as he shifted in his seat. "How's O'Neill?" he asked before Simms could persuade him to go to hospital.

Simms took out a pack of cigarettes and shook one free. He lit it and squared his shoulders toward Craine. "We sent him home. He's suffering from shock but he'll be alright. Said the shooter was about to kill him too before a man and a woman came through the bathroom door. Shooter panicked and ran. Jack Rochelle is the victim. He's dead, by the way, but you probably knew that already. Pronounced at the scene. No one's spoken to his family."

"He wasn't married, no children. I think he had a brother somewhere."

"You knew him?"

Craine nodded. "A little bit." No need to mention Celia. No need at all. "He was a barber on the studio lot. He was also the go-to bootlegger. Most studios have one. I went to see him about James Campbell. I thought there was a connection."

"Why?"

Craine shrugged his aching shoulders. "I had nothing substantial. Campbell and Rochelle did time together in Chicago on a narcotics charge. They knew each other."

"That's what Peterson and Mayer are already telling us. Peterson did some digging—Campbell and Rochelle knew each other, friends until they had an argument over a girl."

"Florence Lloyd? The girl who was murdered?"

"Exactly. You were right to be suspicious. We've got a statement already from some guy Rochelle works with. He was at the party tonight."

"Denny?"

"I didn't get his name."

Craine took a moment to digest, his mind slow, his memory

sluggish. He'd asked Rochelle about Lloyd, was certain even at the time that he seemed reluctant to admit knowing her. It was beginning to make sense. The pieces started to fit together. He pictured Campbell shooting Florence in anger one night before going after her lover, his own best friend. Yet once again he had the feeling that something was missing. Stanley was somewhere hidden in this tragedy. But what role did he play?

He looked at Simms. "What's next?"

"Mayer's going to make a formal statement in the morning; we'll release something to the press shortly beforehand. Nothing's going to make the morning edition anyway, so we have a day."

"So what's the story? Are you making Campbell for Lloyd too?"

"Yes. Love triangle is the angle. Rochelle, Campbell and Florence Lloyd. Blood turns bad, Campbell kills his girlfriend after she's cheated on him. Then he goes after Rochelle. I don't know why Campbell would choose such a public place but he must have really wanted Rochelle dead, that's clear."

"And my involvement? I don't want to be mentioned by name."

"Unavoidable, I suspect." Simms tilted his head toward the cameras flashing further down the hill. The photographers were using magnesium flash powder to take pictures of Craine's car: bright white lights illuminated the hillside, smoke creeping toward the sky. "They're already asking after you. They know you're here. Is there anything I'm missing?"

"It looks like Stanley had a drug habit. He bought off Rochelle. Might have bought off Campbell too. Could explain how they knew each other. At first I thought maybe it was a drug deal gone wrong somewhere—"

"O'Neill told me Stanley had taken sedatives."

"Came up in the autopsy. I asked Collins to remove it."

Simms tapped his fingers on his thighs and looked out through the back doors to check no one was within earshot. "Who else have you told about Campbell's connection to Herbert Stanley?" he whispered.

"I spoke to Gale Goodwin."

Simms sighed. "What did she say?"

"Nothing much."

"Let's keep that between ourselves. Peterson has Mayer in a panic and we don't need to stir things any more than necessary. It isn't relevant."

Craine inhaled deeply. "If Campbell knew him, it could be. Maybe Stanley was involved in this. With Florence Lloyd, I mean."

"It isn't. We've been over this, Craine." Simms said, sounding a little testy. "Stanley's dead. He had a history of depression and he killed himself. Who cares if he knew Campbell, or Lloyd for that matter?"

Craine looked down, examining his sodden shoes. He felt over-whelmed by the burden of fatigue; he knew he couldn't sleep but he was too tired to talk anymore. After a pause, when nothing was forth-coming Simms said softly, "Let's call it a night. I'll send someone round tomorrow with your deposition papers."

He stepped out into the darkness and wandered down the hill toward the direction of the cars, his shoulders hunched, his hands buried deep in his pockets. "Celia would have been proud," he called back when Craine could no longer see him. "You were a hero tonight."

A hero, Craine repeated to himself. He felt anything but a hero.

CHAPTER 23

It took less than twenty-four hours for the D.M.V. to confirm that the Packard 120 recovered at the crash site off Mulholland Highway was registered to a James L. Campbell, born 1903, Chicago, Illinois; his current residence was listed as apartment 409, 112 West 6th Street, Los Angeles C.A. 90013. With no other apparent next of kin, and no fingerprints recoverable from the wreckage, the body was positively identified by his uncle, Conrad Frazer, a dockworker living in San Pedro. The body's remains were incinerated almost immediately after the viewing.

The Loew House shootings were front-page news for three days running. Tabloid yellow press ran headlines such as "M.G.M. MANSION MURDERS," "JAMES CAGNEY ALMOST KILLED IN M.G.M. PARTY SHOOTING," and "KATHARINE HEPBURN SURVIVES BRUTAL SLAYING." Broadsheet dailies made less of the story but praised the police department for their swift apprehension of the killer. A photo of Craine's Fleetwood on the side of the pool with the license plate blacked out made the third page of the *Los Angeles Times*. Craine was referred to as the husband of the late Celia Raymond, a former silver screen star who died at the end of last year. An old M.G.M. publicity picture of Celia was included. Someone had leaked Craine's official police photo to the press and the tabloids had even managed to find a sepia photograph of Craine on the set of a Western fifteen years previous. He was labeled "hard-working, good police," a "hero detective" who was "determined to clean up the streets of Los Angeles."

Yellow press newspapers named the shooter as convicted drugs peddler and freelance photographer James Campbell, but no photograph was included. The victim was identified as Jack Rochelle, a studio barber with ties to the bootlegging trade. The slayings arose out of a dispute over Rochelle's relationship with Campbell's girlfriend, Florence Lloyd, who was also murdered in her home three nights previously.

Broadsheet editorials highlighted that one of the victims worked for M.G.M. studios but under the influence of William Randolph Hearst, most stopped short of mentioning Rochelle's criminal ties or pointing the finger of blame at the motion picture industry or Metro-Goldwyn-Mayer specifically. Rather, the shooting was seen as representative of the violent culture embedded in Los Angeles. In the *Los Angeles Examiner*, Mayer was quoted as saying, "We at M.G.M. are surprised and embarrassed by our association with illegal narcotics distribution. We believe that our wholesome pictures are made by wholesome means and consider this event an anomaly in an otherwise flourishing fifteen years."

The publicity did little to damage M.G.M.'s success at the box office. The studio's latest release, *Goodbye, Mr. Chips*, was an instant critical and commercial success, winning rave reviews and taking the number one spot at the box office. Peterson's publicity team was already drumming up positive press for the imminent release of M.G.M.'s summer behemoth, *The Wizard of Oz*. The date of the premiere had already been announced nationwide: Saturday July 15th.

The Hollywood Enquirer covered only the basic essentials surrounding the Loew House shootings; there was one brief story hidden on page six but neither Rochelle nor Campbell were mentioned by name.

None of the papers attempted to make any connection between the shootings and the suicide of M.G.M. producer Herbert Stanley.

Later in the same week, City Hall-aligned newspapers reported that recorded crime indicated gun-related felonies had fallen by eight percent and drug offenses twelve percent compared to the same quarter in the previous year. According to provisional police figures, all core areas of crime were down, except robberies, which had marginally increased by two percent. Speaking on the steps of Central Headquarters in the Civic Center, Chief of Police D.A. Davidson said the figures gave "a strong indication that the police department are succeeding in making Los Angeles a safer place to live."

On the Thursday, a week after he'd been found dead, Gale Goodwin buried her late husband at Forest Lawn Memorial Park in Glendale. Scores of policemen prevented over two hundred people from entering the funeral chapel where services were held. Only a handful of notable figures from M.G.M. studios and a few close friends were allowed inside. Among those in the chapel were Louis B. Mayer, Russell Peterson and producer Mervyn LeRoy. Gale Goodwin, dressed head-to-toe in black, arrived in a black limousine with close friend Joan Crawford.

Louis Mayer delivered a eulogy to the dead producer before a small cortège followed the casket outside to the cemetery. Stanley's headstone read "Beloved Husband 1887—1939." The press were relentless in their pursuit of pictures and two photographs of Gale Goodwin seen weeping on Crawford's shoulder made the front pages. Mayer was seen beside Peterson, head forward and hands clasped together in mourning. He made a show of posing for photographers before driving away in a black limousine.

No one noticed Detective Jonathan Craine hovering at a distance.

ONE MONTH LATER

CHAPTER 24

June 13th

It was a Tuesday evening in June, and Craine had taken Michael to the Los Angeles Theatre, a weekly excursion that had become something of a routine in the month that had passed since the incident at Loew House. Once or twice they had used their outings to go for dinner or a drive along the Malibu coast road, but mostly they went to the picture house, which allowed Craine an opportunity to spend time with his son without either party having to sit through long periods of uncomfortable silence. Afterward, they'd go to a diner and Craine would read the evening extra as Michael sipped at a milkshake. They never visited their house in Beverly Hills and Michael was always back at the schoolhouse by 10 P.M.

Tonight they watched a Mickey Rooney picture and then went out for a bite to eat. Craine found a diner a short walk from the picture house and they got a booth by the window. He ordered a burger and fries for Michael, grilled chicken and mash potatoes for himself and both of them ate in silence.

"Pretty good food for a diner," Craine said when he was finished. "Apple pie looked good too. We should try some."

Michael could only manage half of his fries. When he was done, he pushed his plate away and took a small book out of his knapsack. It was a pocket Bible. Craine recognized it as one Celia had given him years back.

"You like Bible studies?"

Michael shrugged but didn't lift his eyes off the page.

"Your mother . . . she used to read you the stories when you were very little. You remember?"

Michael stirred, his concentration disturbed. After a few seconds he nodded.

"I was never very good in school. You're smart. Like her," Craine went on, conscious that he rarely held Michael's attention. "You know, if you like stories, maybe in a few years I can get you something on the studio lot. A runner's job. It's about connections in the industry. That's what's important. I help them, they help you."

Michael didn't seem to show any interest. "Have you thought about what you want to be when you grow up?"

More silence. Michael sipped at his milkshake. "You have the opportunity I didn't have. You can do something you want to do. Everyone has dreams, Michael. It doesn't always work out, but it's important you try."

A waitress came over to clear their plates. "Can I get you anything else? How about another milkshake for you, young man?"

Michael looked up. He stared at her but didn't say anything.

"No? Slice of apple pie?" She beamed buck teeth at him. "We got ice cream?"

But when Michael continued staring at her, the waitress stopped smiling.

"He's fine," said Craine, trying to reassure her. "He's a little shy. Just the check, please."

"Sure," she said, unconvinced. "No problem."

When she left, Michael went straight back to his Bible and Craine drank the last of his beer, wondering what went through that little head of his.

At a glance Michael seemed happy. Happier, at least. Despite occasional efforts to engage him in conversation, not a whisper passed between Michael's lips. He had remained mute. Now at least they had developed a wordless form of speaking where, rather than trying to persuade Michael to talk to him, Craine would ask his son simple 'yes' or 'no' questions and Michael would answer with nods and shakes of the head.

"Do you want to see *Goodbye, Mr. Chips?*" he'd asked when he picked him up from the school gates at six sharp. Shake. "Do you want to see *Stagecoach?*" Shake. "*Huckleberry Finn?*" Shake. "*Andy Hardy Gets Spring Fever?*" Nod.

Craine made another attempt to engage his son in conversation. "You like Andy Hardy?"

Michael shrugged then nodded. He'd noticed Michael seemed to be in awe of Mickey Rooney. He had started to comb his hair the same way, dress the same and had even started to mimic Rooney's swagger, almost laughable from a meek nine-year-old. "That's the fourth picture of his we've seen, if you include the one we saw twice."

The Andy Hardy pictures were family films, the M.G.M. specialty. Mostly they were about young Andy Hardy getting into trouble only for his father, the wise judge, to help him learn the error of his ways. He was the model father, and only made Craine feel worse about himself.

Craine had never been particularly close with his father. His own parents had passed away when he was quite young, and he couldn't remember much about either one of them now. He knew his mother as a tintype photograph, his father as a box of medals. Little else about them was either asked or told. For some unknown reason, people assumed that orphans were brought up in Dickensian poverty, when for Craine the opposite was true. A trust fund child, he was raised in an assortment of Catholic boarding schools with wealthy peers he'd long forgotten.

"In that last picture, you remember how they move house? To a different city? Well, I know I talked about it a while ago. My situation has changed a little." Nothing had changed. He'd simply lost the will to move away. "I'm thinking maybe I should stay here."

Michael shifted in his seat. He looked up and frowned.

"I'm not sure about what you want to do over the summer," Craine went on. "I spoke to Father Calloway recently and he said that you could stay there. That way you can spend time with your friends. I figured you wouldn't want to be at home all that time."

Michael looked away. He stared through the window and chewed on the inside of the cheek.

"You know," he said sharply, "this conversation would be much easier if you actually answered my questions. It's pretty frustrating."

Michael's response was to slide out of the booth and walk toward the restroom.

"Michael? Michael? Look, I didn't mean to upset you."

But if Michael heard him, he'd never know. *Dammit*, he said to himself.

There was a folded copy of the *Los Angeles Times* left on the side of the table and Craine scanned the headlines. *Thank God.* After almost five weeks, the newspapers had finally found other news to focus on than Stanley's suicide or the Loew House shootings. At last there were other stories, more newsworthy scandals that could dominate the headlines. Most nationals were increasingly turning to events in Europe, where a peaceful solution to the Danzig Crisis between Germany and Poland looked increasingly unlikely.

He scanned through the news pages. An article lost in the margin of the center pages caught his eye, where an entertainment reporter noted that Cary Grant had a lucky escape while filming a stunt scene for his latest picture, *The Miser*, costarring Gale Goodwin in her first role since the death of her husband five weeks ago. His thoughts stuttered as they always did when he saw a mention of Gale in the press. An image of Gale formed in his mind: dark hair spilling over her shoulders; her skin delicate and even; green eyes you could drown in. He hadn't seen her since that night at Loew House, hadn't dared. For weeks he'd picked up the phone to call her only to put it down almost immediately after. Not that he'd heard from her either. No, that wasn't true—he received some anonymous flowers the day after Herbert Stanley's funeral that he secretly knew were from her. She'd seen him there. But no phone call, no letter. But then, could he really blame her? How was she to know he wouldn't sell his story at the first opportunity? That he hadn't already bragged to other police officers and studio workers about what had happened at Loew House? He was a man unaffected by society's double standards. Public opinion favored him. Men who slept with women were champions, whereas women who slept with men were simply harlots. Idle talk could ruin her career.

But was he really thinking of her reputation, or his ego? He could tell himself that he didn't want to embarrass her, or that it was too soon for either of them to embark on any kind of relationship, but if he was truthful to himself, he was simply afraid of rejection. He was worried that she'd be embarrassed, that she'd regretted what happened and wouldn't want to see him again.

CHAPTER 25

June 14th

"Cameras rolling at nine, Miss Goodwin," squeaked an adolescent production assistant.

"Thank you, Daniel. Oh, and tell Mr. Baldwin the miser's loving daughter is almost ready to be pried from the hair and makeup chair."

Mary, the makeup assistant, laughed. The morning shoot required Gale for her close-ups and she'd been sitting in the makeup chair since 6 A.M.

For the past two weeks, Gale had been shooting *The Miser*, a period comedy of manners loosely based on Molière's play. Since her husband's funeral a month ago, Gale had thrown herself into her work. The long hours of rehearsals and filming were the ideal antidote to the feelings of guilt and loss that had troubled her in those first few weeks.

And then there was Jonathan.

She hadn't heard a word from him since the M.G.M. party. No visit, no letter, no phone call. Jonathan hadn't seemed to her your typical philanderer, if there was such a thing. He was pensive, thoughtful, kind. But then why hadn't he called? It was infuriating. Then and there she promised herself that if she saw him again she'd slap him across the face. He deserved grievous injury.

For weeks after she had thought about that night at Loew House constantly. Once the shoot had begun, however, she had too much to occupy and distract her. Her mind was focused on the issues of the day: her mark, her cue, her timing; the pacing of her words; the gestures of her actions. But then acting had in turn sharpened her imagination, and late at night when she practiced her lines she heard Jonathan's voice in her ears reading the male lead. And when she rehearsed in her dressing room, she would sit there idly dreaming, imagining the scenes beyond the page, replaying that night as she pictured Jonathan whisking her away, his arms lifting her up as he—

"Ooh, it looks like we're getting an extra day's paid leave for Independence Day," cooed Mary.

Abashed, Gale felt her cheeks burning and made a show of normality. "Oh good, what a relief."

"You not enjoying the picture then, Miss Goodwin?" More idle conversation from Mary as she applied Gale's rouge.

"Oh no, I am," she said falsely. "It's exactly what I was after. Just a little challenging at times."

Despite years on Broadway, Gale had never starred in an outright comedy before and had to be trained in gags and timing. The director was an impatient man with a booming voice and Gale found herself in tears some days as he shouted at her in front of the cast and crew for trying too hard to be funny. He also brought his cat on set because he was obsessed with pets and couldn't bear to leave his beloved tomcat, Cecil, at home. Gale was severely allergic, and even being in the same room as that spiteful cat would blotch her skin and make her eyes itch. Cecil, seemingly aware that he caused her stress, enjoyed nothing more than following Gale around. Now, as she was almost ready to be called on set, Gale found herself staring at that mangy little alley cat as he sat regally in the doorway, preening himself.

"Mary, why is that cat so keen to get in here?"

Seemingly offended, they heard an animal growl from the doorway.

"I think he knows you're allergic."

"Even the sight of him makes my skin crawl. I'm watching you, Cecil," she added, when a tentative paw found its way onto the carpet. "Don't think I can't see you. He's the spawn of Satan, Mary, I swear it."

"I don't doubt it for a second."

The same breaking voice from the corridor. "Ten minutes, Miss Goodwin."

"Thank you, Daniel."

"Mary, you couldn't do me a favor, could you? I've left my fan in Costume."

"I'll get it."

"Sorry, I'll never get back down the corridor with this dress."

Another growl from the doorway as Mary left.

"Cecil, what do you think you're doing? You know I can't go near you. Shoo. Go. Get away. Honestly."

She heard the door creak open.

"I said, go away!"

"I'm sorry."

In the dressing room mirror, Gale saw Jonathan Craine standing in the doorway with a neatly wrapped bunch of orchids in one hand. The sight of him rendered her momentarily speechless. He turned to leave.

"Jonathan!" she called out to his reflection before standing up to greet him. "Oh God, not you. I'm sorry, it's the cat." She had to stop herself from laughing. "He's the devil himself, I promise you. I'm allergic, and he's determined to get in here."

Jonathan bent down and fondled the cat's ears. Cecil purred like a broken locomotive and gave Gale a self-lauding scowl to remind her that he was the director's prize pet and she was merely a lowly bottom feeder.

"What's his name?"

"Cecil."

"Hullo, Cecil."

The cat sniffed at his fingers, and deciding Jonathan wasn't edible, focused his attention back on Gale. Jonathan wrapped his hands under his fluffy belly and gently tossed the cat out of the room.

"He likes you. I'm not sure if that's a good thing or not. That's right, good riddance, Cecil."

Jonathan stood there uncomfortably.

"What brings you this way?" Gale said.

"I thought I might come by, see how you are."

He'd waited over a month to come here, and that's all he has to say? Hit the smug bastard, said a quiet little voice inside her head that sounded a lot like Joan's. "Where are my manners?" she said, speaking instead as if they were strangers. "Please, come in."

He offered the orchids and she took them, touching his fingers as she did so. There was a long, pregnant silence as they stood there dumbly, neither one of them saying anything. A better actress could hide the expectation in her face, she thought.

"You really didn't have to bring me anything."

"I saw them. I don't know what you like."

"They're lovely, thank you. How did you know I was here?"

"I'm a detective."

"Oh."

"No, I'm joking. That was meant to be—this isn't work-related. I mean, I was passing by. I thought I might say hello. I asked someone at the studio. They told me you were here."

"I hadn't heard from you."

"I wasn't—I wasn't sure where you were staying."

"The Beverly Hills Hotel. I'm moving home shortly." She waited, but he didn't say anything else. He took off his hat and corrected his misaligned parting.

"Anyway, I'll go, I was only—"

Gale moved closer. "Stay," she whispered. "Please. How are you? I've been reading all about you in the papers. They're calling you a hero."

"It isn't a big deal."

"Well, I'm sure your son is very proud. Sorry, I'm being rude. Can I get you something? Coffee?"

"No, don't worry. I won't stay long."

A tap at the door. "Five minutes, Miss Goodwin." Daniel again. Why couldn't Jonathan have come earlier? Or maybe this was for the best. Short and sweet, not a dragged-out episode where the two of them fumbled over their words for hours on end.

"You're busy. I'm intruding."

"There's no rush. I'm about to do this scene where I have to burst into fits of laughter as Cary Grant falls off his horse and into a pond. I've been rehearsing all morning but I can barely breathe in this dress and my ribs are so sore I'm not even sure I'll be able to do it. He might have to settle for a chuckle. A knowing smile by take six. Oh dear, I'm doing that thing where I harp on again."

"I—"

"It's only that—"

"You go first."

"I never heard from you. After—"

"I've been meaning to call you."

"Then why didn't you? And don't say you didn't know where I was. It's all over the papers."

"I wasn't sure you'd want me to. I thought I might have over-stepped the mark, taken advantage . . ."

"You didn't. Us women, we are capable of saying no, you know."

"Well, I'm here."

"Yes. I'm glad. I've wanted to see you. Very much." He smiled ever so slightly so she went on, "And I must find somewhere for these beautiful orchids. I'm sure I saw a vase somewhere. Ah, yes, here we are, why don't I—"

As she reached up to a vase on the shelf above her dressing mirror, Cecil ran into the room and launched himself at the orchids. Instinctively, Gale screamed and pulled the flowers away, the cat careering into the mirror and knocking over a table lamp.

"Oh Jesus, that godforsaken cat!"

His pride wounded, Cecil hissed at Gale, his tail swishing from side to side. Jonathan laughed, scooped the cat up and shut him outside the door. Feeling another rush of embarrassment, Gale sighed and shook her head, pushing the heel of her hand against her fore-head. "What am I doing? I'm such an idiot—"

And then Jonathan did something unexpected. Lifting her chin delicately with his fingers, he touched her lips with his. Stunned, Gale dropped the flowers to the floor. Her body pressed in against his and she kissed him back.

Maybe she wouldn't hit him after all.

CHAPTER 26

June 26th

The school church opened to local parishioners on Sundays for Mass but today was unusually quiet. The summer break had begun a few days earlier, and most of the other pupils at Michael's school had gone away for family vacations or the upcoming Independence Day weekend. In previous years, Michael had gone home for the summer but his father didn't seem to want him around. He wasn't sure he wanted to go back anyway. He and a handful of other boys would remain at the school over the vacation period and, if he was honest, Michael preferred it that way.

As he entered the nave, Michael went to dip his fingers in the font water. He stopped short as he approached. He could see his mother's face beneath the surface of the water, staring up at him. He quickly placed his fingers inside and her image dissolved in the ripples. He made the sign of the cross.

Michael had been dreaming about his mother a lot lately. More so now than ever. They weren't like most dreams; more like memories. It was her final night that came to him most often, usually as a collection of images that appeared out of sequence, like leafing through a stack of shuffled photographs. An image of his mother's foot protruding through the water might be followed by one of his father on the living room divan. His father had his head in his hands but he must have been talking because there was a man standing above him making notes with pen and pad. Then he might see his mother's pale cream body under the water. In the dream he would picture his mother's hair rising through the water, loose strands floating on the surface. The images sometimes came with voices in his head. His own subconscious asking him, "Why won't she wake up? Why can't I pull her out? Why aren't I strong enough to save her?"

And then he would wake up.

Michael took a seat on a pew near the front. Father Calloway entered, followed by two altar boys, one carrying a cross, the other candles and incense. Calloway arrived at his chair and made the sign of the cross, saying, "In the name of the Father, and of the Son, and of the Holy Spirit." The assembly followed suit, answering "Amen."

After Father Calloway had recited the blessing of the Eucharist, he approached the congregation, placing a wafer into their hands one by one and holding the consecrated wine to their lips. "Amen," each mumbled in turn after they had taken Communion.

Father Calloway was in front of Michael now. He tilted back his head and opened his mouth. He could feel the wafer as it was placed on his tongue. He bowed his head.

At Easter, Calloway had explained to his class that once the bread and wine had been consecrated, they were no longer bread and wine. You were swallowing the body and blood of Christ. Michael had never really known what this meant or how it was possible but Father Calloway said that the Eucharist brought you closer to God.

Michael thought about this now. If he could get closer to God, could he do the same with his mother?

Mamma Rosa's was somewhere between a restaurant and a diner. They served cocktails and Italian food, which O'Neill thought ticked both boxes for a first date. Besides, he'd had lunch here at least a dozen times before so he knew the food was good.

The girl he was meeting was Irish but all of the Irish places in the area were essentially drinking holes. Some he suspected were actually brothels. And besides, Italian food was more romantic, right? Or was that French food? He thought about that. It was definitely French food. *Dammit, Patrick.*

He ordered another cocktail and told himself to relax.

After the Loew House shootings, O'Neill's life had quickly returned to its dull routine. He worked steadily as a homicide investigator, working on four cases and solving all of them in the six weeks that had passed. He spent the evenings alone in his small house in Cypress Park. At weekends he'd go running in the mornings, drive toward the coast for lunch or an early dinner and then drive himself home. Twice a week he'd go and catch a picture somewhere, a musical or a comedy, whichever took his fancy. He'd taken up smoking, mostly because the other detectives at the Bureau did, but that could hardly be considered a hobby and it hadn't improved his social life.

The days merged together. He might as well be forty, or fifty.

And then his mother had called him up yesterday to tell him that a friend of hers had a niece that had moved to Los Angeles a few years ago and that he should take her out.

O'Neill hadn't exactly been over the moon about the idea. After all, who knew what she looked like or what kind of person she was? She could be a psychopathic killer for all he knew. Or outright hideous. Or worse, she could be taller than him. "Count yourself lucky she even agreed to go," his mother had said on the phone. "Girl like that could do a lot better than you, if you ask me."

Better than her own son. *Perfect.*

O'Neill had got there almost an hour early but waiting only made him more anxious so he'd sunk two cocktails and was working on his third when a tidily dressed girl came in and stood waiting by the doorway, trying to catch the waitress' attention. O'Neill noticed immediately that she had a gentle face, a warm smile. She was smaller than him by some margin—*thank God*—and homely-looking without being plump. Her hair was a light reddish-brown and she wore it pinned up like a neat schoolgirl. It made him feel like a schoolboy, giddy and knocked off true.

The waitress pointed in the direction of his table and Patrick gave her a small wave as she approached. They looked at each other with an odd recognition, each knowing who the other was without really knowing each other at all.

"Patrick."

"You must be Grace-Anne," he said, standing.

"Oh, call me Gracie, please."

"Great. Call me"—he realized he had no nickname—"well, call me Patrick."

"Sorry I'm a little late," Gracie began, speaking quickly in a high-pitched but not unattractive voice. "My roommate got in a fight with her boyfriend. She's all flustered but I know she'll go crawling back to him. They're both Italian. Very passionate people, if you know what I mean. They're worse than us Irish. You know how it is."

"Yes. Completely." Patrick had never had a roommate. And he'd never had a girlfriend, let alone a fight with one.

He drained his cocktail and put it next to the two empty glasses next to him.

Gracie looked at them and he saw her looking. "Have you been here long?"

"No, hardly at all. Well . . . an hour, but I got here early. Waitress kept bringing them over," he lied. "Actually, I didn't even order this last one," he lied again.

Gracie looked back at the waitress and whispered, "She's a little rude, isn't she?"

"The waitress? She's okay. A little . . . curt."

Gracie picked up the menu for the first time. O'Neill knew it backward already, had decided what he was having forty-five minutes ago. Spaghetti meatballs for main, a tossed salad on the side to make it seem like he cared about what he ate.

"Would you like something to drink?"

"What are you drinking?"

He winced. "Pink Lady."

"I'll have one too. Sounds . . . interesting."

O'Neill thumbed at his menu. "I hope you don't mind coming here."

"Oh, that's fine. Easy to get to."

"Oh, good. Yeah, I eat lunch here sometimes." Very often, in fact. Sometimes every day.

"So do you know what's good here?"

"The penne comes highly recommended."

"Really? By who?"

"Well . . . the waitress. She said it was good."

O'Neill played with his wrists as Gracie continued to look at the menu. She smiled, then placed it down in front of her. "Decided. Seafood penne."

He'd never tried it. "Good choice," he said, "I'll call her over." O'Neill turned around with his finger in the air but it became clear pretty quickly the waitress was ignoring him. "She'll come over when she's ready," he said, turning back to Gracie. "No rush, I guess."

After a few awkward seconds Gracie said, "Well. It's, um . . . nice to meet you. My aunt and your mom. It's like they're conspiring against us."

"Yes," said O'Neill, "my mother can be very . . . persuasive."

"You needed persuading?"

"No, not me," he said, suddenly worried. "Your aunt."

"Relax, I was only kidding. You know we've actually met before."

"Really?"

"I was six years old. You were eleven or so. I had a birthday party and my aunt invited you and your mom. I remember one of the girls kissed you and you cried."

"Wow." O'Neill couldn't help feeling self-satisfied. "A girl kissed me?"

"And you cried," she reminded him with a chuckle.

The waitress approached their table and brought out a little notepad.

"You ready to order yet?" she asked, scratching her nose with the knuckle of one finger. "I got a cigarette break in five minutes."

Gracie pointed at her menu. "Can I ask you . . . What's the seafood penne like?"

The waitress looked at her with something approaching annoyance. "You like seafood?"

"Yes."

"You like pasta?"

"Yes."

"Then you'll like it."

After she left with their orders, O'Neill leaned over the table. "She really is mean, isn't she?"

Gracie laughed and Patrick chuckled back. That was the second time she'd laughed in as many minutes and he hoped it wasn't the last.

O'Neill wasn't aware of everything they said that evening but he knew he was relaxed enough to talk freely; he was pretty convinced that Gracie felt the same because when their food came he realized that both of them had barely paused for breath.

"So am I right in thinking you work in fashion?"

"God, no. That's so embarrassing. My aunt always tells everyone I do. I work in textiles. A textiles factory. We also make shoes."

"And what do you do there?"

"I'm a secretary. In the shoe department. I graduated from secretarial school two summers ago. This is my second job."

Gracie was honest and open and it made him feel like he could talk to her without constantly worrying he looked foolish. "Interesting," he said. "You like it?"

"Not really. But I do get free shoes."

"That's pretty good."

"Well mostly they're men's shoes."

"Huh. Well, I could always do with another pair."

Gracie held her fork out to one side. With her other she brushed her hair behind her ear. "Maybe if we go out for dinner again I'll get you some," she said quietly with a nervous smile.

O'Neill flushed, with pleasure or embarrassment he wasn't sure. "I'd like that," he said. "I'd like that very much."

When they'd finished their meal and ordered another drink, their conversation took a more personal turn. There was an ease between them and as they got to know each other better, both felt more willing to probe into each other's backgrounds.

When O'Neill told her he was a detective she said openly, "Quite some shadow, I guess. With your father being so famous, and all."

He was surprised by her frankness but not put off by it. "Yeah. I think about him a lot. I guess people compare us. I do too. I think about what he'd do in different situations." People said a lot of things about Quinlan O'Neill, quite a few bad things too, but no one ever doubted his integrity as an officer of the law. He was what people termed "good police." But could they say the same about his son?

Gracie dabbed at the corner of her mouth with a napkin. "So were you involved in those shootings at that Hollywood party? You know, with your job?"

"Um. Yeah. I was there."

Her eyes lit up. "You were there? Is it true what they say? Did that celebrity detective wrestle the shooter to the ground? Held him 'til the police arrived?"

The alcohol must have got to him because his face felt unusually warm. "No. That's, um, not how it happened."

"You're kidding? Those papers make that stuff up, don't they? Like saying Greta Garbo called the police. Wow. I'm so impressed. You're a real hero. I mean, that love triangle thing sounded pretty incredible. Can you believe it?"

"Yeah, yes," he said, not quite believing it at all. "The love triangle." Even after all these weeks, something about the Loew House shootings still bothered him. Unconvinced by the stories in the press, he'd tried to make a connection between Stanley, Rochelle and Campbell but Captain Simms had brought him into his office and instructed him to delve no further into Stanley's suicide or the Loew House shootings. He was cajoled into dropping any attempts at reopening an investigation and was instructed to focus on new, incoming crimes.

He'd felt embarrassed, of course. He'd betrayed his intuition and bowed down to the politics of the department. His father would have been ashamed, but the truth was that these situations had become increasingly common for O'Neill. He wasn't capable of standing up for himself. Late at night he found himself dreaming of avenging these past affronts, replaying conversations in his head, telling his seniors where to stick their orders, altering the course of history with pithy retorts and swift punches to the jaw.

But dreaming changed nothing.

CHAPTER 27

July 7th

Craine's promotion came with the start of the department's second quarter, when senior command could use the occasion to boast of the new administration's latest quarterly crime statistics. Craine would be their talisman, their Buffalo Bill of the coastal West, heroic detective symbolic of the new police department's achievements.

And so it was, at three minutes after noon, in front of a full briefing room of work colleagues and press delegates, that Craine was awarded his two single silver bars by the Los Angeles Chief of Police. Shaking Chief Davidson's large and club-like hand, he glanced to the front row where Celia once sat. She used to come to these events. She was present when he was promoted to Sergeant. That was before she was sick, before she decided she bitterly hated what he did for a living.

His thoughts turned to Gale. If during the first few days and nights their conversations had been awkward, a strange combination of addled laughter and prolonged silence, then they had settled into a more relaxed rapport and began to see each other every spare moment they had, Craine even staying at the house on Easton Drive when Gale decided to move back home. They never met with friends, although she admitted she had told Joan, whom Craine had always known as a gossip. It was a private relationship, and he preferred it that way.

They laughed a lot together, which was novel for Craine. Often they would stay up all night talking about books they had read, pictures they had seen, places they wanted to visit. They were planning a future together. Rarely, though, did they talk about family, past or present. He turned away her questions about Michael, told her very little about Celia. She didn't discuss her marriage with Herbert and he, in turn, didn't ask. Only once, before Independence Day, had Gale pushed him to introduce her to Michael. Craine had resisted. He knew he needed to address some issues with his son soon enough but now didn't seem like the right time. If there was ever going to be a right time. It was as if their old lives had never existed. They were newborns, blissfully happy with new opportunity.

But still, sometimes a voice inside his head told him that this happiness was borrowed and didn't belong to him. The rug would be pulled from underneath him at any moment. And no matter what he told himself, he knew that happiness couldn't be confused with contentment. They weren't the same thing.

His distant reverie was cut short by the cold metal Lieutenant bars thrust into his palms. Flashbulbs blinded him, then the room thundered into applause as the well-wishers rose for a standing ovation. Flanked either side by the District Attorney and the Los Angeles Mayor, Craine posed for pictures, pumping Chief Davidson's hand until he could feel the blood squeezed from his palms like a wet sponge.

He should feel better about this than he did. He felt lousy, but he wasn't sure why. Doubt whispered in his ear. *Maybe because your promotion is an embarrassment, Craine. Maybe because it's a complete sham.*

He shut the screaming apostle Thomas from his head. He should think positively. He had earned a new start. A nascent relationship with a woman he was lucky to have. A career in the higher echelons of the Bureau. He'd made three thousand dollars from his percentage of the studio bonus, and now his efforts were being recognized with a promotion. So what was it that was bothering him so much?

Off the stage now, through the gauntlet like a grinning bride. Posing, shaking hands. Through gold trim and lace piping, he spotted Simms cheering from the third row, his dress blues freshly pressed, the brass and nickel polished. Peterson was behind him, the clichéd wink, hands applauding high above his head, leading the cheers.

Elaine the steadfast, the sturdy constant in his life, dabbed at her eyes with a proud handkerchief. He shook a few more familiar hands, ignored the jealous associates from the Bureau. They'd never liked him anyway. That grousing Patrick O'Neill was at the back, hands by his sides, a sober look on his face. Avoid his scrutinizing eyes like the plague.

But still the doubt remained.

Afterward he went upstairs to the Bureau and started feeling better almost immediately. Elaine helped him pack the few personal possessions he had in his old office and moved them to his new corner office down the hall from Simms. She brought him his mail, presenting him with a sealed package from Chicago R. & I. labeled Private and Confidential.

"This one came in this morning. Should have arrived last month. Not sure what the holdup was."

"Don't worry about it."

"Can I get you a coffee?"

"I'm fine."

"Anything else?"

"Nothing, thank you. Oh, actually yes, my car, the insurance for my car—any news?" In spite of a better parking space nearer the elevator, he was still driving unmarked police cars to and from work. His insurance paperwork had yet to come through, one of those typical administrative holdups that never got resolved.

"It's with Accounts for consideration," she screwed up her face apologetically. "It was an expensive car."

"Yes, yes it was. Not your fault."

"I'll chase them up." She lingered in the doorway. "Congratulations on your promotion, Lieutenant Craine."

A weak smile from Craine as she closed the door behind her. He sat back in his chair and tapped his fingernails on the desk. A wider, better desk, in fact. Mahogany maybe, or good enough to pass for mahogany. Brass knobs. Telephone. Not new. A little old, actually. Was that rust on the dial? He should have it replaced. But now he had a window where he could see buildings, other buildings, not just another brick wall.

LIEUTENANT CRAINE was already painted on the frosted glass. The polished wood floor was covered in a Gulistan rug. It didn't matter that it was cream. Maybe he should embrace Art Deco— modernize. Wasn't this a new beginning, after all? Things were looking good for him. He'd done well for himself.

He turned over the mail package and tore open the bindings: it was the Chicago file on Campbell. He stared at it for a long moment, unsure whether he wanted to look at the contents. Could he be bothered to work today? There was a stamp on one side indicating it was lost in transit. This should have been delivered weeks ago. Inside he found Campbell's Chicago criminal history and a brief employment record. He thumbed through the file. Clipped to a carbon copy of a R.A.P. sheet was a set of black-and-white booking photographs, front and profile pictures taken when Campbell was arrested for distributing heroin. He looked at the man in the photos and shifted uneasily in his chair. Something wasn't right. His fingers tightened round the card. His head started to throb. His office suddenly felt stifling. He looked closer at the lines of Campbell's facial features in the grays and blacks of the prints.

Shaking, Craine dropped the pictures on the desk.

The man in the pictures wasn't the Loew House shooter.

That night, as he lay awake beside Gale in her bed, the migraine slowly returned, that soft pulse behind his eyeballs building into a heavy thump until finally it seemed to shake his whole skull.

Craine tried to tell himself that it was all in his imagination, even though he knew full well that was a lie. If the shooter wasn't Campbell, then who was he? And why would he kill Rochelle? Why would he be in Campbell's apartment? Questions circled around his head like a vicious fever, pulling him away from the safety of sleep like enchanting sirens calling him toward the rocks.

When he could bear the pain no longer, and the very notion of unbroken sleep seemed completely out of reach, Craine went into the bathroom to look for aspirin. The small drawer beside the sink was empty but he found some sedatives in the cabinet behind the mirror. The bottle wasn't labeled but he recognized the pills. They were oxycodone tablets. The same that Celia had overdosed on. Probably the same sedatives that Stanley had taken before hanging himself.

He left the tablets where they were and washed his hands and face, rubbing the back of his neck with a wet hand. He didn't need drugs. The summer heat had left him dehydrated, that was why he was having headaches. He needed to drink more.

He sipped water from the faucet then took off his white undervest, soaked it with water and wiped himself down. Doctors said he'd cracked two ribs in the car crash but they'd healed well and the bruising had all but disappeared. He didn't have any scars, which almost seemed like a shame.

"Is everything okay?" It was Gale, standing behind him. "I woke up and you were gone," she whispered through half-sleep. Her eyes were open but he could tell she was in that dreamlike delirium you get sometimes when you wake up in the night for a few moments before drifting back to the black. He loved that place.

Craine kept his back to her, leaning against the sink and answering her reflection. "Fine," he said quietly, as if he didn't want to wake up the children. The house was empty.

"You couldn't sleep?" she held a closed fist in front of her mouth and yawned. She waited for an explanation but it didn't come. "Too much coffee," she reasoned instead.

"Maybe." But he hadn't had a drop of caffeine in days. When the insomnia first started in New York, doctors told him to try and regain some rhythm to his life: work regular hours; take light exercise; improve his overall sleep hygiene. Their words exactly, and he followed their advice to the letter. They didn't prescribe him pills, which he was thankful for. They told him to avoid caffeine and he did for the most part, drinking a cup or two in the morning to stir him into action but seldom in the late afternoon or evening.

"You coming back to bed?"

"In a minute."

"What's on your mind? Is it Michael?"

He shook his head then considered that he probably should be thinking about Michael.

"Is it Celia? You're thinking of Celia?"

He shrugged. "I often think of Celia."

She had a hand on his shoulder now and he turned to face her. "Is it us? You feel guilty, don't you? You think she wouldn't want you to be here with me."

"It's not like that, Gale."

"You don't have to pretend otherwise. I feel like that sometimes about Herbert. But don't you think they'd want us to move on with our lives?"

"She'd want me to be happy."

"Exactly. She'd want what's best for you. For you and Michael."

"She always wanted the best for me. Apart from my work."

"Celia didn't like you being a police officer? Was she embarrassed?"

"No, she was never embarrassed." Maybe you are though, he reflected briefly to himself.

"Then what?"

"I suppose she didn't like the type of policeman I was." Craine stiffened and stared at the sweaty footprints he'd left on the marble floor. "In the beginning it was different. She thought being a policeman was admirable."

"It is."

"It isn't. It almost always isn't. With Celia . . . it was tricky. She had such high expectations. She used to show me off, you know. Her husband the detective. That's when I started working in the industry.

Helping people. But after Jean Harlow died she didn't like me working the studio cases. They were friends, you see."

"What happened with Jean?"

"She said I'd manipulated the truth," he said, not wanting to go into the details. "There were things that happened with her and other people that most people will never know. I've spent years being a studio janitor. That's not real police work."

"You're too hard on yourself."

"Am I?"

Neither of them said anything and for a moment he thought Gale might leave the room, but there was more to say and he wanted to say it. For months he'd been desperate to tell someone. To share.

"After Celia died, I didn't make it right. I let her down."

"You know that isn't true."

But it was true. Craine had helped M.G.M. frame Celia's suicide to look like an accident. Like he had for far too long, he'd simply followed the studio line. He'd been afraid of standing up to Peterson and Mayer. Afraid of losing his livelihood. He hadn't even had the courage to tell his only son about the truth behind his mother's death.

"Maybe not." He stepped away, embarrassed, and walked back into the bedroom. "I'm sorry, it doesn't matter."

"It does matter," she said, following him. "You should talk about these things."

"It got me thinking."

"You can tell me. I can't help you if you won't tell me."

Craine sat on the edge of the bed. He flattened the sheets with an open palm.

"What is it? Tell me what's on your mind. It can't only be Celia."

"It's not just Celia." He closed his eyes.

"Is it work? I know there are things you see that must be hard. But you can talk to me about it. You can try."

Did he want to talk about it? He needed to talk to someone about what was in his head. "It's Campbell," he said after a brief silence. "The Loew House night."

"The shooting?"

He nodded.

Gale frowned. He felt her pull away. "But he's dead. He died."

"I'm not sure that was Campbell."

"I don't understand."

"I saw his file this afternoon. It was late, should have arrived months ago. Campbell's photograph was inside. He didn't look the same."

"Didn't look the same as who?"

"The man in the car. The shooter. He wasn't the same person. He wasn't James Campbell. Patrick O'Neill was onto something. But I was too shortsighted to believe him."

"So what are you saying?"

"That I think someone else is involved in this. Someone wanted this whole thing forgotten about."

"You really believe that?"

He took a moment to reply. "Yes."

"What are you going to do now?"

Craine leaned back on the bed. "I don't know. Nothing, probably. Maybe I'm wrong. Being paranoid."

Gale kissed him on the shoulder and wrapped her arms around him. He kissed her wrist. Having her here made him feel better.

"I'm sorry. It's just on my mind."

"You look tired. Sleep on it. I'm sure everything was fine." She kissed him on the cheek. "You were a hero, remember."

CHAPTER 28

July 8th

Denny Bergen lived in an apartment complex somewhere in the southern recesses of the San Fernando Valley.

Craine parked his car across the road and checked the address. Blossom Springs, no apartment number. The building was like all those around it: whitewashed concrete on all sides, small, square windows, the walls cracked and hemorrhaging at the base where recent tremors had loosened the foundations.

He shouldn't be here. He had a sense that as his assistant at the barbershop, Denny might be able to tell him more about Rochelle and maybe more about Campbell too. Maybe even shed some light on Stanley's suicide, if he wanted to venture that far. But did he really want to? *I'm developing a conscience*, he thought, *and it's going to get me in trouble.*

The Valley was sweltering in July, and Craine felt his shirt peel away from his back as he stepped out of the car. Thick, leaden heat pressed hard against his skin, barely a gust of wind or the hint of a breeze to lift the sweat from his face. *It must be a hundred degrees, maybe more.*

Craine walked through the gates into an open courtyard. The complex was designed like a motel, with a square central area bordered on three sides by two stories of apartment rooms. He passed a door with a foot-sized hole in the bottom half. Most of the other doors were the same, all the windows cracked or boarded over. He could hear music playing but he wasn't sure where from. In a corner, four boys were playing with a piece of broken glass, holding it over the cement flooring.

"Do you boys know Denny?" he called out to them when he couldn't see anyone else. "You know where Denny Bergen lives?"

They stared at Craine without expression, then went back to whatever it was they were doing. He saw the glass catch the light and the boys cheered: they were burning ants. He wondered what they dreamed of being when they grew up.

A wire cage against one wall acted as a postbox. It was stacked with envelopes, sealed and untouched. They all looked like bills. He reached inside and found one with BERGEN printed across the front. It was from the Los Angeles Department of Water and Power and it said Dennis Bergen lived in apartment 2-D.

Craine took off his hat to wipe his brow and looked around. There were four doors alongside each wall, all beginning with 1. Denny must live upstairs. He took a wrought iron staircase up to the second floor, and followed the black tar paint on the wall directing him to apartment 2-D.

A little girl sat on the concrete up ahead, legs straddling the railings, feet dangling over the edge. She leaned forward and spat, watching as her phlegm fell into the courtyard below. He saw her face when she heard him coming. Her cheeks were dark and sunburned, the palm held above her eyes filthy and blistered. She might have been nine or ten years old. He thought of Michael.

"Hey mister, you got a cigarette?"

"No."

He expected her to say something else but she didn't. One of the boys in the courtyard laughed and called her a slut so she spat at him through the rails, missing him by less than a foot. The other boys fell about laughing.

Craine reached Denny's door and knocked twice. From a few doors down he heard a woman screaming obscenities then a man shouting back then silence. God, I hate this city, he thought, this ever-expanding desert of lost souls. He felt fortunate, which was a rare sensation for Craine. I should be more thankful for the way I live, he said to himself, but I'm not.

The door opened and Denny's long, thin face hovered over a door chain.

"Denny? Denny Bergen?"

"Yeah."

Denny frowned, looking Craine up and down as he tried to place him somewhere in his ragged timeline of wet-shaves and hair pomade.

"You remember me? From the studio lot?"

"Oh yeah," he smiled.

"My name's Craine."

"You're the guy who came—"

"I came to see Jack Rochelle. That's right."

"He died."

"I know."

"But I got you chicken soup."

"I remember. Can I come in?"

"Sure," he said, seemingly surprised by the very notion that anyone would wish to come inside. "Sorry it's a little messy. I haven't been up long."

The apartment consisted of one main room with a single door in the corner: a bathroom or bedroom, he presumed, maybe one leading on to the other. It was sparsely furnished and strangely dark. The blinds were pulled down and there were no lights on inside and no light switches, only holes in the wall with bare wires coiled inside. The room smelt of feces and urine and sweat and God only knew what else. I could vomit, Craine thought. Might even make it smell better. He noticed a cutthroat razor on a round dinner table and felt so strangely angry that he wanted to pick it up and slide it across his own neck. *What is wrong with me?* It's the heat. It's the heat and the sleep deprivation.

"Denny?" a shrill voice hollered from the behind the door. "Who is it?"

"It's okay! It's a friend of mine."

"Which friend? Since when have you got a friend?"

"Don't worry about it. I'll be in in five minutes!"

"I'm hungry!"

"I know!" he shouted. "Five minutes."

Denny led them into the center of the room, then with nowhere else to go, offered Craine a seat on the couch. There was a featherless pillow and a stained sheet on the couch, both covered in small red insects. Bed bugs. Most houses had them. This place looked to be infested.

"My ma," he mumbled, taking a seat when Craine didn't. "She's sick. She stays in bed mostly."

On a small table by the armrest was a picture of an obese woman wearing glasses and a skinny boy on a beach. The boy was Denny.

"You take care of her?"

He could tell from his frown that Denny hadn't really considered that before. As if he'd always thought of it in terms of his mother taking care of him.

"Yeah," he said, almost proudly. "I take care of her."

"You still working at the barbershop?"

"I cut people's hair now," he beamed. "We don't do wet-shaves no more."

Possibly a good thing, thought Craine, looking at Denny's fingers as they clumsily picked at his nose.

"People still coming in?"

"Mostly. Bit quieter I guess, since Mr. Jack died. Not so many of the regulars."

"You know most of the regulars?"

"Most of them."

"Know them by name?"

"I guess. Depends how often they come by."

"Did you ever meet anyone called James Campbell? Maybe you knew him as Jimmy. Did he ever come by?"

Denny shrugged.

"Your police report taken the very night Rochelle died states you said that they knew each other. That they were friends."

"He came round a few times. Before Mr. Jack got shot . . . I mean, before he shot Mr. Jack."

"You were there for that?"

"I was at the party. In that big house? But I didn't see Jimmy there."

"And do you think you could tell me what Campbell looked like?"

"What do you mean? Looked like everybody else."

"Well, was he tall? Dark hair?"

There was a long pause before Denny nodded and stated confidently, "He was tall."

"What about any distinguishing features?"

"Well he wasn't a Negro, if that's what you mean. Looked pretty much like you."

"Anything else? Did he wear glasses? Did he have bad teeth? A mustache?"

"No, he didn't have a mustache." Denny's eyes suddenly brightened in triumph. "Big ears," he spurted out, "he had big ears. Yes, I remember now. He had these great big cauliflower ears. Couldn't help looking at them."

"If you don't mind, I'm going to show you a picture." Craine reached into his jacket pocket and passed Denny the police booking shots from Chicago. "Can you tell me if this is the man you met?"

Denny squinted. "Yes, that's him."

There it was. The blow was softer now, less a realization that the shooter wasn't Campbell than an acceptance of that fact.

"Looks friendlier in person, mind," Denny added, as if he'd caused offense.

"Anything else about him?"

"He always had a briefcase with him. Not much else to say. He was nice to me. I liked him."

"Do you think he killed Jack Rochelle?"

Denny looked confused, his opinion unexpectedly called into action. "Maybe. Who knows?"

"What did he and Jack Rochelle talk about when he came by?"

"I don't know. They whispered, or Mr. Jack asked me to go outside. Sometimes they would go in the back room."

"The room at the back of the barbershop?"

"Yeah."

"You've been inside?"

"Not supposed to go inside. Mr. Jack's orders."

"Denny, you're aware that Jack Rochelle used to do business on the side, aren't you? You're aware that he would sell things, things not to do with haircuts?"

"He didn't tell me much. I never asked."

"But you're smart, aren't you, Denny? You knew. You knew what was going on in the back room."

Denny pulled himself up in his seat. He scratched at the small red welts dotted across his arms. "Yeah, I knew," he whispered, glancing at the door in the corner. "People came and they talked. Mr. Jack said 'Denny, shut your ears,' but you can't really shut your ears. Or if you can, I don't know how."

"I have to ask you, Denny, what happened to the contents of the back room?"

"I wasn't supposed to go inside."

"But do you know what was in there? Denny, I bet there was drink in there. I also think there were drugs. Pills, powder, marijuana plants. Did you see anything like that in there after Jack died?"

"After Mr. Jack died the studio police came and they took everything. That room is empty now."

For a brief second Craine thought about bringing Denny in for official questioning, but there was no point. Evidently, Denny hadn't been working for Rochelle long enough to be privy to Rochelle's business dealings.

"Take care of yourself, Denny. I hope things work out well for you."

Craine crossed back over to the door. He slipped his cuff over his wrist and used it like a glove to turn the doorknob. He was about to open the door when Denny said, "I wasn't supposed to go inside. But I did once."

Craine turned. "You've been inside?"

"Please don't tell anyone," he said nervously. "I have to keep my job. Mr. Jack would have been upset if he knew."

"What did you see?"

"There were bottles, as you said. Cases of liquor. Jars of powder and pills."

"You took some?"

"I didn't want any of those things."

"What, then?"

Hesitant, Denny looked back at the door in the corner.

"What did you take, Denny?"

Denny stood up slowly and removed the cushions from the couch. He lifted up the padded seat, where, through a tear in the material, Craine could see a brown package taped to the springs. "I took these," Denny said without looking at Craine, confiding instead to the floor. "They were in a big book. These ones were at the back. I thought they were pretty and I thought Mr. Jack wouldn't notice."

Denny took out an envelope, folded over at one end and tied tightly with string so it couldn't be opened by idle hands.

"Give me the envelope, Denny."

Denny sighed, perhaps almost grateful to share his burden. He looked again at the bedroom door and pleaded in a heavy whisper, "Please, don't tell my ma."

CHAPTER 29

July 14th

Patrick O'Neill took a call from the San Bernardino county sheriff's department early on a Friday morning requesting a homicide detective from the Los Angeles department—a body had been found in the forests surrounding the Cajon Pass, not far from an abandoned vehicle with a Los Angeles registration.

San Bernardino was a sixty-mile drive on Route 66, the first half through traffic, and it took O'Neill most of three hours to get there in his battered gray Plymouth. He was met by a state trooper in beige khakis at the town's courthouse offices who he then followed up past Devil Canyon toward the southernmost tip of the San Gabriel mountain range.

He was thinking about his date the other week. First dates were always tricky. Although it could be their last date too, considering O'Neill hadn't seen or heard from Gracie since he'd put her in a taxi back to her apartment. "I had a good time," was all he mumbled to her, for some stupid reason, meaning to say that he had loved meeting her and wanted to see her again. He had tried calling Gracie's office a few days later to see if she wanted to meet up again for the July 4th weekend, but she wasn't available and hadn't returned his calls. He guessed that was the end of it.

The highway south of the pass was littered with scree and silt where the roads had flooded and O'Neill had to drive slowly until they'd passed the rockslide. He followed the patrol car as it pulled off onto a dirt track and parked beside a group of local police trucks at the edge of the forest. One of the trucks had a large cargo space with black tarpaulin folded over it. To take the body away, he reasoned.

His escort came over to tell him the chief deputy would be along shortly, then joined a circle of state troopers standing under a tall black locust tree chewing tobacco and smoking cigarettes. One of them had a coffee flask and they were passing round a tin cup, talking among themselves. They gave O'Neill a nod and a weak smile as he stepped out of the car, but he knew at once that he couldn't stand among them. He was a city boy, unwelcome in these parts.

The sun had risen fast; it was a hot, crisp morning and he felt his hair damp beneath his hat. He propped himself up on the hood of his car, took off his jacket and smoked a cigarette he didn't much enjoy. Ten minutes passed and he was starting to wonder why he'd been asked to venture so far away from the city when a middle-aged man in a beige shirt and a white, wide-brimmed hat strolled over toward O'Neill and introduced himself as Chief Deputy Corwin Weddle.

"You from Los Angeles Central?"

"Detective O'Neill."

Weddle tilted his chin but his hands remained by his side. He had a military bearing about him. "Good of you to come out," he said, nodding his head toward the slope. "It's a little further down through the trees there."

O'Neill followed the chief deputy through the forest, stumbling over dead branches and desert plants where the roots tangled among the rocks. After fifteen minutes of walking silently, O'Neill stopped and fanned his face with his hat. Sweat was running down his back and his cuffs had turned brown at the wrist.

He waved his hand toward the rough trail below. "The corpse," he said breathlessly. "What makes you so sure it's one of ours?"

Weddle took the opportunity to take out a pack of cigarettes, shaking one loose then pushing it roughly into his mouth. "Car was abandoned on the side of the road up by our trucks. Burned throughout, but the plates were registered to Los Angeles."

"Where is it now?"

"Scrap heap, probably. The body was only spotted this morning; the car was found six or so weeks ago."

O'Neill found a handkerchief in his pocket and wiped his neck. They carried on walking. "That didn't seem unusual to you?" he asked. "The car being left here?"

"Not really. We get a lot of wreckages left on the side of the road. Dumped mostly so people can try and hitch on the trains. Cars get turned around by the police once they get near the city. No one wants any more people coming into California. Not when they ain't got jobs or food."

They reached a small clearing where an area of approximately fifty feet was roped off. A knot of deputies was gathered in a circle smoking cigarettes. They took off their hats when the chief deputy approached but barely raised an eyebrow to O'Neill.

He got within twenty feet of the men before he had to cover his mouth and nose from the smell of rotting flesh. The stench was terrible, keeping everything away but the flies. O'Neill held his handkerchief over his face and moved forward until he could see the corpse clearly.

It was a dead male, fully clothed, face down in the scrub. In the moist humidity of the summer months, decomposition was very quick to set in and he could tell from the way the body had bloated and ballooned that it was between six and ten weeks old. He was surprised the animals hadn't got to him first.

The corpse was laid out straight, both legs pointing downhill. Whoever he was, he'd been trussed, wrapped wire holding his arms behind him and a limp rope from his wrists to his ankles. There'd been no attempt to bury him.

O'Neill squatted down and tilted the man's chin up. Ligature marks crisscrossed around his neck: he'd been strangled with a rope or cord. There was also a thick black wound across his throat, flies' eggs and maggots already settled in. The strangulation was just the beginning. He'd been finished off with a blade.

"Can we turn him over?" he asked of no one in particular.

A deputy stepped up beside Weddle and together they pushed the body on its back. O'Neill's nostrils flared from the odor as internal gases were expelled from the open jugular. He leaned away and cleared his throat.

The young deputy spat drily and wiped his mouth. "Smells goddamn' awful."

O'Neill took out a printed pad of D.O.A. forms. His neck tensed with the drone of flies. "It's the heat. Decomposition doesn't take long in these conditions."

The chief deputy's mouth tightened. "So how ripe is he?"

"Could be seven, eight weeks old. Maybe more," O'Neill replied, writing over a carbon. "He died mid-May by my estimate."

Weddle looked at O'Neill like he'd just performed dark magic instead of basic forensic biology.

"You can tell all that by looking at him?"

"It's only an estimate. You said you found the car—"

"Last Friday in May. Might have been there for a while though."

O'Neill snapped a twig and used it to peel open the tattered remains of his pants pockets. "Jeans look torn open. No wallet, no I.D."

The chief deputy pursed his lips. "Any way you can figure out who did this to him?"

O'Neill looked at Weddle across the body. "The first step is finding out who he is." When he looked disappointed O'Neill said, "Look, the ideal crime scene is in a house, under cover somewhere. Outside there's little we can do. Nothing to connect him here and nobody else to connect to this location either." He scanned the ground around the body and could see his crime scene was already trampled by boots. There was no means of ascertaining footprints. Fingerprinting would be worthless. Apart from the body, physical evidence was negligible. "We'll need to search the forests," he went on. "Send out teams of three or four, split the ground until we've covered a perimeter of maybe a mile or so. Up to the road, across to the rail line." He pointed to the corpse on the ground. "And have someone take some photographs before you get him out."

"Wait, don't you want to see the rest of it?"

"There's more?"

Weddle beckoned him along a crest then back down through the trees. "We already covered everything between here and the road before you got here."

Further down the slope he pointed to an open suitcase under a thin layer of scabrock. The case was burned through, the insides nothing more than a few charred remains. Beside it, a broken view camera lay in pieces in the dirt and O'Neill stopped and bent down to look at it.

Weddle pushed back his hat. "One of the boys found it shortly before you got here. Camera looks busted. Not much inside the case. Whatever it was he burned it all. Lucky he didn't light up the whole forest."

O'Neill looked at the ground but the wiregrass and surrounding shrubbery showed no signs of fire. "If the fire didn't spread, it might have been during one of the downfalls. When were they, early, mid-May?"

"Seems about right. Barely a drop since."

O'Neill knelt beside the case and began sifting through the contents. There were a few clothes inside but the fabric was frayed and blistered and they wouldn't help identify him. There were three tin containers rolling around the bottom but the metal was brittle and twisted from the heat and whatever had been inside had burned dry. He ran his finger along the inside of one of the containers. His finger was black and oily. Chemical residue.

"Sir?" They both turned to see the young deputy walking down the hill with something in his hand.

"What is it, Darrell?"

"Found this a little further up the slope toward the road. Must have come out of his pockets."

"What is it?"

"Looks like his wallet."

"Does it have identification in it?"

"There's blood all over it . . ." He held it out for both to see and O'Neill took it, holding it by the edges.

O'Neill gently opened the leather and pulled out a set of notes and cards. He wiped the face of a bloodied driver's license and held it out of the shade. The picture was unclear but beside it, printed in smudged ink, was a name he recognized immediately. O'Neill wasn't sure what he was looking at made any sense. The identification belonged to a JAMES L. CAMPBELL.

Craine stretched back in his chair and rubbed his eyes. He couldn't focus. The snatches of sleep he was getting weren't enough, and the migraines were steadily getting worse. He was sitting in his office in the homicide unit, his desk littered with crime reports. In his hands were the two dozen photographs Denny had given him. He sipped at his coffee and started to leaf through the pictures for the hundredth time. The photographs were of girls, naked or half-dressed in fox furs and expensive negligees. The prints were black and white, mostly mediums and close-ups taken with beauty dish lamps and soft fill lighting rigs. They were artistic glamour shots rather than dirty pictures, mainly girls in cabaret dress posing erotically.

He quickly identified a range of different girls: some blond, others brunette, some curvy, others slim but attractive, many disarmingly so. They weren't the hookers he'd seen crawling street corners; they were highly trained professionals working in the sex industry. He separated the photos of different girls into piles. As far as he could see, there were maybe five or so different girls in as many different scenarios. Most were in bedrooms, a few in gardens or on swings; some were of girls in swimming pools. He thought he recognized one or two of the girls but he couldn't put a name or a place to any of them.

He'd spent the past few days considering what to do with the pictures and the new information he had gathered on the Loew House shootings but had yet to form any conclusions. In his imagination he saw Campbell and Rochelle dealing in soft pornography and being killed for that very reason, but his conclusions seemed premature and naive. This involved too many other people. There had been a cover-up, that he was sure of. He wondered nervously who was involved. The studio? More than likely. Anyone else? Had someone actually hired the shooter to kill Campbell, Rochelle and Florence Lloyd? Was it Stanley's last act before taking his own life? Or was it Louis Mayer himself? Who was the puppeteer? He could find no patterns, no rational explanation for what had happened.

Opening the window, he took long breaths of the city air and loosened his necktie. It was drizzling outside, but he could still make out the barred upper floors of the Hall of Justice through the smog. He heard the sound of sirens approaching then fading away. Behind him he could hear murmurings in the hallway beyond the door. Maybe they were whispering about him, spreading rumors, instigating gossip. He tried to imagine what they would say if they could see him now. *He's trying to construct an investigation but he's incapable of doing so. He's not a detective; he's a fraud, a charlatan.*

Turning back to the desk, he picked up Campbell's Chicago file. He had evidence proving that the man they thought was Campbell was actually someone else. The killer had wrongly been identified. So who was he? And where was the real Campbell and why hadn't he come forward?

Pulling his notepad toward him, he tried to make a list of things he needed to do: he knew he needed to re-examine Lloyd's house; he needed to find out why Campbell's uncle had identified the body as Campbell; he had to identify the girls in the pictures; he also had to find out who the shooter really was and who had hired him; finally, he needed motive.

His train of thought was interrupted by two sharp taps on the pebbled glass of his office door. Instinctively he opened his top desk drawer and slid Campbell's file and Denny's photographs off the desktop. A moment later the door opened.

O'Neill was standing outside. His face was dry and sun-blasted. There was dirt and dust in his hair and stains on his knees. He had a large envelope in one hand, his jacket grasped tightly in the other.

"Lieutenant?"

Craine didn't stand up, sliding the drawer shut quietly. "What do you want, O'Neill?"

"Can I come in?"

Craine didn't say anything but O'Neill came in anyway.

"Do you remember who identified the Loew House killer?"

Craine studied O'Neill's face. Did he know about the Campbell file? Why was he in his office, asking him questions about a case that was otherwise considered closed? Craine had thought about going to O'Neill when the file first arrived from Chicago but he'd been wary of having someone else involved. He was used to working alone and wasn't sure he wanted O'Neill to be part of this. Or maybe he was worried that O'Neill would tell him what he didn't want to hear.

Craine shrugged without answering.

"What was his name? Was it a family member?"

"Why?"

"I got a call-out this morning all the way from San Bernardino. They found a body in the Cajon Pass." O'Neill pushed the envelope across the table toward Craine and took a seat in the chair opposite. "He was dumped by the rail line heading through the mountains. Someone had cut his throat."

Craine opened the envelope, pulling out six photographs. They were crime scene glossies, freshly printed and barely dry. The first picture showed a bloated corpse face down in a forest. He glanced at the next photo. The victim's throat was black and open to the bone, maggot-eaten and surrounded by flies. His stomach sank when he saw the man's face. He tried to convince himself that it was all in his imagination but he knew exactly whose body he was staring at. Despite the swollen facial features, the broad nose and large ears were unmistakably Campbell's. He put the photos down on the table. His fingers started to shake so he quickly hid them under the desk.

"And?"

"We found this near the body."

O'Neill pushed a small piece of card onto the lip of Craine's desk. It was a driver's license, soiled and torn but still in one piece. The name was printed across the front—there was no doubt whom it belonged to.

Craine thought for a while before replying. "This isn't the same Campbell." He picked up the photographs. "The Loew House shooter was identified by his uncle as James Campbell. They matched his car. I saw him in his apartment. This is someone else." He pushed the photos away and sat back in his chair. He made a show of looking at the clock on his wall. "Excuse me, if you don't mind I have a few other things I need to be doing right now."

O'Neill dropped his head. Exhaling, he stood and moved to the door. He paused and turned. Craine could see in his eyes he was trying to draw on courage he'd rarely used before. O'Neill took a deep breath.

"It has to be James Campbell," he blurted out quickly. "Why else would he have his license?"

"There could be two dozen other Campbells in Los Angeles, let alone the state. What, you think you're the only Patrick O'Neill in California?"

"It's the same one. James L. Campbell."

"You don't know that."

"Yes I do; it's right here, clear as day."

"You're speculating."

"And you're hiding something," O'Neill said accusingly. He'd crossed the mark now, it was too late to go back; he could only go further. "You're hiding something to do with the Loew House murder. Or Herbert Stanley's suicide—"

Craine interrupted, "That's ridiculous."

But for once O'Neill couldn't be stopped. "Is it? I know what the papers printed was a lie. Worse than that, I was complicit in that lie and so were you. Stanley, Lloyd, Campbell, the shootings. They're all tied together but every time I try to make a connection I get closed down. You and Simms, who do you work for? City Hall? M.G.M.? Because you're not real police; if you were, you wouldn't be determined to sabotage any attempt at a real investigation." He was almost shouting now, his fingers jabbing at the air between them.

Craine glanced at the silver Lieutenant's bar on his left shoulder. "You forget yourself, Detective."

"Forget myself? Do you even remember what you're supposed to be? To protect and serve? That's a joke. Who are you serving? More to the point, who are you protecting?"

Craine rubbed his jaw and whispered a sigh. Even now his natural instinct was to fend off O'Neill's questions, but if he was going to do this, to delve further, he needed help. He couldn't do this alone. "Shut the door."

"Craine—"

"Patrick, please. Shut the door." When O'Neill realized that Craine was ready to talk he stepped toward the doorway, glancing outside to make sure no one was within hearing range. Craine waited for the door to close then motioned for him to have a seat.

His eyes focused on O'Neill's round Irish eyes. "Who have you told?"

"No one. I came to you."

Opening the drawer, Craine reached down and lifted out Campbell's Chicago file, leaving Denny's pictures out of sight. He shouldn't give everything away. Not yet, anyway.

He flipped the mug shot photo of Campbell across the table, face up beside the others. "You're right," he said, comparing the sunken, putrid face to the police mug shots. "The body you found is James Campbell." Opening the folder, he held up the Campbell R.A.P. sheet. "I got Campbell's file from Chicago last week. This is him. There were pictures of him at his place. I should have figured."

O'Neill leaned his head back. "So, if the body at the Cajon Pass is Campbell, who was the shooter?"

"I don't know. But the papers made a mistake . . . *we* made a mistake.

Whoever the shooter was, I think he killed Lloyd, then Campbell and then went for Rochelle at Loew House."

"All three of them?"

"There were no prints at Lloyd's house. No one heard the shots. The guy I saw at Campbell's apartment was firing a semi-automatic with a suppressor. The ammunition from both crime scenes was nine-millimeter Parabellum rounds. That's unusual, the sign of a professional—"

"How do you know that?"

"Ballistics matched them."

"But you didn't say anything before."

"No," said Craine, the edges of his mouth turned down, "no, I didn't mention it before." There was no defense in his voice, only disappointment.

"The body off the Cajon Pass wasn't shot. He was tortured then his throat was cut."

"That's the work of a pro. These weren't random; they weren't crimes of passion."

O'Neill frowned. "You think he was for hire?"

"I think it's possible."

"Employed by who?"

"That's as far as I get."

"And how does this relate to Stanley?"

"I'm not sure. I don't question it was suicide—Stanley was an addict."

"You know that for certain?"

"Rochelle told me he sold to Stanley. I figured a drug connection between all of them but now I'm not convinced. Maybe that has nothing to do with it. Rochelle tried to tell me something at Loew House."

"What?"

"I never got the chance to find out. Next thing I knew he was bleeding to death on the washroom floor." Craine's fingers pecked on Campbell's file. "Look, if I tell you everything I know, will you help me? If we're going to find out why the three of them were killed, we need to know who the shooter was and we need to know who identi-fied his body as Campbell and for what purpose. But for now at least, this investigation has to stay between us."

"What about Simms? What about the D.A.?"

"Forget senior command. This is you and me. You can't tell anybody; your career in the Bureau will depend on it. No one else can know that we're reopening the investigation, do you understand that?"

The jaw muscles in O'Neill's face tightened. His eyes looked wider than usual. Slowly, he nodded his head.

"So what's next?"

CHAPTER 30

Shortly before six o'clock, O'Neill knocked on the door of Conrad Frazer's apartment off Winward Avenue in Venice Beach. Like most of the other doors on the corridor, the frame was splintered, the doorknob broken clean off, probably from replevin actions filed by creditors. Repossession was common in these parts.

When there was no answer, O'Neill knocked again. A low voice called out from inside.

"Who is it?"

"Mr. Frazer? Mr. Conrad Frazer?"

"Yes."

"My name is Detective O'Neill. I'm from the police department. I'd like to talk to you for a few minutes."

"What's it about?"

"You're not in trouble. I only want to talk to you."

"What about?"

"About your nephew, James Campbell."

"He's dead."

"I know he's dead, sir, I'd like to talk to you about him." O'Neill paused, then added, "If you don't mind."

After a long silence he heard four or five deadbolts being slid across the door from inside. When the door finally opened, a squat man wearing soiled jeans and a white undervest stood in the doorway with a tattooed arm held across the jamb. His face was the color of veal. He smelt foul.

"You say you're from the police?"

O'Neill showed him his identification.

Conrad Frazer smiled, revealing several missing teeth and black gums. "Sorry, you never know who's going to come knocking, you know what I mean? You best come in. Close the door behind you."

The apartment was floored with cheap timber. A living area took up two-thirds of the space with a plate-stacked counter and iron sink in the corner acting as a kitchen. The furnishings were minimal; a stained couch was the centerpiece of the room, two varnished wood chairs—functional rather than decorative—were propped up against the wall and an upturned crate acted as a table. The wallpaper throughout was peeled and stained and the place smelt stale enough that he had to breathe through his mouth. He was trying to work out what the stench was when something came running out of the bedroom with an angry, high-pitched snarl.

Cats.

O'Neill looked around the room. There were cats hiding every-where, camouflaged under the couch, huddled in corners, up on the windowsill by the sink. Thin, rangy, with visible ribs and bony legs. There must have been ten or eleven of them at least.

"You have a lot of cats."

"Oh, yeah, these are my babies." Frazer stroked a mottled ginger tabby cat sitting on the couch. "I love my kitties. Don't I, Rover?"

"You call the cat Rover?"

"Yeah, why not?" he said defensively. "Rover's as good a name as any for a cat."

Frazer went over to the kitchen counter and took a bottle of milk from the sink. Four other cats jumped up and ran toward the food bowl. When he turned the bottle upside down the curdled milk slid down the sides like yoghurt.

"Here, Rover, come get dinner." He looked at O'Neill and added, "They like it a little thick."

O'Neill studied Conrad Frazer as he stroked the cats one by one, rubbing the base of their spines with his short, pudgy fingers. He was probably fifty years old but could have passed for ten years older. His hair was thin and lank, his eyes small and bloodshot; when he stood still he planted his feet wide apart and swayed from side to side as if the room was moving.

"Cigarette?" the man offered, reaching for a smoked butt-end.

"No, thank you."

O'Neill felt something on his foot. He looked down and saw a cockroach crawling across his shoe. He flicked it away and shuddered under his coat.

"Do you have much trouble with cockroaches, sir?"

"Nah, not much. Cats eat 'em." Frazer grinned, butt end in mouth, and took a seat on the upturned crate. "How do you like being police? I always wanted to be police when I was younger. Don't know why I never did. Time just goes, don't it?"

"Have you lived here long, Mr. Frazer?"

He shrugged. "Few years. Ten or so."

"And you work nearby?"

"I worked out of San Pedro Harbor."

"Long way to go."

"I haven't worked there for a while. You know how it is."

"Uh-uh. And forgive me for getting right to the point, but do you mind telling me a little more about your nephew, James Campbell?"

"Jimmy? Oh, you know, not much to say. I guess he worked. Photographs, cameras. He always had them with him. Never would let me touch them, though. Said he'd take a picture of my babies sometime but he never did."

"How well did you know him? Personally, that is?"

"He was my sister's boy. My sister lived in Chicago 'til she and her fella died—some accident somewhere. Anyway, I came out for the oil they found here on the peninsula. Not that there was much. Sometime after, Jimmy wrote me a letter saying he wanted to come to California. He came down last year or so. Didn't see a lot of him. Offered him this place to stay but he seemed pretty keen to move somewhere else."

"So you hadn't seen him much before he died?"

"Not since Christmas. He brought me a bowl for my babies. Not the type I would have chosen myself. I guess he didn't know my tastes."

"But you knew him well enough to identify him."

There was a long pause. "I guess. I'm his uncle."

"And you were asked to identify his body?"

"Yeah."

"By who?"

Conrad Frazer stirred. He petted the tabby cat some more, picked it up, rubbed its face against his stubbled cheek until the cat squirmed and jumped away. "I don't want to get into trouble."

"You're not going to get into trouble."

"Well I don't want to talk about it anymore. He was my nephew and he's gone. What's to say?"

O'Neill tingled down one arm. Interviews and interrogations were not his strong point. He tried to sound assertive, knowing that if he attempted to seem threatening he'd fail.

"Mr. Frazer, I'm looking out for your best interests. You're not in any trouble here, that's not what I'm after. But I want to know what happened. And it'll be easier for the both of us if you tell me here and now. You don't want to go down to the Bureau, do you?"

Frazer wrung his hands and looked all around the room, anywhere but at O'Neill. "Well, it happened that these people came and they asked me to go see Jimmy's body."

"And when the men came, did they show you identification, police badges?"

He held up his hands. "No, I mean, they said they were here about identifying Jimmy. Said that I was going to be asked and I should say it was him."

"And then did they take you down to the Coroner's Office?"

"No, they left and then the police came."

"The police came after?"

"Yeah, I mean a few hours later."

"You sure they were police? They had uniforms?"

"They had uniforms and badges and took me in the car. Didn't drive me back though, I had to catch a Red Car."

"So the people that came to your door first and told you to say the body was Jimmy weren't police? They didn't show you any badges?"

Conrad Frazer scratched at his arms and looked back at his feet. "I'm not sure. I don't remember."

"Think. Please, think."

He sighed, biting his lip and bending down to the floor. Two of the cats sidled over to him and licked his fingers. "They didn't show me any badges," he said after a moment. "I guess I don't know where they were from. They didn't tell me any of their names."

"And did they pay you?"

"Can't remember."

"Did they pay you?" O'Neill repeated, more assertive now.

"What's it matter?"

"You're not in trouble, but I need to know. Did they pay you to say it was your nephew?"

Frazer nodded. He spoke quietly. "Three hundred dollars."

"And the man you identified as James Campbell. Was he? Was he Jimmy?"

He closed his eyes for a moment then began to speak. "He was all bloody. His face was all puffed up."

"Was he your nephew?"

Frazer hesitated then said, "Probably was. So hard to tell."

"Was he Jimmy Campbell?" O'Neill asked again, his voice ever so slightly raised.

"I didn't know him well," Frazer stuttered. "People's faces aren't always that easy to remember; people change."

O'Neill shouted, "Was he Jimmy? Was it your nephew?"

Frazer bowed his head. He began to weep. "No," he muttered almost inaudibly, "no, he wasn't Jimmy."

"You said he was but he wasn't your nephew."

Conrad Frazer was a broken man. O'Neill gave him a withering glance then turned to leave.

"I mean, I was, pretty relieved," Frazer explained, his voice choked. "I always liked Jimmy. Figured he'd just gone somewhere else. But I said it was him. I did what they told me to do."

O'Neill sighed. "It doesn't matter. Thank you for telling me. That's all I needed to know."

Frazer, ashen-faced, asked, "Am I in trouble? Please, I mean, I'm only trying to get by here, you know? I wasn't trying to lie on purpose."

Without answering, O'Neill went to the door. He shook his head, took one final glance around the room then pulled back the bolts one by one.

"You shouldn't feed them milk," he said in the doorway.

Frazer looked at him through glazed eyes. "What?"

"Your cats—you shouldn't feed them milk. Milk is bad for them. Makes them sick."

"Are you crazy?" Frazer said, attempting a smile as he wiped the snot from his nose with the back of his hand. "Cats love milk."

Dolores Greer's house was small but tidier than most on the street, the wooden clapboards freshly painted and the front garden well-tended. Florence Lloyd's house stood alone opposite it. In only eight weeks the lawn had grown unkempt and there were crude drawings and swear words painted across the clapboards. The gutters were spilling over and the windows had been patched with plywood to protect the glass and discourage looters.

There was a weathered Ford Flivver up on bricks on the Greer driveway, so Craine parked on the curbside. He was driving one of the unmarked squad cars from the Bureau's motor pool, but the curtains in one of the neighboring houses still twitched. He felt snooping eyes watching him as he walked up the path toward her front door. He suspected Dolores Greer's house didn't usually have many visitors. Craine was evidently a rare find.

He knocked at the door and took a step back. He noticed a black

Pontiac turn into the road and pull up further down the street. Craine squinted against the sunlight. The driver was familiar to him. Red hair, a trim ginger beard. He had seen him before somewhere, he was sure of it. Before he could make out the license plates, the Pontiac abruptly turned in the road, accelerating back toward the junction it had come from.

He considered returning to his car but he heard a bolt being pulled back from inside and an elderly woman in hair curlers cautiously opened the door.

"Dolores Greer?"

"Yes?"

She was small and frail, with wide-rimmed spectacles that magnified her eyes. Craine showed her the tin badge. "Mrs. Greer? Lieutenant Craine from the police department. Could I talk to you for a minute?"

"What about? I told them my car wasn't registered. I don't even drive it anymore."

"Actually, I was hoping to ask you a few more questions about your tenant, Florence Lloyd."

She squinted at his identification.

"Well she isn't my tenant anymore now, is she? You best come in."

Inside the house was ordered and well arranged. Dolores Greer led him into a small parlor with an adjacent kitchen. Twin armchairs upholstered with floral prints overlooked the street. One of them had a doily on the headrest.

He was offered one of the chairs but waved it away politely, content to stand. Craine took out his pad, finding a fresh page as the old lady busied herself in the kitchen brewing tea. Through the window he could see Lloyd's house opposite. He glanced further down the street but there was no sign of the Pontiac.

"Are you sure you wouldn't like a cup of tea? I import it, you know."

"No thank you, Mrs. Greer."

She came back into the room and took a seat on the armchair

nearest the window. "I'm afraid I don't have anything new to tell you. That other young officer asked me an awful lot of questions." She rolled her tongue around in her cheek as if searching for a missing piece of breakfast.

"I understand Florence Lloyd rented the house from you, is that correct?"

"Well, I own both places. My sister used to live in that one but she passed on and never married so I lease out the house."

"And for how long was Miss Lloyd your tenant?"

"Oh, she must have been in there almost two years—two years this summer."

"And what was she like as a person, Mrs. Greer?

"Well, she was a nice girl, I suppose, from what I knew of her. Always paid her rent on time, never asked much of me. Always rushing off this way and that for her work. She had a job, you see," she said as if it was a rarity, which indeed it probably was, even in this part of town.

"You know where she worked?"

"Not sure where, exactly. One of those night restaurants. Out awful late some nights. Sometimes I'd see fellas coming out of her house. All hours they were, barely ever the same one though, I'll tell you that much. Honestly—the youth these days."

"Did you meet any of these people? Could you give me any names?"

"Not really," she said, sipping her cup of tea. "Swanky-looking. Suits, dinner jackets. They seemed okay, so I didn't mention anything. Quite enjoyed having a bit of glamour on the street. Should have seen the cars that came by in the mornings."

"How about James Campbell? Does the name ring any bells?"

"Oh yes, he was the young man who used to come by a lot. Florence introduced me once. They knew each other from Chicago—that's where Florence was from and she said he was her boyfriend. Well, I hope he didn't know about all those other men. I mean, honestly."

"Thank you, Mrs. Greer, that's very helpful. Can I ask you, have you been into the house since the shooting?"

"Yes, a few times. Someone needed to clean up. I'd like it rented out by the end of the summer."

"When you went in, did you notice anything? Anything moved or misplaced?"

"There were clothes everywhere, furniture torn apart. That refrigerator was pulled away from the wall; I only put it in last year. Then I went into the bedroom." She paused at the thought of it and her voice softened to a whisper: "My lord, what a mess it was in." Her hands trembled and she took a long sip of tea before recomposing herself.

"Could you tell if anything was missing?"

"I wouldn't really know. I'm not sure. Most of the furniture belonged to my sister. Anyhow, the police came and took some of it. I boxed most of the rest and threw it out. No point in keeping it now. Can't say I could tell if anything was missing."

"Did you look in every room?"

"Every room but the basement."

"Basement?"

"That's what I said. Door in the floor somewhere, I forget which room. Never went down there. My sister neither, but I know it's there. Pretty big it is too. Good for storage. Seemed to be a big deal for Florence—that I had one, I mean. Few months back she and that Jimmy kept on asking about it. Said she was willing to pay extra to have it cleared out so she could use it all to herself."

"Mrs. Greer, I'd like to have a look around the house if you don't mind."

"I turned the electric off. It's dark over there—I got boards over the windows. Don't you want to wait until I've had a chance to clean up a little? It'll be much nicer in a few weeks' time."

"I'd rather have a look now, if you don't mind."

"Well, okay, I guess."

"Do you have a key?"

"'Course I have a key," Mrs. Greer said, her eyebrows knitting together. "Why wouldn't I have a key?"

Craine stood outside Florence Lloyd's house with his hands buried in his jacket pockets, the high afternoon sun burning the back of his neck. With the threat of earthquakes, most houses in Southern California had shallow, slab-on-grade foundations that didn't have basements. This house was a rarity in Los Angeles. So why would Lloyd be so keen to use the basement? And what might she be hiding in it that the shooter had wanted so much?

He skirted around the edges of the house but couldn't find any cellar windows or visible steps down to a basement floor. There was a small stool outside Florence's window but there wasn't a bulkhead door anywhere on the outside of the house. Behind him, the neighbors watched on, anxiously waiting to see if their house was next on the search list. He should hurry; his car was unmarked and he didn't want anyone calling the police.

Heading back to the front porch, he fished in his pockets for the set of keys the old lady had given him. The first and second key didn't fit; the third turned smoothly in the keyhole. The door swung open and Craine stepped into the hall.

Bare floors, the walls wiped down and broken glass swept up. He tried the light switch instinctively before he remembered Mrs. Greer had cut the power. Except for the light creeping beneath the boarded windows, it was dark beyond the hallway and Craine swept the rooms with a small flashlight he'd taken from the car.

There were four rooms in the house including the bathroom but only four doorways, meaning that the only access to the cellar would be through a hatch in the floor somewhere. Craine investigated the house, moving through the corridor, looking for hinges or grooves cut into the floorboards.

He started in the kitchen: the counters were wiped down; the canned food had been collected and taken away—probably by Mrs.

Greer for her own use. Craine stood for a long moment in the center of the room, turning slowly with the flashlight held by his temple. The black and white linoleum flooring had started to peel at the corners but for the most part it was glued firm and he couldn't see any sign of a cellar door in the floor.

The living room was the length of the house with a low, beamed ceiling and bare, hardwood flooring. After examining the floorboards minutely, he looked over the large moquette sofa: the upholstery had been cut open and fistfuls of stuffing removed. He bent down to look underneath but he couldn't see any hinges or signs of a trapdoor between the base legs.

He left the living room and went down the corridor, standing in the doorway of the bedroom staring at the bed, knowing the killer had probably done exactly the same. He pictured Lloyd on the mattress and was reminded that her body had for a long time gone unclaimed. She was someone who had died alone and may have lived her short life lonely. Craine felt a sudden kinship for the girl whose death he'd filed away and forgotten in a matter of hours.

He circled the bedroom but as far as he could tell it was exactly as he'd left it. The sheets had been stripped and likely thrown out. Where the body had been there was a large brown stain covering most of the mattress. The room smelt of copper, with a layer of disinfectant and cheap perfume where Dolores Greer had probably tried to clean the floor and cover up the smell. She should burn the mattress. Blood never washed out.

Even though the latent prints were never matched to Leonard Stone, fingerprint dusting powder flowered across the doorways and light switches. In the wall cupboard, a dozen long, jeweled evening gowns and six fur stoles hung from the rail. He hadn't noticed them before. Whatever job she had, Florence Lloyd had plenty of money to spend on clothes.

The bathroom appeared undisturbed. The toilet was bolted down and the enameled steel bath was freestanding. The medicine cabinet had several bottles of sleeping tablets but nothing he hadn't seen before. A pinewood dresser stood against one wall. A hairbrush on top, a gold watch and a pair of pearl earrings—nothing out of the ordinary. He went through the drawers but there was nothing in them except jewelry: long bead necklaces, diamond earrings, precious metal bracelets. Whoever had come here hadn't bothered to take them. So what were they after?

He went to leave the room when his flashlight swept across the floor, revealing that the direction of the wood grain was different on the floorboards bordering the fringe of the dresser. Holding the flashlight between neck and shoulder, he tried to shift the dresser to one side; there were wheels on the base and it rolled easily across the floor. He stood there in the darkness and pointed the flashlight at the floorboards. There were two hinges at the lip of the baseboard and he could make out the clear, dark edges of a wooden square cut into the floor.

He'd found the cellar door.

The short staircase that led down from the access hatch had shallow treads and no handrail. Craine padded down carefully step by step, his shoulder brushing against the near wall, the flashlight cutting through the black and guiding his feet down until he reached the bottom step.

He turned the flashlight with his eyes. The cellar ran half the length of the house. It was cool but dry, an unwelcoming oubliette with plain concrete walls and mismatched boards laid loosely over sand flooring. He felt the tug of disappointment. What was he expecting: an opium den? Leather cases filled with greenbacks? Walls stacked high with glassine bags of imported heroin?

He kept one foot on a stable floorboard and pivoted around, flashlight held out like a pistol. There were two metal stands beside the stairway behind him that he hadn't noticed. He recognized them as small arc lights. There was little else he could see of interest. He was about to head back up the stairs when he found what he was looking for: a narrow door in the far corner.

Craine moved across the room, watching his step, angling for the door. Twice the boards cracked beneath his shoes, the balls of his feet digging into the soft sand below. When he reached the door, he slid back a shiny steel deadbolt pinning the door shut at the lintel and twisted the doorknob to the unseen room.

The chamber was no larger than a closet. There was a pewter workbench along one side, a square bath filling the width at the end. A pair of elbow-length rubber gloves were draped over the side. The room smelt of chemicals. He stepped further inside—the bath was half-filled with a foul-smelling liquid.

Looking back at the bench, he noticed a stack of white card: eight-by-ten pieces of photographic paper, empty and unexposed. Beside them were several tin canisters, unopened and sealed.

Peering up now, he saw a red light bulb hanging from the ceiling and a brown gallon bottle on a shelf filled with God knew what. He craned his head back and for the first time saw a set of prints hanging from loose wires spread across the room: photographs, black-bleached and overdeveloped. Craine felt the hairs rise on the back of his neck. He glanced back at the bottle then at the tub. The liquid in the bath was developing emulsion. He was standing in a photographer's darkroom.

CHAPTER 31

"I don't know where you got these from but I shouldn't be doing this," said Crickley, the precinct's only full-time crime scene photographer. "I don't want any trouble."

They were standing under the red lights of Crickley's photography unit, hidden in the lower basement of the precinct. It was a narrow room, low-ceilinged and windowless, the air tainted with chemicals.

"You've got nothing to worry about."

"Like hell I don't. I don't even need to develop them to know what's on these." Crickley ran the celluloid strips between his fingers and held them toward a red bulb. "I mean, for crying out loud ... these pictures—"

"Crickley, calm down."

Crickley pushed nervously toward the door. "Look, I should really go talk to Simms about this," he said for the tenth time, intent on taking the pictures to senior command.

It was O'Neill who was trying to convince him to do otherwise. Craine had said nothing as of yet, his silence all the more intimidating. "Calm down, Crickley," O'Neill repeated. "I need you to calm down."

"How can I calm down? I'll lose my job. Lose my license."

"You're not going to lose your job. No one is going to know," O'Neill went on, with surprising self-assurance. "We need your help. You'd be assisting an investigation."

"Look, I can't do this. I mean, I'm not comfortable doing this. Talk to Simms, see what—"

"Develop the film," said Craine, speaking for the first time. "We won't involve you any further."

"If people upstairs heard about this—"

"You have my word."

Crickley's shoulders sank forward. His ruddy face was dark in the red light, his forehead wet and shiny.

"Whatever happens, please don't let Simms find out."

For over two hours they watched as Crickley worked under the dim glow of the red light, cutting the long, narrow strips of chemical-coated celluloid into five-frame sections then enlarging them using a Federal print enlarger. It was a slow, almost painstaking process, one frame of film at a time by hand, each taking three or four minutes to expose and develop and then several more minutes to soak the enlargement in a stop bath and fixing solution.

By midnight, the developing trays were full, and rows of eight-by-ten prints hung drying from wires stretched across the width of the room. Craine and O'Neill watched intently as the metallic silver came to the surface of the resin paper and the images began to form. Soft at first, blurry, then faster, the lines more defined, the blacks inked darker.

Crickley was right to be concerned.

The images were of a bedroom, Florence Lloyd's bedroom, to be precise, and the content left little to the imagination. The photographs showed a woman sprawled across a bed, wrapped in a sheet and what must only be more flesh. There was another figure in the picture, the back of their head buried between her legs and their face unclear.

The woman had blond hair, almost white, curled up around the ears. It was Florence Lloyd. She was naked in some, hardly more dressed in others and Craine surmised that there was an order here that needed to be deliberated on.

O'Neill shifted uneasily, and even in the red light Craine knew he was blushing. Craine looked at the photographs with earnest interest. There were dozens of pictures in total, the photographer positioned somewhere to the side, Florence Lloyd lying across the bed perhaps fifteen or so feet away. The subjects weren't modeling; they were unposed, stolen snapshots that he assumed were taken without the participants' knowledge.

Before rushing to unnecessary conclusions, Craine considered whether the photos might have been used for blackmail. But the blackmail of whom? The man in the pictures? He looked more closely at one of the prints. The lighting of the photograph was sallow and the images grainy. Florence Lloyd's face was held in rapture but the other figure was shrouded in shadow and impossible to identify. Could that be Stanley?

O'Neill stood at Craine's side. The top of his head came up to Craine's shoulders. "You recognize the girl on the bed?"

"That's Florence Lloyd. I assume Campbell took pictures of her and this guy from the window."

"But how do you know that Campbell was the photographer?"

"I have something to show you," said Craine, walking over to the corner of the room where his coat was folded over the back of a chair and returning with an envelope. He put his hand inside and pulled out a stack of prints, placing the photographs that Denny had given him on the workbench beside the others. "I was given these pictures a few days ago by someone who worked with Rochelle. I have a feeling they were taken by the same photographer."

O'Neill and Crickley glanced at the pictures. O'Neill's faced reddened again but this time with frustration. "Why didn't you tell me you had these?" he said, irritated. "We agreed to tell each other everything."

"I didn't know they were relevant. I'm sorry."

Crickley picked up one of the photographs and examined it carefully. "It's a different camera, but that's not to say it isn't the same photographer. The lighting is different. The girls in these pictures are modeling," he said, comparing the two sets of photographs, "but these new ones we have look like they were taken in low light. Like he was peeping on them."

"The girl on the bed is Florence Lloyd. She was killed two months ago," Craine said, pointing from one set to the other. "If this was blackmail, then I need to know who the other person is in the picture."

"You see the grain on the image," said Crickley, pulling him over to the last of the prints drying from the wires. "That's the silver chloride crystals reacting to the light. It's not stable, you see. The spools are acetate film but it wasn't stored properly and doesn't keep well in the heat. We're lucky we got these developed at all."

Craine looked closer at the enlargements.

"Is this all of them?"

"All that you gave me, but there are some missing from one of the spools. Six, I think. I imagine he developed them."

"Why would he develop some and not the rest?"

"It's a selection process. Printing photographs takes time and money. I'm guessing your photographer would have looked at the entire roll using a loupe and then chosen the best prints to blow up."

"You mean the six photos with the clearest images?"

"Exactly. In this case, I'm guessing they're the six photos where you can see both of their faces. What you have here is the offal, the ones that were no good to him."

"Craine?" This from O'Neill, staring harder at Denny's prints further down the room.

Craine ignored him. "Can we do anything to make it clearer?" he said to Crickley instead.

"No, can't get anything better than this, not with this exposure latitude. Normally I could burn these lighter areas to get a better tonal range but looking at these it wouldn't make a difference."

"Even if you made it bigger?"

"Craine?" O'Neill again.

"The smaller they are, the higher the fidelity to the negative," Crickley went on. "Every time you blow something up you're going to lose quality, and besides, the negative is ruined. In these summer months, the acids in the film break down. I was lucky to get these at all."

"Craine?" O'Neill said for the third time, more insistent this time. "What is it?"

"I've seen this girl before." O'Neill held up one of Denny's pictures, a blond woman wearing nothing but long gloves and a fur stole.

"What?"

"I've met her before. She was at Loew House. The night of the party."

Craine took the photograph from O'Neill's hand and held it toward the light. Exhilaration made his hands shake. "You're certain?"

"I think so," he said before reaching out to take the photograph back for one last check. He took his glasses off and looked again at the picture, his eyes fastened to the girl's face. After a few seconds, he said, "Yes, I'm certain."

"You remember her name?"

O'Neill nodded. "She said her name was Delilah, Delilah Deschamps."

CHAPTER 32

July 15th

There was no Delilah Deschamps filed at R. & I., the D.M.V. or County Parole. There was, however, an arrest sheet and employment record for a Delilah Desmond, aged nineteen years, born in Arizona. She had two prior arrests for soliciting, both in the Venice Beach area, but nothing in the past two years. Her employment record showed sporadic restaurant work and a number of three-month contracts at various studios around town. In that respect she was little different than most of the impressionable ingénues who took the bus to Los Angeles in a bid to break into the pictures, only to find themselves serving plates nine months of the year in the vain hope they might be spotted by a drunk producer.

In the early hours of the morning, after O'Neill matched the photo to her mug shot, they took O'Neill's car and drove to the address listed in Los Feliz.

Delilah Desmond lived in a neighborhood of two-story houses with closely cropped lawns and matching mailboxes. There were functional family cars in the driveways—Packards, Cadillac sedans, Buicks, even a Chrysler. These houses belonged to well-off families. There was money on this street.

The lights were off in the Desmond house but a parked Lincoln Zephyr sat in the driveway. That car cost more than most people's salary.

"Douse the lights," Craine said to O'Neill as they approached the house. "Keep going but slow down."

The Lincoln didn't have a license plate. In the driver's seat a chauffeur had his head tilted back. Dead? No, his chest was rising. Asleep.

Ascending a gentle hill, they followed the beam until they could spot a small turnoff.

"Turn around here. We can still see the house from the corner. I want to see who comes out before we knock on her door."

They decided to wait until morning, each taking turns to watch the house as the other got some rest.

"I don't mind taking first watch," O'Neill offered.

"Go ahead. Really."

Neither one of them said anything for a long time, and after a while O'Neill fell asleep. It felt peaceful without O'Neill yammering all the time, Craine had to admit, though a part of him enjoyed having him around. He glanced at O'Neill as he snored quietly in his seat. His hat was askew, replaced by a palm that he used as a pillow against the window. Most people look vulnerable when they're asleep but O'Neill just looked like a little boy. Yet, at the same time, he was smarter and wiser than most men twice his age. The contrast lent him a disarming quality and Craine liked that about O'Neill. He was sincere and earnest and only seemed to speak in primary colors. O'Neill spoke the truth, and it frightened Craine to hear it.

Around five o'clock O'Neill stirred in his seat and woke up with a start, his knees knocking against the car keys in the ignition.

"Sorry, I forgot where I was for a second."

He took a deep breath and blinked several times, opening his eyes as wide as he could before rubbing them with the back of his hand.

"You want to get some sleep? I'll stay watching."

"I'm okay. Getting light now, anyway. Won't have to wait much longer."

O'Neill shook out a cigarette. He patted his pockets and brought out a book of matches. The car lit up momentarily as he struck a match. Craine wound down the window but there was no avoiding the cigarette burning on O'Neill's lower lip. A thin curl of smoke drifted through the car and caught in Craine's throat. Chesterfields.

O'Neill must have sensed him stiffen. "Rude of me. You want one?"

"No, I don't smoke."

"Pretty unusual. I mean, pretty rare. Everyone at the department does. Truth is, I only started a few months ago. My dad always did. Used to smoke a pipe, one of those fisherman's ones that sticks out sideways so you can see in front of you. I inherited it too when he died but it stays in a drawer now 'cause it wouldn't seem right to smoke it. Even looking at it makes me think of him."

O'Neill was staring at his feet, his eyes lost in the memory.

Craine said, "My wife smoked. She smoked Chesterfields, like you." He paused as an image of her formed in his mind, her smoking a cigarette on the terrace out by the pool. Michael was in the water, learning how to swim. "When I smell them it reminds me of her."

"Oh, I didn't know. I'm sorry."

"Don't be."

O'Neill didn't make a show of stubbing out the cigarette, but he did it anyway.

"You married?" Craine asked.

"No. I mean, I'd like to be but—I haven't met the right person yet. Well, maybe I . . . Doesn't matter. Either way, it'd be nice to have a family. You must feel very lucky to have your son."

Craine wasn't sure how to answer this. In truth he'd never really thought about being a father as some kind of blessing. More of a role he couldn't live up to.

"Does he look like you?"

"A little. Like Celia, really." But Craine wasn't even sure if that was true. Michael had a lot of his features. It was nature's little trick to make you feel responsible.

"I don't look anything like my dad. Unfortunately."

"You want to be more like him?"

"Doesn't every kid want to be like their dad?"

"I didn't."

"Huh. Well, I guess you don't have any expectations to live up to. But I bet your son wishes he was like you. My dad was everything to me, growing up."

Before Craine could consider this, the porch light went on outside the Desmond household and a moment later the front door opened. The driver must have woken up with the light because he heard the ignition turn and then the Lincoln reversed back onto the road. It sat with the engine turning over for a few seconds before a man dressed in a black dinner jacket and loose-buttoned shirt ran down the driveway with an umbrella low over his head. It wasn't raining.

"They were taken around ten months ago, maybe a year," she said frankly after they'd shown her Denny's pictures of her and the other girls.

Delilah hadn't made a fuss at the door, conceding it was better to usher them inside than risk losing face in front of the neighbors. Discretion appeared paramount.

"Either of you want coffee?" They were standing in her kitchen. Delilah flipped the pictures face down on the table and turned toward the cooker, placing a kettle on the stove.

O'Neill, standing awkwardly by the kitchen door, looked at Craine, who shrugged then said, "Black, no sugar."

"What about you, Patrick? It is Patrick, isn't it? We met at M.G.M.'s gala."

"Milk and two sugars," O'Neill added when she'd lit the stove, somewhat shamefaced he'd pretended he'd never seen her before.

Delilah took a seat at the round breakfast table. Her hair was wet and she was wearing a white cotton dressing gown. Without makeup, he almost didn't recognize her from the photograph. "Who took the picture?" Craine asked.

There was a pack of cigarettes on its side beside a cut-glass ashtray and she stared at it long and hard, avoiding all eye contact. "Some guy."

"James Campbell?"

Delilah nodded. "Jimmy, we called him."

"Whose we?"

"The other girls."

"So you knew the other girls?" Craine gestured toward the pictures. "The girls in the other photos?"

Delilah didn't reply, stroking the cigarette pack with her fingernails.

"How did you know the other girls, Miss Desmond? Or do you prefer Deschamps?"

Delilah winced at the mention and opened the pack. "Desmond is my real name," she said, resigned to the approaching questions. A fresh cigarette seemed to calm her nerves. "Deschamps was a name I heard once. I think it was one of my mother's friends. Pretty glamorous, huh? I liked it, so I decided to use it for work."

"Working as what?"

"Why should I be telling you any of this, anyway?"

"I'm only asking what your job is."

She stirred uncomfortably. "You know, it's none of your—"

Delilah flinched as Craine scraped a chair across the floor and took a seat opposite. "It's really a very simple question. We're not after you, here, you're not in trouble—not as yet—but we need to know all the details on this. It's not a matter of you being in these pictures, it's more complicated than that. Three people have died and we think these have something to do with it."

"I didn't do anything."

"What are you? Models? Or prostitutes?" O'Neill asked.

She shot him a look then glanced back at Craine. "If that's what you want to call it."

"That night at the M.G.M. party. You were working?"

She nodded.

"And Florence Lloyd?" asked Craine. "You knew her?"

"I knew her, yeah. But to the clients she was Felicity."

"Felicity? She was a prostitute?"

Delilah's shoulders sagged at the mention of the word. She nodded again.

"So what about the pictures?" O'Neill moved around the kitchen and leaned against the worktop. "Where were the photos taken?"

"Here. Mine were taken here."

"Where?"

"I have a room upstairs."

"Your bedroom?"

"The bedroom is for me, Delilah Deschamps has a room at the end of the corridor. I keep it locked. The photos were taken there by Jimmy. He came round late one evening. Just him."

Delilah swallowed two pills from a brown bottle in her gown. He didn't ask her what they were for.

"What was he like?" Craine said.

Delilah shrugged. "He was always pretty polite, didn't say much. To be honest with you I thought he was a nice enough guy. Although it was a pretty weird setup, I mean with him and Florence."

"He was her boyfriend?"

"I guess so. She said he was. His prick didn't work; some birth defect, she said. Told me she liked that he didn't only want her for sex, you know? But I think he got off watching her with other guys. Anyway, they say he died at that party, but I didn't see him there. He didn't strike me as the type of guy to shoot someone neither."

Craine nodded and sat back in thought. Campbell was the photographer. Lloyd had the means to develop the pictures sub rosa. What about Rochelle? He pondered his next question carefully. "What happened after Campbell took the pictures?" he said, lowering his voice. "He sold them?"

"No, not that I know of. Not the ones he took of us."

"Us?" asked Craine.

"I'm not giving you names."

Craine shuffled his chair closer toward the table. "I'm confused. *Us. We.* You say it like there's a group of you. Like you all know each other personally."

"I only really know Florence and a few others, but the photos of me and the other girls I know of weren't for sale."

"For what, then?"

"For publicity," she said eventually, nursing her elbow in one palm, waving the cigarette in front of her mouth. "Jimmy took the pictures, developed them, gave them to someone else who provided them to clients—"

"Provided for what?"

"I told you, publicity. They use them as—" a pause as she tried to find the right word "—I don't know, like casting photos ... headshots."

Craine and O'Neill shared a look. "Headshots? Like an actress?"

"The clients look at the pictures and it helps them decide who they want. Some guys like blonds, others brunettes, fair, dark, curvy, slim. I told you, they're like publicity photographs."

"Then who are the clients?" Craine persisted.

Delilah looked away, gathering her thoughts for a moment. Behind her the kettle started to whistle and shake on the hob. She looked up at the ceiling then stood up and turned off the gas. "I only let you in here because I didn't want to make a scene. Unless you're actually going to arrest me I suggest you leave."

"You understand we can charge you with pornography, we can charge you with soliciting—"

"Soliciting on what grounds?" she asked sharply. "I haven't told you anything. I know my rights, and if you pull me in I'll deny everything."

"We saw a man leave before we came in here. Do you want us to look him up?"

"We got the license plate," O'Neill added, lying.

Delilah remained standing, tapping her foot on the floor as she considered what to tell them. She poured them all coffee and after a minute or so her expression softened. "I already said no names. You can allow me that."

Craine nodded. "That's fair. Now, what can you tell us?"

Her right hand balled into a fist and she put it behind her back. It took a long pull on her cigarette for her to answer. "They're actors, movie stars, whatever you want to call them."

Craine stole a glance at O'Neill. "You sleep with contract players?"

A shrug.

"For M.G.M.?" O'Neill suggested.

Delilah hesitated. She stubbed the cigarette out in the glass bowl and sat back down. "Not only for M.G.M. Warner's, R.K.O., Paramount."

Craine took a deep breath. "I want to make sure I'm getting all of this right. Campbell took pictures of you and a number of other girls, these pictures were given to studio actors, then they decided which one they wanted to have sex with?"

"Crudely put," she said with a mixture of anger and embarrassment, "but yes, why not?"

Craine looked at O'Neill, who took out the second set of photographs and dropped them onto the table. They watched as Delilah frowned, confused.

"You've seen these before?"

"No, never."

"You recognize Florence?"

"Yeah, that's her."

"She's with someone. Can you tell us who?"

Delilah looked closely at the pictures, taking her time, thumbing through them one by one. "No, it's not clear. I don't even see the second person. It could be anyone."

"What about Herbert Stanley? Was he a client?"

"I wouldn't know."

"You said there was a middleman," O'Neill observed, "someone who provided the photos to the clients. Who was he?"

She ran a hand through her hair and looked at him earnestly. "I never met him."

"Was it Rochelle?"

She shrugged. Craine scrutinized her. He couldn't be sure she was telling the truth.

"I told you," she said defensively, "I never met him. I never heard his name mentioned either. But the other girls at the club said there was somebody and it made sense."

As soon as she'd finished speaking, Delilah closed her eyes. The club. She knew at once she'd given herself away.

"What club?" O'Neill asked before Craine could.

"Say what?"

"You just said the girls at the club," Craine said calmly. "Which club is it you work for?"

"If I tell you, that's it," she said with a look that was meant to engender assertiveness but came across as desperation. Her body shook involuntarily and she went on with a hardness in her voice. "I don't have anything else to tell you. I'm not giving you the names of the other girls, I'm not giving you the names of the clients. I'm not going down to the precinct and you guys were never here—"

Craine held up his hand. "Agreed, Miss Desmond. You have my word. This is as far as we go."

Delilah opened her mouth to speak when there was a gentle thudding from upstairs. Craine followed her eyes as she looked out through the kitchen door, staring at the corridor toward the stairs.

A little girl in a purple nightgown came through the hallway, rubbing the sleep from her eyes. Craine's eyes widened. He looked at O'Neill then back at the small purple figure hovering in the doorway. She couldn't have been more than four years old.

"Hey, sweetie," Delilah shrilled uncomfortably, dashing over to sweep the girl into her arms. "You're up already? How did you sleep? No nightmares, you sleep okay this time?"

The little girl nodded. She stared first at Craine then at O'Neill. It was the look of a girl who wasn't used to seeing strangers in her house. It wasn't the look Craine expected.

"Oh, you don't have to be shy; these nice men are leaving now."

Craine stood and picked up his hat. He smiled awkwardly at the girl before she twisted away and buried her face in her mother's chest. He thought suddenly of Michael. He would probably be waking up right now.

With the girl held tight in her arms, Delilah closed her eyes and pressed a finger and thumb against her eyelids, holding fresh tears in their place. "It's the Lilac Club," she said, her voice tired and strained. "We work for the Lilac Club on Sunset."

"William Wilson's club?" asked O'Neill.

Delilah nodded.

"We'll go," Craine said reassuringly, with a look that told Delilah that she didn't have to worry, she wouldn't be involved, they weren't here to take her away from her daughter.

O'Neill followed Craine as he moved toward the door. "Thanks for the coffee," he said softly. "I'm sorry about what I called you before. This is . . . You have a really nice place here."

"It's just a job," Delilah said once they were in the hallway. "You'd understand if you were in my position. I was fourteen when I got pregnant. I have to provide for her, you see? It's not as simple as going out and working somewhere. There isn't work available, not for a girl like me. I don't have a choice about what I do." For several seconds she lost the thread, momentarily overwhelmed. "She never sees the clients when they come. I'm here when she wakes up; I'm here when she goes to bed. I pick her up from school and I cook for her every night. Sure, question what I do for a living but please don't question my abilities as a mother. I only want the best for her so she doesn't have to grow up to be like me."

CHAPTER 33

Vincent Kinney—Head of Security—walked through the rear entrance of the Lilac Club, down through the basement corridors, past the card rooms and private opium dens until he reached the stairwell. He took the cage elevator up one floor and walked through the main restaurant toward the administrative offices at the back of the building. It was mid-morning but they were already laying the tables ready for tonight's seven o'clock opening. Bing Crosby was due to perform, and several people were busy installing a white piano center stage.

The club manager's driver, Nelson, met him outside the double doors to the kitchen. Kinney kept moving, pushing through the kitchen toward the back offices.

"Is he in?"

"In his office," said Nelson, keeping step. "Are you worried?"

"I'm concerned. I need you and two others. Pick them yourself."

"When for?"

"For tonight."

"I'm not working tonight."

"You are now."

"It's my anniversary," Nelson said, disappointed. "My wife and I had plans."

"Move them. We've had a leak from one of our girls."

The Lilac Club had fifteen contracted escorts and Kinney had personally interviewed every single one of them, using the club's contacts in local police departments and Pinkerton agencies to perform background and credit checks. As Club Manager, Benjamin Carell was keen to hire attractive girls of different ages and appearances to cater to a range of tastes. But an assessment of a girl's erotic capital wasn't really Kinney's concern; he was more interested in finding girls with relatively short criminal histories, stable home lives and no dependence on drugs or alcohol. He refused to consider fame-whores; he dismissed gamblers and junkies, however beautiful, however alluring. Yes, the clients paid for sex appeal, but they also paid for discretion. Most of the club's clients were property tycoons, oilmen, newspaper owners and, of course, rich movie stars. They hired the girls for sex to avoid the common problems they faced with press intrusion, disclosure, blackmail, and infatuation that more often came with sexual relations with a person of their status.

During the five years he had worked for Carell—a relatively long time in any illicit business relationship, particularly when both men were Chicago-born to Italian blood—Kinney had never once made an error. There had been no scandals, no yellow press interest, no police interference. Operations had run smoothly.

Until now.

"Come in," said Carell when Kinney knocked on the door.

Kinney entered and stood in the center of the room. The club manager was seated behind his long desk, as he almost always was, going through the account books for the last financial quarter. Frank Nitti, their Chicago boss, had been upset by recent events and was sending representatives from Chicago to "audit" the club. Unsurprisingly, Carell was anxious that everything be perfect. Like a Shakespearean tragedy, employment contracts in the Outfit were usually terminated through violent means. If the audit went badly, Kinney wasn't expecting his employer to get a pink slip and a handshake.

"We have a problem."

"What?"

"I got a call from one of our girls. She said two detectives were asking about the club. She said they had pictures of other girls."

Carell stopped what he was doing. He paled, as if Kinney had just told him his wife had died. "Christ," he exhaled. "What did she tell them?"

"Nothing. Said they already knew about the club but they were asking questions about Florence Lloyd. Someone's talked. Or someone will."

Carell put down his pen and closed the accounts ledger. He sighed and tapped his fingers against the desk. "Jesus. God dammit," he said, suddenly kicking out against the wall. Kinney had never known his boss to be a patient man. He had a short fuse and a violent temper. He'd seen Carell's wife with a black eye once a few days after she got too drunk and cozy with a jazz singer performing at the club.

"Find Wilson," Carell said firmly, coming to his decision. "If they're onto the club then Wilson's next."

Kinney stepped back and nodded. "Anything else?"

"No. Shut the door on your way out. I need to make some calls."

Craine phoned William Wilson at his main residence but the maid told him, somewhat hesitantly, that Wilson was spending the weekend at the Chateau Marmont.

Modeled on a French mansion of the same name, the Chateau Marmont was the destination of many celebrities around town after a long night of partying on Sunset Boulevard. When he worked studio cases regularly, Craine would receive calls from the hotel on a weekly basis. There was the R.K.O. actor who called his house on a Saturday night when his seventeen-year-old girlfriend started overdosing on heroin. Then the Warner Brothers' producer who got in a brawl with Walt Disney over some actress and Craine had to pay off the uniformed officers not to charge either for assault. Then two years ago, a waitress almost drowned in the swimming pool when one drunk screen siren pushed her in for a joke.

These scenes replayed in his mind as Craine pulled into the hotel's driveway. This was the backbone of my life, thought Craine. How could I bear to be a part of it?

They parked outside the front and showed their badges at reception. A young Mexican concierge who spoke with a light accent led them up to Wilson's room on the fifth floor. Despite asking her not to call up ahead, Craine knew that hotel policy would be to telephone Wilson's room immediately.

They could hear music playing from the corridor of the fifth floor where Wilson was staying. A heavy drumbeat and a clarinet playing somewhere.

The concierge knocked on the door boldly. Three hard knocks that might as well have been a police siren.

O'Neill pulled Craine to one side. "Maybe we should take this to Simms before we go any further. Or higher."

"No higher."

"Why not the District Attorney's office?"

"The Attorney's office isn't as cheap as it used to be but it's still a buyer's market."

"Meaning?"

"They'll cooperate with the highest bidder unless we present our case very carefully."

"You think they'd protect Wilson? And the Lilac Club?"

Craine held up a hand for quiet. The concierge was looking at them.

"Who is it?" Wilson's voice from inside, shouting over a Benny Goodman swing song playing loudly in the background.

All eyes looked back toward the door. "Reception, sir. I'm with two officers from the police department."

Wilson opened the door wearing silk pants and a red smoking jacket emblazoned with his initials. His pupils were dilated and restless, flicking from Craine to O'Neill and back in quick succession. A cigarette between his teeth couldn't disguise the smell of alcohol on his breath. It was 10 A.M. Either he had started early or he was finishing late.

"Craine?" he exclaimed, barely audible over the music. He grinned with recognition and received him with a vibrant handshake. "What a fucking pleasant surprise! Who'd have thought?"

"We need to talk, Billy."

"It's Saturday, for Christ's sake. Don't you ever sleep?"

A joke, of course, not meant to be taken literally. "It's important."

"What's it about? Another *Enquirer* article?"

Craine shook his head. "Relates to an investigation."

Wilson peered out into the hallway and looked up and down the corridor. "Then I suppose you best come in."

They followed Wilson to the center of the room, where two deep couches faced each other, separated by a long, rectangular coffee table. The glass surface was dusted with white powder and Wilson tried his best to cover the marks by tossing a pile of trade newspapers across the table. "Take a seat anywhere you'd like," he said as the music reached its zenith. "The sofa! Sit on the sofa. Not the one on the left, I don't like to face the window."

Craine said, "Can you turn the music down?"

"Can I what? Oh, the music, sure." Wilson swung his hand in O'Neill's direction and whispered conspiratorially. "Who is this, by the way?"

"Detective O'Neill."

Wilson pushed the loose hair from his forehead nervously. "Not a narc, is he?"

"No," said Craine.

"Just curious."

Glancing around the room, Craine took a mental inventory: champagne bottles rolling across the parquet floor; a guimpe shawl on the couch; empty cola bottles lined up in a row; ashtrays filled with smoldering cigarettes scattered around the room.

"You alone?"

"'Course I'm alone. I had friends over last night but they left after drinks and dinner."

They hovered by the sofas as Wilson danced over to a phonograph in the corner and carelessly pulled off the record. He's so high he's almost floating, thought Craine, watching him.

"Look at you, Craine, you look like shit," Wilson slurred, two bloodshot eyes patrolling the empty space between them. "Used to be a real dandy, the debonair investigator." His hand flourished then slapped his leg. "Hilarious! Now take a look at yourself. You look like you can barely stand. Sit down before you fall down. You too, kid."

Wilson returned to the table and took a seat on the couch. "You want to order something?" he said when they were seated opposite. "They try and tell you they don't do room service here but I always get it. Maybe they make an exception for me. What time is it? Is it too early for lobster? Hey, Irish, do you like fish, or shall I see if they can do you some mash potatoes, some boiled spuds, some—"

"We're not eating," Craine said. O'Neill opened a notepad and started scribbling across the first line.

They waited for Wilson to stop laughing. He was sitting upright with his back straight but his arms and head were lurching from side to side as if he were still listening to the music. "Come out with it, then," he said more seriously as he fished through his pockets. "You must have some questions for me if this isn't a social visit." He brought out a monogrammed gold case and lit a cigarette, blowing smoke rings across the table.

"A prostitute died two months ago. It was the same night as Herbert Stanley's suicide. Do you remember it?"

"I remember nothing about a prostitute dying anywhere. I run a trade newspaper, Craine, not a tabloid." Wilson yawned and looked at his wrist in a theatrical display of ignorance.

Craine produced the pictures, first of Florence Lloyd lying provocatively in her bedroom, then the crime scene photographs of her dead body, a shadow of blood and brain matter like a black halo around her head.

Wilson took one look at the pictures and blanched.

"You've seen this picture before, haven't you?"

"I don't know what you're talking about. You're sick, Craine, do you know that? Bringing in photos of some butchery like I'm going to burst into tears and sign my confession. I'm not one of your niggers, you know. I'm not that obtuse. Who do you think I am?"

Craine met Wilson's rolling eyes and tried to hold them still as the smoke drifted between his teeth. He tapped a finger over the glamour shots. "Earlier this morning we spoke to another prostitute who told us she worked with Lloyd at the Lilac Club," he said in his usual sotto voce. "That's one of your clubs, Billy, so I thought you might want to explain a few things to us."

Wilson flicked his eyes down then back up again. His teeth began chattering against each other, his feet dancing on the spot. He knew what was coming.

"I'm afraid I can't help you. What's to explain?"

"Are you involved in a prostitution racket?"

Wilson tried to settle his knee, leaning all his weight against it as if it might spring up at any moment. "Don't be ridiculous."

"We have a girl who claims to work as a prostitute for one of your clubs."

"She's lying."

"Why would she?" said O'Neill. "Who pretends to be a prostitute?"

Wilson twisted on his haunches, bunching his hands together. "I don't own the club anymore."

Craine glanced sideways at O'Neill then back at Wilson. "Then who does?" he said.

"I can't even remember," he said casually. "Some people, out-of-town business types who, you know—" Wilson sprawled back across the couch, leaving the sentence incomplete. For a second it looked like he might be sick over himself.

Craine was losing patience. "I think you're lying. I think you know exactly who it is. And that isn't a problem, because I can get a court warrant and take it straight to your accountant." With men like Wilson, he had to be persuasive without being coercive. He couldn't force Wilson to tell him what he wanted; he needed him to volunteer that information. "Do you really want every payment, every invoice, every transaction you've ever made scrutinized by the attorney's office?" he continued. "With your Nevada project, the Federal Bureau are desperate for an excuse. Don't you think you should make things easier on yourself?"

Wilson began fiddling with his gown, exposing a gray-haired pigeon chest as he loosened the velvet rope around his waist. "I lost some money—the horses, the ships, a few card games," he muttered, fidgeting. "Anyway, I had some debts and I needed the capital for my Las Vegas venture, so I sold the Lilac Club to Frank Nitti and the syndicate." Wilson said, arching forward across the table to flick the ash off his cigarette. "I have de facto control but I'm really only a frontman for the books. The syndicate owns most of it and Carell manages the place. Good riddance, I say. I was bored of it anyway."

O'Neill made notes judiciously. He turned a page then frowned. "The syndicate?"

Wilson waved a hand in the air. Craine had handed him control of the conversation and now he was enjoying himself. "The Chicago Outfit. Frank Nitti and the rest of them."

"Why are they in California?"

"You don't know? You have no idea, do you?" Wilson laughed then cleared his throat. "When Prohibition ended," he went on with surprising alacrity, "the Chicago Outfit had to find new ways to make money because the New York families control most of the rackets. Drugs, liquor, bookie business, it's all taken. This is background, you understand. So Carell and a few others come out to try and make some money out of the studios. He buys my club and fills it with the Hollywood rich and famous. And there's back-room stuff as well—dope and cards and all that kinda thing. You know, I'm surprised you don't know all this already," he added with a glance at Craine. "You're one of them, aren't you? The police lieutenant on the studio payroll."

O'Neill stopped writing and Craine knew he was looking at him.

Ignoring him, Craine said: "None of this explains the girls."

"The girls, the girls, the girls." Wilson repeated the words, rolling them around his mouth. "Ah yes, the girls. Okay, so now the studios and Carell have a relationship, they're starting to scratch each other's backs. At first it's 'Can I get a good table?,' 'Can Bing Crosby play

Friday night?,' 'Can my nephew get a part in your next gangster flick?.' Then Carell starts offering an even better service—"

O'Neill said, "You mean he provided call girls to movie studios?"

Wilson smiled, pointing the cigarette cherry at O'Neill. "Look at chatty over here, he's a regular Sherlock Holmes, isn't he? Careful, Craine, you'll lose him to the Pinkertons. Sorry, Detective, yes, that's exactly what I'm saying. Real pros they are too. All races, all types, all ages, some of them young, still in their teens. They're all beautiful, though, and you need to be born with a celluloid spoon in your mouth, a movie pedigree as long as your arm to get one of them to go home with you." He laughed raucously. "That or a filthy rich newspaper magnate."

"Why would studio players sleep with prostitutes?"

"Why wouldn't they? Think about it, you're a movie star who can have any girl you want—why would you take some sewer girl who's shit in bed, couldn't blow her own nose, and will probably rat to the papers afterward? The Lilac Club isn't like that—it's discreet and the girls are pussy platinum."

"And the studios are okay with that?"

"It's mutually beneficial. Come on, Craine, how many times have you seen some actor get a debutante pregnant, or you got Chaplin or Fairbanks sleeping with an underager and the studios have to pay out for an abortion and keep the family quiet. Carell, he saw a niche in the market. He's solved all of that."

"How many of them are there?"

"The girls? A dozen or so. Less than twenty."

"That's not many."

"Supply and demand. Low supply, high demand. It keeps the prices up."

"How much?"

"Two grand," he confided, leaning forward and engaging them with a wide-eyed stare.

"Two thousand dollars?"

"They have it. That's half a day's work for Cagney, not even. Think of Howard Hughes or any oilman or newspaper owner. High rollers will lose twice that at roulette and think nothing of it. Besides, they can't help themselves. Those photos, they really lure them in. It's like these girls are the stars, does that make sense? But fifteen girls, two thousand a pop, even once a week that's . . ."

"One and a half million dollars." This from O'Neill.

"There he goes again. Exactly. One point five million annually, off the books, tax free."

For a time nobody spoke, then abruptly Wilson said: "All this is pretty crazy, huh? I mean Carell, we get on fine, play cards once in a while; he already told me it's a trial run. This isn't just L.A. This is both coasts. This is blueprints for Las Vegas." Wilson took a drag off a fresh cigarette, punctuating each sentence with a smile, seemingly amused by the whole affair. "Don't you see? Forget drugs or gambling or liquor. His product is human pleasure. And there's so much more money to be made in girls than people think. It's a slave trade, more or less. Genius, really."

Craine's eyes stayed on him intently. He held up the pictures of Lloyd. "Genius? This girl was murdered in her home," he said. "Her boyfriend and Jack Rochelle were dead three nights later. Why, Billy? Why was she killed?"

The question pinned Wilson in place. "That I don't know about."

"Then what do you know?"

"Look, I don't want anything more to do with this. I mean Christ, Carell—he's a businessman first and foremost but—"

"So you're saying Carell was behind the murders?"

"I never said that."

"You might as well have."

Wilson tossed his cigarette case onto the table. After a few seconds' silence he said, "A while back I got a call from a friend of mine that runs another paper."

"Name?"

"No, I'm not gonna give you—"

"Tell us."

"Not a chance. Some yellow rag."

"When was this?"

"This was a few months back."

"When exactly?"

"I can't remember. Easter time. No—later. A month or so before all that shit kicked off at Loew House. Anyway, he tells me this photographer comes to see him with some pictures. Says he's got photos of celebrities with hookers."

O'Neill said, "Who were the celebrities?"

"He didn't say. Movie people, but the photographer never got as far as showing the pictures."

O'Neill turned to Craine, a scenario forming in both their minds. "Could be Stanley. Maybe he slept with Florence Lloyd and the photographs were used against him."

"Hey, it's anybody's guess. It's possible."

"Do you know if the photographer was James Campbell?"

"I never asked and I don't want to know."

"What did your friend do?"

"He told the guy to take a running jump."

Craine and O'Neill looked at him, confused. Wilson explained. "Advertising revenues are down, every paper in town is trying to do more with less. The only people paying for ad space are the studios. God knows I like to wind them up a bit but there's a line. And besides, you're never gonna get in the way of the syndicate."

"Do you think Carell had Campbell killed? And the girl?"

"I don't know. I'm not even going to hazard a guess. That's your job, not mine. Christ, Craine, do you have any idea what is at stake here? With the club and the girls, this is four or five million dollars annually. Don't expect them to file in quietly."

"We'll need you to go on the record."

"There's no way. I'm staying as far away from this as I can. And don't even threaten me with subpoenas because we both know it'll never get that far."

"You're scared of Carell."

Wilson stood and moved toward the door. Their conversation was over. "You bet I am. And so should you be. He'll come for you, you better know that. Doesn't matter who you are. He'll come for you."

Maria Chavez waited at her concierge desk for the two detectives to leave the building. It was common to have police come to the hotel, but something about today's visit bothered her. She'd heard the younger policeman mention the Lilac Club and she knew immediately she should make a phone call.

Chavez lived in Boyle Heights in East Los Angeles, one of the lower-middle-class areas on the bluffs, away from the slums in the Flats. She traveled every day by bus, two hours each way, for half the pay of the white people who worked at the hotel. It was barely enough to make a living. So, for the past six months, Maria had been on the Lilac Club's payroll, seventy dollars a month to keep an eye on the girls who worked at the club. They never mentioned the word prostitute but she knew that the girls who came back with hotel guests were call girls. She understood that times were hard and everyone had to make ends meet however they could. It wasn't her place to judge. Her only job was to call the club when a girl arrived and call again when she left. It was a safety measure for the girls and Maria felt glad she was protecting them.

She picked up the receiver and dialed. Maria heard a female voice on the other end. One of the agents.

"This is the Marmont. I need to speak with Mr. Kinney."

CHAPTER 34

"Stanley slept with Florence Lloyd. Campbell tried to sell the pictures," O'Neill postulated as they drove toward Central Headquarters. "When the papers wouldn't buy them, Campbell tried to blackmail Stanley. Stanley couldn't bear the humiliation and killed himself."

"Possibly. But then who hired the shooter? And what about Rochelle?"

"Carell hired the shooter, maybe on Frank Nitti's order," O'Neill went on. He was less diffident now, a confidence apparent when he spoke. "They wanted Campbell dead for sabotaging their business venture. And Rochelle, maybe he knew too much. He was the one providing pictures to the studio workers, right?"

Craine wasn't convinced. "It's too early to assume anything," he said, aware that he had spent months, years even, walking around slightly blinkered and conscious too that he still might be. There was so much more left to understand.

They were driving down Sunset Boulevard, heading east past the tracts of flat-roofed block-builds as they tried to make their way over to Route 66. The Pacific fog had passed now, replaced with dense city smog that dusted across the windshield. O'Neill flicked on the wipers, smearing dirt in wide arcs across the glass. They were hoping for a short drive onto Route 66 but even Sunset's large, unwieldy roads seemed unusually busy with lunchtime traffic. Young hustlers crowded the streets and sidewalks; a line of grime-gray Fords pulled out from the side streets, the merging traffic and the gathering pedestrians enough to bring the road to a slowpoke crawl.

Ahead of them, a paperboy waved newspapers at a stoplight. Craine called him to the window. "What's all the traffic about?" he asked, paying for a copy of the *Times*. "There been an accident?"

"No, something going on at Grauman's. They closed part of Hollywood Boulevard already."

Then Craine remembered—tonight was the premiere for one of M.G.M.'s films. The first early fans must be already arriving, hoping for a glimpse of the rich and famous on the red carpet. Gale had mentioned it several times. She was going to the after-party tonight. He wondered what she'd say if she knew that he was reinvestigating her husband's death. He hadn't told her what he was up to. Maybe because he knew it would upset her.

Craine instructed O'Neill to take a right down Gower Street then turn onto Route 66 at the Memorial Park. As they did so a set of headlights in the wing mirror caught his lateral vision. He turned back to see a black Pontiac driving about thirty yards behind. He thought he recognized it before a small coupe turned onto the road between them and the Pontiac was lost to the traffic.

They idled at the next intersection before the stoplight gonged and they could turn east, passing R.K.O. and Paramount studios. They went another two blocks before the coupe turned off and Craine spotted the Pontiac again.

"Everything alright? You keep looking behind," asked O'Neill, glancing at him before turning back to the road.

"Keep driving. But hold it under thirty." Craine twisted the rear-view mirror so he could see the Pontiac's headlights behind them. When O'Neill braked, the Pontiac seemed to fall back at the exact same moment. No one drove with such deliberation. Craine squinted but couldn't make out the driver. Was it his imagination, or was this the car he'd seen outside Florence Lloyd's house?

They were building a freeway between downtown and the San Fernando Valley and this part of Hollywood was almost derelict, a hundred-yard expanse of bulldozed desert effectively marking the boundary between West and East Hollywood.

"Take Virgil," Craine said when they'd passed into Little Armenia. "Sunset will be quicker."

Craine was adamant. "Go right at Virgil."

O'Neill flicked on his amber indicators and turned right down Virgil. The Pontiac continued after them, never less than sixty yards behind. For a second, Craine didn't say anything, considering the implications. Should they try and out-chase the car? No, impossible, not in this heap. He unbuttoned his jacket and took out his Browning.

O'Neill looked at him, suddenly worried. "What are you doing?"

"There's a car tailing us."

O'Neill followed his gaze in the wing mirror. "The Pontiac? You sure?"

"I can't be certain. I think it's been following us since Memorial."

"Christ, what do we—"

"You're not going to do anything. Keep going."

O'Neill took a left downhill onto 3rd Street, their chassis swaying as they steered round the sharp-angled bend. Again, the Pontiac followed. Craine felt a tremor of anxiety. He checked the mirror again as they crested the hill but couldn't discern the figure behind the wheel or make out his license plate numbers.

The road leveled out and they continued for another mile, passing St. Vincent's Hospital and a small church hidden behind a row of Italian cypresses. He told O'Neill to increase his speed then looked out for somewhere they could make a sudden turn onto. Before Burlington was a lay-by. He pointed at it and muttered: "Pull over. Right here."

The Plymouth skittered to a halt beside a skinny palm tree. Both men looked around, half-expecting the Pontiac to pull up behind them but it barely slowed down, charging onward. Craine gripped his gun and braced himself as the car drew level. Above the window line he made out a lone man. For the briefest of moments they made eye contact.

Dark red hair and a beard. It was the same man he'd seen on the steps of Headquarters the day after Stanley died, he remembered him now. But who was he?

The Pontiac picked up speed, its headlights tumbling south toward downtown. O'Neill looked at Craine for an explanation but none came.

"Come on, keep going. It was nothing."

"Who was he?"

"I said it was nothing."

O'Neill's eyes were pulsing now. "You think that car was following us?"

"I'm not sure. Maybe."

"But you recognized the driver, didn't you?"

Craine waited until he was sure the car wasn't coming back before answering. "He was there the day you read your statement to the press."

"After Stanley died? Outside the police department?"

"Yeah."

"Should we be worried?"

"If he was going to do anything he would have done it by now."

But a part of Craine knew that wasn't true. Whoever it was that was following them was simply taking their time. He wanted to tell himself that City Hall wouldn't accept a policeman's murder and that Carell would know that. But despite this rationale, a sickish sinking feeling sat in his lower gut with the recognition that at any moment, a black Pontiac could swing out and spray them with machine gun fire. And with what they already knew, it might only be a matter of time.

CHAPTER 35

Benjamin Carell was sitting in the Gold Club Restaurant at the Hollywood Park Racetrack, waiting to hear from Vincent Kinney, his Head of Security. The maître d' had reserved his usual table, a cover for one with a view of the finish line, but he wasn't hungry. He never ate when he was on edge.

Carell heard the starting pistol fire and saw twelve horses career out of their gates and down the long straight that took them to where he was sitting on the first turn of the park's mile-long track. Carell had spotted Louis Mayer downstairs with his wife and Russell Peterson, posing for pictures to drum up publicity for a movie premiere they were holding tonight. Carell was hoping for a quiet word.

Carell saw Kinney arrive like a harbinger of death shortly after he'd finished his cocktail. He approached the table but Carell was already up. He lowered his voice to a whisper. "Not here. Outside."

Carell led his head of security though the restaurant and out onto the balcony so their voices would be lost in the crowd.

"What happened with Wilson?" he said when they were standing alone. Carell could hear the thud of approaching hooves as the horses passed the first lap and the stadium started cheering again.

"It was Craine," said Kinney. "He and another detective—Patrick O'Neill from the homicide department. They went to see him."

Carell was already panicking. "Shit. Who'd you speak to?"

"Concierge. She's on our books."

"Do we know what they wanted?"

"They were asking about the club. But we can't be sure what they know."

"Craine was asking questions before. They know enough."

Carell lit a cigarette and thought about his next move. The events of the previous few months had been frustrating, and Carell knew he hadn't been privy to all the facts. Herbert Stanley's suicide; the loss of one of his best call girls; the shootings at Loew House. None of it seemed to make sense. All of it stirred up trouble, however, and Carell's boss Frank Nitti had expressed displeasure with the attention it had received, even after Carell told him repeatedly that the shootings never came on his order. Now, just as he thought it had all blown over, Craine had returned like Lazarus, intent on ruining everything. Carell wasn't going to stand for it. He considered the Lilac Club his greatest achievement, the product of years of hard work. He wasn't about to let Jonathan Craine take it away from him.

"What are our options?"

"We can wait to see what happens next."

"We do that, it could be too late. Craine takes this to the F.B.I. then it's over for us."

"Or," Kinney continued, "we can deal with Craine now. But killing Craine could be foolish. There'll be repercussions."

"Don't you think I don't know that?"

A waiter approached. "Sir, champagne?"

"No," Carell replied without looking at him.

"Something else? Can I bring you the menu?"

"I said no. Can't you see I'm trying to have a conversation?" Carell was shouting but his voice was barely heard above the crowd. The stress and frustration was too hard to keep to himself. Now finally he had to make a choice. Take his chances and hope that Craine wouldn't pursue it any further, or kill Craine and manage the consequences as best he could. Carell knew that for better or worse, the decision he would make in the next few minutes would change everything.

Another waiter approached. "Sir, champagne?"

"I said I don't want any fucking champagne!" Carell grabbed the waiter by the collar and pushed him away. The tray followed, a bottle of Dom Pérignon and six coupes exploding onto the floor. A table of guests in the club restaurant turned to see what all the commotion was about and Carell gave them a red-faced stare.

Kinney motioned for cool as the waiter quickly got to his feet and ran back inside.

"Calm down, sir."

"Don't you tell me to calm down—don't you ever fucking tell me to calm down. You hear me? Fuck! I need time to think. Jesus." Carell turned in circles, running his hand through his hair. If Craine made a case against him, his business could collapse instantly. But he wasn't alone. Whatever Craine had found involved some of the most senior figures in the state. None of them would want Craine to proceed. But would they really want Craine dead?

"Craine has enough to bring us down, all of us. The feds are already sniffing around. Anything he has they can use against me. We'll be ruined."

Carell was convincing himself of his decision. Craine had to be stopped. But if he was to go ahead with this, he needed the support of City Hall. He had already sent out feelers to his contacts in the Hall of Justice but it wouldn't be enough. He needed to go higher. There were very few men who had the ear of the Mayor's office, the District Attorney and the Chief of Police. Louis Mayer was one of them.

He felt himself hesitate before he said, "I want to talk to M.G.M. I need to know where Mayer stands before we do anything."

CHAPTER 36

"Why?" Simms asked prickly, when they had told them everything they had discovered in the previous few days. They were sitting in Simms' office, the sun squat in the horizon, the Civic Center sitting in a cornsilk glow. During the last twenty minutes, Simms had held back any desire to interrupt either one of them as they outlined what they had found, the conversations they'd had, their theories on the real identity of the Loew House shooter. Simms wasn't prone to petulance and Craine had always known him to be a decent and intelligent man, but still, there was no doubt he would remain protective over the Bureau's reputation. He had listened to their assertions with a scholar's calm; now it was his turn to speak. Craine expected resistance.

O'Neill took the opportunity to answer on behalf of both of them. "We have evidence to suggest that Lloyd, Rochelle and Campbell were all murdered and were part of a much larger illicit trade in prostitution. Isn't that reason enough to relaunch an official investigation?"

"You haven't answered my question," Simms said, raising his head enquiringly. "I asked why. Why would we possibly want to reopen a series of solved murders?" He glanced at Craine, then at O'Neill, waiting for his answer.

Craine's thigh muscles fluttered. He tensed his legs. "New evidence has come to light. Things have changed. Jack Rochelle was killed, right in front of our eyes."

"Yes, and you apprehended a known criminal with a pronounced history of felony and misdemeanor offenses who died resisting arrest.

O'Neill, you were witness to the incident, you saw James Campbell shoot Jack Rochelle at Loew House. Both of you were there—how can you possibly doubt that?"

"It wasn't Campbell. The shooter wasn't Campbell."

"So you keep telling me. How was it not Campbell? The D.M.V. records show that he was driving Campbell's car; Campbell's uncle positively identified his body—"

"We've gone over this. Campbell's body was found by the rail tracks near San Bernardino. His uncle admitted he lied. He was paid to lie."

"By who?"

"We don't know who. But they wanted us to believe the shooter was Campbell."

"And you think Campbell was a victim of the Loew House shooter?"

"Yes."

"And what is your theory?"

"I'm sorry?"

Simms' fingers played with his necktie. It was an eye-drawing brown necktie with a tessellated pattern and it gave Craine a headache. "What is it you propose happened to Stanley, to Lloyd, to Rochelle *and* to Campbell? You're telling me they were involved in illicit activity, and I'm not necessarily disagreeing with you, but they're all dead now and punished enough I'd say, so what good is this information you have? If all you have is another corpse, then all you're doing is tarnishing the Bureau's clearance rate. If you want me to reopen an investigation into four otherwise closed files, I'm going to need reason, I'm going to need motive."

Craine answered for both of them. "Neither one of us believes that the shooter did this on his own. Look at the way they were done: Lloyd, tortured then executed in her bed; Campbell, tortured then his throat cut; Rochelle, shot through the back of the head despite the risks. They were desperate. Rochelle needed to be silenced, and it didn't matter to them that it was a public place. These weren't crimes of passion. They were planned, considered. Our shooter was a professional."

"Then who do you think hired him?"

"We assume it's the Lilac Club."

A small frown formed on Simms' brow. "*Assume.* You think I can grant you a warrant to go into the Lilac Club and roust half the politicians and money men in Los Angeles while they have dinner because you two *assume* that something isn't right?" Simms took a deep breath. There was a pause, much needed, as all of them took a moment to calm down.

"Look," Simms began again, "the Fourth Amendment of our Constitution protects the Lilac Club against unreasonable searches and seizures without probable cause. You two find me evidence to prove why they were killed and we can have another conversation. But until you can give me a motive for the killings, I can't get you a warrant."

Simms waited until Craine and O'Neill had lowered their eyes.

"We're all on the same side here, aren't we?" he concluded tactfully. "And your *assumptions* include a number of people in delicate positions. You understand there's a hierarchy, a carefully constructed house of cards that exists in this city. There's really no need to run around pointing fingers at people. We've created a well-respected Bureau here. City Hall is impressed and pleased. Why go around rocking the boat unnecessarily?"

Craine didn't reply when Simms added, "And you, Craine, I'm surprised at you. You're a company man; don't your Lieutenant bars mean anything to you?"

He could not give him an answer.

There was a soft knock at the door. Simms' secretary entered.

"Lieutenant Craine, there's a call for you."

"I'll take it later."

"I'm afraid it's urgent. It's your son's school. Michael has gone missing."

*   *   *

Guy Bolton

Craine responded to the news that Michael was missing with a grim-faced calm, ignoring the image in his head of Michael's dead body dumped in a gutter somewhere. Father Calloway, embarrassed and apologetic, assured him that he couldn't have gone far and that all necessary steps were being taken to track Michael down. They'd searched the dormitories, the schoolhouse and the classrooms and were now working under the assumption that Michael had left the school premises of his own accord. He had been seen at afternoon Latin and Divinity classes but had not been accounted for at five o'clock chapel. That meant he might have been gone an hour.

Craine instructed Father Calloway to organize a search party. They would split into groups: those who owned automobiles would patrol the roads north and west of the school, while those on foot would head east through the residential side streets. Craine would drive south along Main Street on the off-chance that Michael had taken a bus downtown. Michael knew Broadway relatively well and if he was anywhere away from the vicinity of the school it would be there, he was certain of it.

Craine pulled his car up near Broadway Market and stepped out onto the busy street. If Michael had gone this far, he could be hidden anywhere in the crowd. He pushed through the busy market, spinning around, shouting for his son. He ran from stall to stall, his eyes moving quickly around the marketplace. Panicking, he started shouting louder, weaving through groups of people, reaching out to any child that might be Michael. Mothers pushed him away, pulling their children closer. Other people walked past, ignoring his calls. One or two others stood in doorways and stared at him like he was crazed. No one came to help him.

Craine reached the end of the market square. Michael wasn't anywhere to be found. He tried to ignore his heart's frenzied hammering. The teachers assumed Michael had left of his own volition but there was always the possibility that he had been taken. Craine had spent the past two days asking questions no one wanted answered— he should have realized his investigation might threaten Michael's life as well as his. He'd underestimated how far people might go to keep this buried. Would they use Michael to blackmail him? To force him to drop the investigation? Would they kill him? For a fraction of a second he stood there, pushing the darkest thoughts out of his mind. Then, with numb functionality, Craine walked back through the market, retracing his steps in case he'd missed a doorway or alley somewhere.

When he was convinced that Michael wasn't on Broadway, Craine went back to his car. He had to get back to the school. There was still a chance they'd found him, that he'd be back safe, silently apologetic.

As he stepped down to the curb, a giant billboard framed by light bulbs caught his eye. It was a picture of Greta Garbo, but the motion picture it advertised was old, an early talkie from the beginning of the decade. It was also one of Celia's pictures from the height of her career where she played the second lead. Craine stared at the poster. The film was playing at the Los Angeles Theatre, only two blocks away. There were showings every night, all week.

He knew at once where Michael would be.

Craine went to cross the road but another vehicle pulled out in front of him. The black Pontiac.

He felt a shiver rise up between his shoulder blades as the red-headed man wound down the window. He was only a few feet away and for the first time Craine could really see the details of his face. That scar was more pronounced in close-up, a string of raised pink tissue that curved around his jawline and traveled up beyond his temples. His eyes were both dark, but didn't seem to match.

"You need to be more careful, Craine. You're going to get yourself hurt."

For a brief second Craine expected to see a pistol. Then, before he could even move, the driver put the car in gear and drove away.

*   *   *

For several weeks Michael had been wondering about the possibilities of becoming spiritually closer to his mother. Then, at lunch today, he'd overheard two other boys talking about a picture they'd seen with their parents. *Romance*, it was called. He knew it immediately. It was one of his mother's pictures. He'd listened in for as long as he could without them noticing. One of the boys, David, mentioned that it was an old rerun playing at the Los Angeles Theatre. Michael decided there and then that he had to go there; he had to see his mother.

He left through the school gates before evening chapel, when the teachers were too busy to see him sneak out. He hadn't told anyone where he was going, hadn't said goodbye, but then again he had no one to say goodbye to. He doubted he'd be missed.

He took the Red Car to Broadway, sitting in the rear of the trolley by the window where it was quietest. The trolley passed one stop after another, gathering passengers. Michael stared out of the window at nothing in particular, content to listen in on other people's conversations as he so often did. A woman talked to her husband about the food lines that day. An old man mumbled quietly to himself about nothing in particular as he filled his pipe. Two other boys his age talked about going to *The Wizard of Oz* premiere.

The trolley accelerated toward downtown and the carriage got busier as they approached Broadway and Movie Palace Row.

Getting off at the next stop, he realized the Red Car had dropped him off on the wrong side of the road. Movie Palace Row was the other side, he was sure of it. He went to cross the street but it had been raining intermittently all day and the roads were slick with water. He lost his footing and fell to the ground. A car swerved to miss him as he pushed himself to his feet and ran over to the other side.

Michael took long, deep breaths and tried not to cry. Someone asked him if he was alright but he didn't answer them and walked south down Broadway. The sun was already beginning to set and the sky fell dark under thick rain clouds. He didn't have a watch but he knew that the picture must be starting soon. Where was the picture house? He couldn't see it.

In a sheltered alleyway, two men beckoned him over. They were wearing long coats and large derby hats, their faces bearded and filthy. Ignoring their calls, he kept on down Broadway, looking up at the signs above, desperate for the glowing light bulbs he remembered from the picture house.

A voice called out. It must be the men in the alleyway. He couldn't hear what they were saying, but he knew they were calling for him. He started walking faster, praying they wouldn't come after him. In a moment he heard footsteps behind him. Terrified, he broke into a run, weaving through pedestrians, trying not to slip on the wet concrete.

He reached the curbs when a man grabbed his arm. Instinctively, Michael pulled away. The man grabbed him again, held him tighter and twisted him toward him.

"Michael. Michael, stop. It's me, Michael, it's me."

It was his father. He stared at Michael with fury in his eyes. He took hold of his shoulders, crouched down and pulled his face toward his. Michael had never seen his father so angry before.

"Where have you been?" he shouted. "Where have you been?"

Michael didn't reply. He looked away.

"Look at me. Do you know how many people are out looking for you?" Michael winced as his father gripped him tighter. "Do you understand how worried everyone has been?"

Michael tried to pull himself free but his father gripped him harder and fixed him with a stare. "I'm taking you back," he said, pointing at an unfamiliar sedan at the curbside. "Get in the car."

And then Michael did something he'd wanted to do for a long time. He hit his father. He bunched up his fists and launched them at him, one by one, beating his father's sides until he grabbed his wrists and held him still.

"Stop it. Stop it, Michael."

He let go of his arms and stood up straight. "I'm sorry. I didn't mean to shout. We've been looking for you. Do you realize that? Do you understand? We've been looking all over for you. Please, you need to go back. Get in the car. Please, get in the car, Michael."

Reluctantly, Michael obeyed his father.

Roger Simms had never really considered police work his vocation, but he'd stuck with it and progressed steadily through the middle ranks on tenacity alone. Head of the Detective Bureau was Simms' reward for more than thirty years of service. Besides, what he lacked in investigative ability he more than made up for in political acumen. He knew how the system worked and was savvy enough to recognize that ethics and morals had little place within the department. Justice wasn't an ideal, it was a graph where the thick red line slanted upward.

And yet something about this afternoon's conversations had left him troubled. Until recently, Craine had always strictly adhered to Simms' principles; he was a stickler to protocol. So what had happened to make him revisit the Loew House incident, to question the Florence Lloyd murder and the Stanley suicide?

Simms thought back to that night and the days that followed the murder at Loew House and the Lloyd and Stanley deaths before that. It was inevitable, of course, that the senior ranks wouldn't want such a series of deaths to dominate the headlines for too long, but he couldn't deny that their behavior seemed a little out of place. Chief Davidson seemed genuinely concerned that the news scandals be suppressed; that Craine be brought on board to use his contacts to sway the headlines in M.G.M.'s favor. Then, after the shootings at Loew House, Simms had received urgent phone calls almost daily asking if everything was going smoothly, if the body of the shooter had been identified and duly disposed of, if the newspapers were printing their press releases word for word. Likewise, Craine's promotion had been rushed through, a political maneuver. But with what intention?

Simms was starting to consider whether there might actually be some truth to Craine and O'Neill's tenuous assertions when there was a light tapping at the door. Chief of Police Davidson entered, two hands clasped behind his back.

"Good evening, Simms," Chief Davidson said, that dull monotone voice of his hanging in the air.

Simms shifted in his seat. "Sir."

"Don't get up," Davidson said politely, "I was just passing by and thought I'd show a face. So . . . how is everything?"

"Everything is fine."

"Good to hear it. Thank you for those figures, by the way. Clearance rate looks right on target. First quarter far better than last year, particularly impressive considering recent events."

"Yes, sir, I'm glad you noticed."

"You know, top brass are putting together a steering group to iden-tify action and learning points. I'd like you to come along to our next committee meeting, give us an insight into the fast progress you've made managing the department. Maybe you could help us put together a development agenda for the next quarter."

"Yes, sir. Absolutely."

Davidson smiled and nodded. The Chief of Police was a hulking figure, well over six feet tall, with narrow eyes and broad, toad-like features. "Not a handsome man, nor a charming one," Simms' wife had observed at his inauguration party.

"One other thing. About those recent events," he said, almost as an aside. "That's all done with, isn't it? That's a closed book, so to speak?"

"Yes it is, sir. A closed book."

"It's only because I've had a few phone calls; City Hall is a bit concerned that maybe questions are being asked that don't need to be. One or two of your men—"

Simms blanched. "I've spoken to them," he said quickly, too quickly perhaps. "It's dealt with, sir. Too curious for their own good. Nothing serious. Nothing problematic."

"Great. Swell, as my son would say. Well, I'm sure you have it under control. You know how it is, local elections coming up, don't want to upset the voters, keep those donations coming in."

"I understand, sir."

Davidson's voice became suddenly serious. "But maybe you ought to tighten that leash in future. We don't need any unnecessary worry over this, do we?"

"No, sir," Simms replied, avoiding Davidson's eye.

"Great. Well, I'm glad we're clear. Everything else okay? Your wife . . ."

"She's fine."

"Good, good, glad to hear it. Well, you two must come round for dinner sometime," he added affectionately. "Or maybe golf? You play?"

"A little sir, a little."

"Well, we should, we really should. Nine holes, at least. Weather we've had the past few weeks, we'd be foolish not to. Grab the chance while we can." Davidson pondered for a moment then clicked his heels together and stood at attention. "Carry on, Captain. Don't let me keep you from your work."

When Davidson left, Simms twisted in his chair and watched as the skies opened and heavy rain came down. Maybe he and Davidson would never get their nine holes in after all.

CHAPTER 37

Margaret squeezed her husband's arm with excitement. Their limousine had turned onto Hollywood Boulevard and they could see the crowd of well-wishers outside Grauman's Theatre for the premiere of *The Wizard of Oz*.

The Wizard of Oz had taken a lot out of her husband. A large budget, lots of problems during filming. Once or twice he came home almost in tears. He had aged physically this past year, and she wondered how long realistically he could work the hours he did. It wasn't healthy to dedicate so much time to work, and she hoped now that it was over his life could return to some form of normality. She was starting to resent the studio for taking her husband away from her.

They joined a line of black limousines outside the theater and Margaret felt butterflies rise up in her stomach. It had stopped raining as quickly as it had started and she was quietly thankful. The last thing she needed was the rain ruining her hair.

Margaret felt suddenly self-conscious. She bit her lip. "Do I look okay, Louis?"

"What was that? What are you talking about, you look fine." Louis wiped his forehead with a handkerchief. He was usually a little agitated before premieres but he seemed particularly tetchy tonight and Margaret didn't like it.

"Is everything alright, Louis?"

"Of course it is. Can you let me concentrate a second?"

"Concentrate on what?"

"I need to concentrate on what I'm going to say," Louis snapped. "There's a lot of people here tonight and they'll want me to say something."

Margaret took her arm out of his and shuffled further down the seat.

Her husband sighed and held up two apologetic palms. "Oh, Margaret, don't get upset."

"There was no need to raise your voice."

"I'm sorry, I'm sorry. You look wonderful, did I tell you that? Come on, we're almost here. Are you ready?"

When the car door opened, Margaret was blinded by the flash-bulbs. She shielded her eyes and coughed on the magnesium flash powder drifting through the air. Louis took a gentle hold of her sleeve and guided her toward the press corner.

The theater itself was at the end of the long red carpet. To the right and left, cameramen huddled behind the rope barrier; behind them, there must have been over two thousand people gathered here, all of them screaming, whistling, waving their banners with delight.

"Nice to see you," Mayer said to cheering fans. "Thank you all so much for coming."

More cameras flashed in their direction as Margaret and Louis Mayer began to make their way toward the theater.

"Margaret, Margaret!" She saw one of the photographers raise his camera. "Margaret, smile for the camera. Margaret!"

Margaret's face lit up with excitement before one of the camera-men casually brushed her to one side. She looked back over her shoulder and saw that they weren't talking to her. One of the stars of the film, Margaret Hamilton, had approached the cameras, posing in her Wicked Witch stance. She cackled and the crowd laughed and applauded.

Humiliated, Margaret took her husband's arm. "Please, Louis, can we go inside now? Please?"

"Sure we can, honey, sure we can."

But her husband wasn't really listening, preoccupied with the moment. It was as if Margaret simply wasn't there.

When Craine left the Bureau to go to his son's school, O'Neill headed home. He reheated a plate of meat loaf with buttered beets and mash potatoes and took a seat at the circular table in his kitchen.

O'Neill had learned how to cook from his mother and used to help her make dinner as a child. His father would call him a sissy, tell him he should spend his evenings playing outside with the other boys on the street instead of baking cakes.

Thinking about that, he realized that there were a lot of times his father was hard on him. Unnecessarily so too. He owned his own house. He had a job he was good at. Still no wife, though, O'Neill accepted with an internal sigh. Or a girlfriend. And the only woman I've met since I arrived in Los Angeles that has shown any interest won't answer my phone calls.

He put on a pot of coffee and turned on the radio. A newsreader was reporting from a movie premiere at Grauman's Chinese Theatre. As the announcer segued into a studio recording by Judy Garland, O'Neill's mind started to mull over the events of the last two days. So much had happened since he'd received that call from San Bernardino County that he had barely had a chance to take it all in. Finally he was doing real police work. This was the type of case he'd been waiting for all his life. And despite their differences, he was glad to be working with Craine. He might have an enigmatic quality about him but Craine's skills as a detective were evident in the way he dealt with people—he was a brilliant interrogator, able to persuade people to tell him all their darkest secrets as if he was doing them a favor. Patrick, however, had never been able to manage people very well. His own expertise had lain, and would always lie, in the minutiae of the crime scene.

Considering this, O'Neill cleared the kitchen table. Crickley's film lab had printed copies of the tins of roll film found at Lloyd's basement on eight-by-ten glossies and he took the photographs from his leather work case and placed them on the table beside his coffee cup. There had to be some other clue hidden in these photographs.

There were three rolls of undeveloped film in the tins found in Florence Lloyd's basement and the prints from each of them were now divided accordingly into separate piles. Campbell had used spools of 120 film, each with twelve or thirteen exposures, which meant that the tins contained up to forty photographs in total that he had yet to fully examine.

For most of an hour, he went through the three piles of photographs, ordering the images carefully and slowly. When they looked to be in sequence, he examined the pictures again one by one, pausing whenever anything caught his eye, not wanting to miss any clue, any detail that might prove useful.

The first pictures were of a woman laid back on a bed, partially nude. The woman was Florence Lloyd, Craine had been certain of it. She was undressed but wasn't poised toward the camera. In the following prints, there was a shadow, then the same shadow obscuring the line of sight. In the next photograph, however, there was someone in the bed with Florence. O'Neill looked back through the series of pictures one by one. Florence on the bed alone. A shadow across the room. A figure stepping into the frame. That same figure now in the bed but their face and body almost entirely obscured. Either the cameraman had stopped taking pictures during the previous few moments or there were some pictures missing, pictures that would betray the identity of the man in the room with Florence Lloyd.

The subsequent photographs showed Florence arching back, the figure moving beneath the sheets. Then in the next shot, the sheets fell away and the man's face was just visible through the darkness. O'Neill used a magnifying glass to try and make out the details of his face but the image was grainy and unfocused, as if the camera lens was dirty. It was impossible to make out anything but dark hair and a pale face. Who was he? Was it Campbell or Rochelle? Or Herbert Stanley? Was it someone else entirely?

O'Neill sifted through the remaining photographs but the quality of the images was poor and gave no other indication of the man's identity. Drumming his fingers against the kitchen table, he pushed the pictures away and sat back in silence. He'd found no answers.

Deciding to revisit them in the morning, O'Neill went into the bathroom and turned on the shower. He was starting to undress when the phone began to ring from the kitchen. *Please don't be the Bureau.* He picked up the telephone with one hand and poured himself another cup of coffee with the other.

"Patrick O'Neill," he mumbled.

"Patrick?"

A female voice. And not his mother's.

"Yes . . .?"

"Patrick, it's Gracie."

"Gracie, hi." O'Neill was so taken aback he spun around, his cup catching the doorframe and spilling scalding hot coffee all over himself. *Dammit. Shit.*

"You okay?"

"I'm swell," he winced, trying not to yell from the coffee all over his arm. "I'm . . . great."

He wiped himself down with a dishcloth and ran his arm under the cold tap.

"I'm sorry it's taken me a while to call back. I went to visit my aunt in San Francisco for July Fourth weekend. She wasn't feeling so well so I took a few days off work. My office said you left messages."

"No, that's fine. I called a couple times." Seven, if he was being precise. "Is your aunt okay?"

"She's fine. She acted like she was dying but it was only a bad cold. How are you?"

"I'm great, yeah. Busy, working a lot but otherwise great."

"Great, that's . . . great." They were both saying "great" a lot and worse than that, they were both aware that they were saying "great" a lot.

"Listen," O'Neill began a little more seriously, "I had a really nice time the other week."

"Me too."

"So," said O'Neill, without his usual crippling self-consciousness, "I'd really like to see you again. Would you like to see a picture sometime?"

"I'd like that. Maybe that *Wizard of Oz* picture that's coming out. I loved those books when I was a kid."

"How about sometime in the week?"

"Um . . . I could do Wednesday. Are you free then?"

"Give me one second . . ." Patrick counted to five, searching through his imaginary diary. "Yup. Yeah. Wednesday, I'm free."

"Good, well, do you want to meet somewhere first?"

O'Neill stretched the cord so he could sit down at the table. He slid the photographs away so he could put the telephone down. "How about I pick you up from your office and we go grab something to eat?"

"Okay. You sure you don't mind?"

"No, really I'd like—" But O'Neill never finished his sentence. His fingers were resting on the edge of one of the photographs. With an electrifying realization he saw something in the pictures that he hadn't noticed before. His heart skipped a beat. He stared again at the mysterious face. An idea wormed itself to the front of his mind. He felt the hairs on the back of his neck rise and he shivered with the flicker of promise. They'd made an assumption about the anonymous figure that had led them astray. They hadn't considered all the possibilities. They'd made one simple, unforgivable mistake.

Quite suddenly, like the unravelling of a movie plot, O'Neill knew everything. He knew who was behind all this.

Craine's return to the school with Michael in tow was met with palpable relief from the staff. Father Calloway insisted such an event would never be repeated but Craine didn't want to take any chances. He told Calloway he would take Michael home for the weekend and bring him back first thing on Monday morning.

Driving home, he contemplated the panic he'd felt this evening. He'd allowed his imagination to overindulge itself. He needed to calm down. But there was something else he needed to consider: why Michael had wanted to run away in the first place. Was it simply that he missed his mother and wanted to see her again in some way?

As soon as the front door was open, Michael disappeared down the long corridor toward his bedroom. Still a little uneasy, Craine decided to go round the house, checking the rooms, half-convincing himself he was being ridiculous.

He found Michael sitting on the floor of his bedroom cross-legged with a Bible in his lap. The room was dim, the curtains drawn.

"You can sleep here tonight. I'll take you back tomorrow morning."

The bed was made but otherwise the room was bare. Drawings and pictures had been pulled down from the wall.

"I'm sorry it's such a mess," Craine said, to no response.

Michael's bedroom was a large square with a single bed, a wardrobe and a large clothes chest against one wall. He used to hide in that chest when he and his mother played hide and seek. Celia found him in there once, fast asleep.

"Are you hungry? Do you want to eat something?"

Michael didn't look up. He was pretending to ignore him.

Craine repeated himself and Michael drew his mouth shut, pulling his nose in tightly before giving the slightest shake of his head.

"Listen, I'm sorry, alright? I shouldn't have shouted. I'm not angry with you. I was scared something bad had happened."

Michael faced him and stared at him with glassy, expressionless eyes. They were his mother's eyes and he felt her judging him.

"Brush your teeth before you go to bed. Your old toothbrush and pajamas should be in one of these boxes."

Michael was still staring at him and Craine felt uncomfortable. He knew he was being made to feel guilty. It wasn't necessary. He felt guilty already. I have become my own father, and I hate myself for it.

Craine went back through the hallway and into the pantry looking for something to eat. He wasn't hungry, not really, but he knew the food would allow him to concentrate on the task ahead. Exhaustion always came in ebbs and flows: a light meal would keep him stable for the next few hours.

With great effort he made himself dinner from the bare cupboards he had in the kitchen. A can of soup, a half-loaf of bread with bully beef that the maid must have left. Afterward, Craine put on a pot of coffee and reflected on his meeting with Simms.

It was frustrating, yet not at all surprising, that Simms had refused to request a warrant for the Lilac Club. There was no denying that his rationale was sound. Too many pieces of this puzzle were missing, and questions regarding these mysterious killings would need to be answered before any arrests could be made. If the Lilac Club was indeed behind the murders, what was their motivation for the killings? And Stanley, what role did he play in this?

Craine thought of the Loew House shootings, remembering how Rochelle had asked to speak to him. It was urgent, he'd said. It was important. Craine had been too preoccupied to take his request for help seriously. What was it that he was trying to tell him?

The phone rang, disturbing his thoughts, and Craine answered it on the second ring. It was Gale.

"How are you? I've been calling for hours."

Craine looked over his shoulder to check Michael wasn't in earshot before saying quietly, "I was out. I brought Michael home."

"Is everything okay?"

He decided not to tell her about what had happened. Not now anyway. "Yeah. He's okay. I'm sorry—"

"Don't be. I was only worried about you."

"Are you going to the premiere?"

"I'm only going later. I told Louis and Margaret I'd go to the after-party and I'm starting to regret it. But perhaps I could see you tomorrow? You could come over for an early dinner."

"Sure. I'll call you tomorrow morning."

"I'd like that. Maybe tomorrow you could bring Michael round."

"Yes," he said a little hesitantly.

"Well, think about it, there's no rush. Good night, then, Jonathan. I wish I was there with you."

"So do I," he said with genuine sincerity. "Good night, Gale."

When he put the receiver down, Craine sat back in silence staring at the garden beyond the French doors. He looked at himself in the reflection of the glass and smiled. He was so grateful to have Gale in his life. He should have told her about what they'd discovered but nothing they'd found so far had any tangible connection to Herbert and besides, he didn't want to upset her.

There was the sound of small feet tiptoeing across the floorboards and Michael appeared in the doorway.

"What's wrong? Can't sleep?"

Michael shook his head, stepping further into the living room.

"Take a seat. I'll make you something."

Michael took a seat on the divan and a few minutes later Craine laid out a glass of milk and a bully beef sandwich on the coffee table in front of him.

Michael stared at the sandwich but didn't touch it.

"Will you eat something? Please, I made it for you. You can't starve yourself."

When Michael continued to stare at the plate Craine began to lose his temper. "Is this about the house? Or the summer? Because if it is, I don't know what to do. I don't know whether to stay and I don't know where you should live."

Craine was standing above Michael, his back to the garden. He felt his anger rise then fall in his chest. "I'm sorry," he said, his voice starting to tremble. "Your mother was always better at this stuff than I am. I just want a sign that you're okay."

The two of them remained motionless for what felt like a long time but then Michael leaned forward and picked up the sandwich. He brought it to his mouth and took a small bite followed by a sip of milk.

"Thank you." Craine almost laughed with relief. "I'm a horrible cook. I should bring the maid back but it doesn't seem worth it."

Michael must have been hungry because he ate the sandwich in next to no time, draining the milk afterward like he hadn't been fed properly in weeks. When he was finished, Craine picked up the plate. He was about to go back into the kitchen when he stopped. "It's not the same without her, is it? I miss her. I bet you do too."

Michael looked up and nodded. Craine took a seat opposite him. "I know we've not spoken about it. That's my fault. There are things I should have said. I suppose I've been struggling to . . ." He tried to find the words. "I've found it difficult to talk to you about what happened."

As Craine reached out to touch Michael's shoulder he thought he heard something and stopped perfectly still. From somewhere came the sound of metal scraping. He looked around. No, he was hearing things. Paranoia again.

"I'll get you another glass of milk," he said, turning toward the hallway.

This time Craine saw something in the glass. Movement from outside. There was no doubt about it.

His stomach dropped. Craine grabbed Michael and threw them both to the floor, his chest thudding against the floorboards and the breath knocked out of him.

There was a flash of light from the garden then a thundering as a salvo of machine gun spray took the glass out of the windows and raked the room. For a second there was nothing else but the sheet lightning from outside and the blizzard of noise inside. Craine used his hands to cover Michael's ears. His face was turned away from him but he could feel his frail body shaking as what sounded like a thousand bullets scoured the walls and furniture, the windows and wall lights exploding, glass and metal landing all around them. He felt a sudden warmness and realized Michael had wet himself.

He reached instinctively for his pistol but it wasn't there. Where was it? He tried to be calm and think rationally. The Browning was under the seat in the car. He couldn't defend himself. He had to find somewhere for Michael to hide.

"Stay close to me," he said, lifting his hands ever so slightly and whispering into Michael's ear. "Do exactly what I say."

He waited for the firing to stop then pushed them both to their feet. "Let's go. Quickly, Michael, quickly."

Picking Michael up and carrying him in his arms, Craine scrambled toward the door to the hallway leading to Michael's bedroom. As if responding to his movement, there came the brief chatter of machine gun fire then the sound of someone yelling. "Stop," it said. "Stop firing."

Craine reached the hallway and gathered his breath. Michael's eyes were wide open but he was crying now, snot and tears shiny on his cheeks. Craine pressed his back against the wall, his shoulder beside the doorjamb, the living room now behind him. Pieces of broken mirror against the baseboard gave a partial reflection of the garden outside. Pale smoke like morning fog drifted over the lawn. Then four tall shadows came forward, faces gray and indistinct under low hats and collared coats. They were coming inside. They were coming for them.

CHAPTER 38

Vincent Kinney and three of his men came through the garden and up the terrace toward the French doors, glass blown clear and open to the night.

The living room was empty; they could see it from the lawn but they kept up against the brick wall anyway rather than risk standing out in the open.

Kinney was on edge. The other house hadn't taken long, in and out in a few minutes. His ears were ringing and he was annoyed with himself for missing Craine with a clear line of sight and four of them firing from less than a hundred feet away. He checked his watch: half past eight. On a clear night like this, there's no way the neighbors wouldn't have heard the gunfire. If they'd called the police, they might only have another ten or fifteen minutes. Maybe less; maybe five minutes if a squad car was in the area.

Kinney filled his lungs and turned to Nelson and the two brothers—Anthony and Joseph Gibson. Nelson was the eldest, Anthony and Joseph both younger. They were keen but a little reckless.

"He's gone further inside," Kinney whispered. "We're going in after him. You understand?"

All three nodded.

"Go through the house, check every room you can. Everybody wearing gloves?"

Low grunts. "Yeah," Joseph mumbled.

"Let's go then."

*   *   *

Craine tore down the long corridor leading to the family bedrooms. Michael's bedroom door was open, the lights off. Craine bent down to drop Michael to the floor but he couldn't pry his arms from around his neck. He felt Michael's wet cheeks against his own.

"Let go," he pleaded. "Please, let go."

Michael's feet touched the ground and slowly his arms loosened. Craine pushed the toy boxes aside and slid Michael under the bed.

"Stay under the bed. Stay here and don't make a sound."

Michael shook his head. He was crying. He tried to grab hold of his father's wrists.

"You'll be safe here. Stay under the bed."

Michael shook his head, whining silently.

"Look at me. Look at me. There are men in the house and they're trying to kill us. Do you understand?"

Michael screwed his eyes shut. His body was shaking uncontrollably, his pajamas soaked through with urine.

"Stay here. I'll come back for you. I have to get a gun if I'm going to help us but I need you to stay under the bed and not move a muscle. Can you do that? Can you do that for me?"

Michael nodded but didn't open his eyes. He squeezed his hands over his ears.

Craine checked the hallway was clear before he clambered through the corridors toward the garages, glancing over his shoulder, waiting for the stinging pain in his back, the red mist in front of him that he'd heard about so many times.

He had to get that gun.

Kinney's Thompson carbine, loaded and cocked, led them through the house. He'd seen this gun tear someone almost in half once. Nelson had a trench shotgun, the others Thompson Overstamps with drum magazines. Careful, thought Kinney when they stepped through the living room, broken glass crunching underfoot. Be careful here.

They passed through the living room toward the hallway beyond. Kinney went first, more cautious than the youngsters. It was easy to be fast and careless the first few times. After that you start to figure the situation you're in for what it really is.

They covered each other like he'd taught them, down the dim hallway, each with his own arc. The house was large, with rooms leading onto other rooms and long dark corridors probing out in all directions. There must be two dozen rooms, Kinney estimated, too many for the four of them to cover. Jonathan Craine could be anywhere inside by now.

They reached a broad foyer floored with marble tiles, where the house opened up to three separate corridors. He checked his watch again. They had maybe three more minutes before they needed to get out. He looked at the brothers and pointed his muzzle toward the two corridors leading to the western end of the building. "Split up, one apiece."

He nodded at Nelson to stay with him and the two separated from the others, moving down the wall toward the far end of the house.

Craine's eyes adjusted to the darkness of the garage. After a few moments he could make out the black sedan, the window open just enough that he could reach inside and unlock the driver's door.

He could hear them going through the house, doors opening, kicked off their hinges. There were noises in several rooms at the same time, gunshots rattling from further down the hallway. He prayed they hadn't reached Michael's room.

Guided by the cracks of light spilling from the under the doorway, Craine took the Browning out from under the car seat and held it tight to his chest. He checked for the magazine clip. *Gone.* He scrambled around in the dark for the clip, his fingers searching around under the driver's seat.

The sounds were getting louder. He could hear the footsteps approaching down the corridor. Whoever it was couldn't have been any more than twenty or so feet away. He reached further into the darkness of the car, his shirt fluttering at his chest. He wondered if he'd even feel it if he got shot; would it be the muzzle flash, then blackness? Whiteness, maybe; gates and angels he'd never really thought of or believed in.

Two dark shadows under the doorframe. They were at the door now, probably listening like he was. *Where was that goddamn clip?*

At last Craine felt metal under the car seat. He pulled the magazine out and pushed his index finger against the top to check the rounds were front-facing. Satisfied, he thrust the clip into the butt and racked back the slide. Then, in the same movement, Craine threw himself onto his stomach, pressed his thumb on the hammer and pulled it back until he heard it click twice.

The knob turned; the door opened; an inward rush of light through the darkness.

Craine's eyes caught another's in the doorway. Both raised weapons. He didn't have time to think but he had a brief recognition that sooner or later he was going to die.

Strobes of muzzle flash intermittently lit up the room. A deafening noise and the crack and puncture of a hail of bullets shredding through the body of the car between them. Craine held his arm out straight, pointing the Browning toward the square of light. He squeezed the trigger and clenched his jaw tight against the noise. The gun roared. Empty cases clinked as they hit the concrete and rolled across the floor. He kept firing until he heard a high-pitched keening from the doorway and the man fell back into the light of the hall. He saw the muzzle trailing upward, the gun flashing and more bullets tearing up through the ceiling before the machine gun fell from his hand and clattered to the floor.

At last there was a shrill silence. Bitter cordite hung in the air. Craine's ears were humming so loud he couldn't be sure he'd even heard the scream. Then, from somewhere deeper in the house, the living room maybe, he heard the telephone begin to ring. Regular, urgent, like the sound of a final countdown to God only knows what.

He frisked himself for wounds. I'm okay, he thought, no bleeding. Now get up. He lifted onto one knee, holding the Browning with two hands to keep it level. Christ, it felt heavy, like gravity trying to pull it clean out of his hands.

Unnerved and desperately afraid, Craine turned into the light of the corridor. The floor was slick with blood. There was a short blood smear sweeping from the floor to the wall where a man in a long gabardine coat lay propped up with his hands limp in his lap. The wound was small and round in his chest but a steady freshet of blood ran down his front and pooled all around him. He wasn't moving. His jaw was relaxed, eyes glazed over. He might have been dead but there was no easy way of being sure. Craine kicked the machine gun away, leaned down and put his ear to the man's mouth. Ragged breaths, shallow but still there. He could hear a sucking sound between his ribs. He wasn't dead yet but it wouldn't take long, he knew that much.

Craine straightened and pointed his pistol down the corridor. His hearing was coming back now, tinnitus passing, the whining replaced by a gentle hum. From the other end of the house he could hear the sound of glass under feet, angry whispers and heated accusations. There still were others somewhere in the house. He stepped back and stood there, panting heavily. He had to get to Michael before they did.

Michael lay very still. From where he was he couldn't see anything, but he could hear the gunfire echoing through the house. There were sounds of footsteps getting nearer but then they faded away. A few seconds passed and he could hear nothing but a throbbing in his ears and, from far off, the telephone ringing.

He tried his best not to make a sound but his pajamas were wet and he was shivering with cold. He pulled his knees against his chest to keep himself warm and tried to stop his body from trembling. He had no idea who these men were in his house but he knew that they would kill him. He was alone, abandoned. His father didn't care about him: he had left him to die. He wished his mother was here and started to cry. He bit his lip so he wouldn't make a sound and pushed his ear toward the direction of the door.

Nothing but the drill of the phone ringing.

Most of a minute passed. The voices trailed off. There was shooting further down the hallway, maybe coming from the bathroom or the maid's room. The voices were quieter now, almost distant, and he couldn't make out what they were saying.

Then, from the hallway: the sound of footsteps.

Kinney checked his watch one last time. There was no way the police weren't on their way. Whether they found him or not, they had to get out of here.

Nelson passed him as they moved quickly through the corridor. God knows what awaited them through each of the doors further down the hall. Kinney remained apprehensive. One or two of the lights were on in the hallway and he felt vulnerable. They should have cut the power in the first place. Too late now.

They passed an open door to a bathroom. Nelson swung into the doorway and sprayed the room with automatic fire. Empty. Down the corridor now, the room at the end. The door was closed. He had to be inside. Kinney turned the doorknob, swinging the door open with a light push as Nelson covered. A study. Kinney opened up, firing toward the desk, firing another long burst at the dresser along one wall. Nelson started firing right beside him and he thought for a second his eardrum had burst.

Craine wasn't here. Either he'd got outside or one of the brothers must have found him.

"Go find the others. We have to go."

But as Nelson ran back through the house, Kinney's flashlight probed against another door.

He walked over to the jamb and stood listening. Then he swung round with the carbine in his shoulder and kicked open the door.

A bedroom. A child's bedroom.

Craine moved further inside the house, both eyes open, gun out front in one hand, the other feeling for the wall to keep him upright. Was the floor moving? His legs felt unsteady, the room swaying like a hull in a storm. His feet followed the direction of the pistol, his finger touching the trigger.

He kept walking, concentrating on the space ahead as he approached the corridor that led back toward Michael's bedroom. Covering the hallway, breath sharp and deep, chest swelling, almost lifting him off the floor. He was moving faster now, legs pumping, gaining speed. Don't make a goddamn sound.

Crouched in his hiding place, Michael held his breath and tried not to move. The door creaked open and booted feet stepped into the center of the room. He could hear the man breathing. He might have been only two or three feet away.

He heard shouting. Not from this room; somewhere else in the house.

"Let's go," it screamed. "We have to go!"

The boots stepped back toward the doorway. Michael let out a small sigh of relief but then the footsteps stopped. For what seemed like a long time there was silence before the room suddenly erupted into gunfire, like fireworks going off by his ears. Michael fought the urge to scream. He bit his lip so hard he could taste blood in his mouth. The firing stopped as quickly as it had started and he could smell smoke in the air. The shouting was louder in the corridor but the man wasn't moving. He wasn't finished here.

Michael knew he was next.

He thought of his mother as the gun roared for the last time.

*   *   *

Craine was too late. He had heard the firing from further down the corridor and knew that they had found Michael. When he reached the bedroom door, he heard an ignition turn from somewhere outside, an engine cough to life then the squeal of rubber tires. Were they leaving? He stood there with his gun outstretched, ears pricked for the sound of anything but that goddamn telephone ringing. Nothing.

He stood in the doorway of the bedroom. Under his feet, the carpet was covered in muddy footprints. The windows were shattered, great panes of glass twisting the moonlight across the wall. He felt the cool breeze from the cityscape, smelt the lingering odor of gunfire.

When he was sure that they were gone, Craine turned on the bedroom light.

The bedroom had been raked with machine gun fire, the closet mottled with a line of small holes and the small bed bullet-ridden, feathers scattered across the carpet. He turned away and took another deep breath. He couldn't bring himself to see the body. He should never have left Michael alone. He should never have left him under the bed, knowing that they would kill him if they found him. *Celia put him in my care. I've failed her.*

Craine dropped the pistol onto the floor and his body started to shake. He let out a desperate moan he didn't know was in him.

There was a sound, and for a fraction of a second he thought they were still in the house. Then, from the corner of his eye he saw the lid of the clothes chest open. Two small eyes met his. Craine saw his son crouching inside the box chest and might have cried.

If Craine had ever hugged his son before then he couldn't remember it. But he embraced Michael now, grabbed him and held him so close that he wasn't sure he would ever let him go.

And still the phone was ringing.

CHAPTER 39

There were six cars in the driveway when he got there, most of them patrol cars, two of them from the Bureau. Craine recognized Simms' sedan immediately.

Craine and Michael were in a patrol car, sat in the back behind the two officers who'd arrived at his house barely a minute after he'd put the phone down. It was Simms who had been calling him and Simms who met him as they pulled up behind his Cord.

"Stay in the car, Michael."

Michael grabbed hold of his father and let out a soft noise that might have been a whimper. He had crawled into the box chest not long after his father had left the room. He felt safer inside it and knew he could fit, never knowing it was what saved his life.

"Please, I need you to stay in the car. These men will take care of you."

The boy started crying. He was holding his father's hand now, gripping it tight. Maybe he knew how close he came to dying tonight. Craine still couldn't believe he was alive.

"Michael, it's okay. It's okay, Michael, I'm only going inside the house. I'll be a few minutes, that's all, I promise. I'll be right back. These men will stay with you the whole time. I need to go inside, and then we're going to find you somewhere you can be safe. Look at me, Michael. I won't let anyone hurt you. I promise you. I promise."

Gently pulling himself from Michael's grasp, Craine looked at one of the officers as he stepped out onto the driveway. It was the uniform officer he'd seen at Florence Lloyd's house months ago—Officer

Becker. "Stay with him, Becker," he said with a desperation in his voice only parents understand, "I mean it. I want both of you with him at all times. You know what these men are capable of."

"Yes, Detective," said Becker sincerely. "I won't let him out of my sight."

Simms was informally dressed, wearing an open collar and brown slacks. Even without his suit he maintained a stoical authority, his face impenetrable. "He's passed, Jonathan, he's dead."

"You're sure? Have you called a doctor?" This when they'd made it to the door of the house, a white plywood with a ten-foot lawn that had been sold on the back of a white-picket dream.

"He's been and gone but there was never any doubt. You should know, it's not . . . it doesn't look good. Worse maybe than how it really was. It would have been pretty quick; we can't say he suffered long. We think they came in through the back door, found him in the bathroom."

Craine sighed inwardly. He could barely believe it. "What happened?"

"We got a call from the neighbors, maybe an hour ago. They reported gunfire, said they saw a car outside but didn't see any faces or get any plates. Three uniforms arrived first. No one logged who it was until Henson got here. I called you as soon as I heard, sent the two cars over."

In the corridor, Detective Henson and half a dozen uniformed men were gathered round an open door in solemn silence, photographers clearing space, taking pictures, paying fretting attention to their work. One of the uniforms had a pair of glasses between two fingers and he dropped them carefully into a manila envelope.

They stood back and stared at Craine when he came down the hallway and pushed through to the bathroom. They were standing very straight, with their arms by their sides, hats tucked under their arms. Their eyes followed him, waiting to see his reaction so they could follow suit.

Craine stopped dead in the doorway. What he saw in that bathroom, what he stared at when his eyes refused to look away, stole the breath from his chest.

Patrick O'Neill was lying sideways in the bathtub, naked and pale, his legs twisted unnaturally, his head tilted up to the ceiling in redundant prayer. His face was untouched, his arms and knees as polished and childlike as they'd always been. But his chest was no more, peppered so many times there were no bullet holes, only a gaping wound that rived across most of his torso and left his organs open and exposed.

The room smelt foul, gastric acid and excrement seeping from his abdomen. Someone had turned the tap off but the tub was filled to the top with crimson-stained water, the floor slick and brown where the bath had overflowed. Above his head, chipped and broken tiles showed the extent of the gunfire. He took a margin of comfort in knowing O'Neill likely died even before his knees had buckled but the margin was narrow and he couldn't pretend otherwise. *I never had a chance to truly know him, but he had his whole life ahead of him. He deserved so much better than dying naked and alone, butchered in his bathtub.*

A photographer came and stood beside him and the room momentarily lit up as the flashbulb popped. It was Crickley. His arms were shaking and his eyes were bloodshot but he was going about his work like it was any other day. Craine didn't know how he could stand it. In all the time he'd been a police detective, nothing he'd seen could have prepared him for this. It didn't resemble a crime scene. There was no part of him that could pretend it was a stranger in that tub, someone he didn't know or care about. It was Patrick O'Neill. The boy who wore tweed suits and glasses and wanted justice for victims he'd never really known.

"I'm sorry," said Detective Henson, entering the bathroom and standing next to the photographer. "I liked him. He was a good kid. Did you know him well?"

He wanted to tell Henson that O'Neill had, in only a brief time, made more of an impact on his life than any police officer he'd ever worked with, but instead all he could manage was to whisper, "No, I didn't know him well."

When Crickley and Henson left the room, Craine stepped forward and peered at O'Neill's face. He looked into those gentle eyes, so afraid and helpless, the boy who would have looked away when the door opened and the men with shotguns and submachine guns cut him open from hip to hip. He considered the tenacity that had lived in those eyes and realized he had none of it. He might not be able to go any further without him.

He took one last look at O'Neill then left the bathroom and let the men of the homicide unit close the crime scene.

Back in the hallway, Craine made his way slowly toward the front door, taking in the pictures and furniture that made up O'Neill's life. It was a simple house, but a home nonetheless. Despite the booted footprints and broken glass, he could tell that the place was decorated with care and consideration. It wasn't just the radio, the hung paintings, the furniture. It was the personal touches: the newly painted doorframes; the curtains; the personal trinkets that Craine had completely removed from his own house.

There was a picture on the floor that had fallen off the dresser. Craine picked it up and looked at it. It was a photograph of a man in his fifties with a row of medals emblazoned across his chest. Although he was larger and more handsome than Patrick, the similarity was undeniable. The man in the photograph was Patrick O'Neill's father, the hero cop from San Francisco. What was it O'Neill had said in the car last night? That every child wants to be like their father.

Simms was standing behind him now. He reached out and patted his shoulder.

"Are you okay?" he said, quiet and assured. "Are you okay, Craine?"

Wearily, Craine met his eyes. "What?"

"I said, are you alright?"

He stared at Simms' face, wondering what could possibly be alright. A few deep breaths and a clenched-jaw calm took over him. No, he couldn't begrudge Simms his phatic gesture. What else was there to say? Patrick O'Neill was no longer. Gray and wasted and gone but he, at least, was alive. That had to be enough.

"I'm fine. I just need some air."

Outside, he stood by O'Neill's Plymouth, the fender bent and the paint chipped. He could hear the men working the rooms inside the house, talking noisily among themselves as they tried to clear the crime scene.

"I'll call his mother," Simms said, lighting a cigarette. "She lives up in San Francisco."

"I know."

Simms nodded toward the line of police cars on the curb. "I heard what happened at your house. Your boy okay?"

"Yes. He is. Thank you for asking."

With his back to the house, Craine could see Michael sitting in the rear of the police car with Officer Becker. He felt better for being out in the open air. Being inside came with a sick feeling. Not from the smell or the gore, which he was used to. Not with grief, although he would miss O'Neill. But sick with the thought of finding Michael the same way as O'Neill. Bloody and gutted by strangers, his tiny body left in pieces like a broken doll. It didn't matter that they hadn't spoken to each other properly for six months. It didn't matter that when he looked at Michael he saw Celia. All that mattered was that Michael was the only real family he had.

As he tried to remove the images of O'Neill from his mind, Craine's aching head filled instead with long lists of questions, reeling out like a ticker tape machine. How had they found them? Who were they? Who sent them? What did they want from them? He focused on the last question, and the images of Campbell's photographs started to burn in his retinas. He considered them now, turning them over in his mind as he began to think more clearly.

"Did you find the pictures?"

Simms shook his head. "They're not here."

"You're sure?"

"The uniforms checked."

"Check again."

"They're gone, Craine. They must have took them."

Craine regained his focus, moved away from the house and walked toward the line of police cars.

"We took the man in your house to the hospital." Simms was already coming down the driveway after him. "He's still alive; they've stabilized him and they're prepping him for surgery as we speak. He survives, and we may well have ourselves a court witness."

"Do we know who he is?"

"Not yet but we're working on it. We should have an answer in the next few hours. Craine, there's something else you should know. Billy Wilson's in hospital. He's critical. Looks like he fell from a fifth-floor window."

"He was pushed?"

"We don't know that for certain."

Craine opened the door to the police car and looked down at Michael. He was still shaking like a leaf. "There are some things I need to do. I can't take you with me."

Michael shook his head. He started to whimper and cry again and Craine reached inside and held him by the shoulders. It hurt to see him like this.

"The men who came to kill us . . . I need to find them. I need to find them so that they can't do it again. So that we're safe. Do you understand?"

Michael was drawing in deep breaths. His eyes were red raw from crying.

"These officers will protect you. This is Officer Becker, he's going to stay with you, take you to a place you'll be safe. I trust him. I know you'll be safe with them, okay?" His son's tiny shoulders were shaking. Craine had to pry his fingers off his arms. "Michael, look at me," he said. "Look at me. I'll come back for you. There are things I need to do tonight but I'll come back for you, I promise."

Before Michael's sobs could make him change his mind, Craine closed the door and walked toward one of the unmarked police cars parked in front.

Simms was still with him. "Where are you going?"

"I need to know who did this," he said, sitting in the driver's seat and pulling the door closed.

Simms was by the driver's window now. "Please, Craine, where are you going?"

Craine twisted his head to see Michael still sitting in the back of the police car behind, staring straight ahead. "I want someone to take care of Michael. I want him protected at all times. Don't let him out of your sight."

"Craine, wait. You can't go, we need you here—"

But Craine wasn't listening. The keys were in the ignition and the engine turned the first time. Ignoring Simms' calls, he pulled out and accelerated toward the hills.

He felt suddenly alone again.

It was after ten o'clock when Craine arrived at the hospital. The waiting room was almost empty of patients; only a few drunks and hobos dared sit among the gaggle of police officers minding the first floor.

He nodded to blue-topped uniformed officers as he passed reception. A nurse caught sight of him and frowned.

"Sir, you can't go down there. Sir, where are you going?"

Craine didn't answer, holding out his tin police insignia as he angled toward the self-service elevators with a resolute stride. A doctor tried to stop him.

"Can I help you, Detective?"

"Where is the gunshot victim brought in an hour ago?"

"By the police? He's stabilized. He's going into surgery any second."

"He's alive?"

"He's in a pretty bad way but yes, he's alive. The bullet passed through below his ribs. Missed his spine. Ruptured his lower left lung but he's stable now."

The doctor held the door open as Craine stepped inside the elevator. "It's crucial he's not disturbed during his recovery period."

"Move out of the way, Doctor. What floor?"

"He's not ready for visitors."

"What floor?"

The doctor sighed. "I don't care who you are, I'm calling security."

Craine grabbed the doctor by his collar and wheeled him against the elevator wall.

"I won't ask you again."

"The third floor," he gasped before Craine pushed him into the foyer and the doors slid shut.

When the elevator doors opened, Craine stepped out into a hallway lit by long fluorescent bulbs. He followed signs past a nurse's station. He saw one of them nervously pick up the phone as he swung through the double doors into the surgical ward.

The shooter looked to have his own private room, two uniformed officers standing tall outside the door.

"Has he woken up yet?"

"He's conscious," one of the officers said.

"I need five minutes with him," Craine muttered and they stepped aside.

There was a figure in the bed with his eyes closed, his arms handcuffed to the metal bars on the bedrails either side of him. Glass bottles of saline hung above him on I.V. poles and a central venous line ran down into his neck.

The man sat bolt upright when he saw Craine walking in but there was little he could do. He tried to hold up his hands in self-defense but his wrists were cuffed tightly to the bed. Craine wrapped one palm over the man's mouth and swung his fist into the side of his neck. There was a muffled scream but not loud enough to be heard from outside. Craine hit him again. He'd never been a violent man, never had much of a temper on him but the thought of this man in his house, the thought of how close Michael came to being killed, had let loose something deep inside him.

Craine leaned in, whispering into his ear.

"Can you hear me? Nod if you can understand me. Nod!"

A nod as the man gasped for breath, taking stock.

"Then who sent you?"

The slightest hesitation and Craine pushed his thumb into the man's ribs. A brief, hog-like squeal followed before he pressed the palm of his free hand tighter around his mouth.

"You work for the Lilac Club?"

His head tilted downward.

"Who sent you?"

Two bloodshot eyes looked away. Craine could hear the man's shallow, uneven breaths but his chest was barely rising. He took his hand away from his mouth and moved it toward the bandaged chest.

"Wait, please," he coughed through tears. "I was with Kinney."

"Kinney? The security head?"

"Yes, Kinney."

He looked into the man's eyes and the man looked away. "Why?"

There was a noise from outside before he could get his answer. Through the glass door he could see the doctor from downstairs arguing with the uniformed officers. Craine grabbed a chair from the corner and jammed it under the doorknob.

"Why?" he said, returning to the bedside.

"I don't know."

"I don't believe you."

The man spat blood on himself. He coughed loudly, gasping for air. "We had to. We were ordered to."

The doorknob was rattling now. The argument outside had intensified. The doctor was trying to get in. Craine had only a few seconds remaining.

"By who? Carell?"

A shake of the head. "He gave the order. But someone else instructed him to."

"Who? Someone higher? Frank Nitti?"

"No, a client."

"Who?"

"If I tell you, they'll kill me."

"If you don't tell me, I'll kill you. Now who was it?"

Craine held his bloodied palm up for the man to see before lowering it toward his rib cage.

"He works for the movie studios," the man blurted out.

"You know his name?"

A long pause. "Yes," he said at last through labored breaths. "I know his name."

The Wicked Witch was dead.

For over half an hour, the audience in Grauman's Chinese Theatre laughed and cheered at the picture that almost cost Louis Mayer his career. For a few minutes, the head of Metro-Goldwyn-Mayer had even allowed himself to enjoy the movie with them, jeering when Toto was snatched away from Dorothy by her irascible neighbor Miss Gulch, crying during "Over the Rainbow," applauding with the audience when Dorothy skipped down the yellow brick road with the Munchkins in tow.

People often asked Louis Mayer what the secret to a great picture was. Not a good one, a great picture. Was it lightning in a bottle, or was it a list of tried-and-tested ingredients that allowed M.G.M. to produce critical and commercial hits, time after time? The truth was that it was somewhere in between. You could throw all the money in the world at a producer and he wouldn't make a picture worth a dime. You could hire writer after writer to tighten the script line by line, you could hire the best directors, the most popular actors and actresses—but as much as it pained him, there was no recipe for a hit movie. Not until Dorothy walked through that sepia door into Munchkinland and Mayer could see the faces of the children in the audience light up did he know he had something special on his hands. The hard work had paid off. They'd created something beautiful.

But now, as Dorothy and the Scarecrow sang "If I Only Had A Brain," something else caught Mayer's eye.

Whitey Hendry, almost shapeless in the half-light, appeared

through one of the double doors at the rear of the theater and began whispering urgently to a member of his security detail. From his booth in the wings, Mayer saw the security guard point up toward the balcony.

Mayer shifted in his seat. Something had happened.

"What's wrong, Louis?" Margaret whispered, resting her hand on his.

"Nothing's wrong," he said, standing up.

"You need the bathroom?"

"I have to go talk to Hendry for a second."

Margaret glared at him with disbelief. "Now?"

"Something's come up."

"But it's the premiere," she hissed. "Louis—"

"Please, Margaret, don't yell at me. Not now. I'll be back before you know it."

He met Hendry coming up the stairs toward the wings.

"What is it?" Mayer asked, knowing that something terrible had happened.

"We got word from one of our police informants about twenty minutes ago. Jonathan Craine has been involved in a shoot-out."

The words sent Mayer reeling. "What are you talking about? Where?"

"Carell's men tried to take him at his house. They killed another detective too. Patrick O'Neill."

"The kid?" Mayer said, glaring at him with disbelief.

His silence told him that Hendry couldn't believe it himself. When Hendry nodded, Mayer bowed his head and pinched the flesh at the bridge of his nose. He'd always been wary of associating too closely with Benjamin Carell. Even when he agreed to Carell approaching his contract stars for his escort service, Mayer had been under no illusions about how dangerous he was. But this? Killing police officers? Carell had promised him, sworn to him in fact, that he'd had no part in the Loew House shootings. He'd convinced Mayer that someone else was behind Rochelle's murder and that he'd had absolutely no part in Herbert Stanley's death. So why would he choose now to go after Jonathan Craine?

"Why?" he stammered. "What did they want from them?"

"Carell wouldn't say."

"You've spoken to him?"

"I called him ten minutes ago. He thought we knew. That it was what we wanted. He was trying to protect our agreement. Sir, were you not aware of any of this?"

"Absolutely not."

Mayer stood back and contemplated for a second the sheer scale of these implications. M.G.M. was now involved in the brutal slaying of a police officer. There was blood on his hands, enough blood to drown in. How had he been so foolish as to not see what was happening?

"Sir, he said the order to kill Craine came from us."

"Bullshit, I did no such thing."

But as he spoke, the final pieces of the puzzle slipped into place. He knew of only one person Carell would take orders from on behalf of M.G.M. A person close enough to him to manipulate his every decision. Familiarity had confused things; it had blinded him to the truth. But finally the illusion had dropped. Gone were the questions, the suspicions, the hazy theories behind Herbert Stanley's death two months ago. The answer had been greeting him every morning for the past seven years.

"Sir, Carell believed he was acting on our approval. He told me who the order came from . . ."

"Yes—"

And when Hendry continued, Mayer mouthed the words with him.

"The order came from Russell Peterson."

CHAPTER 40

Russell Peterson lived in a suite on the ninth floor of the Sunset Tower apartment building, the tower block at the peak of Sunset Boulevard. It was a distinguished address even in motion picture circles. Its concrete facade was decorated with chevron motifs and its faceted glass windows offered a view of the city matched only by City Hall.

It was pitch-black outside when Craine walked through the lobby. As he took the self-service elevator up to the ninth floor, he felt the comforting surge of blood through his chest and extremities. Tiredness had given way to a feverish clarity of mind. He was thinking clearly, perhaps for the first time.

He had visited Peterson's suite so many times for casual drinks parties and studio-sponsored charity galas that he felt now as if he was trespassing on home ground. To arrest Peterson was to bite the hand that had dutifully fed him for a quarter of his life. He owed everything he had to the motion picture industry; was he so willing to tear all that apart? He was beginning to understand that his life was changing, going forward with or without him, and he couldn't go back.

When the elevator doors opened, a wide, lamplit corridor stretched in front of him, three doors on either side. There was no one here, no sound of movement, not a whisper in the air. Craine took out his Browning and chambered a round.

Walking briskly down the hall with the pistol beside his right leg, Craine could see that the walnut door to Peterson's suite was ajar; his fingers tingled with anticipation as he pushed the door open.

Craine stepped in and took in his surroundings. He was standing in Peterson's living room. A closed doorway to his right led onto the kitchen and bedrooms. In front of him, half-drawn curtains framed a view of Sunset Boulevard advancing west toward the San Pedro Harbor. All the furniture was intact. Nothing seemed out of the ordinary.

There came a familiar voice. "He's gone."

It was Mayer, slumped behind a green leather desk in a pool of uneven shade as if he'd been waiting for him to enter. If he was surprised, Craine didn't show it.

"When?"

Mayer looked at him despondently. Gone were the vaunted speeches and wide-grinned confidence. He was wearing a long over-coat but his tuxedo was visible underneath; he looked unusually disarranged, his hair damp and tousled, his high forehead flushed.

"Lobby attendant said he didn't come back tonight," he said, speaking swiftly. "Didn't say goodbye, gave no indication where he was going, but we think he's got a flight or a train · ticket booked somewhere."

Craine digested this. He couldn't believe it himself. Was it Peterson in the photographs, or was he protecting someone else? And if it was him, was he so desperate to protect his reputation? He took his time to answer.

"Then why are you here?"

Mayer shifted in his seat. "The same reason you are. A few hours ago Peterson ordered you dead. He told Carell it was on my request. When Carell figures it wasn't—"

"Why? Why did Peterson want me dead?"

"That I don't know." Mayer's head gave the slightest twitch. He wiped his brow with a handkerchief hidden in his palm. "I want you to appreciate that I had nothing to do with what happened tonight. Carell's men were sent on Peterson's demand, not mine."

"Does it ease your conscience at all, saying that? They came into my house. Did you know that? My son is lucky to be alive. They murdered a police detective." As Craine spoke his voice grew louder until he was almost shouting across the living room. "O'Neill was cut in two with shotguns and for what?"

Mayer didn't reply. Something in his look and manner suggested he had given up; he was resigned to Craine's accusations.

"That other detective—"

"His name was Patrick O'Neill."

"I'm sorry for what happened to him. Please, you must understand that I didn't want any of this to happen."

"And Jack Rochelle?"

"No, that was nothing to do with me either," Mayer said, almost contemptuously now. "None of this was. I went along with Peterson's story about the love triangle. He convinced me. We had no idea Peterson was the one behind it."

"Whose we? You and Carell?"

When Mayer nodded, he said, "You sit there pretending you're completely innocent in all of this when all this time you've been playing us like puppets."

"I want to make amends, Craine. I can help you. We've spoken to Peterson's accountant. I have information."

Craine allowed himself a slow nod. "Go on."

"Five weeks ago he made a payment of twelve thousand dollars into an unnamed New York account."

"That tells us nothing. Who's to say Carell didn't hire the shooter?"

"Carell denies it. He has no reason to lie. No, we've already traced the payments. You can't hide twelve thousand dollars that easily. Don't you see? It was Peterson, Craine. Something happened and he had them killed. It all points to Peterson. I had no idea about any of this, I swear to you on my daughters' lives."

"But you knew about the girls, didn't you? You have a deal with the Lilac Club. You encourage your actors to sleep with their prostitutes."

"It wasn't a deal. There was no contract, simply a verbal agreement. Peterson and Rochelle took care of things; it was in their hands.

And I had no choice, you have to understand that. I needed to keep the Chicago syndicates happy."

"Why?"

Mayer tilted his head, looking out of the window toward the sea. His tone dropped. "The unions," he muttered.

"Labor unions?"

No reply.

"The labor unions, Louis?"

"Yeah." He leaned back in the chair. "Carell's got a guy inside at the top. Don't you see? Chicago controls the unions, so they have say over the studios. It's extortion, basically. Warner's, Paramount, R.K.O.—all of us are paying off Carell and Nitti not to raise labor wages."

"Why haven't you said anything? You have political influence. Why not bring in the police? Or the Federal Bureau?"

Mayer fell silent.

"Why? What do you get out of it?"

"The Depression caused chaos," said Mayer, defending himself. "Inflation, mass hysteria over salaries and costs. Budgets skyrocketing. Why do you think half the studios were collapsing? Now there's finally stability. Productions completing on time, and on budget."

"So you're actually saving money? All those taxable dollars you would have paid the union if there had been legitimate wage increases."

Mayer shrugged.

"That's it, isn't it? The syndicate is doing you a favor. I knew you were capable of a lot, Louis, but I never thought you'd get into bed with gangsters."

He wiped at his forehead again. Then he whispered, "How dare you, Craine? After everything I've done for you."

"You deny it?"

"Do you know how many people go to the pictures each week in America? Eighty million. But it's not the pictures they go see, it's the stars. Don't you see how valuable they are? Losing one Stewart, one

Rooney, one Spencer Tracy could cripple us. And the problems we've had, the close encounters. You don't need me to tell you the number of times I've almost lost one of them on some pathetic rape charge. And do you know how much we spend on abortionists each year, how much is wasted on lawyers, on payoffs? Look at all the things other studios have gone through with their leads. What the club proposed, it seemed reasonable. Why not keep them entertained? I don't judge my stars, Craine. So what if I helped give them what they want? I was protecting my employees from their own foolishness."

Looking at him then, Craine realized Mayer was nothing but a pious servant to a system he had helped create. Craine's iconoclasm would never be allowed. There was absolutely nothing in this world Mayer wouldn't do to protect his stars.

"If we bring Carell in on this, you'll agree to testify in court?"

Mayer shook his head. "No."

"You'll be subpoenaed—"

"It won't hold, and you know it. Not with who I know. I don't need that level of publicity and I won't stand for it. No, as far as M.G.M. is concerned, Peterson alone had ties to the Lilac Club. All of this was his doing. No one else from the studio lot will be mentioned by name, I'll make sure of it."

Beyond the living room he heard the sound of a door close. It came from one of the bedrooms further down the hall. Mayer heard it too. His eyes flicked toward the door for a split second, then back to Craine.

Both men stiffened as a set of footsteps approached.

The heavyweight figure of Whitey Hendry stepped through the doorway. In his hand was a thick five-by-seven envelope. Hendry looked at Craine suspiciously before turning back to Mayer. "I found the safe in the bedroom. There was some cash inside, a few watches and some jewelry. I also found this."

Mayer took the envelope from Hendry's outstretched hand and used a letter knife to cut across the seal. He bit his lip when he saw what was inside.

"I've called studio security," Hendry mumbled. "They're on their way."

"Give me the envelope," said Craine, knowing that it contained the missing photographs. He saw Peterson in the bed with Florence Lloyd. He saw Campbell and Rochelle trying to sell the pictures. He saw Peterson picking up the phone and calling New York.

"What good do you hope will come of this, Craine?"

"Show me the pictures." Craine changed his tone of voice. He wasn't asking. "Give them to me."

Mayer handed Craine the envelope. "How noble you'll be in your pyrrhic victory. Do you think you won't lose everything when this all gets out? Your career will be over. Think of Michael. He'll have nothing. Do you think this is what Celia would have wanted?"

"Yes."

Craine's hand dipped inside the manila paper. His palms slid over the gummed seal and he felt the tips of his fingers clinging to the glossy prints. For a long second, he didn't dare take them out.

CHAPTER 41

News of O'Neill's death raged through the police department like wildfire. When word got out that one of the shooters was caught alive and had been taken to the Good Samaritan Hospital, two-thirds of Central's troopers came down to show their support. Day-shift detectives gathered in the waiting room and ignored the opportunity of relief when the night rotation came in at 10 P.M. Ranking officers filed in shortly after, walking stiffly with their starched shirts and polished brass.

Chief Davidson seemed relieved that the press hadn't arrived, and after asking Simms for an update, explained to him very clearly that on no account were any of his men to leak any details to the papers. So far, without reason or motive for the crime, chain of command still had a series of options. There could be any number of reasons for O'Neill's death. Perhaps he shot himself by accident, cleaning his service weapon. Maybe he was suicidal. Then again, he might come from a particularly troubled neighborhood, where violent robberies were commonplace. With so many possibilities, there was no need to go charging off into the night. It was very important that Simms didn't jeopardize the department's reputation with wild accusations that couldn't be substantiated. To put it simply, without unquestionable evidence, the rank and file were not prepared to support a city pogrom of the criminal underworld.

Simms' own officers were another matter. They had rallied around their Captain, and pledged their commitment to bring O'Neill's killers to justice. There were a small number of cardinal sins that were unforgivable in any policeman's eyes, and the murder of one of their own broke their first commandment. Now, like a bereaved family, the Detective Bureau sought vengeance against O'Neill's killers.

Simms felt the weight of the responsibility on his own shoulders. It was his fault. O'Neill and Craine had come to him and he had turned them away. Simms had known O'Neill's father, had served under him briefly in San Francisco before transferring to Los Angeles. He remembered him as an honest police Major, a bear-like figure, well respected but fearsome at times. What would he have said to Simms if he were alive now? Could he forgive the man who had cast his only son away?

Simms lit a cigarette on the steps outside the hospital and took long, satisfying drags as he mulled over his next move. Where was Craine when he needed him?

A black Pontiac drew up outside the emergency exit. The driver's door opened and a man strode purposefully toward him.

"Captain Simms?" he asked, taking off his hat.

The stranger had dark red hair with a trim ginger beard, his stubble high up his cheekbones. Along one cheek, the stubble stopped short of his jaw where a long pink scar crept up toward his temples.

"Can I help you?"

"I'd like to speak to you about Jonathan Craine."

Simms frowned. "Who are you?"

The stranger reached into his jacket as if drawing a gun. For a moment Simms' heart stopped. He wasn't carrying his service pistol.

The man pulled out a metal badge. "My name is Emmett Redhill."

CHAPTER 42

Not long after eleven o'clock, Gale lit her first cigarette of the day. A Chesterfield, a rare treat. It had for a long time been her brand of choice, but Jonathan had asked her very politely one night if she could smoke something else when he was around. It was a strange request but she didn't ask him why; it was pretty obvious. She'd tried a few other brands, Morland's mostly, but they were never quite the same and after busy rehearsals all afternoon she'd felt a few puffs of Chesterfield tobacco were a just reward for a hard day's work.

She had spent the past few hours planning out her evening clothes ahead of tonight's premiere party. It wasn't her picture, of course, and Gale had declined an invitation to the red carpet event, but she was still expected to attend the after-party. Mayer and Peterson had been adamant.

She was planning on traveling alone and meeting Louis and Margaret when the movie ended. A car was due to pick her up at eleven o'clock for an eleven-thirty arrival. She had considered asking Jonathan to join her tonight, but he seemed preoccupied with Michael and perhaps it was too soon for them to be seen in public together anyway. Then again, maybe she was being unnecessarily secretive about their relationship. It would come out eventually, and if the press hadn't spotted them together it was only a matter of time before they did.

She wondered what the papers would make of it. She imagined the headlines: two bereaved spouses find solace in their grief. Not that that was a lie, of course. There had been an initial connection because of shared experience, but now their relationship had gone further than that. She trusted him, completely. She could say in all honesty that she was in love with Jonathan. It was an innocent, childish love that she hadn't really experienced before. Jonathan was such a very kind man, a gentleman in the traditional sense: a man who opened doors for you, who danced well and spoke politely. Not like the animals she worked with, who treated girls like pieces of meat. But neither was he the dour stand-pat she'd thought when they'd first met. Beneath his reserved exterior was a dry charm, an unexpected warmth and subtle sense of humor. All these years she'd been benighted, completely ignorant of what love really was. Now she was devoted to Jonathan wholeheartedly in a way she thought she never would be. She was, for the first time she could remember, content.

Through the window, she saw a car pull into the driveway and park underneath the outside lights. She didn't recognize it at first but then Jonathan stepped out and began walking purposefully toward the house. In his right hand he carried what looked to be a white piece of paper.

She opened the window and shouted down. "The door is unlocked. Come right upstairs."

She heard the door click and then firmly shut.

Gale looked at herself in the mirror and fixed her hair. Taking one last final drag, she stubbed out her cigarette and dabbed perfume over her neck to help cover the smell. As she sipped at a glass of water, she could hear his footsteps reach the top of the stairs then the sound of the bedroom door opening.

"Jonathan, why didn't you call to tell me you were coming, I would have ordered us a late supper."

She turned away from the mirror and went to kiss him. She stopped. Something was wrong.

Jonathan's forehead was sheened with sweat. He was staring at her intently, his cheekbones sharp and defined, his eyes hidden in purple recesses either side of his nose. His entire face looked as if it had surrendered, collapsed from the strain of exhaustion.

"Jonathan, you look awful. What's wrong?"

Jonathan remained standing in the doorway, then, without taking his eyes off her, lifted his hand from his side and dropped a thin pile of photographs to the floor. The prints slid over one another, a trail of exposures Gale had prayed no one would ever see. She took one look at the pictures and felt her stomach drop.

The first of the black-and-white prints showed Gale undressing, a half-naked girl watching on from the bed. Then Gale moved out of frame. The next photo showed Gale moving onto the bed beside her. Three pictures later, Gale was taking off the girl's underwear, kissing her neck, bearing down on her. In the last photograph, the girl lay on her back as Gale pushed her tongue inside her.

"Oh my God," was all she could muster. She could feel her throat tightening and her eyes welling. Ashamed, she clasped a hand over her face.

Jonathan stared at her. It was a cold look, a penetrating look that chilled her to the core. He spoke with a hatred in his voice. "Are you going to say anything?"

Stunned, Gale sat back on the bed. Her voice broke. "What is there to say?"

"When?" he said briskly. "When was this?"

She looked desperately at Jonathan, then at the pictures on the floor. She stared at the gray shades of naked flesh that made her sick with shame. She had pushed that night into the recesses of her memory.

"March. Maybe later."

Jonathan's usual calm was gone. He could barely control his anger. "How long were you with her?"

"Only the once."

He had drawn closer, and she could see his eyes film over. "Someone made you?"

Gale said nothing, then shook her head. Tears came. They ran down her cheeks and into her mouth. "Herbert and I were separated. I was lonely," she said through salted sobs.

Gale thought of the furtive visit to that girl's house after they had met at the Lilac Club. It had seemed nothing then. She and Herbert were living apart. Left alone for weeks on end, she became lonely. She'd drunk too much one night and gone to bed with a woman. Felicity had approached her at the Lilac Club, told her she liked women and thought Gale was attractive. Gale was hesitant but otherwise flattered, a part of her desperate for some kind of physical connection with someone else. So when Felicity invited Gale to her house, she said yes before she could really think about it. Gale didn't feel dirty sleeping with another woman; she'd always been curious as to what it would feel like. Besides, her marriage was such a fraud. Could this really be considered infidelity? She knew so many men who carried on blatant affairs right in front of their wives' eyes. Why were they beyond reproach and not she? Her gaze locked on the photos—like almost everyone she'd ever met, Jonathan had confused her with her celluloid double. She was human. She made mistakes.

Gale wiped at her eyes and spoke through choked tears. "I'm sorry."

"You're sorry? Do you know how many people are dead because of you?"

Gale looked away, visibly confused. "What are you talking about? Who? Which people?"

He pointed at the pictures, a finger jabbing at the naked figure of Felicity. "Don't play dumb with me. You know Florence Lloyd was shot in her house."

"What?" Gale picked up one of the photographs. "She told me her name was Felicity."

"Her real name was Florence Lloyd. She died the same night your husband killed himself."

When Craine told her it knocked something out of Gale. "She's dead? Why? I had no idea."

"It was in the papers."

"I don't read the papers! And I never even knew her real name. I figured she was being blackmailed, like me."

"I don't believe you. You're lying."

Gale shrank away from him. "I'm not lying."

"Lloyd, Campbell, Rochelle . . . Patrick O'Neill—they're all dead because of these pictures."

"O'Neill? The detective? I don't . . . I don't understand—"

"Do you have any idea what you've done? Look at you, you're acting all innocent when you know full well your own husband hanged himself because of these."

She was still on the bed, but Gale's arms were up and thrashing out. "I know! Of course I know! He was my husband. Do you know what it is to feel guilty? To always feel guilty?" Her shame receded and she began to feel angry. Angry at Peterson; angry at Mayer and Jonathan; angry at men and the world they lived in that forced her into this position. "Yes, what am I saying?" she said, turning back to him, "Of course you do—Celia."

"Don't even mention her. Don't poison her name."

"You're using me to make yourself feel better. Dragging up my past doesn't vindicate you of yours. You knew Celia killed herself. Everyone knew. You've been denying it to yourself but you covered it up for M.G.M., didn't you?"

"I said don't mention her name." Craine was shouting now. He grabbed her by the shoulders and threw her to the floor.

There was a silence, during which Gale lay helplessly on the carpet. Craine rubbed his eyes with the balls of his fists. He sat on the edge of the bed in the dimple Gale's slight body had left in the sheets.

"Did you love her?"

Gale relapsed into fits of tears. "No."

"And me?"

Gale looked up at Craine and cried: "Yes, I loved you. I love you now."

"How did it happen?"

Gale shook her head, struggling to explain: "I was at the Lilac Club . . . Herbert wasn't there—he'd left early with a migraine. I met

Felicity . . . or Florence, whatever her real name was. We talked, we went home together. To where she lived. That was it. It was the one time."

"Did you know she was a prostitute?"

Gale frowned, confused. "No . . . it wasn't like that. There was no—I didn't pay her."

"And you never met James Campbell?"

"Who is Campbell? I've never even seen him. I have no idea who he is. You keep mentioning his name but as far as I know he's the man who died in the car crash at Loew House. The one who killed Rochelle over some girl."

"Campbell was the photographer. The girl was Florence Lloyd. This girl. They were in it together."

Gale shook her head from side to side, struggling to believe it. "I had no idea. I was always worried I'd bump into her again. When I found out about the pictures I figured they asked her for money too. I even thought about going to her house."

"And you believed that, even after Loew House?"

"I told you, when Rochelle died I thought it was as the papers said it was."

"You must have wondered whether it was connected to Herbert."

"Yes, I wondered. But I didn't actually think it was. It wasn't my business to get involved." Her voice was coarse from crying. "You have to believe me, Jonathan."

Craine wiped the sweat from his face. "Why didn't you tell me about Florence? About the pictures."

She sat upright against the base of the bed and looked at Craine through glazed eyes. "I couldn't," she said softly. "I wanted to. I was scared. I didn't want you to leave me. I wanted what we have. It's all I've ever wanted."

"You could have told me about her. About the real reason Herbert killed himself."

Gale bit her lip and shook her head. "No, Jonathan," she said through sobs. "No, I couldn't."

Craine took a seat next to her on the floor, each of them unable to look at the other.

"What happened to Herbert?"

"I got a call from some guy. I never knew who."

"Campbell."

"Campbell, then. He said he had pictures of me. He wanted money but I couldn't pay. Herbert had always looked after our accounts. I tried to get him the money but he wouldn't wait. He said he would show the pictures to Herbert. I never thought he'd go through with it."

"Then what happened? He showed Herbert the pictures?"

"Yes."

"When?"

In despair, she replied, "The day he hanged himself. They were delivered in the morning. They phoned him afterward, threatening to take them to the newspapers." She took a moment to gather her thoughts. "I went over. He had the photos in his hand and he was screaming at me. He was drunk and high on whatever it was he'd been taking. He asked me what had happened. I tried to explain myself but he wouldn't have it. He kept screaming at me. He hated me. Said I'd made a fool of him. His career was over and it was all my fault."

"Then what?"

"I left. I went to the Lilac Club."

"Did you speak to Peterson?"

Gale nodded. "Yes," she replied wearily. "I told him what had happened. I could barely look at him. I felt so humiliated."

"What did Peterson do?"

"He went over to the house. He found Herbert dead."

"What time was this?"

"I don't know."

"Think!"

Gale closed her eyes and tried to clear her mind. "Around three in the morning."

"Before the maid found him?"

"Yes."

"And the photos?"

"He took them. He said he'd found them in the study with—"

He cut her off. "Was there a note?"

"He took that too."

"You've read it?"

Gale nodded. "I burned it. All it said was he was sorry but he couldn't forgive what I'd done. Peterson told me he'd destroyed the photos too."

"What happened after?"

"He told me that he'd deal with it. That I shouldn't worry, no one would know. He said I had to stick to my story and that if Louis Mayer ever found out, they'd cancel my contract. I didn't have a choice."

"Did you know Peterson had a deal with Campbell and Lloyd?"

Gale shook her head. "No. What deal? I don't understand."

Jonathan stood up, pacing in front of her. "He paid Campbell and Lloyd to take pictures of Carell's girls with clients. Then they extorted them for their own gain. But they went too far; Peterson had them killed when they tried to sell the pictures to newspapers. He killed Rochelle because he knew he was on to him. I got too close to finding out the truth and tonight Peterson ordered me dead. Men came into my house with guns, Gale. Michael is lucky to be alive. So am I. They killed O'Neill."

She looked at him incredulously. "I can't—Peterson? It can't be true."

"We know it was Peterson. He was behind all of this."

"I had no idea. Jesus Christ." She wiped at her eyes again, her makeup smeared down her cheeks. "All this time. And I went to him for help. I trusted him. Peterson . . . I can't believe it. Peterson . . ."

Craine was looking down at her, searching her face. "Will you testify? Will you go to court and tell a judge what you've told me?"

Gale was shaking. She could barely tell Jonathan what had happened, let alone a court full of strangers. She imagined the newspaper headlines and flushed with the humiliation of it all. She saw no reason for her life to become a common opera for the amusement of others.

"Jonathan, please. I can't." Gale pushed herself off the floor, looking at him imploringly. She was desperate. "My life, everything I have. I'll lose everything. Please, don't ask me to."

He went to leave and she grabbed his arm, twisting him back. "Jonathan . . . no, please, no . . . You can't do this . . ."

"For once, I'm going to do the right thing."

"It's not right. It isn't. What you'll do will ruin lives. No one will gain from this."

She looked at Jonathan and wanted to tell him how much it would hurt her for people to know the intimacies of her life. That she could never get over knowing that everyone across America thought her a tramp. That she loved him so much, and would do anything for them to start again, make believe that none of this ever happened.

Instead she said simply, "If you do this, I'll never forgive you."

Craine pulled his arm free. He remained rigidly silent.

Abandoned to the loss she knew was inevitable, Gale said finally, "You're choosing between me and them, Jonathan. You and I, we have a chance for something better. We can go away, leave here, make a better life. But if you do this, there's no going back. You'll carry this with you forever."

It was dark outside, but Craine could make out car headlights working their way up the hill. He heard the drone of approaching sirens and a few seconds later the sound of gravel under tires. Two round headlights blinded him as the cars pulled into the driveway. More police cars followed until there were four vehicles parked outside Gale's house.

He held his hand up to protect his eyes and watched as a lone silhouette stepped out of the lead vehicle and followed the beam of the car headlights until he was only a few feet away.

"Craine?" It was Simms' voice. "Mayer called me from Peterson's apartment. He told me everything."

"Did he ask you to stop me?"

The corona of Simms' head shook from side to side. "He only wants to protect Gale Goodwin. If she's involved, Carell might try and come for her."

"Where is Michael?"

"I had two cars take him home."

"Who's with him?"

"He's safe, Craine, I promise. He's in good hands."

"Did he look scared?"

"Don't worry, he'll be safe there. We have twelve uniforms keeping watch. I spoke to your secretary. She's been worried about you so she's gone over to look after him."

"Was he alright?"

"He's in shock but the doctors think he'll be fine. It's a lot for a kid to take in. I spoke to him myself. He didn't say anything but I explained what happened as best as I could. I told him you were safe. I told him not to worry."

Craine wanted to be with Michael. Couldn't bear the idea of him being alone any longer. But he needed to be done with all of this first.

"Have you identified the shooter?" Craine asked.

"His name's Gibson. Identified by his driver's license—looks legitimate. Twenty-six years old, employment files we have on him say he works security detail for the Lilac Club. That gives us probable cause but time is against us. We think Carell has chartered a private plane to Chicago."

"And Peterson?"

"We've made some calls," Simms said quietly. "We're trying to find out where he's going."

"What about a warrant? We'll get nowhere without a warrant. The D.A. will stall until it's too late."

From behind him, the sound of another door opening.

"I found someone who can help us."

A man stepped into the light, walking toward Craine until he was close enough to see him. He was wearing a chestnut suit, his dark red hair loosely combed over his skull, his stubble almost a beard. He looked taller now that he wasn't in his Pontiac.

"This is Special Agent Redhill from the Federal Bureau of Investigation. I believe you may have met before."

Craine didn't hide his uncertainty. "You work for the F.B.I.?"

Redhill spoke with a staid demeanor. "I'm sorry we couldn't have met under better circumstances, Craine."

"Agent Redhill has already issued us with a federal warrant. His team will help us arrest Carell. There's no way we can do this without him; Chief Davidson will have none of it."

"That doesn't explain why you've been following me," Craine said, bridling.

"I wasn't following you, I was trying to help you," Redhill explained. "A few months ago I was asked by my seniors to look into the Chicago crime syndicates' migration from Illinois to Los Angeles. We've been interested in Carell for some time. We knew he was up to something but prostitution isn't a federal crime."

"But extortion is?"

"Exactly. I had a sense he was angling for control of the labor unions to extort the studios, but nothing concrete. Then when Stanley died and Florence Lloyd was murdered, I knew I had something to go on. But even after the Loew House shootings, I had no idea it was Peterson who hired the shooter. It was too early to launch a public enquiry."

"So you waited for me to do the work for you."

"No," said Redhill, his jaw unyielding. "I needed to know you weren't going to interfere with our investigation. I needed to know you could be trusted."

"You've been tailing me for days, but you were somehow missing the moment Carell's men turned up at my house? Where were you?"

"I appreciate it's been a long night for you, Detective Craine, but I think your questions might have to wait for a more opportune moment."

Craine lunged at Redhill, grabbing a fistful of his shirt and throwing him against the hood of the car. "You knew what they were up to. You knew they would come for me."

Simms' hand was already at his shoulder, pulling him away before Craine could land his first punch.

Redhill staggered to his feet, his face swollen and crimson. "I couldn't jeopardize my investigation," he said indignantly. "There was no way of knowing you'd be directly threatened."

"You knew it was a possibility and yet you did nothing."

Redhill shrugged, contrite. "I tried to warn you."

"Warn me? A police detective was murdered because you didn't do anything to stop it."

"Sometimes it takes events like tonight to make things happen."

"I can't believe I'm hearing this—"

Simms stood between them. "Enough! Craine, you've done the hard work. From what you've both told me, we can have Carell on extorting the studios over the labor unions, we can have him on prostitution, we can have him on murder."

"And if he falls," Redhill blurted, turning his face to Craine, "God knows who else will. I want to see Nitti inside with Capone. You'll get your revenge, Craine."

"This was never about revenge." But Craine knew in his heart that simply wasn't true.

The three men stood there gathering breath before Redhill asked, "Do you have the pictures?"

If he paused, it wasn't for long. Craine reached inside his jacket and handed Redhill the envelope with the remaining photographs. He wondered if Gale was watching him from the window, her Judas conferring with the priests.

Redhill opened the envelope and glanced at the pictures, his face impassive. Craine couldn't watch. "And Gale Goodwin?" he asked.

"Will be subpoenaed. She'll have to testify, along with Mayer."

"This will ruin her," Simms said sadly.

"It might. But you already knew that, didn't you?" Redhill said to Craine with a questioning glance. "And it didn't stop you from coming."

They heard several police radios bleating simultaneously from all four cars and then a few seconds later a car door opening. Simms was the first to turn toward Detective Henson as he approached apprehensively.

"Captain Simms, we've had a call from Union Station. A few minutes ago a ticket was acquired under Peterson's name. It's a Chicago-bound Challenger train."

Simms looked at Craine, then back at Henson.

"What time does it leave?"

"Tonight. Midnight."

Simms looked at his watch. They had less than twenty minutes.

"Craine, we'll deal with Carell, you—"

But when Simms turned to face Craine he was already lost to the dark, his shoes scraping against the gravel as he sprinted for his car.

CHAPTER 43

Carell ordered his men to destroy everything. Accounts, receipts, payment transfers, balance sheets and employment histories—nothing could remain that could be held up to scrutiny. Burn anything the police might be able to use against them.

There was a floor safe in his office, and Carell removed three thick envelopes. From the first two he pulled out tight bundles of money and slid them into his pants pockets. From the other he removed a thick file of photographs. After tearing the glossed pages into quarters, he tossed the pieces into the tin wastebasket that sat beside his chair.

The telephone on his desk rang.

"Yes?"

The man on the other end didn't introduce himself. Informants never did. "The police already left. You have ten minutes." The line went dead.

There was a bottle of cognac in the bottom drawer of his desk and Carell took it out and tipped half the contents down his throat. The alcohol helped settle his nerves. In a few minutes the building would be swarming with police, and if he left the club with any trace of their business dealings, federal police would hunt him down.

He thought of Russell Peterson and how serious their situation would become if he got away. Peterson had been playing him for a fool all along, using the club to fill his own coffers and do his own dirty work. Now Carell had lost the trust of M.G.M. and the other major studios in town. In turn, he'd soon lose the support of City

Hall. Killing Peterson wouldn't be what Mayer would have wanted, but what he'd done couldn't go unpunished.

He tugged again at the bottle of brandy. What next? He'd already got everyone out of the club. Now he needed to get out of Los Angeles. A private plane was chartered to fly them to Chicago in an hour's time. From there he could beg Nitti for another chance.

Carell poured the rest of the bottle of cognac over the metal bin. He felt tense but his emotions remained undefined. He didn't know what he was feeling, or indeed what he should be feeling. Disappointed, more than anything. Frustrated. Possibly afraid. He took a short-barreled pistol from his top desk drawer and slid it into his inner jacket pocket. He knew that if the police got to him, he'd be offered indemnity to testify against his superiors. He wouldn't allow that to happen.

There was a knock on the door and Nelson entered.

"Russell Peterson is booked on a midnight train from Union Station."

"And Kinney?"

"Should be there any minute."

Carell nodded. Mistakes had been made tonight but Kinney was his top operator, dependable to the end. He tried not to consider the implications of murdering a Hollywood executive. He told himself again it was necessary. Peterson would squeal at the first scent of a plea bargain; he was too involved in this not to be a threat.

"Are the cars ready?"

"They're outside." Nelson nodded and turned to leave.

"Wait—Nelson, give me your lighter."

Carell clicked the flint between his thumb and finger and dropped the flaming case into the bin. The pictures of the club's girls curled and darkened, the images melting away. He should have done this a long time ago.

Carell flicked his blinds shut and turned off the desk lamp as if it were the close of a normal working night. There was nothing else to do.

He walked through the deserted dance hall, past the empty band-stand and the closed bar to the club's lobby. One of his low-rank button men handed him his coat and held open the double glass exit doors.

Outside, four black Chevy sedans were lined up with their engines running. Carell entered the third car from the rear. Arthur Gibson sat in the front passenger seat thumbing the safety catch on a Thompson.

"Good evening, sir," Gibson said deferentially, twisting round from the front passenger seat.

Carell nodded but said nothing. Arthur Gibson didn't know his brother would be killed tonight by hospital doctors on the club's payroll. Then again, maybe he wouldn't care. Traitors had it coming, everyone knew that much.

Michael sat at the dining table in his home in Beverly Hills.

When they'd first arrived back there were four other policemen with long rifles in their hands, two of them walking round the garden and the other two watching the gate. There were more strange men already in the house, men in uniforms who were brushing down the doorframes and taking photographs. Someone else was sweeping up the glass and another man had a pair of long, thin pliers he was using to pull the bullets out of the wall. They'd roped off the end of the house nearest the garage but he'd caught a glimpse from the lobby. There was blood on the floor, he could see that. He wondered who it belonged to.

The dining room was one of the only rooms undamaged by the gunfire. A woman with the policemen had brought some meat loaf and chocolate milk. She said her name was Elaine and that she worked for his father. He liked her blond hair and soft, rosy cheeks. Something about her reminded him of his mother. He wasn't sure what.

Michael forked at his food. Through the window he could make out unknown shapes in the back garden. All of them, the bushes, the line of trees behind the pool, they all looked like men with guns. He told himself not to worry but a part of him expected the room to light up and the shooting to start at any second. Only a few hours ago men had come into the house and tried to kill him and no one had explained why. All he knew was that tonight his father had abandoned him.

"Michael?"

He turned at his name and saw the woman was standing in the doorway. She looked so worried.

"Are you all done? Would you like anything else to eat?"

He sat there dumbly for a few seconds then shook his head.

"Are you sure? Well, it's getting late. Would you like to start getting ready for bed? How about a bath?"

He thought about that and nodded. *A bath.*

When the bath was run and the woman had left him alone, Michael locked the door. He was standing on a large cork mat in his mother's bathroom. This was where he saw her last, of course. He tried not to picture her there, lying naked and still beneath the cold water, but the image rarely left him. And it was there with him now.

Michael dipped a finger into the water. Hot, but not too hot. He slipped off his pajamas and climbed into the tub.

When he was a little younger he'd never really understood that his mother was an actress. She went away every few months, came home a little late some nights but she was always there to give him a bath and tuck him into bed. Usually she'd read him stories from the Bible, occasionally other books. He'd fall asleep thinking of King Arthur or of Cain and Abel, of Isaac, of Jonah and the great whale.

His mother hadn't read to him that final night. She said she would come and say good night but he'd fallen asleep before she'd had the chance. She died, and he couldn't stop thinking that she'd never said goodbye.

He shifted in the tub and his skin squeaked against the sides. Thinking of her now, Michael held his breath and sank, leaving his hands floating on the surface.

He couldn't remember the last thing she'd said to him but he wished he could. He was sure that somewhere, hidden in those words, was the answer to everything. Then the thought crossed his mind:

what would happen if he didn't emerge? What would happen if he stayed here, resting at the bottom of the tub? Would he find himself closer to her?

Michael lay perfectly still. He watched the bubbles rise from his neck then closed his eyes. He felt a great pain in his chest but pushed the thoughts away. He allowed his mind to drift like a branch on the ocean. He pictured his mother's smiling face. His body receded deeper into the water, his mind floating high above. His breathing slowed. He felt calm. He wasn't going to die; he was simply going to another place. Like walking through a door into an unseen room.

Dr. Felton turned a corner onto the surgical ward. He held a clipboard up against his chest, his other arm twisted behind his back so no one could see his hands shaking.

Three F.B.I. agents spilled out of the elevator. Felton turned to stare at a bulletin board to avoid making eye contact. He was wearing a surgical mask but he didn't want to risk anyone recognizing him if questions were asked. And they were bound to be asked.

In his periphery, he could see the agents turn toward the nurse's station. He waited until they were out of sight then continued onward down the hall with his eyes down.

Two policemen stood outside the patient's door talking quietly between themselves. They straightened as he approached and looked at him suspiciously.

Felton held up his clipboard. "Post-op checks."

There was a moment's hesitation, then the two men stepped aside.

He closed the door behind him when he entered but there was no lock; he'd never noticed that before.

The patient lay still on a bed near the window. Two tubes ran into his arms, another into his nose. The lights were dimmed but he could see his eyes were closed. He was probably still unconscious.

"Mr. Gibson," he said softly, approaching the bed.

No reply. He clicked his fingers in front of his face, then clapped his hands. The patient's eyelids fluttered but didn't open. Good: verbal and motor responses were low.

Dr. Felton went to the foot of the bed and looked at his charts. The patient had come out of surgery only minutes ago and was categorized as critical but stable. He'd had a single entrance wound three inches below the sternum. There was no exit wound. The bullet was recovered from his chest cavity. Most of the damage to his insides had been successfully repaired but further operations might be required at a later date. Blood pressure was low but heart rate was stable.

The doctor took a syringe from his left coat pocket, a glass vial from his right, then looked over his shoulder to check no one was watching. He nodded redundantly, as if giving himself the all-clear.

Dr. Felton sank the needle into the 200-milligram bottle of liquid morphine. He filled the barrel and quickly thumbed the plunger. A thin squirt shot into the air. Leaning over the patient, he slid the bed sheet down, exposing a large gauze bandage covering most of the breastbone. His fingers searched along the fringes of the bandage until he found a circle of loose flesh above his waistline.

This dose of morphine would cause respiratory depression within the next minute or so. Cardiac arrest would follow shortly after. Death might only take a few minutes more. There was no chance of revival.

The next doctor wouldn't check on him for at least another half-hour. By then there would be nothing they could do. He doubted they'd even perform an autopsy. Post-op mortality was incredibly high. Fewer than one in five people would survive the night after an operation like his anyway.

Holding his breath, Felton slid the needle into the fat surrounding the stomach muscles and pressed the plunger. He had a watch in his breast pocket and he took it out, his eyes following the long hand as it crawled round the dial. After a minute had passed he put the watch back in his pocket. With his index finger he lifted an eyelid. The pupils were constricting into black pinpoints as the opiates took full effect. He took a penlight from his breast pocket and held it above the man's face. His eyes didn't respond to the light.

Felton leaned closer and listened to the sound of his breathing. Shallow and uneven. He listened as the breaths quickly lost their depth until his chest was barely rising.

The end came quickly, barely two minutes after he'd given him the injection. There was a soft rattle in his throat and a final outward rush of air.

It was done. A thousand dollars for five minutes' work.

The door opened. Felton's heart rose into his throat. He spun quickly to see a nurse standing with one hand still on the doorknob.

"Dr. Felton?"

"Yes, what is it?"

"We have an ambulance arriving imminently. All doctors are to report to the Emergency Room."

There was no small talk in the Chevy carrying Carell to the airport. The motorcade drove the back routes, up Franklin Avenue toward the Rowena Reservoir, avoiding all main roads as they made their way toward Grand Central Air Terminal at Glendale. Carell looked back every few minutes, making sure they didn't have a tail.

He was numb with the speed of recent events. He couldn't believe how quickly his life had deteriorated. He'd never even had a chance to call his wife and daughter. He hoped the police wouldn't arrest them. He'd make arrangements as soon as possible to have them moved to a secure location. And then hopefully soon they could come and join him in Chicago, whenever that would be.

The car headlights picked out the sign to the air terminal. Carell began to feel impatient, checking his watch every few seconds. It was nearing midnight. He gripped his wrists with his hands.

"How far are we from the terminal?"

"Another mile, sir."

His ears pricked up at the sound of a propeller engine. Through the window he could see the taillights of a Ford Trimotor coming in to land. That must be his plane, ready to take off as soon as they arrived. Then, when the roar of the engine subsided, Carell heard a distant whining noise. Another plane? No; he knew exactly what it was. His face bleached of color. It was sirens.

Two hundred feet down the road, three police cars swerved sideways across a small intersection, blocking the way ahead. Doors swung open and faces appeared above the barrier, then long metallic barrels. Shotguns, they were armed with shotguns. It was an ambush.

Carell watched helplessly as the first Chevy hurtled forward at top speed, plowing into the barricade of squad cars, trying to punch a way through.

A row of armed policemen opened up and he saw the car spin out and skid to a stop, glass windows shattering in a bloody haze.

The second car also charged forward, slewing left and right before it ground to a halt. Three of his gunmen came out, shooting down the street toward the squad cars, firing and maneuvering as only ex-soldiers would.

Gibson wound down the window and opened up with his machine gun, shouting obscenities as he riddled the roadblock with automatic fire. Nelson swung right onto a side road but that too was blocked.

More shots rang out and bullets starred across the windshield.

Carell yelled, "Go back. Go back!"

Nelson thrust the car into reverse and twisted his head to the rear. Carell watched through the rear window as the car accelerated backward. It was no use: two more police cars blocked their way. He saw a line of plainclothes policemen raising their weapons from behind their cars. They were surrounded.

Carell lunged forward and dipped his head as a ripple of precision gunfire took out the glass in the rear window. He saw Gibson's head explode across the front windshield. Nelson shouted out in pain as his shoulder was peppered with shotgun spray.

More shots rang out and took out the tires. The car lost traction on the road, skating backward before slamming into a parked truck behind them. Carell was thrown sideways; his head hit the passenger door and warm blood spilled from a small cut on his crown.

"Nelson. Nelson, we have to go." Nelson didn't answer. His body had lolled forward; his head was slumped over the steering wheel.

Carell kicked out. "Goddammit, Nelson! God damn you!" Ignoring the pain in his whiplashed neck, he looked around and weighed his options. Through the side window he could see the police slowly approaching from the opposite end of the street. There was an alley leading onto an apartment block twenty feet to his left. It was his only chance; everywhere else was surrounded.

Dazed and injured, Carell opened the door and wriggled out onto the asphalt. He crawled toward the cover of the alleyway. Shattered glass littered the road and tore at his elbows; he dragged himself to the curb and hid beneath a parked car to catch his breath and pull the glass splinters from his arms. Wiping the blood from his face, he lifted his head in time to see two more of his men cut open with shotgun fire. There were panicked shouts; he heard one final burst of machine gun fire echo off the surrounding buildings, then the firing stopped.

A sudden silence followed. Then, through the ringing in his ears, Carell could hear muffled shouts. The detectives had spread across the street, screaming at his five remaining bodyguards. "On the floor," they kept shouting, "drop your weapons!" He craned his neck to see his surviving men drop their guns and raise their arms, lowering themselves slowly to the floor.

He turned to crawl toward the alleyway when several strong hands grabbed at his feet and dragged him back from his ankles. He looked up to see two plainclothes detectives standing over him, shotguns held squarely in their shoulders.

"Stay exactly where you are," one of them said.

As Carell lay helpless on his back, the remaining men of the club's security detail were manhandled to the ground, wrists girded with iron handcuffs and carried away toward a line of unmarked police cars.

He was considering whether to make a suicide run for freedom when he heard a sharp crack followed by a long burst of gunfire. Carell looked up to see Nelson stepping out of the car, opening up on a row of police cars with a Thompson carbine. His shirt was blood-soaked, his teeth bared and eyes black with hatred. He swung round, firing wildly all around him. The first detective holding Carell was hit in the leg, long arcs of arterial blood spurting across the asphalt. The other was hit in the neck. He clutched his throat and fell to the floor gurgling.

Nelson kept on firing, shooting up the police cars, clearing a path ahead. Carell glanced swiftly to his left and right. The policemen were huddled behind their cars, ducking under cover. Nelson was running toward him now, pushing his way forward. He was coming for him; they were going to make it out of here.

Nelson was only a few feet away when three loud shots rang out and his chest ruptured in a fine spray of red mist. He looked at Carell then closed his eyes—a prayer, a sigh of defeat, perhaps—before his knees buckled and he collapsed to the floor. Nelson twitched briefly then lay perfectly still.

Carell felt neither regret nor shame for the death of his driver and bodyguard, only mild pangs of irritation. Nelson had failed him. All his men had let him down and each of them deserved to die.

He raised his eyes and focused on a wispy-haired man in a white shirt standing over Nelson with a smoking revolver clasped awkwardly between both hands.

Captain Simms kicked the driver's gun away and strode over to Carell, his short-barreled Colt aimed directly at his head. He'd never killed anyone before, never once fired his service pistol in all his years as a policeman. A strange feeling surged up in his chest. Pride, maybe. He'd taken one life to save the lives of his men.

"Get up," he said.

Carell sat upright and propped himself up on the parked car. He shook his head.

"You take me in, they'll do whatever it takes to shut me up. I'm as good as dead."

Simms turned around. Redhill was shouting orders at his agents. One of his men from the Bureau was dead, killed by Carell's men, and the frustration was visible on his face. He wondered how he got that scar.

"We can protect you," he muttered to Carell, not even certain he wanted to. "The F.B.I. want Frank Nitti, not you."

Carell shook his head. "I have a wife and kid to think about." He looked at Simms long and hard, and for a brief second Simms thought he saw a smile forming. He knew then that Carell would never turn witness. As four Bureau agents circled them, Simms realized what he was about to do.

"Don't—"

But it was too late. Carell looked the armed agents in the eyes, pushed himself up, reached inside his jacket and pulled out his pistol. The end came so fast he never even felt the hail of bullets that swept him off his feet.

Simms' ears rang, his shoulders sagged. He wiped Carell's blood off his face with the back of his coat sleeve and looked around, surveying the bloodbath. Four injured officers, two dead; six dead gangsters. All this, for what?

Taking a deep breath, he walked back toward where Redhill was standing. "I want anyone alive put into a car. Get the wounded to hospital. No one else is dying here tonight."

He looked solemnly back at Carell's body for a long moment, then, without saying another word, walked slowly back toward his car.

By far the largest of all main passenger stations in Los Angeles, Union Passenger Terminal was a *mission moderne* to house all of the three major rail companies operating in the West. Tonight the terminal was heaving with throngs of travelers, long lines of people at the ticket counter and crowds of passengers frantically making their way through the platform underpass as they tried to get the last trains out of the city.

Craine made it to Union Station at nine minutes to midnight. He rushed through the ticket concourse, weaving in and out of pedestrians as he tried to find Peterson before he left for Chicago. Unable to see through the crowds, he stepped up onto a wide leather chair and surveyed the room. There were hundreds of people here, blank faces hidden under dark hats and thick coats. Peterson could be anywhere.

Craine elbowed his way through the crowd to the departures board. Four trains departed in the next half-hour, but Peterson should be on the midnight Challenger train from platform two. He had a bare-bones plan of stopping Peterson from leaving, arresting him before he got on the train, but he didn't know any more than that. He couldn't rid himself of the feeling that this wasn't going to be easy.

Then, out of the corner of his eye, he registered a man in a long brown coat darting through the crowd. He turned in time to see Peterson disappear into the underpass leading to the platforms. He couldn't have been more than fifty yards away.

Craine started to run after him as inconspicuously as he could, treading lightly on the balls of his feet, keeping his balance as his shoes slid on the polished tile flooring. He felt a rush of excitement. He'd found him; he wasn't too late.

He crossed the concourse only to find himself at the back of another mass of bodies queuing through the long underpass to the ticket barriers at platforms two and three. He'd lost sight of Peterson.

He stood on tiptoes but couldn't distinguish Peterson through the sea of matching hats. He tried to edge his way slowly forward but the low-ceilinged tunnel was filling rapidly: a late train from Santa Fe had pulled into the station and disembarking passengers were pouring out from the egress gates at platform three. At the same time, a tightly ranked crowd was pushing against them toward the adjacent platform two, forcing their way through the underpass tunnel, desperate to make it through the barriers and onto the Chicago Challenger. Rich and poor alike were left shuffling forward, waving their tickets, shouting at the barrier guards that they couldn't miss their train.

Standing at the platform gates were two ticket inspectors and a uniformed officer waving through passengers one by one. Craine knew Simms would have called ahead and instructed the station to check what tickets they could for a sight of Peterson but there was a chance they wouldn't recognize him or that the message hadn't got through. With so many people and so little time, Peterson could easily talk his way onto the train.

Now what? *Think.* He tried to make eye contact with one of the ticket inspectors but they were almost thirty yards away; he was about to call out when he caught sight of two familiar faces up ahead. One of them he'd seen only once or twice before in passing. He worked the door at the Lilac Club. The other was Vincent Kinney.

A moment of flop sweat panic before Craine pulled down his hat and lowered his gaze. *Why was Kinney at the station?* Carell had sent them here, of course he had. They must be here for the same reason he was. But if they found Peterson before he did, they'd kill him the first opportunity they could.

Raising his eyes quickly, Craine saw the second man take off his hat, pass a hand through thinning hair and look all around him. They were less than twenty feet away, half-way between him and the platform gates leading directly onto platform two. If they moved even slightly in his direction, they'd spot Craine immediately. The man turned back to Kinney and the two men shared a private conversation. He read what he could in their muted gestures: we need to find him, their faces said, we need to find him right now.

Craine steered through to the front of the crowd, brushing people aside, knowing that unless he made it onto that train, Peterson would be gone forever. He glanced up—the second man was still there but Kinney had disappeared. Had he made it through the ticket barriers?

Passengers were shuffling slowly through the underpass toward the gates to the platforms but it was no use, the crowd was too thick; he was stuck where he was. Craine faced back toward the concourse, where the minute hand of the large illuminated clock inched toward midnight: 11:58 P.M. He would never reach it in time, there were too many people. The Chicago-bound Challenger was leaving any moment now. He was going to miss the train.

*   *   *

Sitting under the arc lights of platform two was a Los Angeles Challenger, one of the most highly patronized passenger trains to run between Los Angeles and Chicago. Dragged by a railroad steam locomotive with twelve coupled driving wheels, the eastbound Challenger could complete its run in under forty hours, leaving Los Angeles at midnight and arriving at Wells Street Station shortly before 7 P.M. Central Time two days later. The train was due to depart imminently; wisps of steam rose from the wheelsets and clung to the cool evening air as passengers rushed to board. Finally, the last trolley of luggage was loaded onto the baggage car and the door locked shut.

Russell Peterson was a few feet from the ticket barriers leading up onto platform two. Ahead of him, two ticket inspectors and a policeman stood with a large bloodhound sitting quietly at their feet. A mass of passengers were being ushered through the gates one by one toward the waiting train, and the crowd was becoming restless. Peterson stood in line beside a blond woman and her two children. He was wearing a cheap brown overcoat he'd bought from across the street, but underneath his shirt was damp with sweat. He could feel the material clinging to his back. Trying his best to slow his breathing, he took out a handkerchief and wiped the moisture from his face. He was nearly there.

When he reached the head of the line, Peterson strode forward, stepping in front of the other family. He was almost through the barriers when a voice behind him called out:

"Ticket, please, sir."

Without hesitating, Peterson turned. It was the ticket inspector; the policeman was distracted with someone else. He put his bag on the floor and quickly reached inside his overcoat pocket for his ticket. If he gave any indication of reticence or unease he'd almost certainly be caught out. Neither did he smile or try to appear too casual. Instead, he let out a long exaggerated sigh, reasoning the inspector would appreciate that under the circumstances this was a considerable annoyance.

Peterson handed over his ticket. The inspector studied Peterson's face then looked down at the paper rail ticket, officially stamped and dated but—*thank God*—not named. He prayed that the inspector wouldn't ask for any form of identification. He put his hands in his pockets and thumbed at a pocket knife. He clasped it between his fingers, using his thumb to twist out the blade. He was ready to use it if he had to.

The policemen glanced over. He frowned briefly, a hint of recognition in his face. Then the dog at his feet started growling. Peterson felt a bead of sweat form at his temples and begin its slow crawl down the line of his jaw. *Please make them hurry.* He watched as the policeman rested a hand on his pistol belt and slowly started to walk over. He gripped the knife in his palm, drawing it cautiously from his pocket.

The policeman tapped the ticket inspector on the shoulder.

"Excuse me—"

Behind him, the bloodhound jumped up at the blond woman and started barking and baying at her skirt. The woman let out a shriek, dropping her bags and falling to the floor. The policeman turned and ran over, apologizing profusely as he helped her to her feet.

"Quiet down, you! I said quiet down!" The policeman struck the dog on its hind leg and the hound yelped before falling silent.

The ticket inspector rolled his eyes and slapped the ticket against the palm of his hand.

"Second carriage from the front, sir. Have a safe journey."

Peterson passed through the ticket barriers carrying his single suitcase grasped tight in one hand. He hadn't had time to go home. Once he'd heard that Craine was still alive, he'd known it was only a matter of time before someone realized what he'd done. Every second counted; he was running for his life.

He walked briskly, and had to stop himself from running as he walked up onto the platform, striding past the coach-class carriages toward the first-class sleeping cars near the front of the train. The last of the passengers were boarding and the stationmaster was walking down the train closing the carriage doors.

Peterson stepped onto the iron pedestal and climbed up into the second carriage from the front. The conductor was standing in the doorway. He nodded hello as Peterson squeezed past then slammed the door shut behind him.

Peterson walked past the passengers waving from the windows and went down the corridor to his roomette, a small cabin with a foldout bed and washbasin. He checked the room number against the ticket, stepped inside and shut the door behind him.

Peterson heard the locomotive give a long whistle then felt the coach sway from side to side as the train began to creep out of the station. He took out a cigarette and lit it, inhaling deeply until his nerves had settled.

It had started nine months ago. Mayer had refused him a pay raise and Peterson was fed up of being underappreciated. He'd spent most of seven years saving M.G.M.'s actors from themselves. Their entire star image was his construction, and yet they earned more in a week than he did in a year. So it was time for him to take what was due.

Rochelle put Peterson in contact with James Campbell and the three of them devised a plan. Campbell's girlfriend was a call girl at the Lilac Club. Campbell would take pictures of her with clients and then extort them for payoffs.

Florence—or Felicity, as she went by—was worried she'd get in trouble but the club never found out about it. The key was to only extort those M.G.M. actors that Peterson could handle. Vulnerable, stupid actors who would be only too willing to pay to keep everything hush-hush. They came straight to Peterson, begging the Head of Publicity for advice. All he had to do was convince them that it wasn't worth the trouble. *Don't go to the police. Pay them off. I can talk to the Lilac Club to take the girl off the roster.*

Everything had worked perfectly until Campbell and the girl got greedy. Peterson sighed at the memory, and his thoughts drifted over to the events of the past few months. Hiring Kamona had been necessary. Christ, how could Campbell think that sending the pictures to Stanley would have done anything but drive him to an early grave? Stanley was unhinged. Did they genuinely think that he'd thank them for their discretion, pay them off for not selling the pictures to a local rag?

It was a desperate move to kill Craine but he had only himself to blame. He'd grasped, a little too late, just how close Craine was to revealing his role in this. So with Carell looking for M.G.M.'s permission to go after the two detectives, Peterson gave it to him. After all, if the gunmen did their jobs, there'd be no direct contact to the Lilac Club, so both he and Carell would be able to walk away. And there was no reason for the spotlight to shine on the studio, either. Peterson made it very clear to Carell that Mayer didn't want to be contacted directly and that Peterson would always act on his behalf. There was no reason for Mayer to ever find out.

But nothing ever works out like it does in the movies. Carell and Kinney had failed. Craine was alive, and it was time for Peterson to leave Los Angeles. He told himself that it didn't matter. In two days' time he'd be in Chicago. Maybe he could try and negotiate with one of the Irish syndicates? They hated Carell. He could tell them everything he knew about the Lilac Club in exchange for protection. Or maybe even talk to the F.B.I. Would Hoover grant him immunity if he ratted on the Chicago mob? Maybe—but was it worth the risk?

Peterson drew hard on his cigarette and leaned back in his seat as the train pulled away from the platform. At last he started to relax. Through the window he saw families on the platform waving goodbye to relatives and friends. A girl, a pretty girl, ran alongside a carriage, blowing kisses and waving a handkerchief to some unseen lover. Behind her, he caught sight of a man sprinting down the platform after the train. He looked somehow familiar. *Wait, it couldn't be?* Peterson strained his eyes and pushed his face against the glass. He felt his heart almost jump out of his chest.

It was Jonathan Craine.

Craine strode down the corridor of the Challenger, moving with the sway of the train. When the clock struck midnight, the ticket guards had bowed to the pressure of the crowd and opened the gates to the platform. He'd stepped onto the rear carriage just as the shrill whistle blew and the train lurched forward on its long journey toward Chicago. He'd made it on board—now he needed to find Peterson before Kinney did.

The train rocked from side to side as it screeched slowly up the rail yard, gathering speed, laboring around the first corner as it sped toward the L.A. River. It was busy inside the coach-class carriage, an atmosphere of urgency as passengers with battered suitcases filled the narrow aisles trying to find their seats. It had crossed his mind that Peterson would be hiding among the coach-class passengers, but then again, the risk of being recognized was bound to be too great. He would have paid for a private room in the sleeper carriage.

Craine wove through, breathing the fug of cigarette smoke and perfume as he forced people aside, pressing toward the first-class compartments near the front of the train. There were twelve carriages in total, each with rear and front connecting doors, and twice he almost slipped crossing from one carriage to another as the gyrating metal lips pitched and swayed beneath his feet.

He saw the ticket inspector in the fourth carriage from the front, his narrow face sepia-toned under the glow of low-wattage bulbs.

"Tickets."

"Police," he said, showing his badge. "I'm looking for Russell Peterson. What room is he in?"

"Don't mind who you are or who you're looking for, you can't board this train without a ticket."

Ignoring him, Craine snatched the clipboard from his hands and started up through the carriage.

"Hey, you can't do that!" the conductor shouted after him. "Hey!"

Craine ran his finger down the list of passenger names. The list was alphabetical, the first page ending in Delancey. He turned to the second page. There he was, half-way down: Peterson, Russell. He was in the second carriage from the front, cabin 14.

Vincent Kinney had entered at the front of the train. He'd seen Peterson climb onto the sleeper carriages and knew he must be in one of the private cabins. First class was an amber-lit corridor with a line of doors to his left. There were six cabins to each carriage and Kinney glanced in each of them as he passed, his right hand holding his pistol beside his thigh.

He considered his options. He could kill Peterson now and be done with it, or he could hold him until the train stopped, drag him off onto the tracks and shoot him in the desert somewhere. The impatient part of him wanted to get it over and done with but being reckless helped no one. He didn't have a silencer, and if he was caught, there was no way of getting off the carriage until the train slowed down.

Passing a washroom, he glanced in at two more open doors but the passengers in both cabins were families with young children. The third door was shut. Kinney knocked softly.

"Tickets, please."

There was no reply. He looked to his left and right to check the corridor was empty. He repeated himself and when no answer came he pulled the hammer back on his pistol with one hand and turned the doorknob with the other.

The cabin was empty.

Then, from his left, he saw Peterson dart out of the toilet toward him. Kinney turned his pistol and tried to fix him in his sights but Peterson was too fast and the corridor too narrow. Peterson stepped closer, grabbing Kinney's pistol wrist with one hand, and arching toward him with a metal blade clasped within the other. There was the sound of a train whistle and with it the sound of his own breath rushing out of him as the knife entered his side. Kinney smelt something in the air and suddenly he was on the floor, a burning feeling inside his belly that got hotter and hotter until he could barely breathe.

Pushing through the first-class compartment, Craine counted the cabin numbers as he went: 19, 18, 17 . . . He was crossing between the connecting doors when he heard a confused scream ringing through the next carriage. Before he could reach under his arm for his Browning, the train let out a long, low-pitched whistle and the hydraulic brakes engaged. Craine was thrown sideways, almost falling under the train wheels as the couplings banged together and the Challenger ground to a halt.

He pulled himself up, took out his Browning and looked down the long corridor. There was a woman standing over a man on the floor. Behind them, he saw a door rattle on its hinges as it clanged shut. He looked through the window and caught a glimpse of a figure stepping off the train and down to the rail tracks.

Peterson.

He went to go after him before the woman stepped to one side and he could see it was Kinney hunched on the floor, his chin resting on his chest as if he was asleep.

"Help me," she said, "he's been stabbed."

The hairs stirred on the back of his neck as Kinney turned his eyes to him. He looked at Craine in a puzzled way and then a light went on behind his pupils. Kinney started fumbling at his pant leg. His fingers wrapped around a small metal object, a gun no larger than the palm of his hand.

Craine's first instinct was to run, but thinking of Patrick O'Neill in his bathtub, and thinking of Michael, of how close he came to dying by Kinney's hands, carried him forward.

"Get out of the way, get out of the way."

Kinney wrapped his left hand around the woman's face and tried to pull her body toward him. Using her as a shield, he swept his pistol hand toward Craine.

As the woman screamed, Craine realized he'd been in this exact situation only months before. But if nerves held him back in the corridors of Campbell's apartment block, then this time there was no hesitation. His arm was steady. Craine fired only once but the shot was clean, entering Kinney's skull a little above the eye and exiting the back of his head in a spray of crimson blood that shoelaced across the windowpane.

Craine stood there for a second to be sure Kinney was dead, then, ignoring the woman's desperate wails, he bounded toward the carriage door.

Craine jumped down onto the edge of the tracks, his feet sinking into the deep gravel, his ankles almost giving way beneath the weight of his fall. It was almost completely black outside and he couldn't see more than a few feet ahead. From nearby, he could hear the ghoulish howls of trains rushing through the rail yard and the hiss of the steam as white clouds poured out of the Challenger's couplings and wandered through the night.

Revenge, perhaps the simplest emotion, perhaps Craine's only true spur, was gasoline in his veins. O'Neill's death mustn't go unpunished. The demon in his heart had set to work, images of Peterson spinning in his mind's eye like a carousel. Through the smudges of engine fog he made out a concrete barrier running along the side of the train, too sheer and too high to climb. He paused irresolutely and fingered his collar loose, pricking his ears to the sound of movement. Peterson could only have gone right, back to the rear of the train toward the station or left toward the river. He cocked his head to either side. *Did he go left or right?*

Suddenly he heard something—shoes scraping against the scree. He listened for the rhythm of his step. Peterson was to his left, running for the guard's van and the locomotive coach. He had to be going toward the river.

Craine sidled along the train with his pistol outstretched, his free hand bracing his face against bursts of steam exhaust. He kept his mouth shut and breathed through his nose, gathering pace, his feet finally finding the same rhythm as the man ahead. He couldn't be far away.

When he reached the nose of the engine car, Craine followed the beam from the giant headlight as it probed out across the eddying clouds. His eyes grew accustomed to the light but the steam exhaust was impenetrable and it was almost impossible to see any more than a few yards in front of him.

He walked away from the engine car and stopped on the tracks but he couldn't see or hear anyone. At last a sudden gust of wind began to clear the way ahead; he started to make out the rail lines snaking through the darkness toward two green pinpoints—a signal box flashing beneath a bridge underpass. He hesitated then pressed on, following the tracks, placing his feet down carefully so he wouldn't trip, pausing every few seconds to listen and adjust.

Away from the engine car, the thick clouds of steam were melting into a thin haze and he opened his eyes wide, trying to look for signs of movement. His heart skipped a beat. There he was: a black figure silhouetted against the fog. Peterson was loping across the railroad toward the underpass. He was making his escape to the freight yard and the main road beyond. If he made it onto the street he'd be lost to the city; Craine would never find him.

Bursting into a sprint, Craine scrambled across the tracks in Peterson's direction, arms raised and gun poised. To his surprise, his hands were steady. Dread would no longer fracture his resolve. He wasn't a coward. He wasn't afraid.

Peterson hurried onward, running toward the underpass ahead of him. Hearing the sound of gravel underfoot, he turned around with Kinney's pistol outstretched. Craine was behind him, striding forward, his coat flapping about his sides. He must have found Kinney and followed him off the train when he'd pulled the emergency alarm. He was gunning for him now. There was no going back.

Peterson picked up speed, concentrating on the underpass ahead. From there he could climb out of the railroad and make his way back to his car. To reach it would mean running over open ground, but he had no choice.

He pushed himself harder, desperate to lose his pursuer, grinding his way through the loose gravel between the lines as fast as he could, the rims of his eyes burning with steam and coal dust. He was a hundred feet from the underpass now. He checked the chamber of Kinney's pistol. There was no other option left open. To escape, he'd have to kill Craine.

Behind him, Craine kept step, twice almost tripping on the steel rails as he narrowed the distance between them. When the gap was no more than fifty feet, Craine fired, aiming for Peterson's legs.

The bullets whistled through the air but missed their mark. In response, Peterson swung round and fired three loose rounds. Craine saw the bullets spark against the metal lines but never lost focus, increasing his pace, carrying on through the mist.

Then, ahead of them, he heard the soft chugging of a steam engine. He heard a rumble in the distance and saw the gauzy outline of a freight train. The tracks began to vibrate, the shingles dancing on the spot as a steam engine carrying eight boxcars made toward them, whistling its approach.

Peterson too heard the train approaching up ahead. He continued across the gravel, turning every few paces to fire. He knew Craine was behind him, the distance between them quickly decreasing. Craine was gaining on him every second. If he didn't get across the railroad in time, the train would cut across the path in front and he'd never make it. He needed to get out of the line of fire.

Craine hurried after Peterson, his jaw clamped tight. "Stop," he shouted, his voice drowned out by the train's deafening whistle. "You won't make it."

Running full speed, Peterson hurled himself across the tracks. Craine raised his gun to fire. A deafening noise took his breath away as the freight train hurtled down the tracks between them.

Craine waited intently as the freight boxcars careered toward Union Station. When the final car had passed, Peterson was nowhere to be seen; he had disappeared into the clouds.

Breathless from running, Craine continued slowly toward the underpass and paused. He heard the rumblings of another train up ahead. He strained his eyes through the fog but could see nothing except the signal lights flashing intermittently from green to red.

Through the heavy clouds of steam, Peterson saw Craine stepping forward toward the underpass. He'd waited in the shadows of the bridge, determined to do away with Craine while he could. When the train was less than a hundred feet away, he stepped out to face his pursuer. Craine's eyes were angled away, staring at the approaching train. He was an open target. Peterson took a deep breath and lifted his pistol.

Craine stopped dead as the oncoming train bore down on where he stood, the headlamps cutting through the darkness. Then, at his periphery, he saw a silhouetted figure with his arms raised.

Craine's body reacted on instinct. He dropped to the floor, twisting himself round to face Peterson as a shot rang out and thundered over his head. He heard the click of an empty magazine; there was the slightest pause as they locked eyes, then Craine sighted down the barrel and squeezed the trigger.

The first two bullets hit Peterson square in the chest, the third in the bridge of his nose. Peterson's pistol clattered to the ground and he pirouetted sideways onto the gravel as the train surged past them.

Craine emptied his clip, reached inside his pocket for another, twisted it sideways, reloaded, cocked it. It all seemed to take an age, and when he was finished the silence caught him off guard.

The moonlight made patches of light on the gravel and he cautiously approached Peterson, his Browning aimed toward him. He wasn't moving but Craine could hear a hissing sound in his chest. When he got close enough he could see Peterson staring at him.

Craine's voice was faint and harried, little more than a whisper. "Why?" he asked Peterson. His eyes searched for something in Peterson's but Peterson wouldn't yield. His pupils were glassy now, his life unravelling. "Why, Peterson?"

But he would never have his answer. Peterson gave a final, wintry gasp and then he was gone.

CHAPTER 44

It was after two o'clock when Craine entered the doors to the hospital. He looked like a man in trauma, his stride almost a stagger, his voice when he spoke unrecognizable from the softly spoken law officer that had joined the department ten years ago.

Roger Simms met him in the foyer. He didn't raise an eyebrow at the sight of him, his greeting little more than a nod. He was holding his hat in both hands and his face was weighed down with the burden of bad news.

"Peterson's dead," Craine grunted before Simms could say anything. "It's done. All of it. Over." The police must have arrived at Union Station shortly after Craine did because when he'd returned to the train platform there were almost a dozen officers shielding the ambulance crew as they carried Kinney's body away on a gurney. Doctors from the M.E.'s office pronounced both Kinney and Peterson dead at the scene and a mortuary truck took them away not long after. People gathered to watch as people so often did but it was late by then and the station was almost empty. He'd asked the police about Carell and they told him what had happened.

Simms nodded and looked at him with something that might be pity, but could be something else entirely. Gratitude, maybe, for a reason he would only later begin to understand.

"We need to talk," Simms whispered as he guided Craine through the waiting room toward a corridor of private consulting rooms.

The hospital was busier than it had been earlier on in the night. All around were white hats with gold trim, a few dozen uniformed officers and members of his own unit talking quietly with men in long coats he assumed were from the Federal Bureau. He recognized Redhill giving orders to two plainclothesmen before moving on to talk to ranking officers from the police department. He saw him show them his badge. He wondered where Davidson was. But there were also other men here, photographers whispering with their heads close together. There were press everywhere, more than there should be.

Simms stopped outside a doorway with CONSULTATION ROOM painted on the wood. Craine knew this room. It was the room where doctors told family and friends that their loved one had died.

When they were alone, Simms said, "Craine, I have to tell you something."

Craine wiped a hand across his face, pulling his mussed and sooty hair back across his forehead. "What is it? The uniforms told me about Carell—"

"This isn't about Carell—"

"Then what—"

"Craine, listen to me," he said, his voice clear and lucid, as if he'd rehearsed what he was about to say a hundred times. "There's been a terrible accident."

It took a few seconds for Craine's body to register what Simms had said, and then all too quickly the blood in his face and limbs receded like someone had pulled the plug and his insides were draining away. But if there was a moment of panic, he didn't feel it. He couldn't bear to think those thoughts. Too much had happened for anyone else to die. It couldn't be possible. *Please let it not be Michael. Please let my son be alive.*

Simms was sensitive to what he was about to say, speaking on tiptoes now. "It's Gale, Craine," he said slowly. "I'm so sorry. She left the house and got in her car. They tried to stop her but by the time they realized it was too late. She had an accident not far from her house, came right off the road—" And although he continued speaking, Craine heard nothing more. Simms said something about alcohol and pills in the house, about them pulling her from the wreckage, a word or two about doctors doing the best they could and it not being his fault. And when he could hear again Simms was saying over and over, "I'm so sorry. I'm so sorry, Jonathan."

There were several questions he wanted to ask but his mouth was dry and his face was tingling. A rush of images and emotions stopped him from forming coherent thoughts. Instead all he could manage was a tight and raspy, "Where is she?"

"It's too late, Craine."

"Where is she?" he said again, his jaw clenched so hard his whole head was shaking.

"There's nothing—"

"Where?" He wasn't crying but he wished he was. *Let this feeling out of me.*

"Down the hall, on the corner. I identified her myself."

Simms led him through the intensive care unit. Two nurses made notes on a clipboard outside a large green door. Simms looked at him and he knew this was it. He paused as Simms spoke to a man in a long white coat. Quiet words were issued and then Craine was allowed to enter.

When Simms had told him, a part of Craine hadn't quite believed him. He had a strange sense that it hadn't happened. That this was all a hoax, and that any minute Gale would come walking in with O'Neill right behind her. But all that changed when he stepped through the door.

She was lying on a silver bed in a private room. A white blanket traveled from her feet to the top of her head. He caught sight of her hair and had to stop himself from gagging.

Simms moved toward the door. "I've heard the rumors," he said quietly. "I realize you two . . . were familiar. I'm not sure if it's public knowledge. We'll protect you. The press won't know about it."

Craine's breaths were fast and shallow. "Why was no one there? Why did no one stop her?"

"They tried to, Jonathan. There was nothing anyone could do."

"Did she say where she was going?"

"She ... apparently she wanted to see you. She was driving to see you but she came off a sharp turn. Another driver called it in. Paramedics say she was dead by the time they got there. That's all I know."

A part of him wondered whether she was run off the road, if Carell or Peterson had made one desperate attempt to have her killed, but deep down he knew that wasn't true.

His chest was filling and deflating. His eyes stung as he tried to hold himself together. "Was it quick?"

"I ... I don't know. It's hard to know in these situations. She'd taken a lot of pills. My guess is she barely knew what was happening. I'm sorry."

When Simms took a step back, Craine took a moment to compose himself. Then, slowly, he pinched the sheet and pulled it away from her face.

She was pale, almost luminous. They were always so white when the heart stopped beating. And so still. In the short time he'd known her, she'd never stopped moving.

There were bruises round her neck and face where she'd hit the steering wheel. He wondered what he was doing when Gale's heart stopped beating. Would he have been at the train station? Perhaps it was the exact same moment he'd killed Kinney, or Peterson. An eye for an eye.

Familiar questions ran through his head. Was she drunk? Where was she when she came off the road? How long did it take for the police to find her? Did she die hating him? What were her last words? He tried to recall what she'd said to him. Yes, he remembered. "You'll carry this with you forever," she'd said.

It was true, of course. However he spent the remaining years of his life, there would never be a moment, happy or sad, where he didn't remind himself that it could all have been different. There is a story, a different story, Craine thought, and the ending isn't this one. I burned the pictures and I told Gale it didn't matter, I loved her and wanted us to spend our lives together. He would have realized that she was human, as fallible as he, and that any mistakes that were made weren't even hers. They might have even become closer, left the city and made a new life somewhere new. They could have taken Michael with them. They could have been a family.

But this could never happen now. The decision had been made; the chain of consequences was already in motion. He'd kept the photographs and now Gale was dead.

He'd been so upset with Gale a few hours before, but now any anger he felt was gone. Only regret stood in its place. He had lost two loves in his life and he carried the guilt for both of them. I can't let myself do this again. I cannot lose what little I have left. I cannot lose Michael.

He might have been there a few seconds or several minutes, he wasn't sure. But when Simms said his name and asked if he needed anything, Craine pulled the sheet over her head and turned back toward the door.

Simms looked at him reassuringly. "People are going to ask about what happened tonight. We'll make sure Mayer knows. She'll be protected too, you know that."

"And O'Neill?"

"We got them. We got the men that did this."

Without betraying a hint of emotion, Craine said, "I want people to know that O'Neill figured this all out. He solved this case alone. I don't want him to die for nothing."

Simms nodded. "He won't, Craine. He hasn't."

He left Simms standing in the corridor, walking back toward the lobby where he found himself at the back of a press mob gathered around a long staircase. A doctor in a long surgical gown walked down toward them and explained matter-of-factly that Gale Goodwin had suffered from internal bleeding and blunt brain trauma resulting from a single-car collision. Her car was found off the road less than a mile from her house and she was pronounced dead at the scene of the accident ten minutes after midnight.

The room lit up with the flare and pop of flashbulbs.

"Can you tell us where she was going . . .?"

"Was Gale Goodwin under the influence of drugs or alcohol . . .?"

"Are the police positive it wasn't murder . . .?"

"Will Louis Mayer be making a statement . . .?"

Before the tears could come, Craine broke into a run, pushing his way past the mass of brown hats and probing cameras. He could still smell the magnesium in his nostrils even after he'd left the hospital and sprinted all the way back to his car.

Margaret watched as her husband buttoned up his pajamas and went into the bathroom to clean his teeth.

Louis had returned to his box in Grauman's Theatre just in time to see Dorothy make it back to Kansas, safe at home with her friends and family all around her. He wouldn't explain where he'd been or why and Margaret didn't probe him.

When the picture was over and the audience filed out toward the lobby, she kissed her husband hard on the lips. "I'm so proud of you," she said, "so unbelievably proud."

Louis had been very quiet all night. It must be the stress of it all, Margaret reasoned. He began complaining of a migraine and they skipped the after-party and made their way home. Now, as she sat in bed, Margaret looked at her husband admiringly. Yes, the pictures he made were stressful on their marriage but she was wrong to ever second-guess what his success had given them. It was selfish of her to want him all to herself. After all, Louis' pictures created so much happiness.

"Have some aspirin, Louis. It's in the cupboard. You should really ask Dr. Hendricks for something a little stronger. Seems so silly we don't have a decent painkiller in the house. Try one of the sedatives. Second shelf down."

He didn't answer, but she heard him rummaging through the medicine cabinet.

"Maybe it's the champagne talking," Margaret continued, "but wasn't it wonderful when Dorothy saw the Scarecrow was in Kansas? Do you think they would fall in love? I thought he was delightful. I know you've seen it before, but the audience was in hoots. And the Lion! Oh, he had me in hysterics. I can't wait to talk to Carole about it."

It was such a shame they missed the party tonight. She'd been so looking forward to having a natter with Carole and Clark about the picture. They'd really missed out by not going. Still, there would be other parties. It was surprising anyone wanted to come at all after what happened at Loew House. Thank God nothing like that went on tonight! No, they could throw another little party, a soirée at the end of the summer. She needed a little project to focus on and besides, didn't they deserve a little celebration at M.G.M. after all the difficulties they had with Herbert and all that Loew House nonsense? A dinner party was the perfect antidote. Not too many people. Two dozen at most. A sit-down meal, of course—three courses but keep the food simple; nothing too Jewish or Louis would get mad.

Joan Crawford would come, and Fred Astaire and the lovely Phyllis. Gale, of course. Katharine would be invited but only if she promised not to wear a pantsuit. Who else? Vivien Leigh and Larry Olivier. How nice to add some culture into the mix. Margaret was beginning to run through her invitation list when the phone started ringing downstairs, and then a moment later the telephone on the bedside cabinet began dancing on its cradle.

The dog was already barking when Louis came out of the bathroom.

"Do you have to get it now, Louis?" she asked when he reached out to the telephone.

Louis sat down beside her with his feet dangling over the edge of the bed. "I'll just be a minute." He was very quiet when he lifted up the receiver, muttering "yes" and "no" before pausing to listen for a long time with his back turned.

Margaret stroked her husband's back. For no reason at all she felt lucky for everything she had. After the picture, she'd asked her husband why Dorothy would choose to go back home. Kansas was so gray, so dark, so depressing. Why not stay in Oz? But Louis had been adamant. "No, she has to go back to Kansas," he'd said. "Why wouldn't Dorothy want to go back to America? It has everything Oz has and more." He was right, of course, as he always was. When she first met Louis, he was so poor he had spent his teenage years selling scrap metal. Now they had everything they could ever ask for. Their life was a Horatio Alger tale of rags to riches.

Settling her head back on her pillow, Margaret allowed herself a few proud tears. This was America. This was truly a place where dreams come true.

CHAPTER 45

Throughout the long drive back to Beverly Hills, Craine tried not to reflect too much on the night's events. He knew that tomorrow morning the news of what had happened would be broadcast on the radio, the papers making more of the story in time for the evening extra. There would be brief articles about the Chicago syndicate but they'd be lost beneath headlines about Gale Goodwin. This was a city that not only accommodated tragedies but cherished them. Devoid of a far-reaching history, the City of Angels was content to forge its own mythology, and Gale's loss would be the creation of a legend. This nightmare isn't mine alone, thought Craine—it belongs to all of us. Gale would be the city's lost princess, a starlet who died mourning the passing of her husband only two months ago. Her direct involvement with Carell's criminal enterprise would likely be rumored but ultimately refuted. Inquests would be denied, witness statements edited, autopsies rigged. Mayer's and M.G.M.'s involvement would never be made clear, even if Peterson himself couldn't escape the accusations. M.G.M.'s Head of Publicity would fall on his sword for all of them. And O'Neill. He'd get a medal, Craine would make sure of it. The papers would call him a hero and rightly so; that boy deserved better than what the press could ever offer him.

But still, tomorrow's headlines meant nothing to Craine anymore. He was done with it all. Finished.

The driveway leading up to his house was so packed with parked police cars it reminded him of the parties they use to throw there when he and Celia were younger and happier. As he pulled up outside the front door he half-expected to see Celia waving with a glass of champagne in one hand, but it was his secretary Elaine who appeared in the doorway. She looked forlorn yet exceptionally young in the halo of the porch light. He wondered what she dreamed of at night. Who dreams of being a policeman's secretary? He hoped she found whatever it was she wanted from life. She still had time.

He turned off the ignition and sat unmoving in the silence. Raindrops appeared on the windshield, or was it the early morning dew? He couldn't be sure. It had rained plenty in May and he wanted it to rain again now. Wash it all away so he could start afresh. He didn't expect bow-tied endings; he knew there would be no catharsis but with so much loss it seemed there could be nothing else but a new beginning, in whatever form that might take. His life was moving in a new direction, but he was no longer afraid. It was thinking of his son that pushed him through. I have been saved from myself with your help, Michael. I have discovered unknown strength. Everything that has happened these past few days has made me realize that I've taken you for granted for too long. There is only one act left.

Inside the house, police officers moved in and out of hallways recovering ammunition. Except for the boot prints, the house had been cleaned and tidied as best as uniformed officers knew how. They are men with wives and families, and their efforts are touching, Craine thought. The house was still in ruins, of course, but it made no difference. He had already decided he would sell it. There was no reason not to.

Craine's eyes were caught and held by Elaine's. She looked like she was about to cry. "Where is Michael?" he asked before she could.

"He's in bed."

"Thank you, Elaine. Go home and get some rest. You don't have to go into work tomorrow."

"I'm so sorry—"

"Thank you for everything you've done."

Elaine left the house and the uniformed officers went with her. Craine heard the closing of car doors and the turning over of engines, the cars driving off one by one through the weeping night until only two squad cars and an unmarked F.B.I. coupe remained parked outside.

The house was empty, and Craine wandered through the dark corridors until he came to Celia's bedroom—no, his own bedroom.

Michael was lying in the center of the bed, his tiny body hidden beneath thick sheets, his head nestled in the pillow. The room was dark except for the light coming from the bathroom. The door was open and he could see the floor was wet. A heavy towel was folded neatly on a chair beside the bathtub, Michael's undershirt and socks draped over the towel rack. It looked like a normal bathroom; it was no longer Celia's mausoleum.

Craine sat at the edge of the bed and Michael stirred. He didn't have to look at him to know he was awake. He opened his mouth to speak but no sound came out. The words were stuck in his throat and he had to breathe for a few seconds and wait for his jaw to stop shaking.

In the driveway, under the shadow of a willow tree, a small police light flickered on and off. He'd forgotten that you could see the driveway from here. It had been so long since he'd been in this room. Months. Over half a year. When he was younger, Michael used to come running in here at the weekends, crawling onto the bed and slipping under the sheets. Craine had always told Celia off afterward, said that a boy should learn to stay in his own bed, but he'd never put a stop to it. Michael seemed to enjoy it so much. Besides, the three of them were a family. It was something he'd taken for granted but not something he'd forgotten: that even if fatherhood hadn't come naturally to him, having a family was the single best thing that had ever happened to him. And just because Celia wasn't around anymore, it didn't mean they had to stop being one.

"I never told you much about my father," he began. "I didn't know him very well. He was a hard man, kept himself to himself mostly and in many ways we're similar, I suppose. He died, my mother too, when I was about your age."

He thought for a long time about that. About the strange idea it was to be someone's father. About the way in which he'd struggled to live up to his responsibilities. If I have ever been given an opportunity to change that then it is now. If not now, then never again. Maybe there's no saving me. But there's a life I've created that can live on. I can be the bridge.

He took a shallow breath, knowing that if it was any deeper the tears would come and he wouldn't be able to finish. "I don't think about him much these days, but I wish I'd had a chance to know him. Sometimes I find it hard to remember what he looked like but I've seen pictures of me and him when I was a boy, and I know he looked a lot like I do now. You may be surprised, but I looked like you back then. I always said you looked like your mother, but when I see that picture I know I only wish you did. You look like me."

He looked down at Michael. His eyes were open, what light there was in the darkness reflected in the brown circling his pupils. "When your mother died I know it was you that found her. We never talked about that. I know that you've felt you should have saved her. I can't imagine what that must have been like for you. And I made it worse, not better." He stopped speaking until he could form the words he'd failed to say so many times. His face was growing hot and there was a small out breath as he tried to stop his voice from breaking.

"I went away because I was ashamed of what I'd become. Not because I blamed you." As he spoke, everything that had happened seemed to rise up in his chest and the tears that had sat for so long inside of him made their way to his eyes, resting there for a long time before slowly subsiding.

"You weren't responsible," he went on, delivering the confession he should have given many months ago. "It wasn't your fault. I should have told you that. And I should never have left you. I was selfish, and I wanted to be something I wasn't. I'd forgotten about what was important. About being a father. About you. And I'm sorry. I'm so sorry for everything you've gone through."

His lungs felt so small and shallow, barely able to take in the air he needed to keep his composure. "But now there's only us left, and I have to take care of you. I know that now."

He placed his hand out on the bed sheets and another hand, the same hand in smaller form, came next to it. There is a place for us that isn't here, he told himself. We shouldn't stay in this house just because she was. There has to be a place for us that can have new memories. Through his mind ran all the possibilities of where and how, but it didn't really matter. What mattered was that he'd already made his decision. "I want us to find a house, a new house we can call home. I want you to live with me and we can start again."

His hand moved over Michael's and he held it tight. "I don't know what will happen after that, but that doesn't matter because I'll never leave you again. I promise you, I'll never leave you again. We have each other now, and that should be enough." He took a deep breath and said finally, "I hope I can be enough."

He didn't look at Michael again, standing up to leave without saying another word. He wasn't quite at the door when a voice said, "Good night, Papa."

It was only three words, but when Craine moved back into the depths of the living room, he clung to them, a life raft he needed to hold onto.

Opposite, on the far wall, the photograph of Michael sat crooked above the fireplace, a survivor in the wreckage of their house. Jonathan Craine took a seat on the divan and stared at it for a long time before his breathing settled, his heart steadied and his eyelids drew together with pictures of a better life.

He slept.

ACKNOWLEDGEMENTS

The Pictures is a testament to the help of a great many individuals. It's always an absolute pleasure to work with intelligent, insightful and passionate people and in all three respects I've been incredibly lucky.

I would like to start by thanking my editor Jenny Parrott and the brilliant team at Oneworld. I couldn't have asked for a better publisher.

Thanks also to Sean Gascoine, Georgina Gordon-Smith and Hania Elkington, for picking me out of nowhere, pointing me in the right direction and giving me the encouragement to get there.

I want to thank Mark Bolton, for introducing me to far better writers than I'll ever be. I owe a lot to John le Carré, Graham Greene and Martin Cruz Smith, who in their own way became my creative writing teachers. It's difficult to write a detective story set in pre-war California without also mentioning Dashiell Hammett, James M. Cain, and Raymond Chandler. These authors created the sandpit that I've gleefully been playing in and without them, *The Pictures* simply wouldn't exist.

A special thank you to my literary agent Anna Power, who saw potential in my manuscript, championed this novel and worked so hard to make it the best it could be. You helped make *The Pictures* possible.

Lastly, I'm deeply grateful to my family, my friends and to Harriet Smith, without whose support this book would never have been written.